CONSUMED

Inspired by true events

Hilary LiDestri and Alisa Griffin

TLT Publishing

Chicago

This is a work of fiction inspired by true events. To protect the rights of those who inspired the story, some of the events have been altered, and all names, dates and places have been changed.

THE LITTLE THINGS PUBLISHING, LLC

Chicago, Illinois

Printed in the United States of America

Cover Design by Hilary LiDestri
Interior Design by Cameron Ruen
Edited by Meredith Carey
Published by The Little Things (TLT) Publishing, LLC

The Little Things (TLT) Publishing, LLC
Chicago, Illinois
Visit our web site at:
www.tltpublishing.com

ISBN: 978-0-9844013-1-4

First Hardback Edition: December 2010

[1. thriller-fiction 2. suspense-fiction]
I. Title II. Series III. LiDestri, Hilary VI. Griffin, Alisa

ACKNOWLEDGMENT

This book would never have been born without the interest, support and encouragement of my best friends and family (all the same to me). I am so very blessed to have those in my life that I do. Alisa has been a constant in my world for over thirty years (whether we were together or separate) and this book is the beginning of the path that will bring us together on a daily basis. A special thanks to Randi Ertz, our publisher for taking a huge chance signing two unknowns and to Meredith Carey for her brilliant editing and keen attention to detail. Additional thanks to the entire team at The Little Things Publishing and to those who have read every single version of this book over the past seven years. I promise not to torture you so intensely moving forward. All my love. ~Hilary

I want to acknowledge those without whom I could not have realized this dream: my parents, who instilled in me the love of reading; teachers, in particular Elaine Porter, who helped deepen my appreciation for the written word, and Curtis Stadtfeld, who taught me a new way to write and forever changed my way of thinking; my other family members, biological and chosen, living or passed, who reside in my heart, despite all distances; the TLT family and LH, for believing; and AJR, who has accompanied me throughout this entire journey, providing enthusiasm, encouragement and love. Last, I am indescribably grateful for the realized opportunity to work with my best friend, Hilary, the half that completes the whole, with whom I became intrinsically linked by a bond forged decades ago. This work is but one of our numerous collaborative efforts and I look forward to many more. ~Alisa

For J

the love of my life.

~Hilary

For LMG

Listen to your heart . . . persist . . . and realize your dreams . . .

~Alisa

CONSUMED

Hilary LiDestri and Alisa Griffin

1

Dallasites, welcome to Sustenance. Good luck getting a table—this place will be jammed from open to close. During its inception, some called this concept a risk, an experiment. I, on the other hand, have been restlessly anticipating its unveiling. Once you step inside, you will understand . . .

A noise stopped Lynden cold. The hair on her arms danced, and she sat still in her desk chair. She strained to listen, hands poised above the keys of her laptop. What was it? What had she heard? Scratching? Knocking? Tapping? There it was again. It sounded like a gate opening. A door? Was it inside or outside? Inside. Definitely inside. She slowly reached into the drawer next to her right hand and extracted a small Sig Sauer nine-millimeter pistol.

She fought the urge to deadbolt her office door, crawl under her desk and dial nine-one-one. Most every light in the house was on, but it didn't make her feel any safer. She crept from the office, gun projecting outward in ready position. The house was silent.

She replayed the sound in her head and couldn't place it. Her brain had assimilated the many subtle noises that reverberated through her home, but this had broken through her routine, her concentration, her parameters; something was wrong.

She would guess it had been a kitchen noise. Someone in the pantry? She dreaded the pantry, the rear section of which was a large storage space, the underbelly of the staircase above it, the perfect hiding place for an intruder. She shuddered, trying to shake the fear growing more intense as she eased her way out of the office and through the foyer.

She glanced up the front stairs, the counterpart to a matching flight at the rear of the house. On the blueprints, the design had appealed to her on an escape-route level; in reality, she was repeatedly driven near to madness thinking an intruder was going down one set as she was going up the other. She spent far too much time going up and down in circles, desperate to confirm she was alone. Her paranoid searches were nearly impossible to quit.

She rarely used the back stairs. Out of desperation to break free of the up-one-set-of-stairs-and-down-the-other compulsion, she had begun keeping the carpet combed in a subtle pattern. At a glance, she could detect footprints, though anyone leaving them would be unlikely to notice.

Lynden decided to check upstairs after she secured the downstairs. What if someone heard her breathing or the beating of her heart? She swiped at the sweat beads that had broken across her forehead. She reminded herself she had arranged the house to make concealment nearly impossible.

No furniture was high enough to hide behind; no panels on the windows were wide enough to conceal a man; all doors were kept open and flush to the wall; all showers were either open air, European style, or had glass doors. No shower curtains allowed. All cabinets were too small for anyone to hide in, and her wood-framed bed was too low to the ground for anyone to sneak under. The pantry, stairs, and closets were her major hurdles.

Since being pulled from her writing, she had not heard another sound. One glance at the alarm panel confirmed it was engaged and fully functioning. How had someone managed to get in, and when had it happened? From her position the only blind areas were the inside of the small bar and the other side of the island. She eased forward slowly, trying to reassure herself no one was there, fighting the feeling of certainty that *this time*, someone was, indeed, in the house.

She rounded the tiny bar, which was nestled into a corner between the great room and the kitchen. The gun preceded her, prepared to fire, but there was no one crouching or waiting; no lunatic in a hospital-issue gown, recently escaped from a mental institution, ready to pounce; no Armani-clad mad man ready to spring forth and take her by surprise.

Bracing herself, she whirled around the island and confirmed the entire kitchen, except for the pantry, clear. She made a mental note to get a lock for the door leading to the pantry, so she could be certain no one was hiding inside at a glance. Lynden approached slowly, taking her left hand from the gun to open the door, filled with fear like so many other times. Except this time was different, she was sure—because this time, someone was most definitely in the house.

She crept silently on toward the back of the large closet. Her ears strained for any sound indicating someone's presence—body shifting, light breathing, or stomach growling. She anticipated the clattering of plates, glasses, and silverware that would come as the intruder charged her, sending all of her spare holiday and formal ware to the ground. And yet, not a sound. Closer she crept, and she could see the light fade almost to black as she rounded the corner, dreading the moment her eyes would meet his as he lunged.

She shrieked as the ring of her telephone pierced the silence. Stumbling backward, she fell firmly onto the hardwood floor, leaving herself vulnerable. The phone rang insistently again. She scrabbled out of the pantry, slammed the door behind her, grabbed for the granite top of the island and pulled herself to her feet.

She snatched the phone from its cradle and waited for the machine to pick up. The sound of her own voice asking the caller to leave a message gave her a bit of comfort.

"Lynden, it's Dane. Pick up the phone, girl. I have an offer you can't refuse," her friend drawled. She pressed the button to talk and felt some of her tension abate at the familiar sound of his voice. With phone in hand, she planned to search the house and scream bloody murder if anyone attacked her.

"Dane!"

"What is it, honey? You sound out of breath."

"Oh, I, uh, I couldn't find the hand-held and had to race around. Damn near killed myself! I swear Blanca polishes the floors with olive oil!" She forced a chuckle and leaned around the corner of the pantry to find everything in perfect order. She couldn't help, however, rushing out and slamming the door behind her.

Great room, kitchen, library, and powder room secure.

"Come out with me. I have two passes for the most fabulous VIP club opening." Lynden regretted she would have to tell Dane no, but there was no way she could leave the house at night and come back, especially considering this potential intruder. Letting her guard down a little and asking Dane for help would lead to questions.

"I can't. I'm sorry."

"What? Why? What are you doing? Or is it a who-you-are-doing issue?"

I wish, Lynden thought miserably as she entered the master closet. Running a hand through her full-length dresses, she conducted an eyeball search for protruding shoes. Nothing. That left the rest of the upstairs. Two bedrooms and two closets. Yikes. She would be at this all night.

"No, no, it's just . . . I'm working on my column and I'm already behind deadline," she lied.

"Lynden Hatcher, I have been witness to you writing your column over drinks in a crowded bar so that we had plenty of time to go out to dinner. Give me a break! What's up with you?"

"I . . . I really blew it this month. I haven't even finished the research. Next time." Though disappointed, Dane shifted gears and chatted spiritedly as Lynden scoured the upstairs, baffled by her mystery noise. She didn't bother checking the attic. Since the day she began reading James Patterson's *Kiss the Girls*, in which a family unknowingly had someone living in their attic, its door had been secured by a Schlage padlock.

As she returned the phone to its cradle, she noticed the date, March twenty-fourth, on the word-a-day desk calendar. Tonight's paranoia must have been a subconscious recognition of the day that had altered the course of her life more than a decade ago. She could relax. No one was in the house.

Sipping the last of a bottle of Grgich Hills chardonnay, Lynden paced a bit. She squinted, pretending not to see the cabernet-colored leather book amid the hundreds of other books in the cases lining her great room, where it had been sitting untouched for ten years. In an attempt to desensitize herself to a past that had left her broken and desperately vulnerable, she had put pen to paper years ago and created a journal. Someday, perhaps, she could use her experiences to create a solid work of fiction, make it someone else's story. Prolonging the inevitable, she headed for her favorite place: the kitchen.

She seasoned a small filet mignon with garlic, salt, and pepper; washed some broccoli and put it in the steamer; and whipped up a fresh vinaigrette with red wine, basil, and Dijon. The blanched broccoli would be dilled, the filet medium rare, and the salad a mix of romaine and arugula with hearts of palm, Kalamata olives, English cucumber, and a medley of peppers. She cleaned some baby portabella mushrooms and dropped them in a pan with a spray of olive oil and a splash of Grgich Hills cabernet left over from the night before.

But instead of turning on the burner, she uncorked a bottle of Castello di Monsanto chianti, poured herself a generous portion, and wandered into the library. Instinctually, her hand found the journal and pulled it slowly from the bookcase. *This is not a good time*, she tried to tell herself—but she had already opened the cover and was headed toward the couch.

The first page was titled, "In case I ever forget."

2

It was March twenty-fourth, 1997, the first day back from spring break in the last term of my third year of college at the University of Michigan. As I roller-bladed across campus, the trees were sprouting new leaves, the air was redolent with the splendid smell of freshly cropped grass, and flowers were abloom.

Over break, I had ended a marriage-bound relationship. It had been heart wrenching, but I was starting anew, and it felt good to be free. Later that day, I would resume teaching public speaking and was excited to see my students again. I carefully negotiated, still in my roller blades, the stairs leading to the classroom of my most boring elective that term, Spatial Relations.

Students slowly trickled into the large room, and I was annoyed when someone sat down only one seat away. The whole place was nearly empty, yet he had to plop down so close! The scent of his cologne wafting over was unavoidable, but that he did not initiate conversation offered some relief. When I finally allowed myself a glance at the clock on the wall behind me, I was thrilled the end of class was near.

"Before you leave," the professor said, "give your name and phone number to the person next to you. They will serve as your backup if you miss a class between now and finals and need notes." I scribbled my information on a piece of paper, thrust out my hand with gaze downward, and prepared to make an exchange with the interloper. I looked up and into the eyes of the most stunning man I had ever seen in real life.

"It's Britten. Call me Brit," he said with the air of a man rather than

a college boy. At more than six feet tall, he towered over me. His lemon yellow henley-style shirt and lightweight brown leather jacket beautifully complimented his dark features. Faded, well-worn jeans clung to what appeared to be very fit legs.

His dark eyes searched mine, but I was speechless. I sensed my mouth gaping so far open a Mack truck could drive through.

"Reese . . . Hatcher . . . thanks," I managed. He flashed a smile and turned toward the door, striding away on beautiful brown leather cowboy boots. I watched him walk out, swiftly advancing toward a hot Ducati motorcycle.

I stopped to watch as he saddled up, drawing his helmet down over his head. I looked around and noted I was one of several girls who had halted in their tracks to watch the show. Feeling silly, I put blade in front of blade and headed toward my own classroom.

Much to the delight of my students, I cut class tragically short, anxious to get home and catch up with my roommate Jessica, who had been out of town interviewing for internships for more than a week. Arriving home, however, my first order of business was unwinding in a hot shower.

"Reese?" Jessica called up the stairs just as I was about to step into the shower.

"Just a second," I heard her say from the hallway. She dangled the phone just inside the bathroom door.

"Hello?" I said, slipping back into my bathrobe and opening the door so Jessica could eavesdrop.

"Reese?" that deep, confident voice from Spatial Relations asked. "Brit Holden calling. I apologize for the lateness of the offer, but I would love to take you to dinner tomorrow evening. That is, if you don't already have plans."

"Actually, I do. I have to work on my curriculum for next week. I'm a TA," I said, hoping to sound self-assured. I looked around to Jessica, who was watching me, blonde eyebrows raised.

"In that case, how about I pick you up in an hour for a drink?" When I told him I was only twenty, he said it was no problem. He knew people. I told him where I lived, trying not to hyperventilate before hanging up.

"What's going on?" Jessica begged. I filled her in while I showered.

"Ooh, all of your favorites," Jessica teased. "Bikes, boots, height, class, confidence. I hope he has an extra helmet," she laughed, knowing I would hate the thought of wearing a motorcycle helmet, especially on a first date.

When the phone rang almost an hour later, I grabbed it after the first ring, assuming it was Brit calling to cancel. "Hi, Reese? It's Brit. I hate to be a jerk, but there's nowhere to park, so I can't come up to get you. Would you mind coming down?"

Jessica and I ran to the large bay window and strained to see what he was driving. No luck.

"I can't believe I'm not going to see him!"

"Next time," I said, already hoping there would be one.

Just as I emerged from the building, an enormous black Z71 truck pulled up, but the windows were so dark I didn't know if it was him. I heard the driver's side door open and shut and stood for a moment, feeling like an idiot, until he strode around the back of the truck. I was glad to be standing and not walking, because I likely would have stumbled and fallen down upon seeing him. His stylish long-sleeved shirt was tucked into clingy, somewhat faded jeans. His belt was a perfect match to his cowboy boots, a different but equally beautiful pair than those he had been wearing earlier in class. His short, dark hair was a sexy mess that called attention to his not-so-clean-shaven face. His eyes and mouth broke into a smile when he saw me.

"Wow, you look great!" he said as he reached for my door. The only man who did that was my dad.

The immaculate truck smelled new under the seductive scent of Brit's cologne.

"Oh, I love Depeche Mode," I said, and reached forward to turn up the radio as the music filled the space between us.

"I didn't know this was Depeche Mode. I love music, you'll have to tell me the names of all their albums so I can pick them up. "

We made small talk while I stole glances at him. I couldn't believe he had asked me out. Despite the fact we were roughly the same age, he seemed older *and extremely mature.*

"Have you ever been to The Rack?" he asked. I told him I hadn't but knew it was a sports bar. I was thrilled when he went out of his way to open the door to the bar, speak to the hostess, and secure us a table in the billiards area. I felt compelled to tell him I didn't know how to play, and that seemed to please him.

By the time we were settled and had selected cues, two ice-cold Miller Lites had arrived.

"My favorite," I said, as I reached for my beer.

"Mine, too," he smiled, causing my heart to skip. He clanked his bottle to mine and my lesson commenced. I didn't enjoy the game nearly as much as I enjoyed watching him bend his strong, lean body over the table to make a shot, or feeling him press lightly against me while coaching. We chatted effortlessly while we played, and he introduced me to the many people who stopped by our table. Most were men, but many were women, and under their scrutiny I wondered how many women Brit had brought here before me.

By the end of our third game, I was a little tipsy, as we hadn't eaten.

"I'm famished. Let's go to dinner," he said.

Brit selected the Harvest Grill, a restaurant I'd always longed to go to; it wasn't a student hangout. Most people went with their parents because it was elegant and quite pricey.

"Is this okay?" he asked as we crossed the parking lot. I gave a vague nod as I looked around, drinking in the sprawling ivy-covered patio bathed in the soft glow of an outdoor fireplace.

"Yes, but I'm so underdressed," I said, pulling my attention from my surroundings to look to him in protest. As I turned my head, I felt a hard tug on my hair.

"I'm sorry!" He untangled his fingers from my hair and looked embarrassed. "Your hair . . . it's so beautiful. I wanted to see what it felt like." My heartbeat picked up a bit as his compliment hit home. I realized it had been a long time since someone had paid me so much attention.

"It's okay, you just surprised me," I said, looking forward to the next time he might touch me.

The hostess nestled us into a cozy table on the patio, probably because I was in jeans. The night was cool but not cold. The candle put off just enough light to stun me into silence just looking at him. Brit ordered dinner for us, filet mignon with a wild mushroom reduction served with stacked scalloped potatoes, preceded by a mixed green salad with raspberry vinaigrette.

Wine arrived, Cakebread cabernet sauvignon. I had never had anything but chardonnay and white zinfandel but was more than willing to try something new. The waitress placed giant, balloon-style glasses on the table, and, after opening the bottle, handed the cork to Brit. He squeezed it gently at first, then more firmly as he brought it up to his nose. Something deep within me began humming. He closed his eyes and took another deep breath.

"Mmmmm, amazing, Anita." She smiled and poured our wine as I wondered how well he knew Anita. Once she had gone, he swirled his wine and I copied. He put his hand on mine. "Counter-clockwise. Don't ask me why," he said sweetly, disarming me with a shy smile. I normally would have felt silly being corrected, but he was kind and in no way condescending. He buried his nose in the glass, smelling deeply once again. I followed suit. It had a heady aroma, like wood. My salivary glands let loose and my mouth began to water. I waited to see what we would do next, and he lifted his glass to meet mine.

"Salute," he said in Italian. I swooned. Discreetly, of course.

When he finally brought the glass to his full, already cabernet-colored lips, it was all I could do not to drool. Watching Brit, I rolled a small sip around in my mouth. Even after swallowing, the taste lingered strong on my tongue.

"What do you think?" he asked.

"Amazing. I've never tasted anything like it. Do you always drink this wine?" I asked, impressed with his professional tasting routine.

"I love this particular cellar and year, but I try to mix it up." Words that should have sounded arrogant didn't.

He asked countless questions about my life, and despite my efforts to do the same, he always circumvented back to me. As I marveled over the fabulous meal, he walked me through the odd ingredients and preparation.

When Anita brought the check presenter, Brit opened it and signed the tab.

He didn't put down any money, so I reached for my purse. He surprised me by telling me he had an account with the restaurant he paid monthly. I wasn't sure what that meant.

I assumed we were wrapping up our drink-turned-dinner-date, but instead, a single glass of Cakebread chardonnay arrived for each of us. I should have been hammered, but years of dedication to increasing my tolerance, not to mention my being a descendant of experienced drinking stock, served me well. I was pleasantly tipsy, warm and tingly all over.

As I brought the wine glass to my lips, Brit reached out and twirled a lock of my hair around his finger, leaning in close. "I love the way you smell," he whispered, and my heart stopped for a beat. His eyes, shrouded by long, dark lashes, traveled up and down my body as he took in every facet of my appearance.

As we pulled up to my apartment building, I told Brit not to worry about walking me up. There was no place to park or even pull over without blocking traffic. He took my hand and brought it to his lips. He didn't kiss it so much as touch it to his mouth. "Thank you," he said simply. No lean-in, no awkward moment, no pressure.

I floated up the stairs to my apartment, where Jessica was up watching a movie and drinking a glass of wine. I spent the next hour recounting the evening to her. She listened in rapt silence, right down to the closing of the truck door. Later, as I lay in bed unable to sleep, I realized my heart was going to be broken by this mysterious and seductive man, but that it would be worth it.

3

Much to her dismay, no paparazzi were hovering as Meridan emerged from the Mercedes limousine in front of the Ivy on Robertson Boulevard. Her agent, Roz, had made the reservation for seven-thirty p.m.—prime time for drinks before dinner on a Thursday evening in Los Angeles.

Meridan stood outside the car, glancing around, instinctively prepared to greet her public. She was disappointed to find the guests dining on the patio too engrossed in one another's company to meet her eyes for more than a second or two, as if she were vaguely familiar to them but they didn't quite know why and ultimately didn't care.

She took out her cell phone and speed-dialed as her driver closed the car door.

"Where are you?" she hissed into the receiver.

"I'm pulling onto Robertson now," Roz assured.

"Well, you better make a big fucking deal when you walk in." She ended the call abruptly and headed toward the stairs leading to the hostess area.

A new girl. Great. Where was Gregory? Ignoring the hostess completely, she glanced around the patio, hoping to locate him.

"May I help you, ma'am?"

Ma'am? Meridan cringed at the word, which momentarily distracted her from the absolute annoyance of having to impart effort. Looking around impatiently, she considered taking off her bronze-tinted Gucci sunglasses so the little moron would realize exactly who she was calling "ma'am." It just wasn't acceptable for a star of her magnitude to be dealing with a hostess. As the mushroom cloud of indignation began to form, Gregory appeared, a grandiose whirlwind of homosexuality and reverence.

"Ms. Marks!" the maitre d' half-whispered, the pre-established protocol. He took her hand and kissed it dramatically. "Megan! Why haven't you shown Ms. Marks to her usual table?"

"I, oh, I didn't recogn—"

Gregory cut Megan short with a hand in the air. The gay Heisman.

"I'll do it!" he hissed before assuming an adoring smile. He extended his elbow to Meridan and gushed as they made their way across the patio.

"How good to see you! It's been too long. Tell me whom you're meeting, and I'll keep my eyes open." With exaggerated pageantry, Gregory pulled Meridan's chair out for her and snapped her napkin onto her lap.

"Meridan!" Barely out of her car at the valet stand, Roz gesticulated wildly, her distinctive nasal voice traveling across the crowd. "Meridan!" She was, as always when her client was feeling unappreciated, careful to say the name several decibels louder than was necessary, as it never fell on deaf ears.

A murmur rose and rippled across the patio, balm to Meridan's bruised ego. In her peripheral vision she saw people whispering, shifting in their chairs and pointing discreetly. Finally! She made a mental note never to debut a new hair color *and* new glasses at twilight.

Roz scuttled up the steps, dismissing the useless hostess with a wave, and joined Meridan at her table in the front corner overlooking the sidewalk. It was the preferred spot due to its sight line from the street, ideal for photo opportunities and within an arm's length for signing autographs.

As part of a last-ditch effort to lift the delicate spirits of her client, Roz had planned an evening designed to put Meridan in touch with the one thing that might pull her from the grips of her current self-absorbed funk—admirers.

Meridan's recent foray into the world of film production had not been well received by critics, leaving her outward impenetrable confidence laced with insecurity.

"Where have you been?" Meridan barked.

"Traffic."

"I know, it was a real banshee on the way here," Meridan conceded. Roz, familiar with Meridan's complete inability to master a proverb, dismissed the mangled phrase without even acknowledging it. "Do you realize not one person has asked me for an autograph since I've been here? It's insulting!" Meridan pushed a plump bottom lip out in a theatrical pout.

"You've been here eight seconds. They're just overwhelmed, you know, in the presence of greatness." In just two minutes Roz had tired of Meridan's unending need for attention. It was destined to be a long night.

"Where the hell are our drinks?" Roz snapped her fingers loudly several times without bothering to look for a waiter. Meridan smirked as several waiters scurried inside to find out what could be holding up their gin and tonics.

Roz fished around in her oversized Hermes bag, a gift the previous Christmas from Meridan, and produced a letter. "Mail call!" Meridan noticed the letter was opened, as was normal for communications addressed to her attorney or her film company, Meritime. "Today's letter from your biggest fan," Roz joked, hoping the ardent and prolific fan known only as B would offer high enough praise to bring her out of her mood. "Shall I read?"

Meridan waved a hand through the air, then sat back in her seat, melodramatically pretending to be tired of B's syrupy correspondence, though Roz knew better.

"Dear Meridan, I apologize for not writing sooner." Roz lowered her voice to avoid being overheard. "My days have been consumed by my writing, leaving little time to catch up with you. I feel terrible about neglecting you," Roz continued, embarrassed by the hokey tone of the letter.

"I've been up nights waiting to hear from him," Meridan snorted, leaning forward to swipe her cocktail from the terrified waiter, nearly toppling the beverage-laden tray.

" . . . I was wondering if we could try again to meet in person. I was disappointed things didn't work out last night."

"What?" both women chimed in unison.

"Have you been in contact with this guy?"

"No! I have no idea what he's talking about!"

Roz continued reading. "'What time did you arrive? I was at Geisha House according to plan. Stayed a couple of hours then decided to head home.' According to whose plan?" Roz queried. "Meridan, what are you keeping from me?"

Meridan's hand flew to her chest, appalled. "Nothing! You know every move I make."

Roz furrowed her brow and read further. "Maybe we just missed each other? Hard to say—Geisha House was pretty chaotic last night. Perhaps you didn't feel like going out due to the bad press the new film has been receiving." Roz paused in anticipation of the impending tantrum.

"What? The film is doing great. Have you seen any bad press?" Roz shook her head quickly, reluctant to acknowledge the press so horrible Meridan had not left her townhouse in the past two weeks.

Roz read on. "Let's do dinner. I'll bring us each a copy of my latest script to work from. I'll contact you next week to confirm. B." Roz grimaced as the barrage of insults began to fly.

"Unfuckingbelievable! His scripts are awful! He thinks we had a date. At Geisha House? I love Geisha House. How could he know that? Do you think he spoke with someone at Meritime?" Meridan's face projected sheer disbelief and vexation.

"No one would be that stupid. My God, the very thought!" Upon the approach of a fan armed with a beverage napkin and pen, Roz slipped the letter into her bag.

They decided to order dinner as a steady stream of fans bolstered Meridan's confidence. During a lull, both women dove into their salads.

"I need to tell you something." Meridan's green eyes flashed with mischief in the fading light.

"What?"

"We need to curb any further, I mean, potential, negative press on *As Is*." Roz shrugged and took a bite of her Caesar salad. "We need to put me back on the front pages for something other than that fucking movie." Roz nodded. "I leaked this story to Jack from *Glitterati* magazine this morning."

Roz tilted her head and narrowed her eyes in confusion. "What story?" she asked after swallowing.

"My stalker."

"What stalker?" Roz looked around the bustling restaurant.

"B."

"He's not stalking you."

"Well, he seems a little nuts."

"So?"

"So, if people think I am being stalked, they'll feel bad for me. We'll be vague. We aren't lying, Roz. He isn't right." Meridan's eyes begged for complicity. It was clear Roz had few options outside acquiescence.

"How?"

"I called the police last night."

"What?" Roz gasped, wondering how Meridan had kept this news to herself all day.

"I told them someone was trying to break in. *Total* lie, don't worry, I'm fine." Roz sat in stunned silence as her client outlined her shockingly intricate plot to fool the public using the seemingly harmless delusions of this anonymous, pathetically deranged fan.

"Champagne, ladies, from the gentleman," the waiter announced as he placed two tall crystal flutes on the table.

"What gentleman?" they both nearly screamed.

"Mr. Goldstein. He's using the facilities."

"Jesus!" Meridan brought two fingers to her carotid artery and felt for a pulse. "That scared the shit out of me. It's like I'm waiting for this guy to approach me like we're best friends. Listen, I invited Joel. We need him on board. Pretend you've known about everything all along."

"Meridan, I can't! I'm not a good liar, you know—"

"Ladies." They both stood up to hug Joel and lavish him with air kisses. It was uncommon for him to join them socially.

"I have another fax from B." He held it up and Roz handed him the new letter. While Joel read silently, Roz and Meridan perused the new communications.

Meridan,

Just checking in. I faxed a copy of this to Joel in case you are over there. Maybe you guys are going over the scripts. I worked up some numbers on the Arizona script, and my figures do not include actor salaries. Have your accountant take a look and see if they're anywhere close to what he was thinking. I need to hear back from you before I can work on the next piece of this puzzle. I'm here—not going anywhere, so call me as soon as you can.

B~

Joel sat back in his chair after finishing the letter. He couldn't help wondering where this meeting was headed. Just as Meridan opened her mouth to speak, his phone rang. Not recognizing the number, he answered.

"Joel, Jack Keller."

"Jack!" Joel greeted and Roz recognized immediately the obsequious tone Joel unknowingly reserved for the media. Her eyes darted toward Meridan and she mouthed, "Is this about you?" Meridan nodded, ever so slightly, and stifled a smirk. Roz paled visibly and brought a hand to her mouth.

"Hey, buddy, listen, I need a comment," Jack's voice on the other end of the line said. "We received a tip this morning from someone who put us on the trail of this Meridan Marks stalking thing."

"What Meridan Marks stalking thing?" Joel successfully masked his confusion.

"Don't play coy. Nine-one-one has a record of a distress call from Meridan last night. The cops came out but found no evidence of an attempted break-in. Our source said she's been harassed by a fan for months. What do you say?"

"Right. Why don't I give her a call and see how she wants to proceed?" Joel strained to feign knowledge of the situation.

"Yeah, that sounds good, Joel. Listen, can you have her give me a buzz? I need a comment from her, too. If I know Meridan, she'll try to avoid the questions; she's been quite wily lately. This story's going to run with or without her cooperation. I'm giving her the opportunity to tell her side of things."

"I'll tell her." Joel smiled into the phone before hanging up and slumped over while he kneaded his graying temples.

"Joel—" Meridan squeaked.

Joel sat upright, incredulous. His eyes met Meridan's. "Can you even begin to explain why it is that I'm being informed of your *peril* by the *media*?" Joel's anger was a detail she had failed to consider.

"That's why we're here. Roz convinced me that I needed to start letting people know how scared I've been," Meridan said. "It isn't my fault the press knows. I've been getting hang-ups at home for weeks, and last night I was terrified someone was going to bust a window to get in."

Joel's eyes narrowed skeptically. "Meridan? Do I need to remind you about the night not so long ago when you called me, frantic, begging me to come over? When I did, you presented me with a bottle of wine into which you'd pushed the cork. Now, someone's trying to break into your house, and you don't call. It doesn't work for me."

"I, uh, it was the middle of the night, Joel. Your wife would be furious."

"Have I read all the letters?"

"You read the newest one. He thinks we had a date. He's crazy."

"Jack called this stalking." Joel stated.

"The letters, the flowers, the scripts, the hang-ups and now this," Roz interjected tentatively, in hopes of proving her intimate knowledge of the situation.

"What did Jim say?" Joel demanded in a hushed tone.

"I didn't want to worry either of you. I knew you'd try to make me move." Meridan twirled a long curl between her fingers, assuming an innocent, child-like posture.

"You're damn right, Meridan. Do you realize you could lose your binder if the insurance company gets wind of this? They'll force relocation. No one will hold a contract on an actor who isn't secure. What if you get hurt, or worse, killed?"

In her scheming, Meridan had not considered the negative impact her harmless publicity stunt could have on her career and image, but it was too late to back off now. She had started the ball rolling like shit downhill.

Joel leaned back into his chair and released a long exhalation. Wordlessly, he scrolled through his contact list and pressed send. "Al Roenick, please." He tapped his foot impatiently on the deck, his usually kind face clearly registering annoyance. They'd shut him out. He was more involved with Meridan Marks's career and personal life than he ever would have anticipated when he signed her as one of his first clients nearly a decade ago. Since then, his client roster had swelled, and both his time and tolerance for her neediness were running low.

"Al? Joel Goldstein here. Meridan Marks's attorney? We worked together on that Christian York stalking? Right . . . I have a delicate situation I need help on. Yes, well, my prized client is being harassed. Well . . ." he hesitated. "Stalked." Meridan fought a smile. "Sure . . . sure. Thanks. Actually, she called nine-one-one last night. She's certain she heard someone outside her townhouse attempting to enter. I know. She won't move . . . she's concerned a big mansion, an entourage, or personal security would change her image . . . will do." Joel set down his iPhone and searched both women's faces as they stared blankly, waiting for a cue.

"How do you suggest we address *Glitterati*'s immediate cover story?" Joel inquired.

Meridan avoided looking directly at him. "If they're going to run the story, maybe we should confirm some of the details to make sure my fans know I'm okay and how much I appreciate their support during this difficult time."

"Interesting," Joel answered, shifting his attention to Roz. "Thoughts?"

"She has a point, Joel. We don't need any bad press right now. It wouldn't hurt to garner some sympathy for Meridan."

Meridan smirked and ordered a bottle of Roederer Cristal to celebrate her perfectly orchestrated plan.

4

"I'm telling you, a restaurant by the name of Santi's should not have a Southwestern lobster taco on the menu." Lynden stood her ground in front of the hot-tempered Italian chef, her newest client.

"It is my specialty!" He raised a meaty fist defiantly. She wondered how a celebrated chef hailing from Florence had come to consider such a dish his specialty.

"While that may be true, Santi, we need to name it something else. Like *il crepe di aragosta speziato*." Lynden raised a dark eyebrow, which peaked above severe black glasses. She waited patiently for him to digest the notion, make it his own.

Santi stepped back, one hand over his heart. He stared intensely at her for a moment, then rushed to her, taking her hand and lifting it to his mouth for a quick, moist kiss. She shuddered and tried not to snatch her hand from his grasp. *Be kind, gracious and remember what a huge client he is*, she reminded herself.

"Ah, *bella donna*! You are after my heart! *Crepe*? Ooh, I didn't think of that. I could do a gorgeous pepperoncino reduction! *Brillante*!" Lynden smiled warmly and sighed with relief as he walked away in a frenzy, leaving her standing alone in the skeleton that would become a working restaurant in less than a month.

Lynden turned on a high Gucci heel and headed carefully toward the door—well, the piece of wood serving as one anyway—and let herself out. It was a spectacular day, uncharacteristically pleasant for this time of year in

Texas. Hellish heat typically descended in mid-February, holding the state captive in a caldron until the beginning of November.

Lynden missed the changing of seasons. She missed the smell of spring burgeoning, the never-too-hot summers, the glorious shades only a northern autumn could create. She even missed the brutally cold winters of home.

She had lived in Texas for twelve years. Once she crossed the Michigan border, she knew she would never return to her childhood home. Her parents visited yearly and didn't pressure her to move; they had nursed her through the trauma that propelled her away and supported her absence.

She lifted her face to greet the sun and contemplated the rest of her day. One of her biggest clients had invited her to the grand opening of his restaurant that evening. Lynden was interested to see how the menu would be received, as its conception and implementation had been a raging battle of wills. The rarely-if-ever-attempted culinary leap was a Hawaiian-Mexican fusion.

The preliminary menu Clifton Fox had proposed presented her with a new challenge, so she took the job. The first month was downhill on a greased rail until she finally gained his trust. It wasn't a matter of the food tasting good, as it was exceptional. Conflicts came down to which items should be appetizers and which should be featured, which items would have sides and which side items would be *a la carte*.

A wealthy and successful man, Clifton was used to having things exactly as he ordered. Lynden reminded him frequently he shouldn't have hired her if he didn't respect her opinion. And the row would ensue.

It took what had felt like interminable months to settle the menu. Lynden produced menu after beautiful Photoshopped menu, mocking up and presenting to an ever-unsatisfied client. Clifton worked and reworked each and every appetizer, entrée, side item, and dessert with the renowned Southwestern chef Dane Paige.

Old friends, Dane and Lynden got on famously; he loved to cook and she loved to watch, eat, and learn. Often, once Clifton left for other appointments, Lynden would shadow Dane in the kitchen, internalizing the smells, the textures, and the tastes, memorizing each secret dash and splash. He was a brilliant artist and she was determined to showcase his creations to the best of her ability despite Clifton Fox.

In the end, Clifton was overjoyed; Lynden was overcompensated, leaving her overjoyed; and Dane was a nervous wreck anticipating his opening night.

As she enjoyed the warm sun and cool breeze, she decided she would go early and leave early. This way, she justified, it would be less crowded and she could keep her ear to the ground for positive and negative chatter.

Lynden followed the familiar route from Santi's near the West Village to her home in central Dallas. The top was down on her new BMW 645ci; on a day like today, convertibles ruled the roads. She merged effortlessly onto the North Dallas Tollway, which was loaded with the usual assortment of big-ticket vehicles.

She marveled as she often did at the wealth that seemed to pervade Dallas. The houses were sprawling, monolithic structures on zero lot lines, which made little sense to Lynden, who had grown up in a rural area. She had lived for the past seven years in Highland Park, a prestigious and elegant area, while she saved diligently for a lot on a lonely lane called Strait. Her children would someday play acres from the quiet road, in a back yard that tapered into a tiny creek—much the same way she had growing up.

Though lucrative, her current employment would not catapult her onto Strait Lane, which was reserved for movie stars, people on the ground floor of Internet IPOs, cosmetic surgeons, and old mogul money. She was convinced writing fiction would lead her to her true life's destiny and the accompanying financial success, but she hadn't been able to write a word since graduating with a bachelor's degree in creative writing.

She was grateful Blanca was gone when she arrived home but dreaded all of the touching up she would have to do. The maid came twice weekly and kept the place exactly as required but for a few seemingly minor details. As Lynden entered, she dropped her keys into a small bowl and rearmed the security system before heading into the kitchen.

The clean knives were spread out to dry on towels on the countertop as Blanca always left them despite instructions to put them away before leaving.

Lynden placed the knives in a custom-made drawer, preferring they not be visible at any time other than during cooking or cleaning.

She returned the salt and pepper shakers, which had been put in the spice cabinet, to the ledge of the stove's back splash. She opened the refrigerator and relocated all the large beverages to the top shelf and dairy items to the second shelf, arranging the condiments in the door racks and on the bottom shelf. She wasn't being fastidious, she reassured herself; reasoning instead that the refrigerator needed to be organized to save time preparing meals.

Without pause, she beelined for the laundry room and cleaned the lint trap, dropping a huge clump into the garbage. She rearranged the pillows on the guest bed and reclustered the crystal decanters of alcohol from the straight line Blanca had assembled.

Her own bed required the same attention and she quickly reordered the decorative pillows that adorned her favorite piece of furniture in her house, a glorious Italian canopy bed with wrought iron detailing a crackled wood frame with silver leaf accents and burnished with black ash. She'd seen it in Los Angeles at a tiny gallery on Melrose and pined for it the twelve months it took to be crafted and shipped.

She entered the master closet and reached into the winter sweater storage area, through layers of cashmere, until she felt it—cold, hard and deadly, her most valued possession: a black P226 Sig Sauer nine-millimeter handgun.

She couldn't resist the urge to hold it, poised to fire, lining up the bathtub faucet in her sights. It was a powerful, seductive firearm, and she'd fired more than ten different guns before settling on this one. She had kept her dad's old revolver throughout graduate school, but as soon as she could afford to, she went semi-automatic. As was her habit, she dropped the magazine and un-chambered the round in the barrel.

One must always know the status of one's weapon, she reminded herself. Lynden reloaded the magazine, chambered a round, de-cocked and, as she did each week upon Blanca's departure, slid it under her pillow. It was Lynden's goal never to be taken by surprise.

Back in the closet, the clothing debate was set off. It was too chilly for one of the knockout spring-weather dresses she'd picked up in L.A., but business attire didn't seem appropriate either. She mused, determined to include her new watermelon-colored strappy Gucci heels. Her eyes settled on pink zebra-patterned Capri pants she hadn't worn because, until now, she didn't have the right shoe. A tasteful, semi-backless pink halter completed the outfit, perfectly matching her pink handbag.

She double-checked herself in the mirror and pondered the ensemble. She dreaded attention and tended to dress down to avoid it. Way too much, she decided, and changed into a pair of cropped khaki pants, keeping the top, shoes and purse. This version made her cute at best. She changed out her black glasses for a less severe tortoiseshell pair that matched her hair perfectly.

Her antiquated answering machine showed three messages. Despite all the new answering service options available through her phone company, she clung to the need to screen her calls.

"Reesey . . . are you home? It's Brady, pick up if you're there." The voice silenced for a moment. "Okay, so you aren't home. I'm thinking about flying in on April eleventh, a Friday. Dorrie has a conference in . . . uh, Plano, which is supposed to be close to you. I thought we could have dinner while she's busy saving the world . . . or at least telling people how to do it." He laughed, warming her through.

Brady was a holdover from her former life, the only friend she had allowed to make the transition. She trusted him implicitly; he had been her hero more times than she was comfortable admitting. Much to the chagrin of Brady's wife, Dorrie, they shared a deep bond borne of more than tragedy. Someday she would have someone, too, she reminded herself.

"Reese," she whispered, looking at her reflection in the small mirror hanging above the answering machine. Only Brady still called her by her given name.

The other two messages were sales calls. Grabbing a vintage Chanel pink-and-white tweed jacket, she headed to the door. Blanca had placed the mail on the counter and the latest edition of *Glitterati* magazine had fallen to the floor. *Meridan Marks again*, Lynden thought, staring at the stunning actress that seemed to grace the cover of every fashion magazine and entertainment weekly. *Good Lord, is there a magazine out there* without *her face on it anymore*, she thought in passing as she left for Mexi-Waiian Island. She just could not talk Clifton out of that name.

5

"My God, it's been sheer torture! Where have you been?" Dane wailed from the kitchen across the empty restaurant.

"What's wrong?" Lynden asked, breathless after a quick sprint in four-inch heels.

"Nothing, I just wanted you here and I was worried you wouldn't come!" They'd worked together on many projects and she had brought him to Clifton Fox after stealing him from a stagnant kitchen no longer appreciative of his talents.

"I wouldn't miss it." As a trusted friend, Dane was one of the few men who could touch her without a cloud of darkness threatening to descend. She patted him on the head and gave him a brief hug. The brevity didn't go unnoticed, but Dane had long ago stopped questioning her about her intimacy issues. They were as close as he imagined anyone was with Lynden and he was careful not to press her.

"Can I help?" she asked, unhooking a clean apron from the wall.

Dane grabbed it from her hands and pushed her from the kitchen. "Ah, you insult me! Everything is prepared to perfection. I am merely awaiting my fans," he said with the aplomb of a queen, and she couldn't help but giggle.

"Is Clifton here?" she inquired as she swiped a wedge of avocado from the prep table.

"Are you kidding? I think he slept here." Dane rolled his eyes and they shared a chuckle at Clifton's expense. Ever the officious restaurateur, Clifton delighted in his role.

"The space looks great. There was a time I feared it would be tacky."

Dane's hand flew to his chest in his best "Well! I never!" gesture, replete with a horrified gasp, and Lynden broke into fresh gales of laughter as she left the nerve center of the restaurant to find her client.

The main dining area was large and spacious, the décor eclectic, each piece wildly expensive and personally selected by the Great Clifton Fox himself. The atmosphere was, as planned, festive; their aim had been to relax guests and encourage them to linger.

Across the lavishly landscaped deck strolled Clifton, coiffed and dressed to impress. He was a handsome man in his late forties. He wore a ring on his left ring finger, but his sexuality remained a mystery despite all reconnaissance efforts on Dane's part. Lynden tried not to get involved in her clients' personal lives. So long as they didn't hit on her, she was fine being outside the loop.

"Lynden! My muse!" Oh, the drama. She smiled broadly. "I feared you'd cast us aside for a hot date!"

"I've decided to review you tonight," she said, ignoring his not-so-subtle query.

"Fabulous! Your deep involvement in the creation of the menu will bias you some, *non*?"

"I'll be tasting tonight, regardless of my involvement. I'm starving!" She flashed a brilliant smile, reminding Clifton of someone he couldn't place.

"You should let your hair down!" he said, meaning it literally. Clifton, along with everyone else, was continuously at her to wear her hair down. Habitually, she wore it in either a soft up-do or ponytail, wearing it down only when she was alone. The mere thought of someone running fingers through it, touching it, or smelling it unnerved her.

"What, you don't like it up?" she said playfully, hoping he would let it go if he thought he'd hurt her feelings.

"I do. Most certainly I do." He turned abruptly and headed for the kitchen. His voice trailed behind him, "Dane! Dane! You have exactly fifteen minutes. Are you ready?"

Right. Dane Paige not poised and ready for a restaurant opening that not only would highlight but feature his mastery?

She headed back to the door to grab her camera case. She had decided years ago to shoot all of her own projects; the work the lackeys at the magazine churned out was embarrassing. She preferred a fashion perspective to predictable headshots and lackluster food shots. Her photographs captured the motion, emotion and energy expected of smoothly functioning kitchens and restaurants.

Seeing the camera, Dane came to a screeching halt and posed as Rodin's thinker. She let out a loud and long laugh. Dane always made her laugh.

"Are you ready for my close up, Ms. Marks?" he asked, and she ignored the ever-present reference to the actress. Not a day went by, it seemed, that someone didn't tell her she looked "exactly like" Meridan Marks.

"Give it to me," Lynden said, and Dane launched the food presentation version of Madonna's *Vogue*, which she captured on film. "You're such a diva, Dane!" she said after she finally stopped laughing. Dane was in his element, Clifton was in a great mood, the food looked resplendent, and the staff was giddy with eagerness for the guests to arrive.

Grand openings were the best part of her job. After seven years writing the same widely read column for *Dallas People* magazine, the opportunity to open a restaurant consulting firm fell into her lap. She had been approached a year ago by a gentleman who had suffered two expensive failed restaurant concepts. He bluntly asked Lynden what he was doing wrong and what he needed to change. She responded with candor and was thrilled to later be invited to his third opening, which she gave a well-deserved smashing review.

She loved handing out excellent write-ups to the deserving, but refused to sugarcoat egregious excuses for service, hospitality, or dining enjoyment. Lynden was confident that, despite the name, she could give Mexi-Waiian Island an honestly glowing review.

"Ma'am?"

A waiter in crisp black cotton shorts and a beautiful pink, green, and yellow Hawaiian shirt held out a tray of what Lynden knew were peanut and coconut-dusted jumbo prawns that had been steeped in a decadent, sweet-yet-piquant sauce of Dane's creation.

"Thank you." Lynden smiled as she took a napkin and waited for him to turn away before she took a bite. She was a fastidious eater and hated being watched. Without warning, she heard a voice in her head say, *I love to watch you eat,* and her stomach lurched in response. It happened once in a while, the voice from the past. She had learned some techniques to deal with it. Distraction. She forced her taste buds to take over.

The peanut and coconut were a fantastic complement to one another. The flavors detonated in her mouth as she chewed. The shrimp was moist, exuding hints of sweet and spicy. As to what comprised the sauce, not even she could be certain.

The first guests were flooding the main dining area. An absolute anomaly, the temperature was holding steady at about seventy-four degrees, just the type of weather that sent Texans out in droves looking for that perfect spot to sit outside and people-watch. Clifton couldn't have asked for a more magnificent day.

Lynden relished the "oohs" and "aahs" even though she had little to do with the actual design or construction. Clifton had impeccable taste, and she had learned early on to trust his judgment even when tastelessness seemed to be descending. What could have been done so wrong and so poorly instead had been done to the height of island elegance.

She was proud to be a part of the project and yet happy to be finished. Once she wrote her final review, she could move on. This time, she knew, Dane would not be coming with her in search of a new professional venture. Clifton would never let him go. She chewed quietly so as to be able to hear the comments flying about the patio.

"Have you tried those ribs? I'd bathe in whatever's on them."

"It's Dane Paige, you know."

"It's the only reason I agreed to come."

"The wontons filled with shrimp, bacon, pineapple, and, well, looks like jalapeño are incredible."

"Dane's brilliant. Schaffer never should've let him go. I've never been back."

All good things, Lynden thought, and edged her way to the kitchen. Dane was immersed in a ballet of food preparation behind the line. He ordered his staff with decency, kindness, and respect, and this was but one reason he was loved by everyone he met.

She decided to wait awhile before regaling him with snippets from the guests and wandered out onto the patio.

"Overrated! I'm so tired of hearing how tired people are of being famous," said one well-appointed Highland Park-type, and Lynden inched closer, fearing the first negative comments were about to fly.

"No way!" The throng of gal pals simultaneously challenged the vocal naysayer.

Famous? Like Dane? Lynden strained to hear.

"If she was acting for the love of it, she'd be acting on Broadway. That's real acting!" a St. John Sport-clad woman interjected.

Lynden started to walk away, satisfied they were not disparaging Dane, when she heard something that stopped her cold.

"Well, I love Meridan Marks and feel bad she's being stalked." The women nodded.

Lynden's mind raced. Actresses were always dealing with crazed fans. This was no different. But this was Meridan Marks. *She looks like you*, the voice of fear told her. *It doesn't matter what's going on in Meridan Marks's life; Meridan lives in Los Angeles*, reason challenged.

"I wonder if she's received letters at her Frisco ranch?"

"I didn't know she had a place here."

Lynden grabbed hold of a chair and began counting backward from ten. During deep breaths, she snapped the ever-present hair tie she wore on her wrist, hoping pain would penetrate her paranoia.

She was unaware Meridan Marks had a place in the Dallas area. *Nine, breathe, eight, breathe, seven, breathe* . . . Frisco was just twenty miles north. What if her stalker is from here? What if he grows tired of stalking someone famous? What if he fixates on someone that merely looks like Meridan? She was overreacting. *Six, breathe, five, breathe . . . find something to occupy your mind.*

Suddenly feeling agoraphobic and vulnerable, she whipped her head around frantically, inspecting every guest on the patio.

Dane. She fought the rising tide of panic and forced herself into the kitchen.

"Sweetie! Are you okay? It wasn't something you ate, was it?" he joked, and Lynden shook her head. Looking beyond the woman making fresh tortillas, Lynden scanned the crowd of people cramming the main dining area and spilling into all the ancillary bars. No familiar faces. "Honey, are you okay?" Dane held her hands and caught her gaze in his.

"I am." She laughed, embarrassed. "I think I'm coming down with something." She kissed him on the cheek and promised to call him the next day. Her first concern was getting into her house before nightfall.

Once the doors and windows had been inspected, she confirmed, gun in hand, that the security system was set and functioning properly.

I'm such a head case, Lynden thought as she plopped onto the couch with her copy of *Glitterati* magazine. The press generally doted on Meridan Marks, but little in the volumes of articles profiling America's beloved star had convinced Lynden such rapt attention was warranted. Meridan Marks stared back at her from the cover and Lynden couldn't help but scrutinize. They were virtual doppelgangers.

Lynden downplayed her appearance as much as possible; non-prescription glasses helped hide her striking green eyes. Meridan didn't downplay anything. Her luscious curls were wild in the photo. She wore virtually no makeup on her almond-shaped eyes, as none was needed to enhance them. Lynden herself wore only mascara unless she was going out for the evening, which was almost never.

Meridan's full lips were shaped more into a bow on top; Lynden wondered whether their mouths were the same prior to what must be the result of cosmetic surgery. It was the same top lip Michelle Pfeiffer had and Meg Ryan had recently acquired.

The word "STALKED," stamped in large type atop a photo of Meridan, leaped from the page, assaulting Lynden. She forced herself to read.

LOS ANGELES – Though they awarded her a best actress award for her sober portrayal . . . Lynden scanned for pertinent details, not at all interested in Meridan or her career.

Unfortunately, one person in particular has crossed the boundaries of excess in expressing his appreciation of the actress.

" . . . I have been dealing with it for some time now."

During the past several months the stalker has showered Marks with a torrent of mail and faxes, sending copies to the offices of her production company, Meritime Films; her attorney . . .

And then she saw it. The detail she feared.

. . . on several occasions sent the actress the peculiar arrangement of two dozen white roses centered around a single pink rose . . .

Lynden suddenly closed the magazine and glanced at the door. The compulsion to check the locks overwhelmed her, and she went through the routine on autopilot. Without warning, she began to dry heave and raced to the bathroom and vomited. Spent, she curled up on the floor and tried to convince herself the white roses and the inclusion of the pink was a normal romantic gesture and totally coincidental. An undercurrent of doubt hummed at the back of her brain. It *had* to be a coincidence.

Should she warn Meridan Marks? Was there anything to warn her about? She wished her parents were not unreachable on a Mediterranean cruise so she could consult them. In their absence, her thoughts automatically turned to Brady. He would know what to do.

His voice mail answered and she did not leave a message. He would be in town soon and they could discuss it in person, if she could keep it together long enough.

7

Lynden fired up her laptop and settled with it into the overstuffed couch. Her mind mulled over the year of her life that everything changed—her way of thinking, feeling, responding, trusting, loving, and living as a whole. She was not the same person, not by a wide margin, yet that was not to say she didn't like the person she had become. An old saying entered her mind: "That which doesn't kill you makes you stronger." She thought if this was true, she was one of the strongest women alive.

She stared at the blank screen. One does not simply dash off a correspondence to Meridan Marks. She again perused the article, searching for the attorney's name.

Joel Goldstein, partner in Johnson, Chiavella, Davis and Goldstein, P.A., based in Los Angeles. A Google search for attorneys in Los Angeles revealed a Wilshire Boulevard address for the firm. She scrolled for a direct e-mail contact button and when she clicked on it, the address JRG@JCDG.com appeared in the form of an outgoing mail. She copied it down before closing the window.

She stood up and began to pace, which led to the same routine she went through at least five times daily. Each lock, dead bolt, chain and security device was in place, undisturbed. Her obsessive-compulsive tendencies were just one of many "gifts" from him.

Twelve years had passed, and yet she felt no more comfortable today than she did the day she drove from Michigan to Texas to begin her new life. The last thing she wanted was to revisit her past—any more than she already did every day, anyway—but the danger she was certain Meridan faced left her with no choice but to help.

After setting up an anonymous Hotmail account, she began.

Dear Mr. Goldstein,

A recent article in Glitterati *magazine profiled Meridan Marks's difficulty with a stalker. I'm writing to you because I have information I believe is germane to the abuse your client has been experiencing. I fear her stalker is one of two men (or perhaps both) I encountered in college. These men are brothers and on similar and totally different levels terrorized me for over a year. It sounds as if the harassment is still in its infancy, and I am warning you of the potential for great violence and both psychological and physical damage.*

In the article, Ms. Marks stated her greatest source of fear was not knowing what her "stalker" looked like. I do not have photos but am willing to provide you with detailed descriptions of both men and their names. I will not forward that information at this point until I know you are interested in my help. The danger your client is in should not be underestimated at any point.

Best regards,

She leaned back and read and reread the letter. She omitted her name from the e-mail for her own protection. They would have to be very interested in her identity to research the e-mail address, and even then she wasn't certain her identity could be disclosed. Despite feeling secure in her name change, she had always taken great measures to live anonymously.

She put the finishing touches on the letter and paused before sending, uncertain of whether she should assume any risk. *No one deserves to experience what I have*, she reasoned, and clicked "send".

8

The next morning when I left my apartment for the library, I found a Cakebread chardonnay wine cork outside my door. The fact that it was standing upright told me it had not fallen there haphazardly—I knew it had been placed there. By Brit. Bringing it to my nose, the scent of the wine, while faint, brought memories in a torrent. I observed the date 3-24 written on the cork and would always remember it as our first date. I felt a strong urge to call him, but my upbringing pulled equally hard to stop me. I had been raised never to call boys socially; if they were interested, they would call, my mother had insisted.

Brit was absent from class Monday. I tried to take good notes and was fortunate not to have suffered a strained neck from craning it every five minutes watching for him to saunter into the room. I ached to see his long, denim-clad legs; his stern, scruffy jaw; his intense brown eyes.

Arriving home from class, a message from him explained he had opted for office hours with his business professor.

That afternoon, instead of using my empty classroom to do homework until Jessica was able to pick me up, my teaching partner Scott and I headed out together to get a beer.

"Your stalker," he said quietly and gestured with his head to an extremely handsome guy who sat just outside our classroom and looked up when we passed. Scott had been teasing me about an admirer who lingered outside our classroom daily, but this couldn't possibly be him. I took inventory discreetly. He was tall, with intense espresso-colored eyes. His Rolex was in stark contrast to his sloppy, well-worn attire.

"No way." I shook my head, thinking I should be so lucky to be "stalked" by a man so gorgeous. Scott nodded his certainty while I pondered the myriad excuses for his presence.

I didn't hear from Brit until Wednesday, when he called to invite me to dinner on Friday. Each day had lasted what seemed a year, and I had repeatedly checked the phone to confirm it was in working order. He had seemed interested, yet he was not as aggressive as I had learned most guys were. I thought it odd we wouldn't see each other until our date, but I didn't want to seem needy or overly interested. Despite my disappointment, I cheerfully agreed to the time and told him I was looking forward to our evening together.

Somehow I made it to Friday, and my nerves were humming as the clock crept closer to seven. I checked the wine supply in the kitchen; having consumed such amazing wine with Brit, the overstock of white zinfandel was a touch embarrassing. I opened a bottle anyway, and the first taste told me I had been ruined for cheap wine. Halfway through my glass, I felt a slow warmth inch its way up the back of my neck as I settled onto the couch with my new issue of Road & Track.

The doorbell interrupted my reading, and my stomach took a little dip as I hurried to the door. In all honesty, nothing could have prepared me for the resplendence beyond the threshold. I was grateful that until then I had never seen Brit in black; I would have wanted nothing to diminish the impact of the moment. In black wool trousers that broke delicately over gorgeous black leather loafers, a loose-fitting black silk T-shirt, and a tailored black jacket that matched the pants, he looked as if he had wandered away from a runway modeling gig somewhere in Europe. His dark hair, eyes, and scruff gave him a brooding look that left me completely disarmed. His other hand held three white roses perfectly packaged in pink tissue paper with a small pink ribbon.

"You look amazing. I thought you'd like pink." He smiled, handed me the flowers, and led me by the hand to the truck. I focused on regaining my natural breathing pattern, which was halted when Brit's hand grazed my leg as he helped me into the cab.

Instead of starting the engine, he touched my left cheek. It was a whisper of a gesture, his face thoughtful. "You look beautiful, but I wonder if you could take your hair down for me?" he asked softly, and I did so without hesitation or question. I had scooped my dark mass of curls into a loose, sexy up-do hoping to lure Brit closer if he wanted to touch my hair again. Oh well, I would secure a kiss tonight, one way or another.

During our drive, the day's light sprinkle turned into a torrent for a few minutes, tapering off again by the time we reached Harvest Grill.

"Please, let me," Brit insisted when I reached for my door handle. Instead of offering me his hand to help me down, he swept me into his arms and carried me to the front of the restaurant, carefully avoiding the deep pools of water flooding the parking lot. When he lowered me to the ground, he kept me close, holding me by the waist. His scent roused my senses and I lifted my head, hoping for a kiss. He gazed down at me, his hands firmly gripping my hipbones.

"Let's get you out of this weather," he smiled as he opened the door for me and ushered me inside.

The hostess greeted us graciously and guided us to a small corner table facing a lovely fireplace filled with candles. Brit removed my coat and handed it to the hostess, pulled out my chair and, once I was seated, placed my napkin gently in my lap. It was difficult not to wonder if he treated all women with such care. Had his mother taught him how to treat a lady? Once again, I was reminded I knew virtually nothing about Brit Holden except that he was from Bloomfield Hills, one of the most prominent areas in Michigan.

"I requested this table because you look so lovely in the glow of candlelight," he said softly, almost shyly.

"Oh, thank you. Gosh, I've never been very good at accepting compliments," I said with an abashed giggle.

"Get used to it, because I plan to do it a lot," he said, capturing a stray lock of my hair in his fingers. He rolled it around and stared through me for quite some time.

"You seem preoccupied," I prompted, pulling him from his thoughts.

"I wanted to come for drinks first because I need to talk to you about

something and didn't want to interfere with dinner." Brit greeted Anita with a smile as she presented a bottle of champagne. She uncorked the bottle with a startlingly loud pop and poured Brit a small amount to taste.

"Perfect. Pour," he directed. Once she had, she slipped from the table as I searched Brit's face for any hint as to the discussion meant to follow.

"Salute! To new beginnings." Brit raised his glass and I met it, liking the implication of the toast.

A big sigh followed, and Brit relaxed back into his chair. He took his glass and pondered it for what seemed like an hour. He's going to break it off, I thought. We haven't even kissed and it's over! I silently wished he would have dumped me over the phone or never called me again and I forced an impassive expression.

"I haven't been entirely up front with you," he began, elbows on his knees, leaning forward toward me. I sat back, terrified by what might come out of his mouth next. "I really was busy this week, and I did opt for business office hours, but I also just got back from home. I've been there for two days." His eyes searched mine, and I forced my face to be impassive, masking my swelling emotions. "I went home to break up with my girlfriend." He reached for my arm to stop me from standing or bolting out of my chair, both of which I was too stunned to attempt. "We've been together since high school; it's been bad for years. She doesn't go to school, and having me away all the time has eroded the relationship. Until recently, I had no reason to break it off. We're so used to one another. It's turned into more of a brother-and-sister-type relationship."

Give away nothing, I reminded myself. So, there I had it. He had a girlfriend and even if he did break up with her, he was having second thoughts. And if he wasn't now, he would eventually.

"The day we met in Spatial Relations, I was behind you on my bike while you were, what were you doing?"

"Rollerblading"

"What is that, anyway? Like roller skating?"

"No. Rollerblades are what hockey players use to train in the off season."

"Do you play hockey?"

"No." No longer in the mood, I just wanted to go home. I was embarrassed and felt silly. I'd been so naïve to think a guy with so much to offer wouldn't already be seeing someone. I felt taken, and not in a good way.

"Where did you get them?"

"Does it matter?" I cried. He was stalling.

"Yes. I want to know everything about you," he whispered and reached for my cheek, or my hair, or something. I batted his hand away angrily.

"I can tell you I don't have a boyfriend. I can tell you I didn't enter into this, this, whatever this is, with a boyfriend. I can tell you I didn't have to sample you to decide whether I should ditch my previous relationship!"

Brit settled back in his seat and a smirk played on his lips. The nine o'clock shadow magnified the seductive effect. "May I continue?"

Silence.

"The reason I haven't been in class is because I'm not enrolled in it. I followed you and went in, and, well . . ." He gave me an "aw shucks" shrug of the shoulders that made my heart hurt a bit.

"Are you serious?" I burst out laughing—out of relief or frustration or pure delight, I really wasn't sure. He nodded. The sexy smirk conspired with his eyes, leaving me defenseless.

"I'd planned to go home on Friday and break it off, leaving me free and clear by Saturday night, but I had you on the phone, and you mentioned your plans for the weekend, and like an idiot I asked you out for right that minute. I couldn't wait to see you. I couldn't even wait long enough to break up with my girlfriend. I didn't kiss you, though." He wagged a finger at me, gesturing for me not to be so rigorous in my judgment. Indeed, he had not kissed me that night, nor had he yet—at least not for real.

"One of my friends plays for the Detroit Red Wings; we have the same doctor. He took me to buy the blades. He thought they would be a great way for me to get around freshman year because you can't have a car." My statement was an olive branch. I gestured for him to continue.

"I apologize." His elbows rested on the table and he bowed his head to meet his folded hands. "Have I screwed up? I wanted to be honest with you

from the start." He raised his thick eyebrows in a pleading gesture. I caved. A little.

"Where does it stand? Where is she?"

"She accused me of cheating, which I didn't deny. That hurt her pride. Karis is used to getting exactly what she wants. I haven't heard from her."

"Okay," I said, displaying less emotion and more self-assurance than I actually felt. I decided to let it go. He had been honest. I wanted to be with him; he seemed to want to be with me.

"Okay? Really?" He grabbed my hand and clasped it with the other, holding both firmly to his heart, which I could feel was racing madly. Mine picked up pace to match. We enjoyed our champagne as he intently drilled me with questions about my background until it was time to leave for dinner.

At the door, he swept me into his arms again to carry me over the puddles in the parking lot.

"You're so little. I love carrying you," he breathed through my hair, and I'd have swooned if I were standing. Instead, I melted into his chest and enjoyed the heady scent of the rain mingled with his cologne.

I was anxious to dine at the Wine Cellar. It was no surprise to me when we walked in to backslapping, handshaking, and waves from all around. Brit knew everyone, and they all seemed excited to see him.

The restaurant was charming and quaint, the walls lined with wine racks loaded with bottles, some dusty, some new. Light from custom sconces glowed like embers, candles perched on every surface. The low light was romantic beyond anything I had experienced. Brit led us to what I had to assume was his regular table, which left me with my back to a semi-open kitchen and the whole restaurant before me. Brit across from me was quite a distraction.

"Brit!" A voice bellowed from behind me. I turned to see a young man in chef whites charging our table with his hand extended. Brit rose to hug him and then turned to me.

"Patrick, I'd like you to meet—" he gestured to me with his hand, and Patrick stared at me mouth agape.

"I know exactly who she is," he interrupted. "Does your brother know

about this?" He questioned sternly, meeting Brit's angry eyes.

"Don't worry about it." He dismissed Patrick with an arrogant wave, leaving me shocked and confused.

"Sorry about that, Reese." He affected a casual tone, but anger clouded his eyes as he watched Patrick return to the kitchen.

"What's going on? How would Patrick have any idea who I am? What does your brother have to do with this? I didn't even know you had one." We had spent so much time talking about me and about our shared interests, I wasn't even aware he had siblings. He had the air of an only. He held up his hands as a barrier.

"Whoa! Hold on." Our waiter approached the table, and Brit ordered cheese fondue as an appetizer and a bottle of Grgich Hills cabernet. I was relieved food was in sight, as I was drunk on adrenaline and champagne. My thoughts were getting fuzzy. Had he told me about a brother?

"First of all, I have three siblings. I'm sure Patrick was concerned I was with someone other than Karis."

"But he said he knew exactly who I was," I challenged.

"Yeah, I guess, not Karis? And my brother doesn't know we broke up either. But we did," he finished confidently and met my skeptical stare. I let it go.

Brit explained the fondue was a delectable mixture of Gruyere and Swiss cheeses, dark beer and spices. He dipped a chunk of fresh sourdough bread into the pot, blew to cool it, and offered it to me. When I reached for the stick, he pulled it back.

"Your mouth. I want your mouth," he whispered. I had no doubt he would be my undoing. A barely audible groan escaped his lips when my mouth closed around the cheese-laden bread. My thighs went up in flames. He watched intently while I chewed and I could feel my face grow hot. I was being seduced.

Dinner arrived and we ate heartily. Brit offered me food from his fork frequently and watched me chew until I swallowed each time. I had always been self-conscious eating in front of people, but he made me feel sexy.

"I need to see you again," he announced when our dishes were cleared

from the table.

"You're still seeing me now." I laughed, but he didn't.

"I need to know when I'll see you again," he reiterated.

"Well, I, I'm free tomorrow, I think," I scrambled, knowing I was supposed to spend the evening with Jessica. She would understand, but I felt a brief pang of guilt.

"Excellent." He settled in his chair looking satisfied, the air of a man who had won.

Patrick never reappeared, which I thought odd. Was he so emotionally involved with Brit's former relationship he would be upset by the break-up? When we rose to leave, Brit helped me out of my chair, and when he put my coat on for me, he was careful to pull my hair out from under the collar. At once, he gripped the hair at the nape of my neck tightly, spun me to face him and held me fast in his gaze. I somehow held a startled gasp inside until his warm lips met mine. His tongue forced my lips apart and slipped provocatively into my mouth. I felt I was being consumed, and I gave in to the sensation. My mother's admonitions regarding public displays of affection echoed distantly in my ears. Brit's kiss was demanding, almost possessive, and at that moment I wanted to be possessed by him.

9

It was a warm night, and I had opted for a clingy, double-lined white dress with a plunging neckline. It was much more daring than what I was used to, but things with Brit were progressing slowly enough for me to find comfort and gain confidence in this role he was painting for me. He seemed to find me alluring and sexy, whereas I always had felt like a cute tomboy, or, on my best day, pretty. The too-skinny, rarely-had-a-date adolescent I had been throughout my high school years had taken up permanent residency in the back of my mind, wreaking havoc on my confidence.

The doorbell rang and I grabbed my purse to meet Brit at the door. When he saw me, his eyes widened and his hand flew to his chest. "You're going to give me a heart attack." He held the door jamb for effect, taking a moment, pretending he needed to regain his composure.

Brit's eyes met mine with an intense gaze, and he slipped an arm around my waist and pulled me to him. He stared for a long moment before he brushed his lips to mine. My pulse quickened as it always did when he was close, and I was disappointed when he pulled away. A glance at his sterling silver submariner Rolex told him we needed to hustle to make our reservations.

We'd only seen one another for lunch twice since the previous Friday. He'd wanted to take me out Saturday, but I was so behind on my studies I had begged him to wait until tonight. I still marveled that two weeks ago my best date was meeting at Ranger's for breadsticks and beer.

As we approached the door to Beggar's Banquet, we were assaulted by the wailing of Brit's car alarm behind us.

"Just a sec," he said and turned to the parking lot. I opened the door and headed in. I had never been to Beggar's before. The lights were low, the ambiance enchanting, and the décor reminiscent of an old English cottage. I felt bright white in my dress, like a beacon. The bar was horseshoe-shaped in the center of the room, and I glanced about looking for a hostess stand. I could still hear Brit's alarm and wondered if I should help.

Just as I turned to head out the door, I saw a man stand up from his bar stool; once his face was fully illuminated, a double take confirmed he was my *"stalker"* from outside class. He smiled and I felt trapped. I regretted that the first time I happened to encounter him socially I was with another man. I weighed my options, aware of the awkwardness of the situation. *"What the fuck are you doing?"* I heard Brit growl from behind me. Having not heard him re-enter, I whipped my head around to look at him, but he was looking beyond me.

"You have got to be fucking kidding me, Brit," my *"stalker"* said, sauntering, much like Brit did, closer to us. My nerves jangled like bells I was sure everyone could hear.

"Back off, Ash. This has nothing to do with you," Brit said sternly and grabbed my hand, roughly pulling me to him. Ash stopped in his tracks, but had no intention of giving up the fight. *"You said you were going home, Ash. Why are you here?"* Home? I glanced frantically back and forth between the two, as though I were following a tennis match. Same height, same hair color, same devilish scruff, same watch, although their taste in clothing appeared completely different. Their voices were similar in timbre but not sound, their eyes were different shades of brown but equally intense, especially now.

"This is perfect." Ash turned his back on us and gave Brit the finger on his way back to his bar stool. Brit jerked me through the restaurant to a table in a corner far from the bar. I was too stunned to speak, which was fine, because I hadn't any idea what to say anyway.

"Meet my brother, Ashland Holden. Isn't he charming?" Brit spat as he shook his napkin out of its fan-like fold. He was seething. I had never seen him angry, and I was certain I never wanted to again.

"I know him," I whispered and immediately wanted to snatch the words

back. "I mean I've seen him in the communications building."

"And you remember him?"

"I guess I remember because he reminded me of you," I lied, not wanting to part with the fact that Scott had reported Ash's presence almost daily since school began. I chose to avoid any further discussion and we sat in thick silence for five minutes to a year before the waitress eased the tension.

Brit ordered a double gin on the rocks for himself and a bottle of Kendall Jackson cabernet. As soon as his drink hit the table, he took a long pull on it. He leaned back in his chair and ran his hand through his thick, dark hair while he brooded. I couldn't help wondering what I had become involved in. He was completely unavailable, and I was desperate to break the silence.

"I can't believe how much you look alike. Are you fraternal twins?" The similarities were striking now that I had seen them together. How could I have missed it? I wasn't looking for it. I had become so blinded by Brit that Ash had slipped under the radar. Somehow my statement relaxed his mood a bit, and he softened.

"I'm sorry," he started with a huge sigh, reaching out to me, which flooded me with relief. "No, we aren't twins. My brother . . . it's a long story." Brit looked away, a distant and sad expression clouding his handsome face. Instantly, I recalled Patrick at the Wine Cellar asking if his brother "knew about this," and my mind reeled.

"I'd like to hear it, if you'd like to tell me," I spoke softly, hoping not to trigger anger.

"My brother is a raging alcoholic with some pretty severe mental problems. He's always been, well, unbalanced."

"In what way? He attends a Big Ten university. It would seem he'd have to be competent."

"Oh he's competent; a demented sociopath, perhaps, but competent." Not exactly what a girl wants to hear about a man who loiters outside her classroom.

"I don't follow."

Another long pull from his drink. The ice clanked in his nearly-empty glass. He raised it to the waitress, who had been smart to keep her distance, and she moved quickly to replenish it. I had been hoping he would move to wine instead.

"Ash and I are ten months apart. When I was three and he was four, our parents died in an accident. A semi jackknifed during a blizzard and collided with them." He avoided my eyes and my heart ached for him. I wanted to reach out but didn't. He didn't continue, so I forced myself to speak.

"How old were your other siblings?"

"Ha, siblings." he scoffed. I waited. "Ash and I are our parents' only natural children. We were sent to live with my mother's sister. She already had two children of her own to deal with. The last thing she needed was two more mouths to feed."

My immediate thought was the money. Where did it come from if his aunt had worried about feeding four children?

"My parents' assets were liquidated. We each inherited, I don't know, some money. My uncle's an investor. He invested well, was allowed to use the dividends to help raise us and provide for his own family at the same time. I'm sure it helped cushion the blow of taking in extra kids." Brit spoke with a bitterness I found incomprehensible. Before tonight he'd been nothing but even-tempered, kind and calm.

"We don't have to talk about this," I started, but he shook his head.

"It's better, you know, especially where Ash is concerned. He remembers our parents. He's never been right." He grabbed my forearm and held it a bit too tight. I tried not to cry out. "I want you to stay away from him. He's dangerous." I couldn't help but gasp. Dangerous? What did he mean?

I was grateful when the waitress interrupted to take our order. Without asking, Brit ordered me king crab legs and a Caesar salad, precisely what I would have ordered if I weren't instinctually money-conscious.

"This is a disaster. I'm sorry," he said, pleading with his eyes, and beyond confusion, I felt compassion. So much pain and loss, I couldn't fault him for his emotional display. I couldn't imagine life without my parents. How had Brit and Ash survived such a tragedy? I didn't know what else to say, so we lingered *in silence until our food arrived. The moment it was placed on the table, Ash appeared and pointed at Brit.*

"This isn't over. I want an explanation!" The two men exchanged steely glares, each waiting for the other to fold. My stomach tied itself into a half Windsor and I was terrified Ash would speak to me. Instead, to my horror, he winked at me, which brought Brit out of his chair, tipping it over. I reached for his wrist to try and stop him, but he lunged too quickly for me.

"Bastard!"

I was shocked at the outburst, mostly because I realized I couldn't tell which brother had said it. Ash backed away enough to put some distance between the two of them and fell smoothly into a combative stance.

"How about it, little brother? You want to do this here? Now?" Ash demanded. I could see Brit vacillate between his need to defend me and his unwillingness to become part of a spectacle. "What's wrong? Afraid?"

"Don't be an asshole. We're in public, and I'm not about to allow you to draw me into something." He straightened up and backed away slowly.

"You're worthless," Ash said and turned on his heel. He didn't appear to be drunk at all. He wasn't slurring his speech and his reactions were unimpaired.

Barely containing his rage, the veins at Brit's temples and in his neck were pulsating rapidly. He took his seat and drained his second gin. His disposition darkened even further as he brooded over the confrontation.

As we picked at our food, I attempted light conversation but could not penetrate his mood.

"The crab's amazing. Would you like to try it?"

"No."

"How's your steak?

"Overdone." My appetite had long since abandoned me. He poured us both some wine, shaking his head. "Wow, I'm so sorry. What a shitty night." He smiled at me, the first time since we'd entered the building. My spirits lifted a bit. "How often do you see my brother?"

"Only once." I refused to mention the "stalking," as I was sure it was all

a mistake.

"Hmm . . ." he mused.

"What?" I asked, not really wanting to hear the answer.

"He told me about a girl he was really into. He described her to me. It's only now I'm realizing you're that girl." He smirked. I panicked.

"Maybe not. I mean, I never see him, well, just the one time," I stammered.

"No, no, I see it all clearly now. He thinks I stole you from him." He rolled his eyes as if this was typical.

"I'm sure this is a misunderstanding, Brit, really. Can we forget about it? Please?"

"Yeah, sure." His tone was unconvincing.

10

"Mr. Goldstein?" There was a light knock on the door before it opened slowly.

Joel gazed out over the city from his fifteenth story office window, chatting animatedly on the phone. Swiveling in his huge leather wingback chair, he gestured a silent "thank you" as his secretary Barb slipped the e-mails she had printed onto his desk.

Joel Goldstein, attorney to the stars, juggled several more "critical" calls before settling squarely in front of a pile of paperwork that grew by the minute. E-mails. He hadn't checked them this morning, so Barb had printed hard copies.

He slowly perused the one with "Meridan Marks's stalker" in the subject line.

Something differentiated it from all the other calls and e-mails that had been pouring in from people claiming to know the stalker, be the stalker, be related to the stalker, or be married to the stalker. This was the first person or, Joel assumed, woman, claiming to have been stalked by the same man or, as she proposed, men. The thought of there being two men was disturbing, yet seemed unlikely. That this woman did not ask to speak to, meet or have contact with Meridan made it all the more unusual. Everyone wanted fifteen minutes.

He put the hard copy into Meridan's overflowing filing drawer-turned-cabinet and logged onto his account. He forwarded, via e-mail, all of the stalker-related information he had received, to both Roz and Meridan at Meritime, to Meridan's personal account, and to the police detective not so thrilled to have been assigned to the case.

The police officers and investigators didn't have the slightest notion who the stalker was, and were generally unconcerned. They had found no evidence of a potential intruder at Meridan's home. This had started innocently enough nearly a year ago—letters, postcards, flowers. Joel couldn't help wondering when things had escalated, and why he hadn't heard about it until now—could all this be just a publicity stunt? And could Meridan have devised a plot so clever on her own? Had Roz helped her? Again, he wondered if he'd been cut out of the loop.

He had suggested moving from Santa Monica to Bel Air as a test, knowing Meridan would agree to it only if she truly perceived a threat. Otherwise, he would continue to question the veracity of her claim.

Moving was a long-standing bone of contention between attorney and client. Meridan purported herself the "people's actress" and believed living in a secured environment would alter her fans' perception of her. Being perpetually prepared for autographs, photos and interviews worked to her advantage, as fans didn't hound her the way they did other more elusive actors and actresses. Despite the industry's general lack of enthusiasm toward working with her, the public demanded *More! More Meridan!*

Meridan's draw was undeniable, unless you knew her. Joel found over the years she had become the most self-centered, superficial, vacuous woman he had ever had the displeasure of representing. It had been a cakewalk until the little incident with the bartender. It hadn't been her fault, really. Then there had been the fender-bender on Sunset in front of the Saddle Ranch, tourist capital of L.A., where she entertained fans from all over the country with a foulmouthed confrontation involving four police officers dining there at the time. It hadn't been her fault, really.

Things had calmed down in the months since she'd met Jim Cooper and the two were as inseparable as could be, given both of their busy schedules and Meridan's fabricated relationship with fellow actor Christian York. Joel was relieved to see the Meridan he had known at the beginning of her career re-emerging slowly as the relationship developed.

He tried not to vilify her to anyone, as she had single-handedly brought him a legion of stars that retained him on her word. Joel knew Meridan liked and respected him as much as she was capable of liking anyone other than herself or respecting anyone at all, including herself.

~

"Damn," Meridan said, looking around for whatever it was that had caused her to stumble. There was nothing on her welcome mat. Her eyes settled on a cork resting at the base of the two stairs leading to her door. Slowly, she made her way down the two small steps, nursing her tender ankle.

It was a cork from a bottle of Roederer Cristal. Not unusual. She customarily plowed through several bottles a month; maybe it slipped out of the garbage when the maid was putting it out. She put it in her purse, and, hoping for correspondence from her stalker, she checked the mail before entering the garage.

Minutes later, Meridan stalled her Porsche in front of Lela's, which was packed for lunch as usual at high noon. Everyone turned to see who was getting out of the custom-painted lapis lazuli Porsche 911 with the license plate that read "MS HLYWD." She loved her car and the attention it attracted. Any true regulars would recognize the ostentatious sports car and know exactly who was about to alight; she delighted more in the gasps from tourists. Rumblings went up on the patio but she pretended not to notice the heads swiveling and fingers pointing. She waved at Roz, who was on the phone, as usual.

"I need to go," Roz whispered into her phone before hanging up discreetly and rising to air-kiss Meridan.

"Who was that?" Meridan asked, perpetually nosy about Roz's business.

"Joel. You've received some interesting correspondence. He didn't read any of it to me. He's on his way." Meridan raised her eyebrows and took a big drink of the Bloody Mary Roz had ordered her.

"Listen, Meridan, I wanted to talk to you about the *Glitterati* article."

"I thought it was amazing. I came across so well, don't you think?"

"Yes, you did, splendidly. My concern was that we'd discussed being vague. We didn't want to insinuate B was the stalker, right? I mean, he hasn't really done anything wrong. It just seems like there are a lot of people involved now."

"Duh! The more cooks in the soup, the better. We wanted a media circus."

Roz, as usual, ignored the botched metaphor. "'We?' You."

"I didn't mention the flowers, I think Joel did. I guess it was—"

"Ms. Marks?" a handsome blond interrupted.

"Yes?" She launched a theatrical hair toss and smiled, prompting a well-honed mental eye roll from Roz.

"I just wanted to let you know that we—" he pointed to his table of friends, "think you're very brave, and we totally love you." He gushed and swooned when she squeezed his hand and thanked him.

"Cute boys," Meridan watched him walk away, admiring his lean, toned body.

"Yes, cute *gay* boys," Roz said, a note of disappointment in her voice. "Now, about the article. I feel like we went too far. What do you think?"

"Be quiet, here comes Joel," Meridan hissed.

"Ladies," Joel sang, and held up his hands to interrupt a standard Hollywood greeting. He could do without the drama. "You are not going to believe this." He handed the newest fax to Roz, who leaned in close so Meridan could read over her shoulder. "He thinks you're being stalked by someone else."

Meridan's mouth formed a generous "O" as she read.

Meridan,

Am I to believe what I've read in Glitterati—that you are, as the magazine states, being "stalked"?

There was mention of mail and faxes, scripts, flowers. I'm almost embarrassed to call attention to the fact I am guilty of sending you those same things. You don't think for one second it's me, do you?

You must know—your safety and well being is my utmost concern. All you have to do is say the word, and I will do everything in my power to make sure you're safe.

I don't want to seem blasé about any of this, but it does sound like this is just one of your fans expressing adoration. Nonetheless, Meridan, I am concerned about you, and I feel it is even more imperative we meet—and soon.
B~

"What in the hell is this supposed to mean?" Roz puzzled aloud.

"I spoke with Detective Adler on the way here. I forwarded this to Detective Ford before I came—along with this." He pulled this morning's disturbing e-mail from the anonymous woman out of his breast pocket and handed it to Meridan.

"My God! Violence!"

"Danger!" Both women let out startled gasps as they struggled to absorb what they were reading.

"Joel, this e-mail sounds ominous, but the tone of B's correspondence really doesn't hint that these could be the same people," Roz commented, and Joel nodded in agreement.

"Our guy has never shown any hint of violence. He is polite, adulatory—"

"Except when he tried to break into my house," Meridan interjected and Roz shot her a look.

"Meridan, there was no evidence whatsoever of an intruder."

"Joel, what did the detectives say?" Roz inquired.

"Well, they agree. This guy hasn't tried to contact you personally. He could have called. Hell, if he tried to break in, he knows your address. Why doesn't he just drop by for a drink, for God's sake?" Joel threw his hands up in frustration.

"So that's it? We're just going to ignore this woman? She has information about this guy, or I guess guys. Is it possible there are two?" Roz saw a flicker of actual concern in Meridan's eyes.

"Again, the detectives think it's unlikely the two situations are related, but they did have me e-mail her back thanking her for her offer and letting her know I had passed the information on to you. This way, if it is some fan trying to make a connection, she'll realize you aren't going to call her or contact her. They also asked me to request the names and descriptions she said she could give us."

"So that's it?" Meridan pouted, flouncing back in her chair. "We have a woman telling us not to, what did she say, underestimate the danger I'm in, and you want to ignore it? I don't think this is getting the attention it deserves."

"Meridan, it sounds like you're disappointed it isn't a more threatening situation," Joel prodded, totally unconvinced this "stalking" wasn't a matter of her own devise.

"It's not that. This e-mail is creepy. And there he is thinking someone else is stalking me, all compliments and stuff. I don't like it." Meridan frowned for a moment and, as if someone had told her not to frown or her face would stay that way, she immediately turned it upside down into a forced smile.

"How about we let it go?" Joel offered. "The cops are working on the identity of the woman who e-mailed, but it's a free account, tough to crack. Let's see what happens?"

"I agree with Joel. He might get bored and move on to the next hot thing." Roz regretted her statement the minute it came out of her mouth. "Er—that isn't what I meant. It's just—if we ignore him, he'll go away, right?

11

The letter was taped at about eye level on the outside of her door, unnoticed until Meridan turned around to lock it behind her. She debated removing it wondering if she should call the police. Joel had made it clear the police were reluctant to get involved unless there was a serious threat, so she pulled the envelope off the door. Joel had suggested private security, but only she knew she was more exhilarated by the attention than she was afraid of it.

The thought of driving a man mad with passion was similar to a movie she'd done about an emotionally abused woman who risked her life and those of her children to escape. Her husband was enraged, fueled by distorted love that had manifested itself in possession and obsession. Certainly, Meridan thought, I am the object of desire for countless men and women. Granted, this man was going the extra mile, but like the rest of them, he was harmless.

What kind of game are you playing, Meridan? We keep making plans and each time you blow me off. Initially, I assumed you were trying to stay out of the spotlight, lay low—considering all you've been dealing with of late. And then I hear about you all over town with—of all guys—Christian York!?!?

You don't really consider him to be your type, do you? I'm trying to be patient, but it is absolutely imperative that I see you. Why do you keep pulling away from me? Can you think for one minute of someone other than yourself to consider how that can make a person feel? Pretty bad, Meridan.

Please, think about what you need to do to break it off cleanly with Christian. Do not back down no matter what he says.

B~

Meridan opened her door quickly and stepped back inside. She slammed the door behind her and double-bolted it. Her heart had picked up a few beats, and she sat on the couch to read the letter again. It didn't make any sense.

She picked up the phone.

"Joel, I was wondering if you received anything from my stalker this morning?"

"No, not yet. Why?"

"There was a letter taped to my door this morning." She read him the letter and asked for his opinion.

"I don't like the sound of it. I also don't like the fact it was taped to your door." When Joel again suggested surveillance, Meridan detailed the myriad reasons why that was not an option. Some of it was valid in Joel's eyes. Her primary concern was the façade she had built with Christian York and her real-life romance with Jim.

"What would you like me to do?"

"Nothing, I guess." Meridan gazed unabashedly at her reflection in the mirror above her sofa as she talked. Her expressions vacillated between indignation, wariness, terror and surprise as she spoke. None of the expressions matched her statements or mood in particular; it was a habit. "I have to go to Meritime." She hung up the phone and reapplied lipstick before heading out.

~

"Just read it to me, Roz. I'm far too upset to read."

Meridan,

I wanted to know how things went with Christian. If you don't want to tell me all of the details just yet, I understand. Let some time pass, some water pass under the bridge, turn the heat down and the air conditioning on. What does your schedule look like this week? I'm going to cut this short and finish a story I've been working on. Today. We could meet over drinks. I like drinks. I read somewhere you do, too. Specifically, wine? By the way, when I got to Neiman's yesterday there was nothing left. Naughty girl.

B~

"The guy's a total screw ball—that gave me goose bumps," Meridan laughed and placed the fax on Roz' desk.

"He sounds agitated." Roz mused, after finishing the letter Meridan had brought. "It's weird he would go to your house but not initiate contact."

"He's insane."

"Were you at Neiman's yesterday?"

"Yeah, I didn't notice Creepy there, though. What's wrong with him? Does he really believe what he's saying? Like, we're going to work on some projects? What a freak!" Meridan stood, collected her purse and headed toward the door. Roz marveled at Meridan's cavalier attitude toward the situation. They had pulled America's heartstrings by running that article, and here she was treating it like a joke. Granted, other fans had gone too far in the past, but this guy seemed different.

"Where're you going?" Roz asked.

"I'm off to the Peninsula. Jim's flying home today. I can't wait to see him."

"Tell me you don't check in together!"

"No! Lord no. Sometimes Christian checks in with me then switches rooms with Jim. God knows what he does in there alone." Meridan giggled again. "Probably smells Jim's clothes and tries on his underwear!" Roz laughed with her, but made a mental note to keep closer tabs on Meridan and her schedule until this situation with B blew over.

"I can't imagine Christian finding anyone as attractive as himself," Roz jabbed.

"When you meet Jim, you'll understand. Remember John Taylor from Duran Duran?" Roz shook her head, keenly aware as she often was the decade that spanned their ages. "Well, anyway, same look. That light brown hair with highlights in the front. He makes Christian York look like Steve Buscemi."

"Please! This is *People* magazine's hottest man in the world, what, a hundred years in a row?"

"Jim's amazing, but it seems like we never see each other. You know, all the sneaking around. I don't know if it would work in the long run, but I think I want it to."

"What long run? The one you take when you bolt and leave his heart lying still beating next to his body? Give me a break!" Roz snorted, covering her mouth with her hand. The mere thought of Meridan Marks loving anyone but herself was a joke.

"I'm serious." Meridan closed Roz' office door all the way after peeking out to make certain they weren't overheard. "He's wonderful, but he really isn't into what I do for a living. Not that it matters so long as we all agree that I'm 'in love' with Christian. He's even cool with that. Of course, he knows Christian is—" she mouthed the word *gay* and looked around covertly.

Christian York was one of the biggest actors in Hollywood, a devastating heartthrob whose rugged good looks had made him a fortune—a fortune which neither he nor his "people" were willing to part with by outing him.

Meridan had starred with him years ago in one of her first blockbusters. She had fallen head over heels, only to be crushed during what she thought was a date when he revealed his true self to her. Though disappointed, she was honored to be one of the only people to know the best-kept secret in Hollywood. They had been extremely close ever since, though Meridan still longed to have sex with him just once.

An unusually tall actor, towering over most co-stars at six-foot-two, Christian's smoldering good looks were undeniable whether you were male or female. Luxurious, JFK Jr.-esque hair called like a siren beckoning her to bury her hands in it. But now she had Jim—and Jim was hot and *not* gay.

"If you're committed to this publicity stunt with Christian, you'd better be more careful about your visits with Jim."

"I know. That was stupid. Who'd have thought a photographer would follow me to his place? That was the last time. We usually do the Peninsula. When he comes to my place, Christian comes with. We've been fine at the ranch and the lake, but his schedule is tighter than mine. I wish he'd quit and be my sex slave."

"What does he think about this stalking stuff?"

"He had dinner with Christian and me last week at my place, and he asked Christian to be around more. Of course, I don't think Christian heard a word. He was too busy drooling!" She suppressed a giggle by putting her hand over her mouth.

"Any chance you could share him with friends tonight?" Roz said, realizing for the first time the serious potential of Meridan's feelings for Jim. Until now, Roz had assumed Jim was no more than the latest toy for her fickle client. She dreaded being out of the loop even for a moment, and realized she was suddenly intensely curious about the man who'd humbled her client a measure.

Meridan had been dying to get her hands on Jim all week. They had been able to talk only a couple of times due to his erratic schedule. Who was the movie star here, anyway? "I suppose it isn't out of the question. Dinner or drinks maybe?"

"What time is it now?" Roz consulted her watch. "Eleven. When does he come in?"

"Noon. I'm to be naked in bed," Meridan taunted wickedly.

"Rough life, Meridan," Roz said, not entirely free of envy.

"I know," she responded. "Let's say Skybar for drinks. How about eight? But no drinking like wild dogs! I don't want any failure to launch later. Can you call and make reservations? Make sure you don't use my name. We don't need a mob scene." Roz rolled her eyes. First of all, had she ever used Meridan's name on a reservation? *And*, she couldn't help thinking, *how exactly does a wild dog drink, Meridan*? At this point in her career, Rosalind Lescher had as much power as Meridan Marks herself. After seeing Meridan's impressive performance in her first film when she was only twelve years old, Roz had contacted Meridan's parents and asked for permission to meet. It seemed three hundred years had passed since. While she and Meridan were, for all practical purposes, the best of friends, Roz at times felt she could cheerfully throttle her spoiled, self-centered diva of a client.

Once alone, Roz examined the newest fax. It was disjointed, delusional. Did he really think Meridan was acting in accordance with his wishes? Joel said the scripts he had sent were pages and pages of senseless fiction. No plot, no direction, no character development. What could he do for a living that he had so much free time?

Either way, she had to admit it was most likely the man had no intention of harming her client. He was just harassing her. He could have called Meritime or even Joel's office; instead, he took a passive role, asking her to contact him, yet offering no contact information. He probably was afraid to actually meet her, so he was deluding himself by pretending to ask for dates to which she'd never show.

12

The hotel valets greeted Meridan with nothing less than a spectacular display of acrobatics, all trying to be the first to reach her car door.

The concierge bolted from his desk chair, startling the clients already seated at his desk to check in. "Ms. Marks! I have your key for you. I've arranged for a cheese plate and a bottle of Cristal to be sent to your suite."

"Steven, I don't want to interrupt. You're obviously busy." Striding to the concierge desk, working the lobby like a catwalk, Meridan drank in the dumbstruck couple who had been there before her, but had immediately risen to their feet to make way for America's favorite actress.

"I'm Meridan Marks. I apologize for interrupting you," she said, shaking the hands of both speechless guests. "Steven, it's imperative that if anyone other than Joel, Christian, or a man named Jim should ask for me, I'm not here. Please inform the staff." She smiled warmly.

"The stalker?" asked the female guest, finally finding her voice.

"Don't you worry, I'm well protected and kind people like Steven help watch my back." With a wave, she traversed the length of the lobby to the elevators, leaving Mr. and Mrs. Davis from Wichita awestruck in her wake. Meridan heard Mr. Davis say, "She is the most courageous and . . ."

"Gorgeous?" his wife filled in as they fell out of earshot.

Once inside the spacious suite, she sprawled on the bed to call Christian.

"Hi, beautiful," he answered, bringing a smile to her face.

"Jim's home and I wondered, well, Roz wants to meet him. I was thinking . . ."

"Drinks with your hot man? Count me in. I'm at the studio until seven, but I can meet you after. Where will he be?"

"I'll be with him, by the way, and just so you know, he's straight and desperately in love with me," she laughed. What an odd situation this was. Christian, her fake gay boyfriend, lusted for Jim, her straight real boyfriend, and she lusted for both of them. Delicious! It would make for quite a titillating story line on the big screen. Hmm . . .

"Well, stud, I must go and prepare myself for a long afternoon of mind-altering sex."

"Bitch."

"Skybar at eight, love." Meridan hung up the phone and hopped into the shower. She could barely keep her mind off Jim while she lathered up; she couldn't wait to have his hands on her. Days seemed like years when they were apart. She knew it had only been a few months, but he was so real, they were so real, so distant from her life. He adored her, and she couldn't help but think about the future. It looked very bright.

She swathed herself in lotion and perfume and donned the new, barely-there negligee she had purchased at a trendy little shop on Melrose. The owner was a friend of Roz's daughter; the stuff was irresistible.

A hearty knock set her stomach aflutter, and she couldn't help running to the door. Without thinking, she threw it open, giving the room service attendant an eyeful.

"Whoa!" she shrieked, slamming shut the door. "Leave it outside, I'll get it later! Put it on the room. Add twenty percent!" she barked. Good Lord! All the legalese she went through to keep nudity out of her films and she had just flashed a waiter. She looked down at herself to see how much he'd really seen and concluded there wasn't much left to the imagination. Oh, well. *Made his life*, she giggled to herself.

She slipped into a pair of Prada spikes, a perfect cap for her long slender legs. The height of the heel made her calves taut and her quadriceps take shape. She admired the look in the full-length mirror next to the king-sized bed. The negligee was semi-transparent pink and black leopard print. It had a demi-cup, which offered a tantalizing amount of cleavage, and an extremely short skirt.

She was primed for Jim's arrival when the doorbell rang. The room was candlelit, the champagne poured and the cheese ready for a post-coital snack. That is, if she herself wasn't the post-coital snack.

"Babe, it's me." His deep voice resonated, causing a shiver to slip down her body, and she couldn't open the door fast enough. "Well, if it isn't America's sweetheart," he said mischievously, holding her at a distance to drink in every detail. "For me?"

She was so filled with desire she couldn't speak. She pulled him to her for a deep kiss, her hands buried in his thick, chestnut hair, her body vibrant with desire and need.

"Make love to me," she whispered.

"I want to tell you something."

"Later," she begged, as she dragged him to the bed. He watched her long legs as she pranced like a prize-winning horse. Running a hand up the back of her thigh he moaned upon realizing she wasn't wearing underwear. Clenching tightly to her tiny skirt, he stopped her in her tracks. She turned, startled at the tension as he closed the distance between them in an instant. "Over there," he gestured to the chaise longue dimly lit by her premeditated candlelight. Condensation was pooling around the champagne on the table adjacent to the chair. He effortlessly hoisted her into a horizontal position, and she released a deep groan as she grasped his hair and kissed him voraciously—each taking sips of air between deep kisses—their longing being nourished, yet catalyzing more want in its place.

"Jim, please . . ."

He began working down from her full lips into the hollow of her neck, lavishing her with delicate attention, his right hand creating balance on her hip and his left firmly at her jaw poising her noble chin in the air. Her head tilted back, mouth slightly open, mumbling pitiful and indiscernible sounds. She was no longer Meridan Marks, Academy Award-winning actress; she'd been reduced to a pool of steamy lust, begging to be indulged.

"Jim, please, take me," she pleaded, breathless.

He continued to the notch above her sub clavicles, and then lingered in the tiny fissure between the two most perfect breasts he'd ever seen. Her nipples were plump, erect with desire, straining against the sheer fabric of her lingerie.

Unable to resist he used the scruff of his chin to pull the demicup down releasing her breasts and began to devour her with intermittent deep kisses, biting her gently and watching her respond.

One hand reached into the champagne bucket, pulling out a solitary cube of ice, the warmth of his hands melting it on contact. Drops of electricity seeped from his fingertips, showering down on her. Before the drops were able to cascade down the curve of her abdomen, he quickly collected them with his tongue, releasing his own groan of satisfaction.

Meridan managed to grasp his hair tightly, holding him fast to her breast as she told him exactly what she wanted.

"Mmm, that's some dirty talking coming from such sweet lips." He smirked, coming close to planting a kiss on them before denying her.

"No, I . . ."

Before she could utter another syllable, Jim slid further down until he was on his knees between her bent legs, her titanium spikes planted firmly in the carpet. Her breath was racing, calves tight in anticipation of his next move. He placed his hands on the inside of each of her knees and spread her legs wide— she moaned as his hands began to move their way toward her epicenter. He lifted her tiny skirt and found her inner thighs soaked with want.

"Mmm, I see you're ready for me."

"Oh yes . . . I need . . . please."

Jim slid his tongue up her thigh, delighting in her abundant offering, emitting a deep sigh.

"Meridan, you taste exquisite. I've missed you so much."

"Please."

In compliance, he buried his mouth into her. She could feel the scruff of his chin bearing down on her; her hips began to undulate in concert with each of his motions. His tongue was her keel, and he grasped her ass with his strong hands, creating an even deeper penetration. Meridan lifted her hips to meet him—to ensure his comfort, stopping was not an option; she could feel herself losing control as he slid his fingers deep inside her. In an instant he identified her trigger. How could he know her body so well in such a short time?

All conscious thoughts vanished as she was broadsided, her body seized with overwhelming pleasure.

"Oh, my God, yes . . ."

Meridan's body froze for a long moment, then convulsed uncontrollably as she was overtaken by her climax. Jim continued with his tongue, causing her to writhe with pleasure on the precipice of pain. Overcome with a hunger for air, she drew in a deep breath as her body settled back into the chaise longue.

"Jim, how do you . . . I want you to . . . " Meridan was gripped by an aftershock, cutting her inquiry short. "Oh, my God . . ."

After turning her over and firmly placing her hands on the back of the chaise, Jim pulled himself to his feet. Still catching her breath, Meridan looked back at him as he began to slowly unbutton his shirt. He offered her the profile he knew she found irresistible.

"So fucking beautiful," she breathed.

"Mmm, thank you baby." She bit her lip in anticipation, her eyes riveted on the flush of red on his chest his arousal had created. *I did that*, she thought proudly.

He unbuttoned his shirt, unveiling his perfectly sculpted chest and abdomen; hip flexors plunging down where she knew she wanted to be. He freed his body from his shirt and unbuttoned his jeans revealing his own want barely contained by his simple white Calvin Klein boxer briefs. Meridan gazed at the specimen before her.

"Mmm, I need you right now," she began to sway her ass back and forth like a hypnotic metronome. Growing impatient she turned to him to help him with his underwear and he stopped her.

"I've got this."

He slid his fingers down the elastic of his boxer briefs with his right hand and exposed himself completely. Meridan was certain she'd never become accustomed to seeing him before her—he was majestic.

"Mmm, I want that inside me . . . Now."

With his left hand he grasped her hip. Meridan arched her back to him—her wetness luring him. As he plunged into her depths Meridan yelped with a mélange of pleasure and pain. Jim grasped both of her hips and began to pound with abandon.

Meridan felt every muscle in his body begin to tense as she felt his climax beginning at his base. As he grew closer, the intensity increased and Meridan shocked herself with a string of perverse gasps.

Jim's body convulsed suddenly—surprising him, leaving him uncharacteristically without lusty utterances. Meridan tightened inside and encouraged the continued involuntary thrusts as he released inside her.

"Oh fuck, Meridan."

Jim collapsed on her back, and Meridan in turn collapsed onto the lounge under his weight. As Jim began to relax, he extricated himself and Meridan whimpered as what was full became void. She turned her body, allowing him to lay his head on her breasts; tangled beautiful bodies covered in each other's fluids.

"I love you," she heard him say, and new warmth spread through her.

"I love you, too," she whispered, without hesitation. She smiled knowing no dream could be better than her reality.

13

"Sounds like a confused fan to me, Joel," Detective Ford shrugged, placing the new faxes on top of the towering stack of previous faxes, letters and scripts. "What's that?" Detective Ford nodded to a huge pile of paperwork on another desk nearby. "You got another movie star in trouble?" he snickered.

Detective Ford had long ago grown tired of the politics that went hand in hand with his job in L.A. He spent more time trying to keep things under wraps than he did uncovering them. He was not at all concerned for Meridan Marks's safety, though his wife was reveling in telling the other wives and neighbors he was handling the "case." What case? Just another overpaid, overindulged movie star looking for attention.

"Actually, I do have several bankable stars on my roster, but those are cards and letters from fans offering their unwavering support and love to Meridan Marks. Those are from this week, post-*Glitterati* article." Detective Ford's eyes bulged as Joel made a broad sweeping gesture toward the huge mound.

"You gotta be shitting me! That stuff on the floor, too?" Joel nodded. "I guess I need to take it all with me. I can have my people make sure none of it matches the stalker's MO." He sighed heavily. Detective Ford had spent enough time with the rich and famous to understand they were actors because they could do little else. It galled him to think of spending his day reading sympathetic fan mail written to a woman who seemed to enjoy her predicament. Joel enlisted Barb to box up fan mail and "stalker" correspondence for Detective Ford.

"Joel, can I be honest with you?"

"I'd be disappointed if you were anything less."

"Is there the slightest chance this whole thing is a fake? Is Meridan Marks or any of her people capable of making this up?"

"I regret I've been going over that possibility too often. Meridan's taken some serious heat over a couple flops. I wondered myself if this wasn't a scheme to catapult her into the spotlight for something other than failure." He paused and leaned back in his chair, debating his next statement. He wondered why Detective Ford was asking. The police had copies and detailed records of all "stalker" activity. Was there something they had seen in particular?

"I know Meridan better than most people do. She's been my client for what seems like several lifetimes, if you know what I mean." He paused for effect. Detective Ford snagged the implication. "She's shallow, vacuous, and insecure, if you can believe it. Her need for attention is staggering and endless, and, furthermore, she can be cruel and hateful. I'd appreciate if none of this leaves the room." Detective Ford nodded his complicity. "I want to strangle her more often than not, but honestly? She loves what she does, she adores her fans—well, let me tweak that a bit. She loves the *attention* she gets from her fans. And I've never detected a scheming bone in her body beyond the norm. You know, tipping off the press when she's dining out and feeling neglected, the usual."

"What about the fact that he always faxes from a public place? He hasn't called any of you personally requesting to speak with her, and, further, he asks her to call him repeatedly, yet he has never given her a number." Detective Ford shook his head. It didn't add up. "It's almost as if her 'stalker' isn't stalking."

"What about the woman who e-mailed us? The one who recognized the bouquet, the one who thought it could be the work of brothers?"

"I've looked at what amounts to limited information, Joel, and other than her suspicions she may have been harassed more than ten years ago by one or two men who have a fondness for a certain floral arrangement, there's nothing solid. We can't even come up with one guy, let alone two! It doesn't steer me from Meridan or someone in her camp. She seems too happy about all this."

"She offered names and descriptions."

"She didn't return your e-mail."

"Yet."

"Maybe she's hoping to strike a chord with Ms. Marks and develop a bond." Both men sat in silence for a few moments mulling over the conversation.

"At no point did she ask for interaction with Meridan. This woman wants little or nothing to do with getting involved."

Detective Ford nodded noncommittally. "Well, until there is a serious act of aggression or a physical threat, or even something amounting to more than ranting, faxing and minor harassment, there's very little I can do. There are other options, you know."

"Meridan won't go for any bodyguard stuff. I've been trying to get her to move into a more secure location. If things become dangerous, I'll force the issue."

"She seems like the type who'd enjoy the hype of security."

"I may have to tap into that logic." The men shook hands and agreed to keep one another informed. Joel hated being duped. He hoped this wasn't going to blow up in Meridan's face, and closed up shop for the day with an uneasy feeling. What had those men done to that woman? What did they have in mind for Meridan?

14

"This seat taken?" When she looked up to see him leaning on the top of the booth grinning down at her, Meridan's heart skipped a gear and jumped into overdrive. They were the first to arrive. She had been anxious to see him, her mind still buzzing from his confession. He'd been gone when she awoke.

"I *am* expecting some people, but there's no reason why you can't keep me company," she answered and he took a seat next to her.

"What's new on the stalking front?" Jim asked after ordering drinks.

"Let's put that on hold. Why don't you tell me again what you said right before I nodded off. I'm afraid it was a dream." She seduced him with her eyes and her provocative mouth.

"Oh. I don't remember." He brought his hand to his chin and furrowed his brows.

"You beast!" She swatted at him playfully, and he reached under the table to give her knee a squeeze. He reminded himself to keep it clean, as he was with Christian York's girlfriend, and leaned in close to whisper in her ear.

"I said, 'I love you.' Mer, I do. I've been wanting to tell you for a while."

"Jim!" Christian bellowed, approaching the table with outstretched arms. Jim jumped to his feet to share a huge, manly hug that, for Christian, was very satisfying.

"Hello, darling," he said, leaning in for a wholesome kiss from Meridan.

"Hi, babe," she replied, casting a glance toward Jim to monitor his comfort level with the situation. He winced, but only slightly.

"Why don't you sit next to your girl, and I'll sit over here next to Roz," he offered, and everyone eased into position. The cabana was the best in the house, overlooking the entire pool area, offering prime people-watching opportunities while at the same time showcasing its prominent occupants.

"Great table, who do you know?" Christian smirked. "Roz!" he called, rising to meet her, and after a brief embrace led her to the table by the hand. "Jim beat you here," he announced loudly so as to satisfy anyone wondering about the relational dynamics. It was not unusual for the staff of top restaurants to tip off the press and receive payment for what they'd witnessed.

"Jim, so nice to finally meet you," Roz said discreetly, extending her hand. Meridan observed a thorough blush overcome her agent.

"You as well." Jim stood and kissed her on the cheek. "How lucky could one man get, eh, Christian?" he played along.

"No doubt." Christian beamed and Meridan wondered how *she* got so lucky, knowing Roz was thinking the same thing. Both men were decked out in the finest, Jim in Prada and Christian in Armani.

"Meridan was just bringing me up to speed on this stalking thing," Jim said, taking a small sip of his martini.

"What a mess that is." Roz shook her head.

"It's not that bad, Roz." Meridan reassured Jim.

"None of us are too comfortable with it, Mer," Christian offered and quickly ordered a round of drinks, a double Tanqueray on the rocks for himself.

Meridan relished their concern. It made her feel so loved and protected to be here with her favorite people and to have them so worried. "I'm totally fine. He sends flowers and crazy letters, but he isn't *dangerous*. The *Glitterati* thing got blown way out of proportion. You know how the media is."

"What's really going on?" Jim turned his attention to Roz, who sat somewhat in a daze.

"Uh, well, there have been the flowers. He's sent some scripts to Joel and he faxes Meritime and Joel's office almost daily. He's convinced they're in contact. He chastises her for missing dates and asks her to call constantly, but never leaves a number. A lot of it is rambling." When Roz met Jim's gaze, she felt the butterflies in her stomach take flight. *What did Meridan do in her previous life to deserve Jim?* she thought. *She sure as shit isn't lighting the world on fire with her charitable behavior in this one.*

"It doesn't sound too bad," Jim said.

"Well, Meridan hasn't been totally honest with you then. He taped a letter to her door yesterday. He followed her to Neiman Marcus or something, because he knew she was there. If we just knew what he looked like or who he was, we could issue a restraining order or something," Christian said, squeezing Meridan's hand protectively.

"Jesus." Jim looked Meridan straight in the eye. "Are you afraid?"

"I know I should be, but I'm not. He's harmless." She winked at him, her heart fluttering at his concern.

"Meridan, I think it's important to keep this quiet." Roz said, honestly regretting her complicity in the machinations that had led to the article in *Glitterati*. "It's critical we don't make him angry or incite him in any way."

"Maybe I should just meet with him."

"No!" Christian, Jim and Roz insisted simultaneously.

"Don't be absurd," Jim added. "That's the stupidest thing I've ever heard. In addition to being dangerous, do you really want to condone this behavior?"

"No, I guess not. Let's drop the subject. Certainly there are more interesting things to discuss than me?" she asked coyly, though no one believed she meant it.

15

"Gia Androvaldi, Ms. Hatcher," she said, approaching with an outstretched hand. "It's an honor to meet you. As soon as I made my decision to move forward with this project, I told Daddy I had to have you on board." Lynden couldn't help blushing a bit under the compliment.

"Well, thank you. I hope we can make some progress today that will begin to address your concerns and your aspirations. Your name is spelled G-I-A-D-A in your e-mails. How do you pronounce that?" Lynden asked, smiling warmly at her potential mega-client.

Ms. Androvaldi was not at all what Lynden had expected. Dallas seemed so homogenized at times, it was a rarity to find a woman that stood out, but Ms. Gia Androvaldi did just that. At a willowy five foot ten, she hardly needed the four-inch Michael Kors titanium-heeled pumps she had coupled with a gorgeous black Gucci pantsuit.

"*Gee-ah-duh,*" she said in a decidedly Italian accent. "It means 'jade.' Supposedly, when I was born, my eyes were more green than blue. My parents thought naming me Giada would call on the Fates to keep them green instead of changing to blue like my mother's or brown like my father's. Alas, the Fates were not listening. The only person who calls me Giada, or can pronounce it properly, is Daddy." Her light brown hair was flat-iron straight and blunt cut at the shoulders, a dramatic look that set off bright blue eyes artistically enhanced by the smoky charcoals and grays of her makeup. A very full bottom lip almost engulfed a less plump top lip, setting her mouth in what would have been a perpetual pout if not for her electrifying smile. Lynden directed Ms. Androvaldi

CONSUMED

to her interior office.

Ms. Androvaldi took inventory, carefully assessing Lynden's style, and seemed pleased with the décor and ambiance. Lynden was proud of her work areas, which she had decorated herself.

Lynden's office was spacious but not too grand. The floor was dark-stained concrete with a lovely tone-on-tone brown multi-textured area rug. A large semi-circular couch with a high back faced a plasma screen and full complement of audio-visual equipment. At the back of the office sat her workspace, a monolithic piece of artwork from a gallery in Sarasota. Lynden considered it more a sculpture than a desk, despite its extreme functionality.

Her iMac's giant monitor glowed at the ready. Two elegant modern chairs covered in a luxurious bronze fabric rested in front of the desk. One large wall was lined with custom-matted and framed articles featuring Lynden and her career. She detested the self-aggrandizement, but felt it was important for clients to trust her qualifications immediately. The other wall featured some of her favorite write-ups, in most cases those of the restaurants that had stood the test of time, due in part, perhaps, to her favorable reviews. This helped create the aura of her prophecy: if Lynden Hatcher could predict a winner, she could create one.

"Your office is stunning. Who did you hire, and can we get them to help us with my place?"

"Well, in a way, you already have," Lynden said, lowering her gaze bashfully.

"No. You didn't do all this, did you?" Gia gazed around, taking in every little detail. "I can see that you have impeccable taste. I already feel like I've made the right decision," she smiled.

By design, Lynden thought.

"Excellent," Gia declared, giving the office her seal of approval and selecting one of the mini chaise longues as a seat. Lynden removed her jacket and offered a beverage to Gia, who, given the options, chose Conundrum white wine. After pouring them both a glass, Lynden perched on a chaise to face the striking Ms. Androvaldi.

"I appreciate you seeing me last-minute. I didn't mean to drive you nuts with the e-mailing, but my schedule has really been out of whack. I just graduated from SMU law school and, if you can believe it, my dad brought me on interim for his company! I just passed the bar, for God's sake! I'm not ready to be chief counsel for a company that large! Anyway, he offered me the job and was devastated when I turned him down. My degree is business law, but I want my own business. Of course he understood, but was looking forward to working with me every day. He made me promise I would at least set up shop downtown so he could stop in constantly." She rolled her eyes dramatically, and despite her verbosity, Lynden was quite taken. She didn't interrupt, allowing her soon-to-be client prattle on about herself.

"Daddy insists on funding my venture, although I intend to pay him back within a year. I've already drawn up the papers with interest. If I know him, he'll just hold the checks. Dads!" Another roll of the glittering azure eyes.

"So, tell me your thoughts."

"Well, I hate to be so run of the mill, but my passion is wine. I spent an entire summer in Tuscany and, quite frankly, if it weren't for Daddy, would have stayed forever. I want to somehow translate that charm and elegance into an upscale wine bar and eatery. The same as everyone else, huh?"

"No, not really. Of course there are some notable wine lists, menus, and bars in Dallas, but as yet no one has captured the warmth and style indigenous to that region."

"You've been?" Gia's eyes lit up as if Lynden held a juicy piece of gossip.

"Briefly. I assure you, however, I've been to each and every attempt to recreate it in Dallas and would delight in the opportunity to help you fulfill your endeavor."

"Well, I want it to have a similar feel to your office, really." She stood up and towered over a still-seated Lynden, which reminded her to sit up straight. Gia strode to the center of the room and turned in a lazy circle. "There is such warmth and panache here. Each piece, while not a matched set, seems to blend seamlessly with the carpet and the window panels. The feel is luxury and custom." She met Lynden's eyes. "I adore custom and thrive on drama."

Indeed.

For the next three hours, the women pored over the details, from furniture to square footage to location, location, location. Gia had done her homework and selected an enviable space with a huge price tag in the most up-and-coming area of downtown. The space was just over five thousand square feet with a loft area that added great depth and movement.

"What do you think?" Lynden asked. Gia had been held rapt by her concepts and ideas and had taken volumes of notes, interjecting rarely.

"I think you should partner with me, because this is going to be a monster success!" Lynden had never really considered entering the arena. She was more comfortable formulating concepts and implementing them. It was an interesting offer. "I'm serious. Would you ever consider getting more involved in day-to-day operations?"

"I don't know. It's a compelling offer. If you're serious, I would give it some thought."

"What else?" Gia beamed.

"The lighting is critical. It must be low and recessed. We have to create the illusion of secrecy. The more selective and expensive a place in Dallas is, the more sought-after it will be. As you know, Dallas is the home of hundreds of professional athletes, actors and actresses." Gia bounced up and down in her seat and clapped like a four-year-old looking at her new pony.

"Why haven't you already done this for someone else?"

"No one has asked. Believe me, all facets of this concept are being done, but not all together in one place. That's the trick. Additionally, you're providing me with the financial latitude to blow the competition away. Do you realize how much time I waste justifying the stock of the menus and the cost of designing paper products and signs? And it doesn't stop there. The owners want to bicker over the price of the leather or vinyl on the barstools."

"I don't know if you've heard this before, but money truly is no object on this project. I ask only one thing. I'm a stickler for quality. I want the finest, but I want it to be commercial grade and easily replaceable in case of damage. I want excessive overage on fabrics and all materials used—tile, marble, or paint."

"Done."

Both women stood up, and Lynden envied Gia's extra couple of inches in height.

"Can you have a proposal to me by a week from Friday? Daddy wants a hard number." Gia grimaced, fearing she would be rushing Lynden.

"I'll have it to you by Monday." They shook hands and the words "unlimited budget" buzzed through Lynden's head. She would have to seriously consider her level of involvement. It was an interesting proposition, but one that would markedly change the way she conducted her life. Operations involved early mornings and late nights, often alone, the thought of which made her stomach turn.

Before leaving, Gia turned to Lynden with a curious expression. "What about the name?" she queried.

"*Consumare*," Lynden offered.

"'Consume' in Italian," Gia marveled and repeated the word a few times out loud in her perfect and seductive Italian accent. "It sounds sublime. You're a genius."

~

Once safe in the confines of her home, Lynden forced herself to check the Hotmail account she'd been avoiding. Since e-mailing Joel Goldstein, she had convinced herself she'd been hasty in her suspicions. Her heart fluttered when she saw a response from the attorney. It was a request for the names and descriptions she'd offered; but after mulling it over, she decided to leave it alone. Meridan was a strong, well-insulated woman. She would be fine.

Lynden cracked a bottle of 1997 Grgich Hills cabernet and settled in with the journal.

16

"Special delivery," Jessica announced as she bounced onto my bed. My head was crashing due to lack of sleep and too much drink. I opened one eye and leveled it on her.

"What?" I croaked, afraid to hit my head with full volume. She held out a small box to me.

"I bet it's from Brit," she smiled. Jessica had been asleep when I arrived home the previous evening. I had been dying to wake her up, to bask in her sanity, to seek advice and comfort. Today would do.

"Aren't you going to open it?" she beamed, as I stared at the box. I smiled and opened the other eye. Not too excruciating. Perhaps I would live.

I lifted the lid of the small, white box, and inside was a Kendall Jackson Reserve cork, stained with cabernet it had protected for three years prior to being sprung. I lifted the cork to my nose and the scent caused me to dry heave.

"Sorry, too much of a good thing," I chuckled and made a "cheers" gesture with the box. I noticed a card, which read: 'My sincerest apologies for an abominable evening. It could have been handled better and it won't happen again. I'll pick you up at seven for dinner- Brit.' My stomach flip-flopped as relief washed over me. Last night? Perhaps I had imagined it all, my senses heightened by the wine. Things were not nearly as bad as I thought.

"What's that all about?" Jessica asked, reaching for the card. I decided a second opinion was critical and gave her an overview of the evening. "The stalker is his brother?"

I nodded. "I was so stunned when he got off his barstool I didn't even notice the similarities, which are striking. I couldn't believe he was approaching me, finally, after all of the lingering and loitering. Brit was furious when he saw him. I don't really know how to describe the intensity."

"They were fighting over you right there, in Beggar's, in public?'

"Not really. There was some loud talking and a few accusations, but it had little to do with me, I think."

"Wow, that's intense," Jessica marveled. I was not so amused. "Those poor boys. I can't believe their parents died. And I can't believe I still haven't seen him."

"You're barely ever here!"

"Tonight at seven I will be."

Jessica barreled past me to answer the door when Brit knocked. When she entered the living room with Brit in tow, her face clearly portrayed awe. After introductions and polite chitchat, he took my hand and led me to the door.

"You look so nice. I love the way you dress. Not too many girls bother to dress around here," he said. I had decided on my favorite black blazer with white polka dots and jeans with boots. "Would you like to come to my place? We could listen to some music and talk?" he asked, and despite reservations about being alone together so soon, I said yes.

His apartment was huge, and not loaded to the ceiling with college-level crap furniture—it was beautifully furnished and decorated. A supple, camel-colored couch with harvest-colored throw pillows ran the length of the wall separating the living room from the kitchen. Two cabernet-colored leather chairs with matching camel and harvest throw pillows were flush to the juxtaposed wall. What looked like original photographic art, signed and dated, adorned the walls. A dining table was set for two and a fragrant arrangement of flowers completed the setup.

Most impressive, however, was the wall of CDs; there must have been at least a thousand of them. A large entertainment center housed a state-of-the-art Bang and Olufsen system. I noted Cerwin Vega speakers and a large television. I couldn't imagine owning such extravagant things at this age.

"Do you have a roommate?" I felt compelled to ask. Granted, Brit had

nice things, but he didn't act rich or snotty.

"Sure, his name's Kevin. He's never here. This is sort of his official crash pad, but he virtually lives with his girlfriend. They have been together since, like, third grade," he called from the kitchen, and returned with two ice-cold Miller Lites.

"So, all this stuff is yours?" I couldn't help but ask.

"All but the microwave. Kevin never eats anything that can't be prepared in five minutes or less." He offered me a seat and unwrapped the new Depeche Mode CD I had mentioned liking. I feared the potential of its sensual overtones and wondered if I was being sucked into something I was unprepared for. It was as if everything I ever dreamed of, and then some, had come to life.

We chatted for what seemed like hours, and I eventually realized it was dark outside and I was growing hungry. I suggested he take me home, not wanting to assume we would be dining together.

"Not until I feed you," he murmured in a tone so low I had to ask him to repeat himself. "I want to feed you," he said slowly, with purpose, and reached out to brush my hair out of my face.

Moments later, he was bustling about the kitchen, adeptly stuffing chicken breast with spinach and feta cheese, sautéing mushrooms and tossing a salad. He made cooking look easy and I delighted in his explanations as the aroma of freshly baking garlic bread filled the room.

"These bread-making machines are amazing. I could never bake bread from scratch," he said, but I was certain there was very little he couldn't do.

We sipped Heitz Cellars chardonnay while we dined.

"Tastes like apples," I whispered unintentionally, and he leaned in as if to hear. When I looked up, he slipped his hand into my hair, cradling the back of my head in his large hand, and brought my face up to meet his. When his lips touched mine, they were cold from the wine, soft and delicate; mine were on fire. His tongue slid over my lower lip.

"Yes, apples."

As I carried the empty dishes to the kitchen, he followed with a newspaper article and my wine.

"I saved this for you." I took the paper and saw a team photo of the Detroit Red Wings. *"Which one is your friend?"*

"Mmm." I swallowed my wine and pointed to number twenty-four. *"Bob Probert."*

"Wow, he's a good looking guy. How is he in bed?"

"What?" I choked, wine shooting into my nasal cavity.

"You heard me," he challenged.

"I never slept with him. I barely know him!"

"You barely know me and here you are. This could easily turn into an overnight date."

"If that's what you think, we need to talk! I guess I shouldn't have come here."

"I'm totally kidding, relax!" he laughed.

"Listen," I began tentatively, not knowing how much I wanted to reveal. *"Six months ago I was a virgin."*

"Right!"

"Why do you say that?" I was offended but curious.

"A girl that looks like you, a virgin at twenty? It just isn't conceivable." He eyed me suspiciously over his wine glass and took a long drink.

"It's true. I dated someone for a year and a half. We waited a long time, until I knew it was right, that we were right."

"So why are you here with me and not with him?" For a half a second, I wondered that myself.

"It didn't work out." Brit examined my face. I didn't want him to think I was pathetic. I wanted to be strong, but felt swept away by my interest in him.

"Hey, I'm sorry. I guess I'm a little curious about your life before me. I was just giving you a hard time."

We had more wine and he lured me to the couch where kissing became intense.

"Brit, I . . ."

"I didn't ask you here to have sex," he said between kisses. *"But that doesn't mean we can't do other things, does it?"* He tested me by slipping a

hand up my side and near my breast. My body was on fire and I wanted him to touch me. My lack of resistance prompted him to graze my breast. My nipple was taut against my thin bra, and he drew in a deep breath after brushing it with his thumb. "God, I have wanted to get my hands on you!" Just as I thought he was going to tear my shirt open, the front door pushed open and Katie and Kevin walked in. I scrambled off Brit. A high school response; we were, after all, dating.

"Sorry," Katie said with little sincerity, looking me over thoroughly.

"No problem, we were just going to bed," Brit said proudly and pulled me after him to his bedroom. I was having second thoughts.

"Brit, I'm on my period," I started to explain, and he pulled me to him by the wrist. He placed my hand on his massive erection and forced it to stay there.

"I need you to touch me," he whispered into my ear. A thrill ran up the length of my entire body and settled between my legs.

"Can't we just make out?" I asked, lifting my head for a kiss. Perhaps he thought he would have better luck persuading me after getting me into a horizontal position, but he resigned to my suggestion. He handed me a pair of boxers and a T-shirt. I changed in the bathroom, putting on his clothes over my bra and underwear.

Climbing into bed, I was shocked to see he was wearing only boxers. His body was hard and lean and smooth. He settled into the curve of my body and started to kiss me. I loved the rough feel of his scruff. His hand settled on my breast again, and my senses jangled. He pinched my nipple gently and I couldn't help but moan. He pinched more forcefully and kissed me while grinding his erection into my hip.

"When?" he whispered.

"I don't know," I said, honestly, and he pinched me. Hard.

17

Meridan saw the letter taped to her door from a distance and wondered when he had come, and how close she had been to seeing him. She'd left the Peninsula tragically early for an appointment with Joel. Her departure at seven that morning had awakened Christian, asleep on the sofa bed across the room, from a deep slumber. Jim had left in the wee hours to avoid being seen and had sent Christian back to her room.

Joel had given Meridan the latest details on her upcoming contract negotiations and then broke the news to her the studio was considering going with a more "protected" actress. This had shaken her. How could she maintain her image in a Bel Air mansion with a mile-high gate and security cameras everywhere? Joel had hinted the part in question could end up being her arch nemesis Harley Ryan's first major dramatic role if Meridan wouldn't consider a move. She had never imagined the studios could control her to this degree. Maybe it *was* time to move.

This time the envelope was stuck to the door by some type of crusty glue. She tore it off and, as she closed the door, made a mental note to have the maid clean off the residue. As she digested his words, she reached for the couch and eased into it, suddenly dizzy. She couldn't tear her eyes from his hate-filled diatribe, even for a moment.

What the fuck is going on? Meridan, I gave you explicit instructions to break things off with Christian York. And my instructions were such that you could have done it in a sensitive way. And then I fucking see you with him at

Skybar. What a cozy fucking double date you and Roz enjoyed. Who is that fucking joker she is dating? Aren't you two the talk of the fucking town with your pretty boys?

Honestly, what was going through your mind? Help me, Meridan. Help me help you. I thought I was being supportive. I am fucking furious right now and on top of it confounded by what you keep doing to me. It no longer makes sense.

I'm out of here. This shit needs to stop—now.

B~

Her phone jangled and she read the caller ID. Meritime Films. Undoubtedly, they had received the same fax. Great.

"Roz?"

"Meridan, sit down."

"I am."

"I need to read you something, and you're not going to like it."

"I already read it. It was stuck to my door."

"This one was to me." Roz said, obviously stricken.

"What?" asked Meridan, her voice laced with unmistakable jealousy.

Roz,

What the fuck do you think you are doing? I know you are responsible for cooking up this little romance between Christian York and Meridan. You are causing her great confusion, and she feels torn. Her loyalty to you makes it difficult for her to go against your wishes. She has asked me to contact you directly. Meridan loves me, and she has felt pressured by your insistence that she date that joker for months.

It really hurts that you disregard my feelings for Meridan. Your actions serve to negate the time and effort I have put into our relationship.

You are such a nosy fucking bitch. Don't even think about turning your new boyfriend loose on me, either. I saw you all last night, laughing at me. Who do you judgmental bastards think you are? I am tired of the harassment.

Release her from her obligation to see Christian York, or I will deal with it myself. We belong together, and not even the great Christian York can stand in my way.

B~

"I don't know what to say."

"Meridan, I'm worried. He's angry. Further, he's convinced you two have a relationship. How does that happen?"

"I don't know," Meridan said distantly. The hair on the back of her neck stood at attention and she couldn't shake the vulnerable feeling that had settled over her. "I can't believe he saw us. Thank God he didn't pick up on any vibe between Jim and me. I can't place him in danger. Is he threatening Christian?"

"He's threatening someone," Roz said, for the first time fearing for her own safety. "I'm going to forward this to Joel. Why don't you bring me the letter you have, which says what, by the way?" Meridan read the letter to her, and Roz instructed her to come to Meritime immediately.

By the time she arrived at Meritime, Joel had faxed over another letter from B.

Joel,

I have to wonder what your role is in this relationship between Meridan and Christian. I thought we were working together on this project and I trusted you. You can't profit from me unless I trust you, and I have to be honest—the whole situation is disturbing. I met with Roz this morning and she has assured me she will instruct Meridan to break it off with Christian.

I have to tell you my creative process has been stifled by this new development. I told Meridan days ago to take care of this, and just last night she was with Christian. I am going shopping right now, but I demand to be informed when it is done. Just call me after four and we can move forward with the agreement that we agreed upon.

B~

"What are you thinking?" Meridan wondered at Roz.

"At this point I would be more concerned with Christian's safety than yours."

"Thank you very much!" Roz indulged her with an apologetic look. "Christian York is so insulated the FBI couldn't get within thirty feet of him."

"Maybe that's what you need. Some insulation. It could be good publicity," Roz added, pandering to Meridan's need for drama and attention.

"Maybe you're right." Meridan began to nibble on her thumbnail.

"I am right. The police can't do anything right now. You just need a presence. We don't want this guy anywhere near you. What do you think?"

Meridan sat back and envisioned herself with a huge, ear-pieced bodyguard. It would look kind of cool, and, truth be told, the guy actually was starting to creep her out. On top of that, news about it would spread like wildfire.

"Check with Joel. Have him call that guy he used when Christian needed some extra protection. He was hot." She stood and exited Roz's office. "Did you remember to book my appointments for today?" Roz rolled her eyes. Had she *ever* forgotten to book manicure, pedicure, hair cut, color and up-do on the day of a premiere?

~

"You won't believe this, but Cameron Riley actually called *me*. When he read about this in *Glitterati*, he wondered if we needed help. I put him off because she refused. How did you do it?" Joel asked, trying to mask his veneration. He never expected anyone to convince Meridan to take protective measures.

"I created an impressive picture of a victim driven to hire protection from a deranged fan. You know she can't resist drama." Roz smiled into the phone.

"I've put in a call to Elaine Worthing about a new house."

"Yikes. Does Meridan know that?"

"We talked about it this morning while perusing the daily rantings of a madman," he chuckled. Roz tried to join him but couldn't. She sensed things were about to spiral out of control.

18

Christian let himself into Meridan's townhouse when she didn't answer. He disengaged the alarm and was surprised she wasn't waiting impatiently.

"Mer?"

"Hey!" she called out from the master bath on the third floor of her lofted townhouse. "Sorry! I just got out of my ice-cold shower! My hair and makeup looks so fabulous, I didn't want to risk steam!" He trudged up the ten stairs from the entryway and headed toward the refrigerator on the main floor.

"Can I get you a drink?"

"Yes! I've had a hell of a day! You will not believe what I've had to deal with! You would think Devin Madison would have been jumping through his own asshole to get me ready for this premiere, yet he was too busy with that harlot, Harley Ryan. I swear the woman is the bale of my existence!" Meridan's customary massacre of a colloquialism was lost on the equally inept Christian, who popped the cork on a bottle of Roederer Cristal, knowing it was one of her favorites. He reached for two flutes from the cabinet next to the bar.

Waiting for Meridan to come down, he flipped on the TV to pass the time. The station was set on Entertainment First, and, before the image on the screen even materialized, he delighted in the comments being made about him.

"The crowds started gathering here in front of Graumann's Chinese Theater at nine this morning. As you can see, people are jockeying for position and speculating as to how Christian York will make his grand entrance. Word is Meridan Marks will be in attendance with her man on his big night, despite being recently plagued by an unknown madman. Jordan, back to you." The blonde bobble head had over-annunciated and gesticulated her way through the blip, distracting Christian completely. The camera panned the mob scene comprising his fans, and it cheered him to see them lining both sides of Hollywood Boulevard, nearly toppling the stanchions.

"What are you so happy about?" Meridan asked seductively, demanding his attention as she waltzed down the stairs from her loft. She was radiant in a fuchsia crepe halter-style dress Christian had no doubt was a custom design by Donatella Versace. He stood and gave her the standing ovation he knew she required, and once she reached the bottom of the stairs, he gestured for her to spin for him. The backless dress nearly exposed buttock cleavage and had a slit up the back all the way to the upper thigh, revealing a tan and toned left leg. He marveled at how it stayed on her body at all.

"What can I say other than *phenomenal*? You must write Donatella a personal thank-you for this little number! I'll have to light my hair on fire just to get noticed!" Meridan beamed and feigned humility.

Christian always knew how to make her feel special. She only wished Jim were there to personally remove the dress later. She had called him earlier to tell him to watch *Entertainment First* so at least he could be jealous he was not with her.

"Thank you," she smiled, as she took the frosty flute from her friend. A long sip was the salve she needed to assuage her still-bruised ego. "I'll tell you, when I heard Harley was the one keeping Devin to herself today, I told them I was leaving. Of course, he raced in and tried to console me, but the damage was done. He ruined my special day and I'll never go back. Where the hell does she have to go anyway? It isn't as if she ever graces the public with her presence." Meridan's voice oozed sarcasm and she included a heavy eye roll. Christian shrugged his shoulders, captivated by the montage of his career on the screen.

"Yikes, do I look old? Look how young I was!" He gasped, placing a hand over his sumptuous mouth.

"Hardly, darling. You're hotter today than the first day I met you. Don't you think we'd make a great couple?" Meridan approached him and squared the knot in his tie, careful not to block the television. "By the way, if I haven't told you how fabulous you look tonight, you do." She admired him in his classic black Armani suit, which he had paired with a black shirt and black tie. She loved dark men. "What time do we need to be there?"

"I have the Maybach out front. We need to show at eight or so. We'll do interviews and autographs for fifteen minutes and sneak in after the house lights are off. I insisted on that; I'd hate to be harassed. We've got a few minutes to finish our champagne."

"Finish? How about take with?"

Christian stood, offered his arm to Meridan and escorted her down the stairs to the waiting luxury ride.

"This car is so fabulous. You made the right choice," she said, easing into the seat. She reveled in the supple leather and the new car smell. There was a built-in champagne chiller and cup holders to accommodate wine glasses or champagne flutes.

"I'm really excited about tonight."

"Will Sean be there?" Meridan asked, referring to Christian's on-again, off-again lover.

"No, he's furious with us, as usual. I swear, sometimes I don't know why I keep him around at all," he whispered. Meridan cocked an eyebrow at him and they both burst out laughing. Meridan knew the intimate details of their sex life and knew exactly why Christian kept Sean around. "He's tired of the charade, blah, blah. He wants me to come clean and admit my sexuality. I think he just wants to be acknowledged publicly as my lover instead of being shuttled around and hidden all the time. Woe is fucking me."

They both laughed and Meridan imagined Sean at Christian's sprawling Bel Air mansion, surrounded by every snack item ever created, eating half and petulantly throwing the other half at her and Christian's faces on the enormous projection TV.

All treats would be washed down with gallons of green appletinis. It was a wonder Sean didn't slip into a coma or die of insulin shock. There would be pouting, crying and screaming; they wouldn't speak for days. Sean would wallow in self-pity at the center of the Grecian-style pool that adorned Christian's spacious grounds and deepen an already deep tan borne of doing, well, nothing.

Once the sun became too much to bear, Sean would go on a wild shopping rampage, leaving Rodeo Drive in desperate need of restocking. AmEx would recognize Sean and Christian were in another tiff, even though for the record they knew Sean as Christian's personal assistant. Woe is him, puh-lease!

"How is John, er, Jim?" Christian asked, more than interested.

"Stop picturing my—" she mouthed the word *boyfriend*, "—in his underwear!" She gave him a playful little shove, careful not to spill.

"I'm not. I was thinking of John Taylor," he replied with a wicked smirk.

"Stop your mind from wondering!" She lowered her voice as they were used to doing when discussing items pertaining to lascivious details outside the bliss of their relationship. "He's mine."

"He's hot, and I mean radioactive hot," Christian chuckled decadently, picturing Jim Cooper in nothing at all, his sculpted body that from which the image of Adonis himself could have been created.

"You don't even *know*." Meridan reached out and closed the window between them and the driver as Christian reached out to lock the intercom.

"Do you love him?"

"I do. I know it hasn't been that long, but he is so okay with everything, you know, my life, you, the business. He makes me feel normal. Well, as close to normal as you can be when you're a Hollywood A-lister. When I'm with him, I don't feel like I have to look perfect, act perfect, say the right thing. I can just do what I want instead of what's expected of me."

"He doesn't expect anything from you?"

"Just for me to make time for him when he can make time for me. It's a perfect arrangement. He really likes you. I guess that's what keeps him from getting crazy jealous. I mean, let's be honest, your girlfriend is, as far as the whole world knows, deeply in love and in a committed relationship with *Glitterati*'s hottest man in the world, what, a thousand years running?" Christian pretended to blush; a true act-off was in progress inside the Maybach.

Neither one was very good at humility, grace, or self-deprecation.

When they pulled up to the theatre the line was short, just a couple of cars in front of them. Christian poured them another glass of champagne.

"Holy shit! I can*not* fucking believe it!" Meridan gasped, gaping, and Christian contorted himself to get a look. Just in front of them, Sean alighted from a stretch Escalade, resplendent in a white summer-weight Versace suit with a black shirt and what had to be custom black and white cowboy boots. He offered his hand and out he pulled the devil in Dolce: Harley Ryan.

Harley Ryan and Meridan Marks had battled for every romantic comedy lead for the past seven years. Harley had secured most of them, forcing Meridan to branch into dramedy and drama. It had been a valuable, not to mention award-garnering, career move for Meridan. She was grateful to have found her acting niche, even if by default, but always in the back of her mind worried Harley would one day eclipse her.

Four years Meridan's junior, Harley had a captivating and effortless universal appeal virtually non-existent in Hollywood. Worshipped by all with whom she worked, she generally avoided the public and the press. Her apparent unavailability created an elusive and provocative air. Her fans undoubtedly loved her, but seemed to love the "Mystery That Was Harley" even more.

Comparatively, Meridan took every opportunity to work the public like a politician running for office. Despite being America's favorite actress, she instilled in her colleagues a feeling of intense aversion. There existed an ocean of contrast between the persona Meridan vigorously maintained and the person she was to the people who truly knew her and to those forced to accommodate her. The foundation of her career was her success working the fans.

Christian inhaled what seemed to be all the air in the car, and his anger detonated.

"This is fucking war!"

Sean offered the glorious Harley his arm and helped her up onto the red carpet. Despite her virtual inability to move in her second-skin corseted animal print gown, she made her way to the bay of deafening fans and began signing autographs. Christian and Meridan were nearly blinded by the flashes. It was an aberration for Harley Ryan to appear in public, let alone sign autographs.

"This is fucking rich! My two exes, together!" He snatched his iPhone from his inner pocket, dialed furiously, and waited for some poor soul to answer. "She can't have me, so she goes after Sean. She'll never get over me," he said, and he probably was right; it was the primary reason Meridan had agreed to "date" Christian. By aligning herself with him, Meridan would keep herself even more in the public eye as an individual commodity and as half of a high-profile couple. Their relationship would both protect Christian's sexual identity and further Harley's humiliation.

Poor Harley had fallen for Christian during the shooting of their first and only project together. They had "dated," which for Christian was a strategic move to obtain free straight press. Harley, on the other hand, had invested wholeheartedly in their "relationship." Heartbroken and more than a little embarrassed, she did not attend their film's premiere following the breakup, but had instead become more reclusive. Until now.

"Who the fuck invited her?" Christian demanded into his phone. "Get them the fuck out of there. Move them through the crowd. This is *my* premiere and no one, I mean *no one*, will take the spotlight from me tonight, especially not that strumpet or, should I say, those strumpets. Call AmEx. Cancel my card in his name. Send a locksmith to my house and change every lock. Call the garage door people and have them change the code. Call the alarm company and bar his access code. Change mine to, um, 0210, that's Meridan's birthday, make a note of it. If he has any accounts in L.A. on credit, cancel them." He threw his phone on the floor so hard Meridan was not certain of its survival.

As furious as she was at having her thunder stolen by Harley Ryan, she felt horrible for Christian. No matter how angry he was, she knew he had genuine feelings for Sean.

"Christian."

"No. I've been trying to get rid of him for months. He's a crybaby opportunist and I'm tired of refereeing between you two."

"I try to be good with him."

"It's not you—it's him. He's crazy jealous of you."

"What if he tells someone?"

"He signed a non-disclosure agreement."

"Those are broken all the time."

"Not this one. I'll sue him until he's ruined. We've shared an accountant, so I can destroy him."

"I hope Harley doesn't know he's gay," Meridan smirked, and they both cracked up at the thought of Harley being destroyed by another gay man.

"He honestly thinks he will waltz back into my home tonight all smug. Bullshit! I need a man."

"As much as I love you, you can't have mine."

"Bitch."

Meridan's door was opened for her, and miraculously, Harley and Sean had been ushered in already per Christian's instructions. Fans were bobbing anxiously in anticipation of Christian and Meridan's arrival. The moment she was fully in view, the crowd erupted. She waved enthusiastically, an impossibly wide smile lighting her gorgeous face. She waited for Christian, who kissed her on the cheek, and the cacophony of chants and screams grew ever louder. Christian waved, the flash bulbs popped. They turned in all directions, their smiles never fading, giving each and every photographer and fan a perfect view.

In unison, they headed to the fan bay to the left of the red carpet, feverishly signing photos and shaking hands. Meridan leaned in to kiss an older gentleman on the cheek, but the photographers were too busy trying to outmaneuver one another to snag the best PR shot of the day.

Christian's true personal assistant emerged from the throngs and escorted them to the first of what looked like hundreds of media setups. It was all well-organized, and they were to spend one minute or so with each team.

"Welcome, Christian and Meridan!" gushed the perky blonde *Entertainment First* correspondent. "Don't you just love the way that rolls off the tongue?" Christian and Meridan beamed. "Okay, Meridan. I guess I don't need to ask—Versace?" Meridan nodded. "Christian? Armani?" A laugh from all. "Are you surprised to see Harley Ryan here tonight, Christian?"

"Not really, Heather. She's a huge star. That's what this is about, right?"

He laughed gregariously, prompting Meridan to move toward the *Sophisticate* magazine photographers eagerly anticipating their arrival.

"He's here!" exclaimed *Sophisticate*'s entertainment reporter amid a lightning storm of camera flashes. "Christian York and his lovely, longtime love, Meridan Marks. How are you both?" The usual perfunctory responses around. "Meridan, are there any further developments in your stalker case?"

"Well, Macy, this night is about Christian . . ."

19

The next day was glorious, and Meridan raced to get herself ready. A bit hung over from the night before, she launched into her rigorous morning routine. There was a lot of work involved in preparing Meridan Marks for public display. She twisted her long, curly mane into a loose but sexy knot and applied her makeup expertly.

It was a cool seventy degrees at nearly noon, which required layers. By two it could be high eighties or still seventies, so she selected a Dolce & Gabbana tank top, matching Capri pants and a denim jacket. After rifling through twenty shoe boxes, she settled on a pair of two-inch Jimmy Choo pumps.

The Ivy was slammed, as could be expected, and Meridan didn't see Roz at their table. She approached the restaurant slowly, giving everyone time to recognize her. A couple of fellow actors waved, and she graced their tables with her presence. There was an abnormal charge in the air, and Meridan glanced discreetly from behind her Gucci shades to see who else was dining. It didn't take long to identify the energy source: Harley Ryan.

Harley knew better. The Ivy was hers for lunch! Harley had Caffé Roma! Meridan knew for a fact Harley lunched there often and had paparazzi on staff to report her comings and goings in an attempt to seem like a public figure.

"Harley, darling! You look fabulous," Meridan oozed saccharinely, bringing Harley to her feet.

"Meridan, you look absolutely divine today," spewed Harley, as she reached to anoint each of Meridan's cheeks with an air kiss. "And to think that

I'd been concerned about you, with all I've been hearing. What's this about being stalked, you poor dear? Come here." The two actresses embraced, putting on quite a show for the guests of the Ivy. "It was all I could do to pull myself from bed this morning," said Harley. "I just got home a few hours ago, but I was starving! Last night was glorious. We went to the premiere of Christian York's new movie."

Still smiling, Meridan looked at Harley, attempting to digest what she was hearing. She fought murderous thoughts, which included yanking every last hair from Harley's overdone mane.

"I wonder who he took to the premiere?" Harley added.

Barely able to resist slapping Harley in the face, she ignored the jab. "Dearest, so sorry, but I have to run. Roz just arrived, and we simply have to put our heads together and figure out how to deal with my latest crazed fan. Christian's barely able to work, what with his fear for my life. You know how it is. Oh, silly me. You don't."

Ever the actress, especially with a captive audience at hand, Meridan affected worry and dismay and headed for her table, leaving Harley to turn several shades of rage. She waited as the maitre d' dashed over to pull out her chair.

"What is this?" He picked up a cork that stood on end in front of Meridan's place at the table. With an embarrassed swipe, he slipped it into his pocket. "I apologize, Ms. Marks. I don't know where that could have come from. You are, as usual, the first person to use this table today."

Her mind flashed to the cork on her doorstep that had nearly broken her ankle a few days before.

"Can I see it?" He reached into his jacket pocket and produced the cork. Grgich Hills. Christian's favorite cabernet. Had they had Grgich Hills last night? "Has Mr. York been here today?" she asked.

"I haven't seen him. Should I ask the staff?"

"No. He probably left this on my table to remind me of him. Such a doll," she said, dropping the cork into her purse. She made a mental note to thank Christian.

"Meridan!" Roz crowed, working her way through the tightly arranged tables. "Oh, Harley! I didn't see you! How are you?" she called out, as she glided past Harley's table. Meridan smirked at the jab Roz had delivered and wished she had been the one to do it.

"That Harley Ryan is really impressed with herself," Roz said, as she sat down heavily in her chair.

"I can't imagine why. She hasn't even won an Academy Award," Meridan sniffed, glaring at Harley, who now was being deluged by fans.

"The Academy doesn't generally hand out Oscars for romantic comedy. Sweetie, she did you a favor. She single-handedly boosted your career to the next level. We should be sending her a bottle of champagne to thank her."

"She's so full of herself! I wish Christian had stayed. That would have driven her wild."

"Christian was here?" Roz looked around, hoping for a glimpse of the man she had considered to be the absolute male—before she'd met Jim, of course.

"He left a wine cork on the table to remind me of our evening." Meridan found it easy to fantasize about Christian being heterosexual. Just one time! Was it too much to ask?

"How was last night?"

"Okay. Until she showed up with Sean."

"What?" Roz shrieked and slapped a hand over her mouth.

Meridan leaned in to give Roz a detailed play-by-play, delighting in Roz's full attention.

"Was Christian too upset to kiss?"

"Absolutely not." She raised her perfectly shaped eyebrows coyly, knowing Roz was consumed with jealousy. So good to be Meridan Marks. So amazing to make out with Christian York! So disappointing to go home alone.

"How does Jim feel about all of that?" Roz whispered, effectively concealing the satisfaction it brought her to be able to reel Meridan back into reality now and then. *Hell, if I can't have Christian,* Roz thought, *there's some satisfaction knowing Meridan can't actually have him either.*

"He knows I'm faithful."

"Unless Christian had a moment of bisexual weakness," Roz snorted and leaned in. "Would you do it?"

"Are you kidding me?"

"Eat up. We have an appointment with another member of your fan club."

Meridan cocked her head. "I didn't know I had a fan club."

"I was being facetious—never mind. Cameron Riley. Your new personal security."

"Mmmm. Out of Jim, Cameron, and Christian, who would you rather have sex with?"

"Jesus, Meridan. I don't know." *All of them*, Roz silently decided.

20

Meridan,

    Congratulations on winning the Academy Award for "The Losing Game."
I consider myself to be a true cinephile, and so it is with confidence I declare—
few actors in the history of the motion picture industry have proven so adept at
capturing the very essence of a character and bringing that character to life.

    You are a remarkable actress, Meridan, but I find I'm drawn in time and
again by your compelling beauty. You have the rare gift of being pleasing not
only to the mind and the eye—but also to the soul.
B~

Meridan,

    I want to start by apologizing—there's no excuse for the things I said to
you. It is still critical I receive proof of your breakup with Christian. See what
the thought of losing you does to me? Forgive me.
B~

"Is this the last of it?" Cameron Riley asked, his massive hands tented in front of his mouth as he digested the series of letters he'd just finished reading. Towering at six-foot-four, he was an imposing man with a shaved head and striking features. His name connoted Irish descent, yet he had an olive skin tone and dark features. His shoulders strained against the confines of his sport coat. Overall, he was an imposing figure.

"Yes," Roz, Joel, and Meridan answered in kind. A nervous laugh escaped

Meridan, and she covered her mouth with a pale, delicate hand. He was better looking than she had remembered. She thought he'd been hot then, with hair, but bald—so Vin Diesel.

"I see a threat. Not the same threat the police are looking for, however. They need him to make an aggressive *physical* move. I consider this pretty aggressive, and I don't have to play by the same rules the police do. He's clearly unstable. I see moments of clarity; he's an educated man. He must have a job, because he's able to keep up the floral arrangements, the faxes and the postage for all of the mailings. Still, not stable." Cameron shifted his tremendous mass in the chair he engulfed.

"What's the next step?" Joel asked, all business.

"I'm with Ms. Marks in public. We create an illusion of impenetrability. Chances are, at least in my experience, that once this little creep gets a look at me, it'll jolt him back to reality. He'll realize there's no way around me. This could be over immediately."

"Do we want to catch him? Will you post yourself outside her home and watch her?"

"That's up to you. We can start slow and become more aggressive if that doesn't scare him off."

They all nodded in unison and the papers were signed. Joel handed Cameron a check to cover his fees and expenses for the next week.

"So, where are we going?" Cameron asked after hoisting himself from what now, standing empty, appeared an impossibly small easy chair.

"We? Are we going together or are you following me?" Meridan asked.

"I'll shadow you. When we're in public, I'll be next to you. No one will be allowed to touch you without dealing with me." A little thrill raced through Meridan. It was pretty enticing; so many people she knew had bodyguards, and, until now, she thought the idea silly. This smoldering, sexy man would be by her side at all times. Perhaps it was time to consider overnight duty.

"We have a meeting at Meritime," Roz announced.

"No. It was cancelled. Besides, it's gin-and-tonic-thirty." Roz looked at her watch and realized it was, in fact, the end of Meridan's work day. Four-thirty was really all anyone could expect.

"Where to?" Cameron asked.

"How about Madeo?" Roz knew what Meridan was up to. They had overheard Harley discussing her happy hour plans for today. Roz grabbed her coat. There was no way she was going to miss the Clash of the Titans.

Madeo was bursting with Hollywood's A-list, as per usual. Meridan scanned the tables for Harley but didn't see her. Damn!

"Three, Ms. Marks?"

"Two? Three?" Meridan asked her companions.

"Two," Cameron stated, and once the ladies were seated, he took his place behind Meridan's chair. As if the guests weren't already abuzz, the sight of Meridan Marks with a bodyguard was whipping them into a frenzy.

"Shit." Roz averted her gaze.

"What?" Meridan leaned in to hear Roz.

"Jack."

"I guess this was unavoidable." Meridan concealed a grin. "Jack!" She waved and Roz grabbed her arm.

"What are you doing?" she hissed. "We aren't asking for attention on the matter!"

Meridan gestured to Cameron and tossed Roz a "you have got to be kidding me" look. "Well, hauling the Titanic around with us will put up some red flags, Roz. We might as well nip this in the butt."

"Bud."

"What?"

"It's bud. Nip it in the bud, not butt."

"Really?"

"Jack, good to see you." Roz stood and shook Jack's hand warmly. Meridan followed suit.

"Friend of yours?" Jack gestured to Cameron.

"I guess you might as well know," Roz started, offering a seat to Jack. "Can this be off the record, at least for now? I mean, we could promise our cooperation, if there's anything worthy of reporting, but right now there's nothing." Meridan lifted her eyebrows, warning Roz that she sounded like she was lying.

"Jack," Meridan interjected. "I've hired a bodyguard. Nothing is going on, but it's better to be safe than sorry, right?"

"So, no news? Have you heard from him?" His eyes shifted between the women, looking for chinks in the armor of their united front.

"Flowers, the usual. Nothing new." Meridan shrugged her shoulders, and her eyes lit up when she saw Harley Ryan saunter through the restaurant. As could be expected, the staff fluttered about the actress and led her to her table.

"Gotta go." Jack bolted from his seat, leaving Meridan seething.

"What's going on with Harley that's such a big deal he needed to leave us? She pretended she didn't see us. You can't miss Cameron, right? Do you think she saw us?"

Roz shook her head busying herself with the drink menu. In her peripheral vision she watched Meridan obsess over the flurry of activity across the dining room.

"I'm going to the bathroom," she announced. Roz couldn't believe it was taking this long to reclaim the available attention. Cameron helped her from her seat, and Roz couldn't resist watching Harley's face when she "noticed" Meridan. Ever the actress, she smiled broadly and offered a wave, which Meridan pretended not to see.

Harley's entourage insulated her from several clamoring fans. Perfect. The battle of the sheltered. Roz ordered Meridan's favorite appetizer, calamari, and gin and tonics all around.

Meridan took the long way from the bathroom so she would have to come closer than necessary to Harley's table, relying on the closely situated tables as an excuse.

"Harley? This is crazy! We don't see each other for years and then twice in one day?" Meridan leaned in for an embrace.

"Looks like our paths are going to cross more often. Who's your boyfriend?" Harley asked, unable to keep up the façade she hadn't noticed him looming about.

"That's cute, Harley. You know Christian's my boyfriend. He insisted I hire some protection. This stalker has become very threatening," she whispered her lie to keep from being overhead by Jack. Harley rolled her eyes, but it was visible only to her people. "You know how it is," Meridan smirked.

"Yes, I'm still reeling from my last brush with him."

"Who?"

"Your stalker. Sweetie, I reread that article in *Glitterati* after lunch and I'm pretty certain it's the same guy who harassed me last year. Is your bodyguard single?"

Meridan gritted her teeth and said her goodbyes.

"I don't know who she thinks she is," Meridan fumed after returning to her seat. "She's convinced that my stalker used to stalk her! How crazy! We look nothing alike, we *are* nothing alike—well, we're both very famous and adored by millions, but that's it. She's just trying to break my thunder, as usual!"

"Why did we come here if you didn't want to see her?"

"I wanted her to see Cameron," she pouted, jutting a thumb backward at her new bodyguard.

Roz's phone rang and she fished it out of her purse.

"Yes? I see. Interesting. Please dispose of them immediately. Who delivered them? Courier? Call them and find out if they have any idea who ordered the delivery. Find out how they paid." She snapped her phone shut. "It seems he's *very* sorry," Roz reported.

"What did he send me?" Meridan perked up with the spotlight back on her.

"A dozen arrangements. The usual ones. They're at Meritime."

"Ms. Marks?" The waiter startled Roz and Meridan out of quiet contemplation. He handed her a two-page fax. A cover page read CONFIDENTIAL FOR MERIDAN MARKS. Cameron leaned in and noted it was sent from a Kinko's nearby. He added the number and time of the fax to the list he had compiled from all of the other faxes.

Meridan,

I am very concerned about your new companion. I wonder if perhaps

*you have hired him to protect you from your stalker . . . I'm surprised you
didn't run this by me. I am a big guy myself, though not trained in the art of
bodyguarding. I wondered if he would be joining us for dinner this week? I
need to know what day and if he will be eating or just looming.*

*I'm not crazy about the way he's looking at you. I'm hoping he will
continue to keep this relationship professional. With Christian York out of the
way, I don't need anyone else vying for your time. If I don't hear from you by,
let's say, noon tomorrow, I will pick a day and time for us to meet.*

*I suppose you'll be enjoying the calamari. You eat too much Italian. I don't
know how you maintain that glorious figure of yours.*
B~

Roz reached to take the fax from Meridan, who sat speechless at the
realization B had been there, close enough to know what she had ordered.

"Watch her," Cameron said as he left to troll the restaurant. Roz nodded
and put her hand over Meridan's. She couldn't help but notice the buzz
generated by Cameron's intense and thorough examination of the guests. She
also couldn't help noticing this was the first time Meridan wasn't noticing.

"He's watching me," she whispered, her eyes flitting about, frantic
and aimless. Roz continued to pat Meridan's hand, stunned that she wasn't
concerned or even aware that Harley Ryan was nearly breaking her neck trying
to ascertain what was happening. "Why is he doing this to me, Roz?"

"He's confused, obviously."

Cameron returned. "I spoke with a waiter who recalls a tall, dark,
attractive man who dined alone a couple tables over."

Meridan hung her head low; she had to learn to be more observant.
She'd been so wrapped up in leering at Cameron and taunting Harley, she
hadn't noticed any attractive men. Maybe she'd have recognized him from
somewhere.

21

Once Cameron had Meridan secured at the Peninsula, he took off to run down the fax locations while Roz kept an afternoon appointment with the real estate agent. He left his protégé Noah in charge, a third-degree black belt and gun enthusiast. His explicit instructions were to inform him when Meridan heard from Jim, who had been contacted. Noah was not to allow Meridan to leave the premises, and Joel, Jim, and Christian were the only male visitors allowed.

"Hey, Cam. Jim called. He's going to stop by Meridan's and pick up some clothing and be here about seven. Meridan's kind of out of it. Does she do drugs? Prescription or otherwise?"

"I have no idea, but if she didn't have an open script for Valium she'd be the only actress I've ever met who didn't. Have Meridan or Jim call me later to coordinate where and when I'll take over for him."

"Any luck?"

"Hell, no. This guy's a ghost. I've been to the county courthouse, the Bar Association, the Visitor's Bureau, the public library . . ."

"Could he be a lawyer?"

"I haven't the slightest idea. All those places have plenty of fax machines and no one knows anything."

"I can't believe you aren't on around-the-clock detail. This is Meridan Marks, for God's sake!"

"Turns out it was a huge struggle to get her to agree to protection. Her people are trying to take it slow. They hired me because I've never been an alarmist and I'm not going to start now. They want Meridan to feel secure and insulated, not suffocated. I'm not even sure I should be wasting my time trying to locate this guy. All we can do at this point is identify him and maybe issue an order of restraint or file a complaint of some sort. If anything, we risk exacerbating the situation. He's already seen me, so if he finds me snooping around in his life, he won't be happy. I don't want him taking his anger out on Meridan. That letter today pissed me off. He was close enough to know what she ordered, and I didn't notice anything."

"Hope you don't get fired on the first day," Noah jabbed.

"Right. Take care of her."

"No problem, man. It sure does suck having to babysit one of the most beautiful women in the world."

"Don't I know it?" Cameron signed off and tried to settle on a course of action. He was hired to protect Meridan Marks only during the day. Once she was safe in her own house or in the company of someone she trusted, he was free to leave. It didn't seem comprehensive enough.

22

Noah opened the door and Jim burst through, heading directly for the bed, where he knew Meridan would be perched. She was a wreck. Her hair was askew and she was nibbling on a once perfectly-manicured nail. He gathered her into his strong arms.

"I'm here, babe," he cooed. She was limp in his embrace. "Is she on something?" He looked to Noah, who had set about marshaling his belongings to leave them in peace.

"I don't think so. She's been like this since I got here. She's been staring at the TV like she was in a trance or something. I don't know her, so it's difficult to say what's normal." He gave a small wave and Jim nodded his thanks.

"Mer, are you okay? What happened? I'm worried about you. Did you take something?" He barraged her with questions, which went unanswered. She curled into his lap and rested her head on his chest.

After a few minutes, Jim sensed Meridan's body gradually softening. Her breathing regulated to a slow cadence and he thought she had dozed off. He moved to reposition her on the bed, but she held him tightly. "I'm scared. I know I said I wasn't before, but I am now," she whispered.

"Tell me what happened." He rocked her gently as she brought him up to speed, from the venomous attacks the day before to the apology, the dozens of flowers and then, finally, the fax to Madeo. While listening intently, Jim eased himself back against the stack of undisturbed pillows on the bed. Even the small distance between them caused her tension to creep back, and she curled tight into a ball, her arms wrapped around her knees. "He was there. Right there, while I was. He was watching me, looking at me."

"This is making me crazy. I should take some time off work."

"Can you?" She brightened as he opened the calendar on this phone.

"I leave in the morning for Atlanta—"

"Can I come?"

"Have you forgotten the photo in *Glitterati* of us holding hands? It's up to you. I'm ready to blow the lid off this relationship the minute you are. I'm not afraid to be Meridan Marks's boyfriend, but you have to be ready not to be Christian York's girlfriend."

Meridan sat back with a huff, arms folded across her chest combatively. This was a mess. She wanted to end the charade, but her public relationship with Christian was critical to both of them. She needed not to worry Jim so much that he insisted on staying in town. Once this whole thing blew over, they would sit down and work out both relationships. In the meantime, she had to make sure Jim didn't get frustrated enough to leave her for good.

"I have a trip to Manhattan over the holiday I can't miss. It's my cousin's wedding at the Plaza. My family would kill me."

"Wedding? Can I go? I think it's about time I met your family, don't you?"

"Mer, we talked about this. Listen, you deserve the full treatment when you meet them. I can't bear the thought of you playing second fiddle to anyone. That, and my cousin would castrate me for bringing the most beautiful woman in the world to her wedding." He chuckled a bit, hoping she would understand.

"I wouldn't wear anything dramatic," she promised.

"Babe, you could wear the awning from the hotel without a belt and still rock all of New York City. I'm literally flying in from Atlanta, attending the wedding and flying home as soon as it's over. But I'll be just a phone call away from you."

"You're going to be gone, like, a month?"

"Please! After the wedding's over we'll take a trip out to Chicago and meet everyone. I'll be gone a week or so, my annual team meetings."

"Are you embarrassed of me?" Meridan begged for reassurance.

"On the contrary. I spoke to my mother and told her I am deeply in love, and that she would meet the girl of my and everyone else's dreams soon enough." She acquiesced at his kind words.

"I'm not usually this needy. It's just the whole stalking thing is dragging me up the wall."

"Driving."

"What?"

"Driving you up the wall."

"Right, yeah. I'm exhausted. I don't even sleep anymore. On top of everything else, I miss you. I wish you didn't have to travel so much."

"Me, too, but I could kiss Joel and Roz for convincing you to hire some help. I can worry about you one ounce less knowing you're protected."

"I feel pretty comfortable at home and even more comfortable here with you," she said, raising a sculpted eyebrow in a tempting arc.

Within seconds, she was tearing at his dress shirt, unbuttoning each button and savoring the expanse of his tight, muscular chest. She inhaled his scent deeply, wiping away the anguish of the day.

She settled back and surrendered while he disrobed her, watching lustily the way his long, lean limbs bulged and worked as he removed her blouse and jeans. Anxious to have him inside, she helped remove her undergarments.

After, when they lay spent on the king-sized bed, Meridan propped herself on one elbow and examined her boyfriend.

She thanked Gavin Mast frequently in her thoughts for introducing her to Jim. The party was huge, even by Hollywood standards, a post-premiere bash at his mega-mansion recognizing the potential of *The Losing Game*, which Gavin had directed and co-produced. Meridan was to be the guest of honor at what had been described to her as a small cast gathering at Gavin's house, but she arrived to find more than five hundred of her "closest" friends and industry people awaiting the grace of her presence. It was a magical night in all respects, a magnificent celebration of her performance and a testimony to everyone's faith she would bring home an Oscar for them all.

Halfway through the evening, she had noticed Jim watching her across the dance floor. She flirted a bit with eyes she knew to be irresistible, luring him to her. He had approached with an air of confidence that rivaled her own, and, without words, he removed the drink from her delicate hand and replaced it with one of the two flutes of champagne he had carried with him. He toasted her silently and they drank, their eyes riveted to one another. He led her to the dance floor, where they cut the tempo in half and danced lazily.

When the music ended, he diverted his eyes and said goodnight. As he walked away, she felt her heart, already attached to him, ripping out of her chest.

"Wait!" she called, but the music had fired up to full volume, drowning out her voice. She fought her way through throngs of well-wishers until she was close enough to touch him. At that very moment, he was whisked away by a fetching woman. The two of them spoke for what seemed an eternity until the woman finally departed. Seizing the opportunity, Meridan bolted to him.

"We didn't get the chance to meet formally." She extended her hand to him, which he accepted readily. "I'm Meridan Marks." Unable to refrain, she turned her thousand megawatt smile on him, rendering him momentarily speechless.

"I know who you are," he said.

"I don't know who you are."

"Jim Cooper."

"Well, Jim Cooper, what brings you here tonight?"

"You."

"Really?" she asked, barely able to speak.

"Yes."

"Aren't you the smooth one?" She shot him a crooked smile and lifted an eyebrow, intrigued.

"Yes."

"Not to mention a man of few words."

"At times."

"Could I interest you in another dance?"

"Absolutely."

Over the course of the evening, she learned everything about him.

Born and raised in Chicago, he had a pleasant yet forceful Northern accent. He was the only child of parents still married after forty years. He attended Northwestern University and majored in advertising. He had been sent to the party by his biggest client to prospect Meridan for a new fashion fitness line. She'd found that funny considering she didn't exercise. She had always turned down every endorsement offer she'd received, but promised to consider his. In the end, the company, having gotten wind of her lack of athletic prowess, selected a professional volleyball player to represent its line.

In the months to come, Meridan pursued him as best she could without interfering with her "relationship" with Christian. He was interminably understanding about her professional and personal obligations. She returned the favor by not giving him a hard time about the amount of travel involved in his work, and meeting him on location when possible, which was difficult given her major-league star status. They'd been busted once and Jim had become somewhat of a mystery man to the media. They really couldn't afford any more screw-ups.

Jim turned his back to her in the failing light, and she snuggled up to him and shared his warmth. She never wanted this to end. Jim brought out the best in her. She fell asleep fantasizing about the proposal that couldn't be long off. She needed to start thinking about how to deal with Christian and their inevitable breakup.

23

The time that had passed since Lynden had received Joel Goldstein's e-mail had blown by. The new project with Gia Androvaldi was a completely consuming and welcome diversion. So long as she was working, she could keep her fears at bay. She'd managed to convince herself Brit and Ash were not stalking anyone and, despite an e-mail from the LAPD requesting the names of the brothers, was steadfast in her determination not to get further involved.

Lynden was racing toward Addison to meet Gia at Mercy Wine Bar. She needed her to see what Lynden considered *par excellence* in the wine bar arena. It didn't surprise her Gia had done no research, let alone traveled anywhere north of Highland Park, as most Dallas residents didn't; however, this particular restaurant was a destination point no matter where you resided.

The tollway was clear, but a frantic call from a client had kept her in the office ten minutes longer than planned. As she reached for her cell phone to call Gia, it rang. An incoming number with an Atlanta exchange. Brady. She cringed as an image of him broken and bandaged in a hospital bed assaulted her, and answered quickly so his voice could erase the horrific image.

"Brady!"

"Reesey! How are you, baby girl? Neurotic?" Her grin grew wider as she basked in him.

"No. Most of that is gone," she lied.

"How many times have you washed your hands today?"

"Let's see, a few times this morning, each time I went potty, and after lunch?" This time she was being honest. The hand washing was tough to shake.

She always felt sticky. "Thanks for reminding me, though, you harpie!" Brady laughed thunderously, warming her through. "When will you be here?" she asked, with no attempt to disguise her excitement.

"Friday, if that's okay? I'm, I mean, *we* are staying at the Hotel Crescent?"

"Oh, you'll love it. It's a beautiful hotel with a shopping annex and tons of restaurants and bars close by. As a matter of fact, my new project is right down the street."

"I'll e-mail you the details. Same e-mail?"

"Same." She paused and contemplated telling him what had transpired but decided to wait until she could look him in the eye. There was no doubt he would be furious with her.

He hung up leaving her calm and nostalgic. She loved that he still called her Reesey. It reminded her of a time when she didn't fear the dark, wash her hands twenty or fifty times a day, or compulsively prowl about the house, confirming her safety. The only drawback to having Brady in her life was being reminded of her disturbing past.

She screeched to a stop in front of the valet stand at Mercy, having almost missed it. She'd returned several times with Dane since her initial glowing review and hoped the owners would be in.

"Sorry I'm late," she called to Gia, who was on the phone. Gia waved back excitedly and raised her index finger. Both Glen Agritelley and Vincent Havard stood to greet her, and she shook hands warmly with both proprietors. They chatted briefly and Lynden was happy to see business was booming for them. Seeing Giada place her phone on the table, she approached to make introductions. Glen was genuinely delighted to hear about Giada's venture, and Lynden enjoyed watching Giada at her winsome best. Both men were quite taken, as was she.

"Absolutely charming," Gia breathed as the gentlemen took their leave, and Lynden nodded in response. "How are you? That was Daddy," she reported, but Lynden had already ascertained that from her tone. Gia worshipped her father, and that worship was mutual. Over the course of their meetings, Gia had shared bits from her past—her mother's death when she was four years old and her father's subsequent remarriage.

"I'm good. Listen, I wanted to go over a few things with you."

"Of course! The first thing we need to discuss is how we're going to outdo this place. It's gorgeous, and the menu is fantastic!"

"It's not a matter of outdoing anyone. Mercy has a great many things to offer, but so do we. Let's work on developing a clearly articulated concept and filling seats. In the meantime, I spoke with the head of PR for the Dallas Storm; he's an acquaintance I've cultivated for years. Anyway, he's on board for throwing an early season premiere party at your restaurant." She paused long enough to order a glass of wine. "It will be tight, as the grand opening will be the following night, but I suggested a cross-promotional soft opening."

Gia responded with her usual clapping. "Daddy's anxious to meet you. He thinks you're brilliant and I can't agree more." Gia raised her glass to Lynden just as the waitress delivered Lynden's drink. "*Salute*," she smiled, and Brit's face flashed into Lynden's mind. It had been the first date. "In keeping with our Italian theme."

"Yes." Lynden downed her wine quickly, hoping to soothe her fraying nerves.

Gia fished a large green olive from the dish on the table and popped it into her mouth. She settled back in her chair, eyeing Lynden suspiciously.

"What?"

"Well, two things really. Number one, are you going to partner with me? Number two, are you dating anyone?" Lynden appreciated her in-your-face method of communication.

"Number one, I have not decided. I have a number of concerns. Number two, I really don't have time to date." A second glass of wine appeared and she thanked the waitress. The sauvignon blanc was cool and crisp. She sipped.

"What concerns?"

"I don't want to give up my business. I've worked too hard to walk away from it. I love what I do and have no interest in day-to-day operations."

"Okay. I don't want you helping other restaurants compete with me. How can I persuade you?"

"I don't consider myself capable of generating competition."

"I do." Gia reached into her briefcase and pulled out a thick legal document. She placed it carefully on the table. "I expected this answer and have a solution. I want to be in business with you. I think you're invaluable; you have all the experience and I have none. I've drafted an agreement that would serve as, well, a non-compete, if you will. It would limit you to handling four concepts per year, none of which could be similar in any way to mine." Gia spoke animatedly, as always, which Lynden found charming. "The agreement demands you are on staff for all PR, marketing, promotional and creative aspects of the restaurant. Your presence would be required at any type of function of your devising, and you would serve as general intellectual counsel. You're the big picture person. In exchange for this, I make you a twenty-five percent partner with no investment on your part other than your mind and your time." She pursed her lips and narrowed her eyes as she waited for Lynden's response.

Lynden crossed her long legs and relaxed to think. She had realized the first day she met Gia Androvaldi that she intended to get whatever she wanted at any price. She didn't want to tell Gia she usually managed only three concepts a year, so she wouldn't be giving up much there. Gia hadn't mentioned her column, so no loss there. She would be paid profits on a concept she believed in and conceptualized, no problem there. Next stop, Strait Lane.

"Gia, I appreciate your offer. Would you be offended if I had my attorney look it over?"

"I would be disappointed if you didn't." Gia raised her glass to Lynden, wearing the smirk of a woman who intended to win. "I would be willing to increase the share of partnership if you wanted to invest." Lynden returned the gesture from a distance and sighed deeply. Things were really starting to hum for her. She felt confident, barring any serious restrictions on her time or intellectual parameters, that a week from today she would be partnered with Gia Androvaldi.

24

"Hi, I'm Jeff Atwood," he said plopping into the chair next to mine. I smiled, feeling comfortable for the first time since arriving at Brit's apartment. I was delighted to be invited to meet his friends.

"I'm Reese."

"Damn, I should've known you were taken," he said playfully, and I was glad someone recognized I wasn't just a random chick at this party. "You're Ash's girlfriend. He was right about you. You're gorgeous!" My face turned red.

"Thank you, but I'm not seeing Ash, I'm seeing Brit."

"Unless there are two girls named Reese who look like you, and unless Brit broke it off with Karis, you're seeing Ash." He laughed. I stood and silently combed the room for Brit, who was nowhere to be found.

"Excuse me." I followed the sound of Brit's voice coming from the kitchen, but stopped short upon hearing my name and strained to hear more.

"You just better hope Ash doesn't show up here." Kevin and Brit were engaged in a heated conversation. Confused, I wanted to get to the bottom of the situation.

"Why?" I interrupted. They both looked at me as if I had caught them in bed together.

"Why what?" Brit asked, a portrait of innocence.

"Why does it matter if Ash comes here?"

"Reese, why don't you go grab a beer? This is between Kevin and me," Brit said.

"It does concern me. It does not, however, concern Kevin. I need to speak to you alone. Now." I had none of the conviction I was voicing, but I hoped I would convince them otherwise. Kevin took the lead.

"Reese, if you must know, I was telling Brit he better hope Ash doesn't show up because I'll kick his ass." He saw my skeptical expression and continued with what I already determined to be a lie. *"Last night we were out . . . Ash got drunk as usual and got us kicked out of the Harvest. I tried to help the bartender calm him down. He was a raving lunatic and he started in on me. He was name-calling and being a bastard. I'm tired of his shit."* He shrugged his shoulders and walked out of the room. Brit gave me a *"see"* gesture that didn't clear up my conversation with Jeff.

"Brit, did you break up with Karis when you told me you did?"

"Yes! What? You don't trust me? Where is this coming from? What have I done to make you not trust me?" He stormed out of the room, leaving me alone and miserable. He was right. I'd never heard Brit mention Jeff. Perhaps Jeff didn't know they had broken up; they had been together so long it probably seemed impossible. I left to find Brit and instead ran into Jeff.

"Reese, are you all right? Did I say something to offend you? I didn't mean to." He placed his hand on my arm and seemed sincere. I felt my eyes well up.

"Listen," he continued. *"I'm a really good friend of Ash's, and I've been dying to meet you. He's told me all about you. He should be here soon."* His voice trailed off as if he had just gotten a thought. *"Is he here? He told me he was bringing you."*

"I'm not seeing Ash," I whispered.

"You know, dating. I know he can be a little difficult, you know, with the drinking, but he's a great guy and he loves you."

I grabbed my keys and bolted to the door. No one asked where I was going. No one cared. I raced to my car, humiliated Brit wasn't running behind me. He didn't care about me. I was a pawn in some twisted game with his brother.

My apartment was blissfully empty, and I crashed on my bed. I willed Brit to knock, but he didn't. I listened to the machine pick up countless phone calls *that weren't from him. I had pissed him off. It was over. I nodded off around midnight.*

25

I awoke to thunderous knocking on my front door. I leapt out of bed confused and disoriented but, thankfully, not hung over. Still wearing my clothing from the night before, I ran to the door.

"Reese, open the door!"

"What do you want, Brit?" I asked through the dead-bolted door.

"I want to talk to you."

"Then you should have called or come over last night."

"Don't fuck with me."

"Hey, dude." I heard my neighbor Mark's voice from next door. "What's your problem?" I silently prayed for Mark to go back into his apartment, but knew he was probably on his way out to bike.

"Don't you fucking worry about it, Greg LeMond! Reese, open the door!"

"Reese? Are you okay?" Mark asked.

"Of course she's okay, asshole. Go back into your apartment and mind your own fucking business."

"Look, dude, you need to leave. If she wanted you to come in, she'd let you in."

"I didn't fucking ask your opinion. If you want me to beat it out of you, keep talking!"

"Brit! Please stop it!" I threw open the door and he came at me so fast I shrieked. Instead of hitting me, he pulled me into a tight hug and kicked the door closed behind him.

"Reese? Are you okay?" Mark asked.

"Yes, I am." I hoped I was. "Sorry."

"Don't ever leave like that again!"

"What?"

"I've been sick all night wondering what I did to make you not trust me. I couldn't think of anything." He pulled away and took my face in his hands. Tears tumbled down his face. I started to get choked up myself out of relief.

"I couldn't believe you left. Everyone was looking forward to meeting you. I was embarrassed and angry at first, but by this morning, I was terrified it was over!"

"Oh, my God, Brit." Tears filled my eyes. I couldn't believe what I was hearing. *"I don't know what to say. I met Jeff Atwood and things got so confusing. He insinuated you were still with Karis and . . ."*

"Jeff's a friend of Ash's. I haven't seen him in months. I'm not surprised he didn't know we broke up. It's none of his business anyway!" Brit grew stormy again, and I shrank away. *"You should have trusted me!"*

"I did. I do . . . I want to, but I'm confused." I tried to put some distance between us, but he held my wrist tightly.

"Don't walk away from me, Reese. I want to know what's bothering you." He guided me to the couch and directed me to sit.

"Jeff insisted Ash was dating a girl named Reese that Ash had told him all about, and that he was in love with her." I was babbling in my attempt to get it all out.

"Listen. My brother's fucked up. The truth is, he probably is in love with you. We saw you at the same time at Shakespeare's. We were there with Patrick and Kevin; you were there with some friends. Ash said he thought you were hot. We all agreed. Patrick said he had seen you in the communications building, maybe the year before. Ash said he was going to marry you. I thought he was fucking around. When you left, I followed on my bike. I found out where you lived. You know the rest," he confessed.

"Why was Patrick mad at the Wine Cellar?"

"Apparently, Ash had been trying to work up the nerve to talk to you for weeks. I didn't know that. Ash and I aren't very close. He drinks a lot; he's

unpredictable, volatile. He, Patrick, and Jeff are close though."

"So, while your brother was working up the nerve to talk to me, you swooped in and made a move?" I challenged.

"First of all, I didn't know he was trying to make a move. He didn't bring you up to me again. Is it my fault I have more balls than he does? Why? Do you want to be with him?" he accused, instantly furious.

"No, I . . ."

"This is bullshit. What kind of game are you playing?"

"Me? I haven't been able to get a straight answer out of you in weeks!"

"You didn't ask."

"I didn't want to upset you!"

"Well, now you have. Not only is my brother walking around telling everyone he's dating you, which makes me look like a fool, I have to worry about whether he believes it." He paused for a moment before turning to the door and leaving. It was over.

26

In the hours following Brit's sullen departure, I set about getting my life back in order. I felt a deep sense of loss, but knew I would not make any attempt to make repairs. I was incapable of calling, let alone groveling to, a man. I showered, and washed and dried my hair. I gave myself a facial. I cleaned the apartment and listened to the answering machine as it collected volumes of messages for my roommate. Most times it was nice to have my space, but right now the silence just meant loneliness.

I spent the afternoon preparing my lesson plan for the next week. Scott called, and I lied to him about my big night meeting all of Brit's friends. Mark knocked on my door that evening around six. I had forgotten to go over and apologize for the scene created earlier. When I opened the door, he extended a note.

"This one was on your doorstep. I hope it isn't from that crazy asshole who was here earlier. Is that who you're seeing?" he asked.

"Not anymore," I answered, sleepy with depression. "Hey, thanks for helping me. He isn't an asshole. It was my fault." I gave him a weak smile and closed the door.

I opened the note reluctantly.

Harvest Grill—7 p.m.

My heart soared. I looked at my watch and saw I had less than an hour to get myself ready to meet Brit. I dressed carefully in a black evening suit. The jacket had a chiffon collar, which veiled the cleavage created by a scalloped-cup teddy.

When I arrived, the hostess immediately escorted me to the table. I was frantic because I was ten minutes late. Brit let out a sigh of relief and a nervous chuckle before kissing me on the cheek.

"I thought you weren't coming," he said quietly.

"I'm sorry I'm late. I didn't get your note until six. You have my neighbor to thank for me being here."

"You look amazing. Next time I'll hug him instead of trying to beat him up," he laughed, and the tone was set. We gazed into each other's eyes, and, for the first time in weeks, I felt comfortable. We were on the same page. We huddled close like lovers, and I entertained the possibility a day would soon come that we would be.

"I met the coolest guy last night. His name is Tracy Ellis. He came to the party with Jeff Atwood, do you know him?" I shook my head no and he continued. "He's an exchange student from Brazil. Can you imagine?" I shook my head that I couldn't. "Man, that would be so cool. His father is British, but he grew up mostly in South America. He told us all about it. I want you to meet him, maybe this week? I think you'll really like him." I nodded, looking forward to meeting someone who didn't know Brit with Karis.

"I feel like I can't get close enough to you. I want to be inside you," he whispered.

"What?" I said, involuntarily.

"Don't panic," he said. "I meant your mind. I want to know everything about you. I want to feel you next to me at all times."

The night was wonderful and we got on well. Dinner was fabulous, as always at the Harvest, and there was no mention of Ash or anything unpleasant. He begged me to stay with him that night and promised to be on his best behavior. We went back to his place and listened to music. It wasn't long before he extended a hand to me and gestured toward the bedroom.

"Brit, I . . ."

"I promise I won't touch you." His hand over his heart caused an odd mixture of relief and frustration. It wasn't that I didn't want him to touch me. I just wasn't ready to have sex. I wanted to be more to him than sex. I was

afraid he'd leave me once he'd conquered me. Had I unintentionally created a
challenge?

"Stop where you are," he said in hushed tones in the dim light of his room.

"Why?" I giggled.

"I want you to take off your clothes."

"Brit, you said—"

"First your jacket."

"Brit."

He clicked off the small lamp, which was glowing softly, and settled into the
large chair in the corner of his bedroom.

"Is that better?"

"No. I don't want to."

"I'm not asking you. I'm telling you."

I was experiencing equal parts of fear and excitement. My heart thundered
in my chest.

I unbuttoned my jacket slowly, letting it fall open.

"Now, unzip your skirt, slowly." I did what he asked. Probably too
slowly, but I was mortified. "Let the skirt drop on the floor and step out of
it." I realized not for the first time that night I was wearing thigh-high black
stockings, their elastic eliminating any need for a garter belt. I was acutely
aware my undergarments belied my chaste intentions.

I heard his breath catch in his throat as I let the skirt fall. I wondered how
clearly he could see with the minimal light from the window.

"Now, the jacket. Take it off."

"Brit, please. I'm embarrassed."

"I'm turned on."

I debated running to the bathroom and locking myself in, but feared it
would spell the end. I let the jacket fall and there I stood, clad only in my black
teddy, thigh-high stockings and very high black pumps. I innately feared leg fat
oozing over the bands of the stockings.

"Now, sit on the bed, with your legs crossed." I still couldn't see him
clearly, but heard the rustling of fabric. I sat on the bed feeling foolish and

vulnerable. I heard low, moaning sounds that, despite my current state of mind, I found arousing. I heard his zipper and then his belt.

"Oh, God, that feels good. Just thinking about you gets me hard. I think I've been hard since the first time I saw you." I had never seen a man masturbate, but now, hearing it, I was captivated.

"Come here," he said.

"I can't."

"Just come closer. I need to see you, smell you." I could see in the vague backlight his hand continuing to stroke. I started to get up, but he stopped me with his voice.

"On your knees," he demanded so sharply I instantly dropped to my knees and silently prayed he didn't want me to give him head. I didn't want to be some cheap slut to him. I wanted more. I could smell him and it was dizzying.

"Just kneel there in front of me. I can feel your lips on me," he panted, the stroking motion becoming faster and faster, his breathing more jagged.

"Oh, God, Reese, oh, my God!" he climaxed with a roar and fell silent for a long moment. When he clicked the light on, I instinctually averted my eyes.

"Look at what you made me do," he said. I didn't want to look, but I couldn't stop myself. He had tucked himself back into his underwear but his bare chest, like a chiseled sculpture, was spattered with white. As he stood, his ejaculate began to run the length of his torso, slowed only by the trail of hair that led from his navel and disappeared into his underwear.

He pulled boxers and a T-shirt from his dresser and tossed them to me as he headed into the bathroom.

"You're staying. I promise I won't touch you."

I heard the shower running and feigned sleep when he came out. Despite feeling more sexually alive than ever, I was terrified he would try to pressure me into sex. True to his word, he didn't touch me.

In the morning, he served freshly baked cinnamon raisin toast and juice in bed and the incident from the prior evening was not discussed.

27

"Hey Joel, Cameron here. Listen, I took over for Jim this morning early at the Peninsula. Everything was fine until we got a fax."

"Do you have it with you?"

"Yeah, I thought you'd want to hear it."

Meridan,

I guess you forgot about our dinner at Geisha House last night? You act like you are trying to tell me something. I had the scripts ready, I made you your own copy in case you forgot. I had highlighters and paper clips. You are so selfish sometimes. Why are you at the Peninsula anyway? I am feeling a bit harassed by this.

Why don't you make it up to me and meet me for dinner Monday night. I have made arrangements for two at Katana. I'm assuming your new bodyguard will not be joining us? After all, you have me to protect you. I've been giving this a lot of thought and decided you need to give me a key to your place. I didn't see Christian around anywhere, so I am not going to get mad about you staying there.

I wanted to let you know I saw a familiar-looking guy at the valet on my way in. It could be the guy. He was tall and good-looking—if you are into the California rock star look. He kind of looked like Roz's boyfriend. Very suspicious. You should probably call Roz and find out if she knows where her boyfriend is. I'll give her a ring later.

B~

"He's talking about Jim. He saw Roz, Christian, Meridan and Jim at Skybar."

"I remember the letter. Charming guy."

"I don't like this. He's too close."

"You don't need to worry. She's currently destroying Melrose Avenue with Noah, and as long as she's with one of us, she's safe."

"What do we do about Katana? I just talked to Detective Ford, and they remain unwilling to get involved in what they consider a harassment case. We can't take any type of legal action because we have no frigging idea who he is!"

"I spoke with Meridan and she won't participate in any type of sting."

"I agree, but don't you think it's time to bust him?"

"Hell yes, the little fucking coward. But get this: I called Katana to check for any reservation under B someone or Meridan or Marks. They're not open Mondays."

"What?" Joel said, incredulous. He ran a hand over his salt-and-pepper stubble in frustration.

"The guy badgers the shit out of her and sets a date on a day the place is closed."

"What does that mean?"

"Could mean he's toying with her. Maybe he thinks she'll show up. You can enter the main gates and get all the way across that outer deck only to find the door locked. This leaves you in the dark in a semi-isolated area. I only know this because I showed up before they were open one night."

"You don't think he's thinking of kidnapping her?"

"That would be the upside."

"Killing her?"

"I don't think immediately. He seems to want more from her. He wants to consult, talk, get to know one another, have a relationship. This sounds more to me like he'd want to keep her. Captive."

"Fuck. This is creepy." Joel released an exasperated sigh and reclined in his chair. He observed his reflection in his banker's lamp, disappointed by the dark circles that had taken permanent residency beneath his eyes.

"I have a tentative plan. I'm going to call back and prod them about reservations for anyone for any night with that initial or any reference to Meridan. Roz told me they were there a few weeks ago, but said she never uses Meridan's name. Maybe the hostess will remember something? Let me tell you, though, despite my considerable charm, they were not too cooperative."

"Maybe you need to use your considerable charm in person, maybe shirtless?" Cameron erupted into laughter, appreciating the brief respite from the grave discussion.

"Perhaps. I think getting them to part with the info, though, will require an Act of Congress."

"It's Katana, Cameron. Very heavy hitters dine there," he gushed sarcastically, drawing another chuckle from Cameron. "Hey, seriously, this guy must have some cash, look at all the flowers . . . and those corks are from some pretty nice bottles of wine. He seems cultured and sophisticated and, well, insane."

Cameron laughed. "It's refreshing to be around someone who can actually construct sentences."

"I'm a whiz at proverbs, anecdotes, and axioms, too. Have you been graced with any of Meridan's attempts?"

"Hell yes, she told me there were too many cooks in the soup in reference to this situation. I'm thinking, cooks in the kitchen? Right idea, wrong implementation?" Joel snorted and chortled.

"Classic. I've got to remember that one. It's one for Meridan's Moronic Solecism Hall of Fame. She's a quick brain melt, isn't she?"

"No, she's okay. I do feel my vocabulary slipping a bit. Is aneurismal a word? She told me she was feeling aneurismal. She makes shit up and then I get confused."

"I guess that would be the adjective for aneurism, because we need one? Do you ever feel aneurismal, or do you just get one? Maybe she knows something we don't? One for the medical books?"

"Oh, and she's a little full of herself."

"You think? She thinks the saying 'beauty is only skin deep' is a compliment. Not that she could spit it out unmangled." Cameron roared.

"Okay, enough. We shouldn't completely roast her."

"I know. As big a pain in the ass as she is, she's our pain in the ass."

"Yes, I forgot to thank you for bringing me into this quagmire."

"You offered. Hell, I haven't gotten this much work done in ages."

"Okay, so I'm thinking I send Noah to the bar at Katana, have him linger, try to get a look at the reservation book in case I can't make any headway. B might frequent Katana and Geisha House as he mentioned both in the faxes. Maybe he talks about her or asks about her. He can't be that hard to spot, eh? Beady little eyes? Unibrow?"

"Simian-like arms?"

"Shit, you crack me up, Joel. I have to go and marshal the troops—well, troop. Will Melrose ever be the same?"

"You've never seen buying power like that."

"If she has a handbag to match every pair of shoes, I can't believe she hasn't outgrown that little townhouse."

"Let's just say it used to be a three-bedroom place. Now it's one-and-a-half."

"Later, man."

"Hey, what's the plan for tonight?"

"She told me she wants to go to Skybar and Katsuya with Roz. I'm not sure what order. They're both really small places, not too much trouble she can find, eh?"

"This is Meridan Marks."

"Point taken."

28

"I better call and let them know we're running late," Roz said as Meridan slouched exhausted in the backseat of the limo.

"Hey, better late than unfashionable."

Roz half-smiled as she realized Meridan's unintentional massacre and subsequent combination of two different proverbs actually made sense this time.

"Yes, this is Roz Lescher. I have a reservation for two at seven. I also need extra space for security . . . Just one. Perfect. I apologize, we're on Sunset right now. It won't be five minutes." She hung up and helped herself to the open bottle of champagne. "This has been a hell of a day. Cheers to it being almost over." They clinked glasses and downed the icy beverage.

Cameron took advantage of the momentary silence to broach the subject of the next night's reservation. "Katana isn't open tomorrow night."

"Was there a fire?" Meridan asked.

"What?" Cameron and Roz asked at the same time, both wondering how she had made the mental leap.

"It's never closed. Well, except on Mondays."

"And tomorrow *is* Monday," said Cameron. "I find it odd he would tell you he made reservations for a day the place is closed."

"What are you thinking?" The worried look on Roz's face suggested she was formulating the same conclusion he had.

"I believe he was trying to lure her."

"Why?" Meridan asked, riveted.

Cameron reminded them of the tricky grounds and low light at the proposed hour. "It would be a good place to . . ."

"Attack me?" Cameron nodded. Meridan pondered this and shuddered visibly as if a massive chill had pervaded the limo.

"Now, nothing to worry about. We've curtailed his efforts. He could've lied. Maybe he's never even been there, much less tried to make a reservation. We don't know, and I don't want speculation scaring you."

"I am scared." Meridan slumped in her seat and gazed into the twilight.

"Noah is at Katana now trying to bleed the bartenders for info. Strange that he suggests places you frequent. Perhaps he's asked about you."

"Here we are, ladies," the chauffer chimed from the front. They had opted for a discreet mode of transportation to Katsuya, and limos were a dime a dozen in L.A.

"Ms. Marks, Ms. Lescher, so good to see you!" The host fluttered about, making space for Cameron. Meridan enjoyed the fuss, but even more, she liked when Cameron stationed himself behind her chair, earpiece and all. She felt like the First Lady.

Roz ordered for both of them and turned the conversation to Meridan's current favorite subject, Jim, hoping to lighten the mood.

"We had a wonderful night after the fiasco at Madeo. We had a little tiff about him not inviting me to his cousin's wedding. I guess I understand. Would you just die if you were the bride, you'd waited your whole life for this moment, and in walks Meridan Marks?" Roz kept the eye roll mental and nodded. "I think he's going to propose soon."

"Shut up!" Roz banged the table, causing Cameron to reach inside his jacket. "Sorry." Roz looked up to see him pull his hand away from what she feared was a gun.

"I'm serious. He promised to take me to Chicago in the next few weeks to meet the family. He also told his mom I was the woman of his dreams and that he was deeply in love with me."

"What did you do in your former life to deserve this one?"

"I don't know, but I'm really glad I did it." The women shared a giggle and enjoyed their dinner. After an hour, the waiter cleared the table and delivered the check presenter. Inside was an envelope with Meridan's name written in black ink. Seeing it, Roz was out of her chair, trailed by Cameron, headed toward the host, who could confirm only that a fax had arrived for Meridan and had been placed in an envelope.

Meridan looked around the restaurant, filled with a mix of curiosity and anxiety. How could he have known she was here?

"Open it," Cameron told her, unconcerned about obtaining prints, as thus far B had left none. He leaned in close and Meridan could smell his cologne. *If I weren't terrified*, she thought, *I might be turned on.*

I can hardly wait to see you tomorrow night. I am assuming you will be there, as you have not called to decline my invitation. Oh, could you straighten your hair and wear it down like you did in "As Is"? You look so hot in that movie, and I'm not embarrassed to admit I masturbate during it. I can just imagine you on your knees in front of me, your mouth hot and wet. Man, I plan to get some of that tomorrow.

No panties, I need easy access.

B~

"EWWW!" Meridan shrieked before balling up the note and throwing it onto the table.

"I'll take that." Cameron reached over and plucked the paper from the chili sauce.

"What the fuck! Where is he?" Meridan yelled and flew from her chair, nearly racking Cameron's privates in the process. He tried to ease her back into her seat, but she was incensed. "Stop it, Cameron! I want to know where he is! He knows where I am every minute of the fucking day."

"Mer . . ." Roz stood and tried to corral her friend.

"No, Roz, I've had it! I can't handle this anymore! It's driving me crazy!" She took one last look around the room before fleeing to the bathroom.

"Should I go?" Roz asked Cameron.

"Nah, let's give her some time. She really needs to unwind, and this didn't help."

"What's up with tomorrow night?"

Cameron sat down for the first time during a meal, and rested his strong chin on a steeple created by his large hands, his lips a thin, tight line.

"I have a weird feeling about this."

"Like what?"

"Does Meridan have any major projects in the works right now?"

"Well, she just finished a film that's looking good for another Oscar."

"Is it possible someone's trying to shake her tree?"

"I'm sorry?"

"Fuck with her? Throw her off her game? Drive her nuts? Ruin her public image?" He gestured toward the teeming onlookers anxiously awaiting Meridan's return. He gave a nod to the guy who had bolted outside and was talking animatedly into a cell phone. "Friend or foe outside?"

"I don't recognize him, but that doesn't say much. There are so many moles in Hollywood. You can't take a shit in your own bathroom without having all the minutiae detailed in the press." Cameron snorted and threw her a smile. "As far as conflict? Meridan is envied in this town. Not too many people like her, but people who *hate* her? I know Sean Chaison is not a happy man right now."

"Isn't that Christian—"

"Right. And then there's Harley Ryan—"

"Her nemesis."

"No doubt about it—they are Israel and Palestine.

"Interesting choice of enemies."

"How so?"

"Which one is Palestine?"

Roz pondered his question for a moment, realizing for the first time Cameron was more than just a gorgeous, monolithic bodyguard.

"Well, Meridan has been all but forced out of romantic comedy by Harley."

"But Harley isn't being harassed."

"Well, permanently displaced would be Harley. She was devastated Christian dumped her, but things really turned nasty when he took up with Meridan! You're brilliant! Could this be Harley and Sean teaming up? It was a huge surprise to Meridan and Christian when Harley and Sean showed up to his premier together."

"Weirder things have happened. Look at Nancy Kerrigan. This smacks of conspiracy to defame, humiliate, or embarrass. Sounds like at least two people have major axes to grind. Further, if they've hired someone to help, and they get a line on Jim, they could expose Meridan and Christian as a fraud without breaking any confidentiality agreements."

"Now that I think about it, Jim has been too present. Meridan is always flying off to meet him someplace against my better judgment. They've been nearly busted a few times, to the point Christian is a constant companion when Jim wants to visit Meridan. Hell, I am surprised Jim hasn't been paired in the media with Christian. Exposing this, with proof—because believe me, there have been rumors about Christian for years— would devastate both their careers. Wow, that's a lot to digest, but it all fits. Should we talk to Meridan about it?"

"Not right now. She's in quite a state."

"Yeah, you're right. Let's give it a few days, let this 'date' pass and see what happens. He usually freaks out and gets mad. How's it going with her anyway? Are you getting along?"

"I pretend I'm dealing with a spoiled four-year-old," he retorted. Roz roared, sympathizing greatly.

"So you've been witness to some of her legendary misspeaks."

"That, I have. This morning she was yammering on, and I asked her if she'd always been so reticent and she says, 'Yes, since I was little.'"

Roz snorted. "You have no idea. The vocabulary building workshop—too hard. 'No one uses those words anyway,' she tells me. The interest in college which lasted a day . . ."

"Isn't being beautiful enough?"

"When she heard Harley Ryan was a Mensa candidate, she flipped. Well, after I told her what it meant." They shared a snicker at Meridan's expense.

"Can we go?" Meridan demanded sharply, having returned to the table.

"Sure, sweetie. How are you?"

"It was nice of you to come in and make sure I was okay."

"I wanted to give you some privacy." Roz dreaded the coddling she was going to have to provide Meridan.

"Can we go to Voyeur? I need drinks."

Once inside the limo, Meridan apologized for the scene she'd made. She reported that the guy on the cell phone was Jack Keller's new assistant. Roz knew she was secretly hoping to prompt another article. A true press hound, Meridan knew a good scene made good press, and sympathy was better than envy.

"What should we do tomorrow?" Meridan asked.

"Work?" Roz suggested, unnerved by the amount of time being devoted to non-work related matters.

"On what?"

"Maybe reading some of the scripts that have piled up at Meritime since this whole thing started to bubble over." Meridan gave an uninterested shrug and sipped champagne. "Really Mer, we need to get something in the hopper."

"What's a hopper?"

"I don't know, it's a saying."

"No it isn't."

"Yes, it is. I think a hopper is, like, I don't know, but it's a saying."

"I've never heard it," Meridan challenged.

"That doesn't make it not so."

"Notso?"

"Not space so."

Cameron enjoyed the exchange almost too much to interrupt, but saw Roz crumbling. "A hopper is the box in which a bill to be considered by a legislative body is placed."

"What in the hell does that have to do with scripts?"

"Well, a great deal," Roz continued, grateful for Cameron. "We need to get something generated. We need to select some things to consider for production."

"We don't have a hopper."

"Jesus Christ, Meridan! It's just a saying!" Embarrassed, Meridan straightened her back and put her nose in the air.

"I know," she said, not risking any further discourse on the subject.

"Voyeur," the driver announced. It was a skeleton crew at the valet stand and front door, which initially annoyed Meridan until Cameron came to the rescue, offering her a hand.

"Allow me," he smiled, and she giggled a bit. She charged through the open front doors, not waiting for Roz or Cameron.

Cameron's phone chirped as he approached the table. "Noah. Any news?"

"None. I got a shot at the reservation book when I told the hostess I'd left my AmEx the night before. She was gone forever. There were no B's, but plenty of parties of two with reservations in names that started with B. We don't know if this is a nickname, a nick-initial, a last name, a first name. One thing for certain is there was no Meridan or Marks on the books."

"What about the bartenders?"

"Well, there's only one, it's slow. He's pretty cool. I asked him if any big celebrities ever came, and he ran down the list for me. Meridan was on the top. I asked him if he gets that question all of the time, and he gave me the 'if I had a dime' line."

"Frustrating." Cameron retreated to the pool to get a little privacy. "We got a fax at Katsuya. It was pretty graphic. Even gave *me* the creeps. He's still insisting they're on for dinner tomorrow."

"I'm ready to wrap this up."

"Me, too. I could use a little less Meridrama." Noah chuckled.

"How should I handle tomorrow night?"

"Linger in the lobby of the Mondrian. You will have an unobstructed view of the entire front of Katana."

"Right. I can't wait to bust this bastard. Luring a woman like that."

"Later."

"Anything going on at Katana?" Roz asked hopefully. Cameron shook his head.

"He should be fairly obvious, right? Total gomer?"

"Gomer?" Cameron snickered. "Where did you pull that out from?"

"Third grade," snorted Roz.

"Oh, what, and you're quite the lyricist," Meridan snorted, and Roz and Cameron squelched rising tides of giggles.

"Linguist," Roz coughed, and Cameron erupted.

"What?"

"Nothing, honey. You're so clever." Meridan straightened up a bit and basked in the "compliment."

"Ah, drinks." Meridan clapped like a four-year-old child presented with a birthday cake, and Roz buried a smile in her hand, thankful none of them had driven; it was going to be an evening soaked in gin.

~

"Do you want me to help?" Roz asked Cameron, who was completely supporting a very intoxicated Meridan.

"I've got it. Maybe I should stay?" In her semi-lucid state, Meridan ran her hand over Cameron's head and leaned in as if to kiss him.

"Yes, stay," she slurred, and Roz shook her head strenuously.

"Get her up to her room and get out or you are going to find yourself in a bind." Meridan was gazing longingly at Cameron, not digesting the dialogue going on around her.

"Understood. Do you have a key to lock the door behind us?" Roz nodded. Cameron scooped Meridan up in his arms and made his way to the front door.

"I think it's time you and I got to know . . . each other . . . better," Meridan managed on the way up the stairs. Cameron knew a weaker man would have crumbled. It was dark and his hands were full so he made his way carefully through her bedroom.

"The bed's over there." Meridan flung her arm toward the bed and he tried to follow. He inched slowly across the dark room, nearly breaking his ankle on God knew what. When his shins solidly connected with a piece of furniture, he stumbled forward and was relieved when they landed on her bed.

"Weee!" Meridan gave a drunken sigh. As Cameron felt around for a bedside lamp, Meridan laced her long legs around his torso. With one hand deflecting extremely forward gestures from his intoxicated client, he was finally able to locate the switch with the other. "No!" Meridan whined when the room was softly illuminated. "Stay with me," she demanded while reaching for his belt.

"Do you want to change or go to bed like that?" Cameron dreaded her answer. Meridan leaned back on her bed, propped on elbows, legs akimbo. He wasn't sure if she was contemplating or passing out.

"Wait here. I am going to put on something just for you." He helped her from the bed and guided her to the bathroom. Once she'd closed the doors, he bolted. He figured she'd be mad but wasn't likely to remember his rebuff in the morning.

"That took forever." Roz said as they locked the door behind him.

"I barely made it out alive."

29

The damn smoke detector needs batteries, Meridan thought, and tried to
resettle into her slumber. The beeping penetrated her alcohol-induced haze
like a white-hot needle piercing her left eye. The pillow over her head did
nothing to mask the sound. Opening her one good eye, she realized it wasn't
yet light outside, meaning she had plenty more time for snoozing but only after
remedying the battery situation.

Sitting up, she looked around, trying to orient herself to the noise. It
seemed to be coming from the wall. Where was the smoke detector? On the
ceiling, right? Aren't they always? Her eyes slowly adjusted to the dim light as
the intense pain in her eye quickly pervaded her entire head. She tried to recall
the evening. Drinks, dinner at Katsuya with Roz and Cameron, drinks, faxes,
letters, flowers, and that noise, that infernal noise!

She stood and reached out to the bedside table for assistance. The room
tilted, causing her stomach to whirl. And then she saw it. Not red or green on
her alarm panel but yellow. Though dreading it, she clicked on her bedside
lamp and squinted as she waited for her body to assimilate the fresh stimulus.

She crept closer, addled by her crashing headache. The yellow light was
blinking and beneath was the word TROUBLE.

What does that mean? Does it have to do with a loss of power? A glance at
the side table clock, which, not blinking, read 5:07 a.m., confirmed the power
had not gone out. Did it mean someone had invaded her home?

Ignoring her pain, she lurched for the phone to call the alarm company and
was startled to find no dial tone. She hung up and tried again. Nothing. Perhaps

the batteries were dead, but she had no intention of leaving her suite to find another phone. Instead, she locked her bedroom door in one deft motion and pressed her back to it.

Her heart hammered in her chest. She knew he was in her home. The fun and games were over, and he was ready for action. He finally had tired of toying with her and was making his next move.

She prayed her cell phone was somewhere in her room while she tried to piece together the vestiges of her homecoming the night before. Had she remembered to plug it in? Doubtful. She was forever running down the battery due to her forgetfulness. Was it in her purse? Or, horror of horrors, in the car?

She pressed her ear to the door and heard nothing but the occasional car passing in the early morning outside her window. How long had that light been blinking? How long had she been in TROUBLE? Where was he?

Her eyes searched the room for her purse. Which one had she used? What had she worn? The dresser. She snatched the hot pink Gucci bag from the top of her small dresser and scoured the contents. No phone. Damn. Ahh, pink Jimmy Choo clutch. On her knees, she fished her hand around inside. No phone. Fuck. She pressed her hands to the sides of her head to stop the throbbing for a moment so she could think straight. Jeans, a T-shirt, and Gucci sandals. She needed to look for her signature tan clutch.

Easing the heels of her palms from her temples, she remained motionless, hoping the thundering inside of her head would lessen. Memories began rolling in. She had taken off her clothes in her master bath and, if her nickname Dialing While Drunk held true, she would have been on the cell phone while undressing or as she was falling asleep. She crawled to the bed and felt underneath the cool sheets until her hand closed around her phone. *Please let there be some battery power*, she thought desperately.

"Nine-one-one, what is your emergency?"

"This is Meridan Marks, I'm at 901 Montana. I woke up to the trouble light on my alarm. I'm not sure what *that* means." She was breathless and panicked, and she knew her fear resonated in her voice. For once, she was not acting or thinking about acting.

"Ma'am, we'll send someone over right away. In the meantime, you could call your alarm company. Sometimes the warning light comes on when there is an interruption of power or phone service."

"Yes, thank you. Please hurry. I have a stalker. I'm afraid he's here now." She hung up without any further discourse and sought the number on the alarm panel. I'm being stalked, she thought soberly. Currently. Where was he? My God, was he in her room? Her bathroom? Had she locked herself in here with him? With her back against the small lingerie bureau, she forced herself to lean down and look under the bed. It didn't seem a fully grown man could wedge himself under there.

Okay, so he's not in the bedroom or bathroom. The closet? What should I do? her mind screamed, prompting pain to detonate behind her eyes. Paralyzed by fear she sat against the bureau, her eyes never leaving the dark cavern that was her walk-in closet. What used to be a modest closet had become an enormous room after knocking out the wall separating it from the upstairs guest room. *So many places to hide*, her mind reminded her, and she wondered for the first time why she didn't own a gun. In a moment of clarity, she sprang to her feet, pulled a pair of panty hose from her bureau, slammed the French doors closed and wound the panty hose tightly around the two knobs. That would slow him down, she reasoned, perhaps until the police arrived.

"Ace Alarms." She whispered, relaying the relevant information the technician requested.

"Yes, ma'am. It appears your phone line is not operable. Have you had an interruption in service?"

"What do you mean? I was asleep. I don't know."

"Is the account paid to current?"

"Are you kidding me? Do you know who you are talking to? Could I finance a ten million dollar movie if I couldn't pay my phone bill? Don't you normally send someone out when this occurs? I mean, for God's sake! What if someone cut my phone line?"

"That's entirely possible ma'am. I'll call nine-one-one immediately."

"I already have!" she said, hanging up. It was official. He had cut the phone line. He was here. She could feel it. Why couldn't she hear him? What was he doing? Shouldn't he be trying to bang down the door? Was he just ransacking the place for mementos? Surely not. He had made it abundantly clear he was in love with her. Was he going to rape her? Questions swirled about her already swimming head.

She sat ramrod straight against the bureau and waited in petrified silence for the police. What was he going to do? Was he downstairs? How strong was the lock on her door? If she survived, she vowed a dead bolt would be placed at the top and bottom of her bedroom door. That would hold her over until she moved out of this place altogether. The highly secure house in Bel Air looked appealing for the first time. It seemed to be taking longer for the police to arrive than it had for the pyramids to be constructed.

How had it come to this? When had it spun out of control? Two weeks ago, he was a fan. Two weeks ago, she was living a completely normal life; a normal life for America's leading lady, anyway. She wanted to go back. Just two weeks.

"Miss Marks?" Her heart faltered upon hearing her name spoken just on the other side of her bedroom door. "LAPD, ma'am."

"How do I know?" She crawled toward the door so she could hear more clearly.

"You called nine-one-one approximately eight minutes ago?"

"You could have overheard me."

"Ma'am, this is Officer Janis Simmons and Officer Kenneth Martin." Upon hearing a woman's voice, Meridan threw open the bedroom door and raced into the small sitting room just outside.

"Thank God you're here! Is he here?"

"Ma'am?"

"My stalker? I told the nine-one-one lady." Meridan flipped the hall light on and instantly realized she was standing in front of two police officers in nothing more than boxer-style shorts and a camisole.

"Oh, excuse, me. I was afraid to change. I'm afraid he's in my closet."

Officer Martin held up a hand and gestured for Officer Simmons to search the bedroom area as he headed down the stairs to secure the ground floors.

Meridan perched on the bed while Officer Simmons crept through her bathroom preceded by a huge weapon. She was dizzy with fear but half hoped the lunatic would leap from the closet and be shot dead by Officer Simmons.

"Clear." Meridan heard a voice from downstairs, and soon after, the same response from her bathroom. Officer Martin re-entered her bedroom holstering his weapon and nodded at his partner.

"Ms. Marks, why don't you change? Take your time. Your home is secure. Meet us downstairs when you're ready—there's something you need to see," his voice was tight. Meridan nodded, vertigo descending, and closed the French doors to the bathroom behind her. She had seen enough.

30

Clad in jeans and a T-shirt and unable to escape her hangover, Meridan made her way to the first floor.

"What is it?" she asked the officers hovering over her dining room table.

"I'm afraid it's a little graphic, Ms. Marks," the female officer offered as she closed her pad. Meridan looked around; everything seemed to be in perfect order. Her eyes returned to the dining area and Officer Martin's back.

"What's happened?" she asked. Officer Martin stepped aside so she would have full view of the dining table. She squinted her eyes and tried to make sense of what she was seeing—one of her PR photos and a pair of her baby pink Cosabella panties, covered with something.

"Where did you find this?" she shrieked, her eyes darting expectantly from one officer to the other.

"Right here, ma'am. It has the appearance of . . ."

"What?" One dark brow arched impatiently and she made her way to the table. "Is this . . . ?" She furrowed her brow at the milky, mucosal substance and quickly averted her eyes.

"I would say so."

"What is it doing here?" She inhaled slowly and teetered, her face paling, prompting Officer Simmons to grasp her elbow and assist her to the sofa. Meridan sat stupefied until Officer Martin spoke.

"I would say, at least upon the preliminary findings, someone cut your phone line, disabling your alarm, and entered your home. Most likely this person brought the photo, unless you have some lying around, and it would seem this person is male, as there appears to be, ah, ejaculate on the items."

"Those are my underwear. He was in my room?" She wondered, horrified, if the panties indeed were taken from her bureau or whether they were taken from the floor, dirty. She burst into a torrent of tears.

"Ms. Marks?" Officer Simmons sat down next to Meridan offering her a tissue. "This is nothing to be embarrassed about."

"Isn't it? Isn't it really? Somehow, something I have done, or maybe it's just being me, has driven this man mad. He's fallen in love with someone he doesn't even know." She stood up suddenly and began to pace. A thumbnail found its way to her mouth and she nibbled. "Do you realize how close he was? If I had walked to my door I'd have seen him, doing that." She extended a long, well-toned arm and pointed to the mess on the table, her other hand covering her mouth. "What if I had woken up while he was in my room? What would he have done? I need to call someone. What time is it?" she asked, her feet cutting a distinct path into the thick, plush carpeting.

"Five-forty in the morning," Officer Martin offered after consulting his Seiko.

"I have to get out of here." She ran both hands through her disheveled hair.

"Ms. Marks? There's a note."

"A note? What does it say? No, I don't want to know. Yes, you better tell me." She inched her way toward the table where Officer Martin was standing. He gestured to the spattered, almost illegible note scratched on a piece of paper from her own kitchen note pad. It sent a shiver through her to think of him, whoever he was, lingering in her house, touching her things. Had he watched her sleeping? Had he touched her?

All my love for you, Meridan. See you soon. There is fun to be had. B

"He's insane." She backed away and picked up her cordless phone, forgetting the line had been disabled. "Damn it!" she cried, hurling it onto the couch. "I need my cell phone." Meridan dashed to her room leaving the two officers alone to call for back up.

The phone was on her bed where she'd left it. "Joel, thank God you're awake!"

"Meridan, it's five-thirty in the morning. What are you doing up?"

"Joel, he was in my house!" Her voice was a rising crescendo of hysteria as she began to recount her harrowing morning.

"Jesus, Meridan, slow down. I'm pulling over."

"I can't Joel. I am . . . I don't know what to do."

"Did he hurt you?"

"No. I mean . . . I don't know. It doesn't seem like he came—" At the mention of the word "came," Meridan started to chuckle. Once she started, she couldn't stop. It was the most inappropriate time to giggle and she knew it. Joel didn't say anything until he felt he needed to interrupt.

"Meridan. What's going on? Are you okay? Why are you laughing? This doesn't sound like a humorous situation to me. Can I speak to one of the officers?" Officer Simmons had made her way up the stairs toward Meridan's bedroom, alarmed by the sound of what could be shock or hysteria setting in. Meridan thrust the phone at her.

"This is Officer Simmons."

"Joel Goldstein, I'm Ms. Marks's attorney." Joel listened in horror as the officer elucidated. "Why didn't he do anything?" Joel muttered unintelligibly.

"Detectives Ford and Adler are on the way."

"Thank you. It might help if you gave her a drink." Officer Simmons looked over at Meridan, who had curled up in her bed.

"Do you want to speak with her again?"

"No. Tell her I'll be there shortly. Expect her bodyguard Cameron Riley as well. I'll call him personally."

"Yes, sir." Officer Simmons hung up the cell phone and approached the bed.

"Ms. Marks?" Meridan did not stir. "Is there anyone else you would like me to call for you? Your attorney and bodyguard are on their way."

Meridan wanted no one but Jim. She needed him, his strong protective arms around her.

"Can I use my phone?" she asked the officer.

"Sure, hon." She handed Meridan the phone and went to the dining room to wait for the detectives.

Meridan held the phone to her chest. Jim would be so worried if she called; he would drop everything to get to her. He'd miss the wedding. His family would hate her before they even met her. If she didn't call, he would be furious. Perhaps she should wait until tomorrow; maybe they could meet somewhere. She would take Cameron with her. She was finally grateful she'd hired the personal security Joel had suggested repeatedly since this whole situation had started its downward spiral.

The cell phone rang, startling Meridan, who, surprisingly, had dozed off. *Jesus*, she thought, *I'm losing it.*

"Roz!" Her voice caught in her throat.

"Meridan, my God! Joel just called me. I'm on my way." Silence. "Mer?" Finally, she heard the quiet sobbing of her friend. She chastised herself for leaving Meridan alone the night before. She should have insisted Cameron stay, or at least stayed herself. What had happened?

As she flopped down onto the bed, Meridan glimpsed something colorful peeking from under her pillow and slowly removed it; she gaped, having never before seen the enormous silk scarf. "What is this?" An ear piercing shriek caused Roz to nearly drop her phone.

"What? What?" She demanded.

"Oh, my God!" Meridan screamed, setting the officers in motion bolting up the stairs to her room.

"Ms. Marks?" They entered to find her holding the scarf by her thumb and index finger as if it were a rodent by the tail.

"Ms. Marks?" Officer Martin tried to jolt her into speaking.

"It isn't mine." In one swift motion, she flicked it to the floor and leapt from the bed. Roz's frantic voice called from her phone, which had dropped onto the floor.

"Meridan! What's going on?"

"What else is in there?" She pointed to her rumpled bed prompting the officers to strip it completely.

Meridan raced to her closet and pulled out suitcases and garment bags, mumbling to herself as she emptied her bureau—underwear, pajamas, socks, lingerie—not bothering to fold anything, just unloading what appeared to the officers to be a bottomless pit. She gave a start when the front door slammed.

"Meridan?"

"Joel!" She ran for the stairs and Joel's open arms. He stood motionless and allowed her to cry.

"Mr. Goldstein? There's been a development," Officer Martin started, but Joel held up a hand to silence him. He slowly guided Meridan down the few stairs, aiming for the couch in the living room but deciding against it once he'd eyed the dining room table. He sat her down on the bottom step and knelt before her.

"Meridan, stay here and let me get you some Kleenex." She nodded and he took the wadded up tissue from her hand. Once out of Meridan's sight line, he gestured for Officer Martin to join him in Meridan's bedroom. "What's going on?"

"Ms. Marks was on the phone when she found that in her bed. She says it isn't hers." He gestured to the puddle of silk on the floor.

"He left it there?" Joel's body shuddered involuntarily. They had really underestimated the potential danger here. What if he had strangled her with the scarf? He wondered briefly why she hadn't heard him before realizing she had most likely passed out drunk.

"Jesus." He ran a hand through his thick, dark hair and looked around the corner to make sure Meridan was not listening. "Has she been checked?" The officer gave him a confused glance. "This guy was in here, put something under her pillow, had time to jack off. Is it possible he touched her? Meridan probably had a few drinks last night. Who knows how long he was in here or what he was doing?" Officer Martin nodded his understanding.

"She hasn't mentioned feeling, you know, violated. Perhaps you should ask her?"

"Joel? Meridan?" The front door slammed behind Cameron.

"Up here." Joel called and started down the steps to meet him at the landing where Meridan sat.

"Are you okay?" Joel heard Cameron ask Meridan, who simply nodded. Cameron met Joel's eyes and gave him an "Is she?" look. Joel shrugged his shoulders.

"Mer." Joel squatted down next to his client and took her hand after giving her a new wad of Kleenex. "Do you think he touched you? Do you feel like he did?"

"No."

"Okay. Cameron? You help her pack her things. Take her to the Four Seasons. I have already arranged privacy. No one comes back here until we sort this mess out."

"Can I talk to you for a sec, privately?" Cameron asked Joel. It was time for him to unveil his suspicions regarding the situation at hand.

31

"I'm sorry you had to answer all those questions," Cameron said, breaking the silence. Meridan had said little to nothing since leaving her townhouse, and had shuddered visibly at her dining room table and the mess B had left for her. He was relieved all parties were as receptive to his theory about Harley Ryan and Sean Chaison as Roz had been the previous evening.

"Actually, your take on the situation makes more sense than anything, and just talking it through with the detectives made me feel a lot better about everything."

"It does shed some light on things, doesn't it?"

"Hell, yes! I couldn't figure out why he'd be right there, you know, excited and all, but not rape me or hurt me. Probably couldn't get it up because he's gay."

"Well, there is always the chance they hired someone."

"That's why Detective Ford suggested Jim keep a low profile. The easiest way for them to expose Christian, if that is their angle, is to prove I'm involved with someone else. I mean, who would believe I'd step out on Christian York? As good looking as Jim is, he isn't Christian York. I mean that from a movie star standpoint. Detective Ford promised me he wouldn't share details about Christian and Sean and I with anyone but his partner."

"He's a good guy. He's the one who referred Christian to me in the first place, and now he's given us some protection. At least for now." Cameron searched his rear view mirror for the unmarked sedan and noticed it had fallen a couple cars behind.

"I feel protected with you, Cameron." A bat of her long lashes caused a strange flutter in his stomach. He'd dodged a bullet the night before and hoped she wouldn't continue to make advances.

"They'll be stationed outside the room, and Noah or I can stay if you want."

"At least for a couple days? Until we see what happens? Detective Ford said they would be all over Harley and Sean."

Pulling up to the cargo area of the Four Seasons, Cameron handed her the large hat and sunglasses he'd taken from her townhouse. "Let's get you upstairs. You can take a hot bath while I make some calls."

The suite was magnificent, but Meridan, accustomed to such luxury, hardly noticed. "Can you call down for a bottle of champagne? I feel like celebrating. Roederer, if they have it." She closed the door behind her to shut out the conversations from the other room. She lit the candles lining the tub and immersed herself into the clouds of bubbles. She let her thoughts drift to Cameron and felt a bit guilty.

"Meridan?" Cameron knocked a while later.

"Come in."

"Oh shit, I'm sorry." She lifted her eye mask as Cameron turned around suddenly, almost dropping the champagne bucket. Looking down, she smiled noticing her breasts were totally exposed.

"Sorry," she lied while resituating the bubbles.

"Here you go," he said turning tail as quickly as he could.

"I'm all wet. Could you please open it and pour me a glass?"

"I don't know if I can pour it. It must be pure gold for three hundred dollars a bottle." He tried humor to distract him from the stirring in his pants.

"Cristal, my favorite." The heady aroma of the candles and her throaty voice negated his efforts. He tried unsuccessfully to avert his eyes from her legs, terrified she would notice his growing erection. While he fumbled with the cork, Meridan savored each moment of his discomfort. Suddenly, the cork shot out, ricocheted off the back wall and dropped into the water above her pubic area. *Perfect*, he thought.

"Wow, that was awesome. I feel like I could explode right now, too," she said coyly and tossed him the wet cork, which he absently slipped into his pocket.

When the door slammed shut behind him, Meridan laughed long and loud for the first time in days. It was good to be famous, beautiful and desirable. She would immensely enjoy a roll in bed with Cameron. Here they were at a charming and intimate hotel, sharing a room. He had seen her nearly naked. He'd never been far from her mind while he was guarding Christian or even after. If only she'd met him before . . .

"Meridan? Telephone. It's Jim."

"Come in, I'm covered," she laughed as Cameron opened the door tentatively. He inched across the floor with his arm extended. He handed her the phone, kept his gaze to the floor and made haste for the door. Nice ass, she thought.

"Baby!" she sang into the phone.

"What're you doing? It sounds like you're in a barrel."

"I'm in the bathtub thinking very naughty thoughts about you," she lied.

"Really. Tell me more. Wait a minute. Did Cameron just come in the bathroom?"

"I have bubbles all over me," she purred seductively. "He didn't see a thing. Well, I don't *think* he did."

"I suddenly feel very far away."

"I need you."

"I can't wait to see you."

"I mean now."

"What's wrong?"

"I want you inside me."

"Not good. I don't want you all worked up when you get off the phone. You might jump Cameron."

"Don't be silly. I want you. I was just lying here touching myself, wishing you were here."

"I miss you, and, believe me, I wish I were there, too. I bet you look so sexy, all hot and wet." She felt a pang of guilt for not yet telling him what had transpired that day.

"I have bad news."

"What?"

"We're at the Four Seasons. He broke into my house last night. He used a pair of my panties to get off and left them on my dining room table." She paused and bit her lip.

"What!" he roared, causing Meridan to fumble the phone nearly dropping it into the water; it skittered across the marble floor.

"Hold on," she yelled and reached for the phone just out of her reach. Hoisting herself up on her knees she leaned over the edge of the marble tub.

Cameron, hearing her shout, burst into the room. "Are you okay?" he asked, unnerved at the sight of her long, wet body, ass in the air, breasts hanging heavily, hair across her right eye.

"I dropped my phone. Sorry." She pushed back on her knees with considerable effort and bared her entire body to him. She smiled as he closed the door.

"Sorry, babe."

"What the fuck is going on there? Is he in there with you?"

"No," she laughed, trying to make light. "I dropped the phone and when I yelled for you to hold on, he thought something was wrong. He was trying to help."

"Did he see you naked?"

"No, he just handed me my phone. I'm covered."

"What happened today?" She enjoyed the fact that he sounded frantic. Served him right for leaving her. She brought him up to speed with tremendous drama and detail.

"I'm surprised you heard the beeping. I talked to you when you were in bed . . . you were pretty hammered."

"Oh, that explains why my phone was in the bed. Did we have phone sex?"

"I did. You passed out. Are you okay, Mer?"

"I'm fine." Meridan finished filling in the blanks.

"No more fun and games. When I get to L.A., you're moving. We're getting the most secure alarm and surveillance system in the world. Tell Cameron not to leave your side, well, except when you're in the tub, or bed."

"That isn't all." She delicately outlined Cameron's conspiracy theory. "Cam and Joel think it would be better, for the time being, if you and I cool it."

"What? Why? We're always careful."

"Well, if it's Sean or Harley or someone they hired, we can't risk being caught together. It would kill my reputation."

"Nice. How long?" Her heart thumped a bit knowing he was pressing his full lips into a thin line of frustration.

"I bet by the time you get back home, this thing will be over."

"What about the lake?"

"No way, I'm under a microscope right now."

"I'll give it a few days, but we might have to re-evaluate your priorities."

"What do you mean?" Meridan felt insecurity rear its ugly head.

"You're letting your career get in the way of your personal safety. Further, your career seems to be more important than our relationship."

"I will work this out. I promise. Let's not be hasty. Just a few days. I miss you."

32

Meridan emerged from her bath to find Cameron, a knot of frustration, pacing and growling through the suite with cell phone in hand.

"What's wrong, Cam?" Meridan slunk across the floor, her voice more of a purr.

"I'm feeling a little useless. Can I call Christian? I want to run this by him if that's okay."

"Sure." She handed him her cell phone, which was a little worse for wear after skittering across the bathroom floor. "It's under Chrissy. You know how bad it would be if anyone found my cell phone and people's real names were on there?"

"You're in awfully good spirits."

"Oh, there's nothing like a long, hot bath and a big, strong bodyguard to take your mind off your troubles. Oh, and add brilliant sloth to that list." Cameron stifled a laugh and hoped she meant sleuth. Actually, he had missed the gym a few times since this whole thing blew up. "I'm feeling really good about the whole thing." She flounced onto the couch, ignoring how her robe split open, revealing far too much leg for Cameron's comfort. He headed for the next room to make his call as she flipped on the TV and swilled champagne.

"Christian? Cameron Riley here."

"Hey, Cam, glad you're on this. Is Meridan okay? I talked to Joel, so I know she's safe, but I can't reach her on her cell."

"Sorry," Cameron said, looking at the phone face. "It looks like she does have some voice mails here. We've been a little busy with the police most of the morning."

"I've been going crazy answering the press calls, frantic trying to reach her. Don't forget, she's my 'girlfriend.' It doesn't make sense to the press that I don't know what's going on. 'No comment' is the order of the day."

"Fuck!" Meridan exclaimed from the next room.

"Hold on, Christian. Meridan, what is it?"

"My house." Images of the front of her townhouse, cordoned off to keep the press at bay, were on the television screen. "What's wrong with Joel? Why didn't he keep this quiet?"

"In his defense, you're the one that called nine-one-one, Meridan. Once it's out there on the radio, anyone can pick it up."

"My life was in danger, or don't you remember? He probably didn't choke me because he ran out of time!"

"I have Christian on the line."

"Can I talk to him?" she asked, reaching for the phone with both hands. "Christian! My God, you can't imagine what I've been through!" Cameron shut the door of the front room and turned on his own television to "E" for information. He'd deal with Christian later.

" . . . It's no news that Ms. Marks has been beleaguered by a stalker for months. We have no information as to her whereabouts now, but we're hoping she is safe and tucked away from this mad man. Back to you, Jackie."

Cameron clicked off the television. If every nut job in L.A. didn't know where Meridan lived before, they did now. That place was officially sold.

His phone chirped.

"Joel! Where've you been? I've left messages everywhere!"

"You and every fucking media rep in the country. This is a shit storm. The press picked up Meridan's call and it spread like wild fire. They're going ahead with a second article at *Glitterati* and Jack Keller wants a comment from each of us. I've given it considerable thought and decided it's the best thing. If we can let this guy know the amount of protection she has, how well insulated she'll be from this point forth, it'll scare him off. What happened last night is unacceptable."

"I agree," Cameron interjected, hoping he wasn't being blamed for the debacle at Meridan's townhouse. "I never saw this coming. Any news on our candidate for the World's Most Annoying Crackpot Stalker Award?" He chastised himself for leaving her alone at all, but overnight protection had not been ordered. He'd locked the door, for God's sake. Joel sighed on the other end of the line. Cameron pressed his ear against the door and heard Meridan chatting animatedly.

"Actually, that's why I'm calling. The caretaker at Meridan's ranch just called. Before I decided on the Four Seasons, I had called him to ready the ranch. He found a cork on her master bed with a note."

"You're fucking kidding me? What did it say?"

"Hold on, I have it right here. *'Can't wait to see you. All of you. It took everything in my power not to take you right then. B.'"*

"I just got goose bumps. Was that it?"

"Yes. Detective Ford is all over it. How's Meridan?"

"Actually, she's emotionally and I guess psychologically attached to the idea of the stalker being someone she knows. She has no fear whatsoever of Sean. She's been in a great mood since we talked about it. There has been a whole case built in her head. Is she always so . . ."

"Stupid?"

"No." Cameron laughed deep and loud. "Flirtatious."

"Oh," he joined Cameron. "Only when she wants something. You're in trouble. Jesus. Good luck with that. She's like a battering ram when she wants something. Try to remind her of Jim."

"He called. It's mitigated the effort."

"Did he flip out? I just left him a message telling him what was going on and asked him to stay put."

"I don't know how he took it. Meridan's talking to Christian."

"Keep your shirt on. Bodies are her weakness." Both men laughed at her expense, and, upon hanging up, Cameron felt better than he had all day. He could still hear Meridan yammering away, snippets of the day being hyperbolized. Meridan, the unwitting victim.

33

"That was Jack Keller from *Glitterati* on my voice mail. I was right, that was his new errand boy at Katsuya," Meridan said, fully sated from an amazing dinner on the terrace.

"I talked to Joel and he's making sure Al, Noah, and Roz comment," said Cameron. "I agree. The more involved we seem to B and to the public, the better chance we have of forcing his—I guess I should say his or *their* hand."

"Mmm, I can't wait to expose those scheming assholes, Harley and Sean. It all makes sense to me. They want to ruin me. I'm sure Sean blames me for he and Christian's breakup, and Harley has never gotten over Christian. Sean probably thinks he can get Christian back if he's outed. It makes sense they would join forces to get me out of the way. Does that mean that I'm supposed to call Jack back?"

"Yes."

She scrolled through her contacts and located the number. "Hi, Jack Meridan Marks."

"Meridan. I appreciate you getting back to me, you little fibber."

"What did I fib about?"

"You told me you would call me if there was anything going on. When I saw you at Madeo you said it was just a precaution, your hunky personal security."

"At that time it was. I know you already talked to Joel. The fact is things have gotten crazy in the last few days. I knew that was your guy at Katsuya, how unfortunate for me . . . bad timing. Hell, maybe *you're* stalking me."

"If only I'd thought of it."

"Anyway. I'm fine. I don't want my fans to worry. It's been a little stressful, and I must say that I lost it a little over dinner the other night. It's just that he's everywhere."

"What does he look like?"

"I have no idea. I've never seen or heard him. He faxes, leaves letters at my houses, sends flowers, scripts, he's left messages and wine corks for me at the Ivy, faxed me over drinks at Madeo, and now this Katsuya incident."

"You poor dear. What can I do to help?"

"Just be honest."

"Any chance I could see some of the correspondence?"

"The police have all of it."

"Hmmm. So, what happened yesterday, really?"

Meridan gave a vague account of the prior day's activities.

"What did the note say?"

"Uh, er, something about catching up with me later, sorry he wasn't here, the usual. He always talks like we've just talked and arranged to meet. It's a little creepy."

"What else?"

"Not much really, I just want it over. I'm a very busy woman and can't have my life side-saddled with things like this."

"Right. Okay, call me if there's anything else. I need to talk to that hunky hottie who is guarding your body."

"He's right here. Ta." Meridan bid farewell and handed off her phone.

34

Morton's of Chicago was classic. Despite all the new hip steakhouses cropping up all over the metroplex, Morton's was still one of Lynden's private joys. She loved the men's club atmosphere in the Dealey Plaza location, the pomp and circumstance of a tuxedoed maitre d', the primarily male management and staff, and the large booths lording over the unfortunates bound to the tables in the center of the room.

Lynden had managed to beat both Gia and her parents to the packed steakhouse and was greeted warmly by the maitre d', Robert Reed, who recognized her immediately.

"Ms. Hatcher! How splendid to have you as a guest this evening." He covered the short distance rapidly and shook her hand firmly. "Will you be dining alone?"

"Actually, I'm waiting for Mr. Androvaldi and his family."

"Ah! My favorite customer!" Robert gushed. Lynden was certain every customer was treated as his favorite. "Mr. Androvaldi is in twice, three times a week." He directed her to the bar and ordered a glass of Roederer champagne.

"New on the menu. You must have some, on me!" Just hearing the brand of the champagne spoken aloud caused a touch of vertigo, and she reached for a bar chair to steady herself. "Ms. Hatcher! Are you alright?"

"Yes, yes, I'm fine." A flush of embarrassment warmed her cheeks, and she tried to laugh it off. "I haven't eaten much today."

"Sergio! Half Alex for the lady," he barked to his bartender, who took off without waiting for Lynden to respond.

To avoid further prodding, she seated herself after thanking him quietly. Therapy had enabled her to read and write about wines and food from her past, but it had not erased all of the triggers that could tilt her world.

She could manage the sound of a cork popping, but if a man's voice was a certain depth, tone and timbre, the words spoken could shake her visibly. She listened as Robert spoke to another guest nearby, but couldn't discern any similarity to Brit.

"Sorry!" Lynden recognized Gia's breathless voice and turned to find her dragging by the hand her stepmother, who was tiny between daughter and husband. "Lynden, this is my mom and my daddy."

"Lynden! Finally." Mr. Androvaldi boomed, extending a hand that could have engulfed two of her own.

Lynden reached out to shake it. "Mrs. Androvaldi, Mr. Androvaldi."

"Luca and Nina, please!" the elegant Nina Androvaldi insisted.

Lynden nodded. Robert escorted them to their table and then left to fetch a fresh round of drinks.

"Lynden, Giada told me the good news!"

"What good news?" Lynden looked to Gia, who busied herself with her glass of champagne.

"That we're partners, silly." The half Alex appetizer arrived, temporarily interrupting the conversation.

Wary of disappointing anyone, Lynden offered a cautious answer. "There's a very good chance," she said honestly and took a sip of her champagne.

Without ordering, the table was deluged with items both on and off the menu. Though he was an obviously revered guest himself, Luca seemed to be impressed by the attention Lynden commanded without saying a word.

"Dinner with a food critic. Giada, remind me to invite Lynden everywhere we dine," he roared, winking at Lynden.

Examining him, she was drawn to his immense personality. Most everyone in the restaurant came by to bid him hello, and the back slapping, hand shaking and compliments to the ladies abounded. Nina Androvaldi preened like a princess—well, a queen; the princess role was filled. Lynden wondered how

Mr. Androvaldi found the time to lavish both women with such attention. He was magnetic. Just like Brit.

"Lynden," Luca called, jolting her from wandering thoughts, causing her to spill champagne into the bacon-wrapped scallops. "Sorry, sweetie, didn't mean to scare you." He lowered his voice. "I just realized," he pointed at her and nodded, "you look like that actress I love. Honey, what's her name?" Both daughter and wife snapped to attention and answered.

"Meridan Marks." They looked at each other and laughed.

"Gia, I'm Honey, you're everything else." Nina chuckled, patting Gia on the hand; the affection between them prompted a wave of nostalgia for her own parents.

"Why didn't I see it before? Actually, the similarity is uncanny." Gia leaned to view Lynden at different angles.

"Luca, it appears someone has beaten you to her. The poor girl is being stalked!"

"I read that a couple of weeks ago in *Glitterati*." Gia nodded.

"No, this was today while I was at the spa. This week's *Glitterati*. Things have escalated."

"What?" Lynden's sharp tone brought everyone to attention. "What did the article say?" She fought the rising panic that was whirling like a tornado, ever closer.

"At first he was writing letters, sending gifts, almost courtly behavior. But now . . ." Lynden, Gia, and Luca leaned in, awaiting a big secret.

" . . . He's broken into her home. Not just in L.A., but here, at her place in Frisco. He left a cork on her bed! She's being terrorized!" The rest was dissonance. Lynden couldn't hear anything else through the crashing in her head. The cork confirmed Brit was the one stalking Meridan Marks. "Excuse me," she whispered. Trying to hide her panic, she managed to push away from the table and navigate the crowded, spinning dining room.

Once inside the sanctity of the restroom, she collapsed on the floor of one of the large stalls, bending over the toilet bowl as a variety of appetizers spewed forth. The force of her sickness caused her to breathe too heavily, and darkness threatened.

"Ten, breathe, nine, breathe," she started. She heard the door open.

"Lynden?" *Oh, my God,* she thought. It was Luca.

"I'm okay, I'll be right out. Sorry," she issued before depositing yet another torrent into the bowl. The sharp pain on her wrist caused by the snapping of a hair tie helped, as it always did, to clear her mind.

Lynden stared at herself in the mirror. Train wreck. She needed to return to the table, excuse herself and get home. Her own copy of *Glitterati* would be waiting for her with the whole story.

"Gia, Mr. and Mrs. Androvaldi, you'll have to excuse me. I haven't been feeling up to par all day. It feels like the flu coming on or some type of stomach virus. I'm sorry to have disrupted your meal. I should get some rest." She bowed out gracefully and Luca grabbed her purse, insisting he escort her to her car. She squeezed both women's hands and waved as she left.

"You really don't have to wait with me," she said graciously, secretly grateful he stayed with her while the valet retrieved her car. The darkness was so vast outside the light of the awning.

"What kind of gentleman would I be, allowing you to wander around at night alone?" He nodded to the valet, letting him know he would be helping the lady into her car.

"I'm sorry for this." She smiled wanly as she settled into her seat.

"Nonsense. You be careful. There are a lot of crazies out there." He slammed her door and stepped away so she could pull out.

If only he knew.

35

The drive home had been sheer hell, her stomach still a nest of malaise. As she pulled into the driveway, Gia called to be certain she had arrived safely. Upon opening the garage door, she engaged the second setting of her side-view mirrors, which provided an unobstructed view of both edges of the garage. No one could slip in unnoticed.

She checked and rechecked the house and took a shower before slipping into cotton pajamas and curling up on the couch with the magazine and a glass of Trinchero cabernet. From her copy of the latest issue of *Glitterati*, amid several pieces of mail, a beaming Meridan Marks waved to her fans. Underneath her picture in huge print loomed the disturbing word "TERRORIZED!" Lynden's stomach lurched as she visualized Brit lurking in the shadows, watching Meridan. Was he thinking of her? Was Meridan just an accessible version of her? How accessible can one of the biggest movie stars in the world be?

She retrieved her laptop from the library and refilled her wine glass. Repositioning herself on the couch, she knew it was time to do the right thing.

Dear Mr. Goldstein:

I apologize for my reluctance in the matter of Ms. Marks's stalker. I've decided I would be remiss if I didn't avail myself to you and the authorities in an effort to circumvent what will most assuredly become a violent and perhaps deadly situation.

The two men you are dealing with are brothers: there is not a doubt in my mind that one or both of them is behind these machinations. Though the Michigan Police were unable to trace the names, I knew them as Britten and Ashland Holden. Both men are about 6' 4", with short dark hair and brown eyes. They are what most people would call very handsome men.

It sounds as if exception is being taken to Ms. Marks's refusal to meet and/ or return the affection. This is just the beginning of a serious situation. Though it may be a common gesture, Brit used to date the corks he left for me. If you doubt the veracity of my claims, perhaps this will give me further credence. If there are dates on the corks, do they coincide with her consumption?

Against my better judgment, I am including my cell phone number in case you need to reach me directly. Please do not do so unless it is absolutely necessary, as I have spent the past twelve years of my life building a safe, impenetrable existence. While I empathize with Ms. Marks's plight and wish to help in any way that I can, I cannot put myself in jeopardy.

I hope you understand my concerns.

214-555-7989

Unable to fight the urge to wash her hands, she did so thoroughly, refilled her wine glass, and returned to the couch. The journal beckoned. Its leather cover was cool in her hands. She had marked where she left off with a beaded tassel bookmark.

36

We met at Paddy's so I could meet the guy who was taking Brit away
from me. I was growing wary of Tracy Ellis; I wondered where and with whom
they'd been all week. Brit assured me they were just hanging out, listening to
music, trading stories about culture and whatnot. Brit wasn't the type to admire
or envy anyone, but he talked incessantly about Tracy and his life in Brazil. I
hadn't seen Brit all week other than for lunch a couple of times.

Tracy Ellis was not what I expected; at about five-foot-eight, Brit towered
over him. His hair was a thick mop of dirty blond curls. He wasn't attractive
or well kept, making it difficult to imagine his family was as wealthy as Brit
had reported. He shook my hand, and as soon as he opened his mouth, I
understood.

His accent lured me in, and, regardless of the topic, whatever issued forth
from his mouth sounded worldly, exotic. Tracy had a way of making you feel
like the most important person on earth. When you spoke to him or answered a
question, he devoted every bit of his attention to you, quietly listening to each
word instead of seeking an opportunity to butt in.

"Brit was right about you. You are the perfect woman. In every way." He
raised his mug of beer. I blushed.

"Now do you see why I wouldn't let you meet her?" Brit smiled and
looked to me. "You aren't going to try to steal her away, are you?" Tracy
laughed, and so did I.

"Don't you get tired of being the luckiest man in the world, Brit? I mean,
really. You're great looking, funny, intelligent and now this," Tracy gestured

toward me.

"No," Brit said, taking a long drink of Tanqueray on the rocks.

"Reese, Brit tells me you're a writing major. That's fascinating. I detest putting pen to paper for anything. I'm truly the worst writer. It's almost like the sight of that blank sheet of paper is too much pressure." I burst out laughing knowing only too well how he felt.

"You may be a better writer than you think. If you're that in tune with the pressure of putting pen to paper, you may have too much to say rather than too little." Chin resting on hand, he was entirely focused on me. "If you could just write with that accent of yours, it wouldn't even matter what you said. People would eat it up." Tracy and I laughed, but Brit was quiet.

"If you'll excuse me." Tracy headed toward the bathroom.

"You're right, he's really cool—" Brit reached out suddenly, snatching my wrist and holding it tightly.

"What the fuck are you doing?"

"What? I thought you wanted me to like him?"

"I want you to like him, not seduce him." My wrist screamed for relief.

"I'm sorry. I didn't realize I was doing anything. Please, Brit, let go of me. We were just talking." His grip relaxed a bit, and I pounced on the opportunity to make it right. "Brit, I can't imagine being attracted to anyone but you. I was just being polite. I have no interest in any other man." I leaned in to kiss him, hoping to stamp out the flames that flickered behind his eyes. My intended peck became a deep, long, and consuming kiss.

"You are mine," he whispered in my ear when Tracy approached the table.

"Should I leave you two?" he winked at Brit, the equivalent of a male high five.

I took an ancillary role for the remainder of the evening. Tracy attempted to engage me, but I diverted the attention to Brit. I glanced at my watch and realized if I left, I could catch Jessica for a drink.

When I looked up, Brit's eyebrows were raised. "Late for something?"

"Yeah, hot date?" Tracy laughed, and Brit turned a frosty glare on him.

"I, well, you boys seem to be so involved, and I really should go say bye to *some friends who are leaving to start internships."*

"Where?" Brit asked.

"The Landfill," I answered. He smiled and stood up to help me out of my chair and into my jean jacket.

~

I walked into the Landfill knowing there was a chance Jessica wouldn't be there. It was slammed. I spotted her talking to a guy I had never seen, and she waved me over.

"I can't get rid of this guy," she said in my ear when she hugged me. "Where have you been? I've been waiting forever!" I gave her an apologetic smile and sat down.

"Well, Randy,"

"Steve," he corrected.

"Steve. My friend is here and we really need to speak, privately. If you could excuse us?" She batted her long blonde lashes and he left begrudgingly.

"I had no idea you were coming!" She beamed. It seemed like years since I had talked to her and I needed to. "I thought you were with Brit tonight. I got your note."

"I was. I was supposed to meet his new best friend tonight. It was a bust." I sighed.

"Why? Didn't you like each other?" She moved her chair in closer for the story.

"Actually, he was really sweet, funny, charming and that accent is enough to make you weak."

"So?" I hesitated to tell Jessica about Brit's volatile mood swings. I didn't want anyone to dislike him or judge him unfairly. No one in my life really knew him well enough for me to start painting a bad portrait of him.

"It's like Brit thought I was flirting with Tracy." I said, embarrassed. I didn't even know if I knew how to flirt, let alone when to do it.

"That doesn't sound like you," she reassured.

*"I know!" I gushed. "I was just telling him I bet he would be a great
writer. He tells the most amazing stories about Brazil. Brit nearly came undone.
I mean, we worked it out, but he was really mad. I don't want him to think I
can't be trusted. If he doesn't like what I do when I'm with him, how can he
trust me when we aren't together?"*

*"He's here," Jessica pointed behind me. For the first time I had the
opportunity to watch how a large group of people responded to him. It wasn't
just women who gaped; men took time out of their conversations to take note
of Brit. We watched him walk through the sea of people who parted for His
Majesty. He strode through the quagmire rather than struggle like the rest of us
did.*

"Wow," said Jessica. "Sorry."

*"It's okay. Just looking at him makes me wonder what he's doing with
me." Both of us watched riveted as he sidled up to the bar. The female
bartender abandoned thirty impatient and demanding customers to focus
entirely on Brit.*

*"Don't be silly. Honey, you're a very charming and beautiful woman. I
bet Tracy was flirting with you, and Brit was mad at him but took it out on you.
He's probably here to apologize."*

*The entire female population of the bar gave a collective sigh of
disappointment when Brit headed to our table with three drinks in hand.*

*"Ladies." He flashed a dazzling smile and bent down to kiss me. I felt all
eyes upon me.*

*"What are you doing here? Where's Tracy?" I questioned, sensing I was
being checked up on.*

*"I was going crazy wondering if you were okay. I can't believe I was such
an asshole and let you walk to your car in the dark!" He gave me a deep and
repentant gaze. I was junk, and so was Jessica. A hand fluttered to her heart.*

*"Brit, I've been navigating this campus alone for years! I appreciate your
concern though." I felt radiant.*

*"If anything happened to you, I don't know what I'd do." He leaned in for
a deeper-than-appropriate-in-mixed-company kiss, and I melted into him.*

We spoke awhile until he rose to leave.

"Where are you going?" Jessica asked, disappointed.

"I'm going to leave you girls to your chat as long as you both promise me you'll have someone walk out with you."

"He's so amazing," Jessica sighed. We watched Brit pass money to the large bouncer at the door, point to us and wave. The bouncer saluted him and Brit sauntered out. I took in the stares of envy. "You should go over and surprise him tonight. I think he's in love with you, Reese. Maybe it isn't time for sex, but time to, shit, I don't know. How you can keep your hands off him?"

"I don't want to be just another girl to him. I'm afraid he'll lose interest as soon as I give in."

~

Though I tried to talk myself out of it, I went straight to Brit's. I had come by unannounced before and hadn't been shot or anything, but was nervous surprising him. What if he was with a girl? How embarrassing. No, how devastating. I let myself in with the key Brit had given me, relieved neither Kevin nor Katie's car was in the lot.

I slipped into bed in my bra and underwear, but Brit was sound asleep. It felt amazing to be close to him, to smell him, to feel the heat rising off of him. It wasn't long before I fell into a deep and comfortable sleep.

37

A single ray of sun peeked through a crack in the blinds and settled on my left eye, forcing me to wake up. I extended my leg to search for Brit and found the bed cold and empty. I sat up and let my eyes adjust to the darkness, realizing he must have already gotten up. I used his toothbrush, which was already wet. Surprisingly, I did not detect the scent of coffee brewing and fresh cinnamon raisin bread rising in the bread maker.

I emerged with Brit's T-shirt over my bra and panties and headed for the kitchen. Despite it being ten in the morning, the rest of the apartment remained dark with the blinds shut. In the dim light I saw the faint outline of Brit asleep on the couch. An early riser, I guessed he had probably grown tired of waiting for me to wake up and lay back down to read.

I crept to the couch, not wanting to wake him. I took off the T-shirt, lifted the blanket and snuggled into him. He was warm and, as always, I marveled at his size, next to which I felt dainty and vulnerable at times.

"Mmmm," he murmured as he stirred. My back was to him, and he brought his arm around me, positioning it in my cleavage. Instantly aroused, I wondered if this would be it. His large hand slowly moved over my breast, down my side and landed on my hip, which he gripped firmly, pulling me close to him. His touch, more hungry than usual, matched my rising interest.

My breath quickened as he skillfully unfastened my bra, which sprang open in the front, releasing my breasts. He caressed them, brushing his thumb over my nipple, which rose to meet it. His kisses traveled from my neck to my breasts, where they grew frantic and desperate. I felt like I had waited an eternity for this moment.

"Brit," I moaned, my body in flames as he fondled my breasts with his hands and tongue. Fervent, hot kisses burned a trail down to my stomach. A bolt of desire shot straight downward when his tongue slipped into my belly button. I could feel myself growing wet and my hips began to gyrate softly. My jutting hipbones begged to be nibbled, and he complied.

He reached a hand into my underwear, and I resisted the urge to push his hand away. His fingers played over the exterior, and I could feel I was ready to be entered. His thumb found that spot and began to massage it gently. Without warning, he replaced his thumb with his tongue and moaned softly like the night he had pleasured himself in front of me.

My God, I wanted him. I loved him. My eyes were closed and I was slipping into oblivion. As I neared climax, he replaced his tongue with his thumb and poised his body over mine. Just as I catapulted into the throes of ecstasy, he plunged himself into me.

"Oh, Brit!" My body rose to meet him. I clung tightly to him and he remained buried within me as the shuddering of my body subsided. I wondered if he was afraid of climaxing too quickly when he slowly withdrew himself almost completely and drove himself back into me.

The front door shut loudly, and I cried out as I squirmed from under Brit's body and onto the floor. Kevin! Damn it. I fished for my T-shirt and was horrified to see Brit come around the corner, his arms loaded with grocery bags.

"What the fuck?" he boomed, snapping on the overhead light. My head swiveled as Ash sat up on the couch. I swallowed the small amount of vomit that came up in my throat and stifled a scream by clasping a hand over my mouth. Ash rubbed his eyes sleepily, his hair a tousled mess. My God, what had just happened?

My mind was reeling and I felt dizzy. I held the T-shirt fast to my chest, hoping to God that Brit wouldn't realize my bra was undone behind it. I looked down to confirm my panties were still on my body.

"What the fuck is going on?" he roared again, his head snapping back *and forth between Ash and I.*

"I . . . I . . ." I couldn't speak. I was apoplectic with fear, revulsion, and confusion.

"What the fuck are you doing here, Ash?" Brit's voice shattered the momentary silence created by my failure to explain.

"I crashed here. I got drunk and your place was closer, so I walked." He feigned great difficulty waking up. I could feel his hands, his mouth, on me. I was trembling with the knowledge that less than a minute ago, Ash had been inside me. I wanted desperately to run as far as I could from both of them.

"Reese, what are you doing? Where are your clothes?" he demanded, throwing the bags on the love seat. With his hands on his hips, he fashioned an excellent barricade.

"I got up, you weren't there . . . I came out here. I thought he was you." Tears poured from my eyes. I used the coffee table to help me stand as my head began to swim.

"I took my T-shirt off and was about to climb onto the couch with you, when you walked in."

"Did you touch her?" Brit charged Ash. "You fucking bastard, I'll kill you." Ash was surprisingly spry for someone attempting to shake the fog of sleep. He lunged at Brit and they collided. I fell backward, and shrieked when a bolt of pain drove up my spine. I clasped my bra and scooted into a corner near the window. Fists were flying and connecting.

"You've been trying to get your hands on her since I met her." I was sickened that I couldn't tell who said it.

"Stop it! Please!" I cried. "Brit, please! It was my fault!" I was yelling at the top of my voice. My throat strained and tears coursed down my face.

Their fight was halted and they both turned to me. Panting, bleeding and a general mess, they put some distance between them.

"Get the fuck out of my house and don't come back!" Brit roared at Ash, who shrugged it off. I averted my eyes as Ash pulled his jeans on over his boxers and slipped his shirt over his head, bloodying it. He grabbed his wallet and turned for the door. Brit turned his attention to me and shot me an "I'll

deal with you in a moment" look.

I watched Ash walk toward the door. In the last second before he left, he threw me a wink over his shoulder.

I let my emotions loose then and was stunned when Brit leaned down and wrapped his arms around me. I clasped my hands to my head as if trying to keep my brains from leaking out and sobbed until I couldn't cry anymore. He didn't say anything. What had I done?

38

*I barely made it to the bathroom before vomiting the contents of my
stomach, which amounted to little more than alcohol, digestive acids and the
thirty gallons of adrenalin that had mainlined into it during the fight between
Brit and Ash. I dry heaved until my body collapsed, exhausted. I couldn't help
but cry. I had consented to sex, but with the wrong person, and dreaded the
consequences of Brit finding out.*

*Brit held me while I cried and apologized for overreacting. If only he knew
why I was crying. He justified his violence by saying Ash had been asking for
it, whatever that meant. I was secretly happy Brit had gone after Ash. Hell, I'd
wanted to myself. I couldn't say with certainty how things would have ended if
we hadn't been interrupted, if I would have realized at any point it wasn't Brit. I
was so ready, so completely in the moment. I shuddered to think of Brit walking
in to find his brother driving into me.*

*Even hours later, I couldn't shake Ash's face, covered in blood, his dark
hateful eyes, and the wink. The fucking wink filled me with revulsion. His hands
had been on me, he had been inside me, and I was certain Ash was far more
sane than people realized. A long, hot shower did nothing to cleanse my mind
or body. I had been adulterated.*

*I attempted to do my homework, anything to create the verisimilitude of
normalcy. He had been inside me. His mouth had explored the most intimate
parts of my body. It never occurred to me Ash was on the couch that morning.
Just over a week ago they were poised for combat in the middle of Beggar's,
and now Ash was crashing at Brit's place like nothing happened?*

Feeling depressed and lonely, I called my dad. He asked me to come home for the weekend, and I wanted nothing more than to run away from the situation and envelop myself in the warmth and familiarity of home. I opted instead to invite my dad up to school for the night and told him I wanted him to meet Brit. Keeping Brit with me would lessen the opportunity for him to interact with Ash.

Dad picked me up and took me back to the lobby bar of the Hyatt, where he was staying. I spoke of little else than Brit during the ride, and Dad listened intently without interrupting. He inquired about the money and I explained the tragedy that had befallen the brothers. He seemed sympathetic but wary of this guy who had swept his daughter off of her feet.

Brit walked in, wearing a suit, which made me wonder where he had been. He leaned in to kiss me on the mouth, and I quickly averted his attempt. My faced flushed and I looked to Dad, knowing what his reaction would be.

"Brit, this is my dad, Mike Hatcher." I leaned back so they could shake hands across the table.

"Hey, Mike, good to finally meet you." My stomach tightened at Brit's use of the first name, abandoning his normal regard for etiquette. "What prompted you to come and visit our girl?" As if it had never occurred to my dad that someday there would be a rival for his girl, his jaw clinched.

"Well, Brit, my daughter felt it was important we meet," he said as he waved down the waitress. She arrived with a double Tanqueray on the rocks and asked what my father and I would like. I ordered while Dad eyed Brit suspiciously.

"Come here often?" Dad asked after the waitress left.

"No, actually, never. She used to work at Harvest Grill. Honey, don't you recognize her?" He smiled, placing his hand over mine. I quickly pulled away. I hadn't warned him to keep his distance. Dad was overly protective and hadn't liked any guy I'd dated.

"What are you drinking, Brit?" I cringed at the tone of utter distaste when Dad said Brit's name.

"I'm drinking gin with a twist of lime, Mike," Brit returned with a smirk. I fought the urge to bolt for the door.

Dad sat back in his chair with his arms crossed. *"So tell me again how you two met. Do you have classes together?"*

"Actually, I met her by accident, through my brother. He was under the impression he had proprietary rights over her. I had to set him straight."

"That's an interesting way to put things."

"To be honest, I don't have much time or need for classes anyway. I'm just going through the motions."

Dad raised his eyebrows. *"Is school keeping you from something bigger and better?"*

"Well, I'm not sure how much Reese has told you, but I came into money at an early age. I have other plans for my life."

"I suppose one could make quite a life for themselves, you know, having come into some money. They could do well for many years if they planned it right. I certainly wasn't as fortunate as you at such a young age. My family was quite poor when I was growing up."

"And look at you now. You seem to be doing very well."

"Yeah, look at me now," Dad said, shooting me a look. *"I managed to work very hard and invest early and often, mainly stocks and bonds."*

"Not me, man. Real estate is really the only way to go."

And so the excruciating evening dragged on. I was curious but also grateful when Brit announced he had a prior dinner engagement and needed to leave.

"Who are you meeting?" I asked, wondering who warranted a suit.

"Ash." Panic spread through me like hot lava. It was over. This was it. *"Our attorney's in town and needs us to look over some papers."* He thumbed through the cash in his hand and I noticed for the first time the bruises and cuts on his right hand. I wondered how Ash's face compared.

"I'll get this, Brit," Dad said flatly, annoyed a twenty-year-old guy would attempt to pick up the check.

"No, really, Mike, I got it." He dropped money on the table, kissed me on the cheek, grabbed his jacket and extended his hand. My dad stood and reluctantly shook Brit's hand. I sat, bracing myself for an outburst.

"What the fuck was that?" my dad thundered once Brit's huge frame had disappeared down the escalator.

"What do you mean?" I asked, knowing full well what he meant.

"What fucking kid drinks gin on the rocks? Doubles, no less! Does he have a drinking problem? How long has this been going on?"

"Brit's had a really bad day. He got into a fight with his brother this morning--"

"No," my dad stared me down. "He's a disrespectful punk. Just because he has a few nickels to rub together, he insults me? I don't want you to see him again and that is non-negotiable!" He was shaking with anger and his face was red. I hadn't seen him this mad in years.

"What are you saying? Don't you trust me?"

"I trust you, but I don't trust him. There's something very wrong with him," he said, pointing at the chair Brit had been sitting. "I don't know what, but he's . . ." He trailed off, taking a long drink of the beer he'd been nursing.

"Dad," I said softly. "Brit was not himself tonight. He's really a very sweet, kind, caring and considerate person."

"I think you're wrong. I think he's exactly who he was tonight. I've never been more unnerved in my life. I'm going to my room," he said and rose to leave. I was the only patron remaining in the bar.

I dragged my heavy heart home and opened a bottle of wine. I waited anxiously for either Dad or Brit to call. Neither did.

I didn't hear from Brit until the following night. I had stayed in bed all day, replaying my version of his evening. I tried several times to reach Dad by telephone but got no answer. I almost burst into tears when the phone rang.

"I need to see you for dinner. I'll pick you up at seven," Brit said without offering any excuse for why he hadn't called earlier.

39

"Sorry to summon you so early, but I thought you'd be interested in seeing this immediately." Joel and Detective Ford addressed Meridan, Roz and Cameron in the large sitting area of Meridan's suite. He handed them all copies of the e-mail he had just received.

"What's this?" Meridan asked.

"Another communication from the woman claiming to have been stalked by your stalker."

"When did you get this, and why hasn't she responded sooner?" Roz asked.

"A half hour ago, and I think the answer to your second question is addressed by her directly."

"The corks do have dates on them," Meridan said quietly as she laid the e-mail on the table.

"We need to look at them and determine if there's any significance to the dates."

"Let me call Detective Adler and have her fax the evidence list to Joel." Detective Ford offered. "Initially, when you looked at the corks, did anything strike you as odd?"

"They were all from bottles of wine or champagne I drink. I looked at the dates, but I thought they were printed on them." She rolled her eyes to the ceiling and appeared deep in thought. "I guess the one that really stuck out to me was a cork from a bottle of Cristal, because it's a three hundred dollar bottle of champagne."

"Didn't we drink a bottle at the Ivy a few weeks ago?" Roz asked, nodding as the thoughts formulated in her head. "We did. Joel, you were there."

"I don't remember the date but I recall paying a hefty bill. Let me check my AmEx account online," Joel said, anxious either to discard the e-mail and the woman or to move forward with the additional information in the e-mail.

"Okay, here it is. March twenty-fourth, five hundred and thirty one dollars. Now we just have to wait until we can get confirmation of the date on that cork."

"If it matches, we have a name on this guy?" Meridan looked hopeful.

"Well, we have a name on a guy or two guys. I'm going to be honest— it isn't much. This girl I went out with in college used to date everything I touched—napkins, matches, corks."

"It's curious to me, however, that the initial 'B' matches the name Britten." Detective Ford pointed out.

"I find that interesting as well." Cameron said.

"Does this eliminate Harley Ryan?"

"No, this doesn't, but I need to bring you up to speed." Detective Ford opened his notebook and dreaded telling everyone they'd come up with nothing.

"We met with Sean Chaison and Harley Ryan. They both have solid alibis for every date in question. It seems Sean is very, uh, *active*. They were both concerned for Meridan's safety and offered to help in any way they could."

"Now we know they're lying," Roz spat.

"We'll continue searching for any type of evidence they hired someone to harass Meridan."

"Why has it been so quiet? We haven't heard from him since he broke into my house."

"If it was Sean and Harley, maybe we scared them," Joel offered.

"What if it's this guy or guys?" Roz turned her attention to Detective Ford.

"I'm afraid that's where we are right now. I don't want to alarm anyone, but the conspiracy theory isn't ringing true to me."

"What did he do to her?" Meridan spoke softly, her gaze riveted to the e-mail. The others were surprised by her compassion.

"Who?" Joel asked.

"What did these men, what are their names—Britten and Ashland? What did they do to this woman? The first time we heard from her, I didn't believe her. Now, I know how it feels to be stalked. What's in store for me?"

"Meridan! Stop this! He hasn't made any threats; he hasn't made a move to hurt you," Roz pointed out, but felt her own ripple of fear as Meridan voiced hers.

"I just wish I knew what she went through."

"Meridan, what's wrong with you? You've been so upbeat about this."

"Something in this e-mail clicks. It seems real," Meridan answered, not feeling upbeat at all.

"Should we call her?" Roz asked Joel.

"No. Let us have a crack at these guys," Detective Ford said.

Joel turned all his attention to his distraught client. "Meridan, it's unfortunate this woman you do not know went through something horrible at the hands of some men many years ago, but there is no relevance to our case yet."

"I guess I'm just feeling sympathy pains for someone who's endured what I'm going through." Roz stifled an eye roll. Here was the Meridan they all knew and loved.

"What now?" Roz asked.

"Why don't you ladies go out and enjoy the day? Do not under any circumstances go anywhere you would normally go. Are you okay with that, Detective Ford?"

"No problem, as long as she doesn't mind her detail tagging along." Detective Ford rose to discuss the orders with his men and make a few calls.

"Why don't you go up to Malibu or have lunch at Shutters? That would be fun, huh, Mer?"

Meridan considered his proposal. It would be nice to get away for the day, away from all of it, to be somewhere B couldn't find.

"Can we take your car?"

"What?"

"Obviously, we can't be seen in mine. Just switch with me today. Come on, I probably paid for it anyway."

"I don't care, fine, whatever, just let me get to work for God's sake or I won't be able to afford the payments!" he smiled, throwing her the keys.

"Joel? Do you want me to go, too?" Cameron asked, committed to his role in the protection of Meridan despite the unnervingly quiet few days.

"They'll be fine. Perhaps you could get with Al and start working on all this? I don't know how long they are going to extend protection to Meridan. I'd like to wrap this up."

"No prob," he said and escorted the ladies to Joel's brand new Mercedes 600 convertible. He opened the door to allow Meridan to slip behind the wheel. He was relieved it was an automatic. He had seen her drive a stick and knew the damage she could do to a transmission.

There was little conversation on the way to Shutters, the day too amazing to muck up with conversation about B or anything else. Roz felt herself unwind completely, thoroughly enjoying the wind in her thick, dark hair.

"This is an amazing car, Mer," she yelled over the wind and radio.

"I should get one of these. It's time for a new car anyway, and I'm getting pretty tired of driving a stick."

"Great idea. You could still do the custom paint. It's kind of your trademark."

"Check into it for me, will you?"

"Gladly." Roz smiled, hoping never again to be in a manual vehicle with Meridan.

"I haven't been to Shutters in years," Meridan said as she pulled into the parking lot.

"Do you have a reservation?" the hostess asked, and Meridan took off her sunglasses. "Oh, my God, Meridan Marks! How wonderful of you to join us! Please, come this way, ladies." She seated them and left to place their order for two tall mimosas.

"We'd better be careful," Meridan laughed when she saw the size of the drinks. "Joel won't be too happy if the police have to drive us home." She nodded toward the two cops a couple of tables away.

Both indulged in the special of the day, lobster salad. Meridan's phone rang midway through the meal, and she squealed with delight when she saw Jim's name appear on caller ID. Roz marveled at the tone Meridan took while speaking with Jim. She'd never seen her so wrapped up. She secretly wished Meridan and Christian would call their charade quits so Jim would be around more.

"Where is he?" Roz asked when finally Meridan completed her syrupy conversation.

"Miami. He's pitching Pepsi a new ad campaign. It's the biggest opportunity of his career. Hell, I'd offer an endorsement if it would get him home faster."

40

"You look gorgeous!" Brady hugged her tightly.

"I can't believe you're really here!" Lynden smiled from the inside out. They hadn't seen each other in years.

He pulled out a chair for her at a small table in the courtyard of Breadwinners.

"I'm serious, Reesey, you look beautiful!"

"I guess fear agrees with me," she hedged, unsure of how to open the conversation.

"Fear? What happened? Have you heard from him?" Brady's face displayed a full range of emotion within seconds, settling on deep concern. Reese's gaze rested on the jagged scar running through his left brow and disappearing into his hairline, ending, she knew, near the middle of his head.

"No, not directly. You won't believe this. Actually, I'm having a hard time digesting it," she began. "I read an article in *Glitterati* about Meridan Marks. She's being stalked." Brady settled back in his chair and examined Lynden.

"You look like her. I never thought of it before. I guess because I know you. You're more beautiful, but I see it."

"I . . . there was something in the article that struck a chord with me." She shifted uneasily in her chair, suddenly uncertain whether she wanted to discuss the issue. "Many times she has received a large bouquet of white roses with one pink one in the middle."

"The last bouquet," Brady said softly. He had been the one to tell Reese the details of Brit's home invasion. Through the years she had pondered the final bouquet and wondered why it was different from his normal monochromatic scheme.

"Is it a common arrangement? Do you think?" Lynden asked and took a drink of her beer.

"Hell, I don't know. It gives me the fucking creeps to even think about it. If you could've seen the apartment . . ." He stopped abruptly, realizing his insensitivity.

"It's okay. I know how bad it was. My parents got the photos, and I looked at them during therapy. I feel thankful every day that I wasn't there." She looked at the scar and thought of him lying in the hospital bed, moments after they had been told he wouldn't make it through the night.

"It's not your fault," he said and took her hands in his. But it was. If it weren't for her, Brady never would have been involved.

"I'm sorry." Lynden took a deep breath and tried to lose the past in the present.

He clasped large hands behind his head and searched the sky for answers. "Was there any more information?"

"I'm afraid so. There was a second article about escalating threats. It mentioned gifts of wine corks." Brady buried his face in his hands and sat quietly.

"What are you going to do?" he asked, finally meeting her eyes. Her contrite expression caused him to erupt, propelled by fear, not anger. "What *did* you do?"

"I tried to reach you, but you weren't home. I wrote to her attorney after the first article. I told him I feared she was being stalked by one or two men who had stalked me." Brady sat listening, shaking his head. "I didn't sign my name and I used an anonymous Hotmail account."

"What the fuck is wrong with you? How could you get involved? You saw the pictures. You saw *me*. If you had been home, you wouldn't be alive. Do you understand that?"

"I just couldn't sit back idle while he tormented her. No one deserves that. I got an e-mail from the attorney asking me to reveal my identity, to forward descriptions and names. I decided not to. Until I read the second article last night. Then I was sure. Brady, it's him. Or them. I don't know which, maybe both. It sounds like Brit, but who knows? They're so similar. I don't even like to think about it!" At the sight of her tears, Brady's anger abated quickly. He reached over and pulled her into his arms, but she resisted. She wiped her tears away and sat back.

"Don't feel bad for me yet. You're not going to be happy with me." They locked eyes, and Brady sat back and waited for her to regale him with her recklessness. "I forwarded the names, the descriptions and my cell phone number."

"Reese, what if they call? What if they want to get you involved in this mess? Are you prepared to see him? Can you actually be face to face with him again, after all of this?"

"No. At the same time, I can't bear for her to be the one who ends up home when he finally does snap. He's capable of murder." Lynden knew Brady was the last person that needed to be told what Brit was capable of. "Don't you want to put them away?"

"Not if it means jeopardizing your life. Fuck her, you don't know her."

"I know you don't mean that."

"I kind of do. You can't kick a sleeping dog like this, Reese."

"I gave them everything I knew, and I'm hoping that will help to locate him or them and stop all this madness. It's as good as over, Brady." She had debated whether to part with the last nugget of information, but felt a need to justify what Brady undoubtedly considered careless behavior. "Another thing that made me act was that he has stalked her here."

"What here?"

"She has a ranch about twenty miles north. He's followed her."

Brady let out a quick sigh and massaged his brow. "I don't know what to say. I guess maybe you did the right thing. You must've had a stroke when you realized he might have been here. Fuck. He could be anywhere." He covertly looked around, never wanting to be caught by surprise again.

"He's not here," she laughed hollowly. "I'm shadowboxing again. I can barely leave the house for fear that I'll see him. I can't live like this anymore. I've forwarded the necessary information, and hopefully they'll act on it. Once he's in custody, it'll be over forever."

"Are you forgetting the fact the police were never able to track him down? Do you recall neither of them were registered students at Michigan? Do you recall that as far as anyone knew, they didn't exist? Do you recall the police determined they were using false names, not just to you, but everyone? I think you're wrong. I don't think this is the end of it." He reached for her hand and wondered whether or not to tell her his news.

"What? Please don't be mad at me, I'm doing this for both of us."

"Dorrie and I are separated," he stated nonchalantly, causing Lynden's jaw to drop open.

"What?"

"I know. I can't believe it myself. I guess we grew apart. Two separate careers, no kids to hold us together." He shrugged and took a long drink of the beer that had until now gone untouched.

"Brady, what's going on?" she implored, grateful for the diversion.

"She told me she was in love with another man, had been for five years."

"I didn't realize you were having problems. Am I really so self-absorbed you feel you can't come to me?"

"What man wants to admit he hasn't had sex with his wife in years?"

"Years? My God, you're a loaded chamber!" They both burst out laughing, providing much needed relief.

"Years, and, yes, I am. What about you?"

"What? Nothing about me." Lynden tried to curtail the inevitable discussion of her romantic life. "Are you hungry? I'm starved!"

"For affection?" He quickly brought the subject back around.

"Actually, I'm seeing someone." She wondered where the lies were coming from.

"What's his name?"

"Clifton Fox." She answered firmly and without pause. Her client may have a high profile in the Dallas restaurant scene, but Brady wouldn't know who he was. Satisfied, he dropped the subject.

Mid-meal, Lynden couldn't help but ask him again about the separation.

"Are you going to get a divorce?"

"I guess so. We're in couples therapy, but not making much progress. The doctor told her she needed to break it off with her, I guess, boyfriend. The other man." Through his cynicism and sarcasm, Lynden could tell he was hurting. She knew he loved Dorrie.

She gazed at Brady, admiring his looks. Well over six feet tall, his toned and fit body caught the attention of every woman in the restaurant when he walked in. Though the scar was brutal, it added character to an otherwise flawless, pretty face. It made for a more rugged Brady. He would be fine. He was a great looking guy, had a great career, no kids, and was still in his mid-thirties.

"No worries, handsome. It won't be long before someone snatches you up." She looked at him, and, for the first time in fourteen years, saw not just a friend but a man. His chestnut-colored eyes searched her face. "What?"

"Nothing."

"Tell me."

"Dorrie isn't with me. There's no conference. She's on vacation with him. I couldn't stand to stay at the house while she was off fucking someone else." Lynden reached for his hand. He was so abject, pitiful.

"What can I do to help?"

"Spend some time with me? I'm here to see you. Well, that and running away from my problem." He smiled and squeezed her hand. Something in his eyes sparked a tiny flame in her stomach.

41

I could scarcely pull myself together for dinner. My mind worked frantically, creating excuses for Ash's version of events, scenarios that had played out the night before during their dinner. My stomach was tight with tension when he arrived at seven. When I opened the door to him standing with a bouquet of white roses, I was flooded with relief.

"I missed you," he said as he handed me the flowers. My heart soared and my eyes began to water as I arranged them in a vase.

"Where's Jessica?" he asked. I told him she had gone home for the weekend. He surprised me by coming up behind me, pressing my hips into the counter. His hands slid up my sides and settled on my breasts.

"I want you now," he whispered into my ear.

"Brit, I—" He spun me around and kissed me hard. His hands reached under my blouse and he grabbed one of my wrists when I tried to stop him.

"Don't," he insisted, pulling me to my room.

My body was turning on me. My nipples were hard, responsive to his touch. My mind screamed for me to stop him. I couldn't get Ash's face out of my head.

"Lay down." He pointed at the bed and started to unbutton his shirt.

"Brit . . . please." Tears welled in my eyes.

"You can climb into bed with my brother, but not me?" I choked on my own saliva when I took a sharp breath and began to cough.

"Brit," I begged, tears spilling down my face.

"We've been seeing each other for two months. I've barely made it past

first base with you, and I catch you almost naked, ready to fuck my brother?"
He shook his head in the dim light. Ash had not told him. More tears came,
from relief.

"Is that what he told you?" I choked.

"Lay down," he ordered.

"No. Please, I want to talk to you."

"I'm done talking, I want some action." He placed his hands on my
shoulders and knelt before me. I could barely breathe, I was crying so hard. His
hands settled on my knees after a slow crawl downward. He was silent for a
long time. I wanted him to leave.

"Hey, babe," he said softly. "I'm sorry, I'm just really frustrated. Seeing
you and Ash like that really fucked me up. I've been a fucking mess since then.
I can't get it out of my head. I wanted to kill him last night at dinner. It was a
good thing for him he came and left with our attorney."

I started to calm down a little, my breathing leveling off. My nose was
running, and I felt blotchy. Brit left the room to retrieve tissue for me and held
me while I calmed.

"Reese, I'm in love with you," he said gently, and I burst into tears again,
this time of joy. His hands slowly spread my knees apart.

I didn't resist. He loved me. I couldn't believe it. His hand slid up my
naked thigh, and he rose to kiss me. I plunged into the kiss, wanting him. He
eased me back onto my bed and settled on top of me. His tongue explored
my mouth and I tasted gin. This taste would forever remind me of him, I was
certain. His hands tore at my shirt, desperate to free my breasts. With one hand
on the back of my head, fingers intertwined in my hair, he held my mouth fast to
his, devouring me. I let one hand travel to his pelvic region, massaging, as his
hot, wet mouth moved to my breasts. I was awash with pleasure.

He slipped a hand under my skirt, forcing it up over my hips. His fingers
quickly and adeptly worked their way into my panties.

"You are so wet," he whispered, and I gasped when he slid his finger
deep inside me. My back arched against his hand, forcing it deeper. He worked
another finger inside. I was disappointed when he withdrew but shocked to hear

him sucking on his fingers, licking me off of them.

"You taste amazing," he breathed and kissed me. Tasting myself on his lips, I was pleasantly surprised; it wasn't offensive. "That is so hot," he said, continuing to pleasure me as he lavished my body with kisses, sucking and biting gently.

I worked his belt feverishly. I was ready. He helped me get his pants down and sat on the edge of the bed.

"Get on your knees," he said. I was completely under his control and I didn't feel capable of resisting.

"Do it." I pulled out all the stops, working him expertly. Brit soon became rigid, his hands clenching my hair as his breathing accelerated. I waited for him to call me off so he could enter me, but instead he came suddenly in my mouth. I forced myself to swallow, and my desire went out like a flame.

I curled up next to him and could feel his heart beating wildly.

"I don't want to know where you learned that," he said.

"Cosmo," I said lightly.

"We'll leave it at that." He kissed me on the head and apologized for not being able to stop. "I've been so worked up over you for months, I can't believe I didn't come in my pants," he laughed. Most men weren't so flippant about the concept of premature ejaculation. Brit, ever confident, strode out of the bedroom and into the bathroom.

~

We gazed at one another across the table. My body was humming with arousal, and I hoped we'd be taking another crack at sex when we got back to his place.

"Hey, guess what?" he said over his wine glass.

"What?" I asked, hoping he was going to tell me again he loved me.

"I talked to Tracy last night after my miserable dinner, and I'm going to Brazil for the summer!" My heart pounded and my face grew hot.

"What do you mean?"

"I already talked to my attorney. He's setting it up. Isn't that great?" He settled back with his wine glass and my thoughts swirled in my head. *What about me? What about us? Why was he leaving me? Why was he doing this to me?*

"I don't know what to say," I said, looking away. *"I don't feel well. Can you take me home?"* He was completely unconcerned about my sudden sickness. I bolted from his truck the minute he stopped at my apartment.

The next morning there was a wine cork outside my door. I threw it away. I avoided his calls for two days and threw myself into school. I tried to reach my parents; I'd left messages that went unreturned.

Brit called several times a day, but I deleted the messages without listening to them. I knew I was ending the relationship but didn't care. I was devastated he had made plans of such consequence without consulting me, and I assumed nothing but the worst in trying to determine his reasoning.

Immediately after Jessica returned Sunday evening, the phone rang. She answered and, not knowing about Brit's latest news, called to me.

"Reese, it's Brit."

"Hello," I answered, nonchalantly.

"Why are you avoiding me?"

"I guess I'm trying to reconcile you telling me that you love me and that you're leaving for a three-month vacation during the course of a single night." I felt so confident on the phone where he couldn't touch me. Jessica's eyes were wide.

"Hmm . . . Well, I don't know what's going on with you, but maybe we should take a break." My legs buckled under me, and I sat down hard. There it was.

"Okay." I said and started to hang up.

"Don't you want to talk about this?"

"No."

"Listen. Karis came up last week—"

I ran from the kitchen and hurled myself onto my bed. I cried until my throat burned and my eyes stung.

CONSUMED

"Sweetie?" Jessica let herself in. In her arms was a large grocery bag, just the sight of which reminded me of Brit that horrific morning. She sat down and emptied the bag of its contents—coffee ice cream, Mountain Dew, Reese's Pieces, and microwave popcorn—all of my favorites.

We gorged ourselves while rehashing the details of the past week. I omitted the incident with Ash out of sheer disgust. By evening's end, I had accepted and found some relief in the fact it truly was over. Through bittersweet tears, I recalled the day I lay on the same bed, knowing he'd break my heart but convinced it'd be worth it. I'd been so wrong.

42

*The term ended and I knew Brit was leaving after his last final for
a summer in Brazil. I enrolled in classes to distract me from my absolute
loneliness. I made time for friends I had put on the back burner since the day I
met Brit, but mostly I dulled my grief with far-too-frequent naps.*

*With each day of Brit's absence I sank deeper into the depths of abysmal
depression. Nothing in my life held any joy for me; I drifted through my daily
routine more like a dark apparition than myself.*

*It burned that I should stumble onto such an amazing man and begin such
a fulfilling and exciting relationship only to lose it all. It was impossible not to
torment myself with unproductive accusations. Why we were over didn't matter.
All that was left to truly ponder was: Where was I supposed to go from here?
JFK Jr.?*

*I bolted upright in bed at the shrill ringing of the phone. Without thinking,
I fumbled for the receiver. "Hello?"*

"What are you doing?"

*"What do you want, Brit?" I asked, barely able to force the words out of
my mouth. A month had passed since our relationship ended, and he'd been out
of the country at least two weeks. I had never expected to hear from him again.*

"I wanted to know how you were."

*"Fine, thanks for calling." I dropped the receiver into the cradle and
made a futile attempt to hold back tears. The phone rang again, and I grabbed
it. "Don't ever call me again!" I said and hung up. As an afterthought, I
removed the phone from the cradle. I couldn't deal with any more calls.*

The next morning, I almost twisted my ankle on a wine cork waiting for me on my front mat. A thorough examination revealed a handwritten date. I knew I'd forever remember 3-24 as our first date. After a quiet lunch, curiosity got the best of me, and I drove by his apartment. His truck and motorcycle were parked in their usual spots, normal whether he was home or away. I drove to a pay phone and called his apartment, promptly hanging up when Kevin answered.

I returned to my apartment to find three white roses beautifully wrapped in pink paper and ribbon. There was no card; there was no need. I knew who they were from and that he was not in Brazil.

There was a dated cork outside my door each day. Three days passed before he called again.

"Hello," I answered.

"Did you get my flowers?"

"You shouldn't have."

"I feel bad about how things ended."

"It was a very clean break. It was time," I lied.

"Yeah, about that . . ." I waited for him to continue, but he didn't.

"Why didn't you go to Brazil?"

"I am in Brazil."

I wondered who had made the deliveries and feared Ash lurking about. "Why are you calling, Brit? I'm very busy and need to go." I hated the way I felt, the longing, the sadness.

"I made a mistake."

"We all do."

"I didn't realize it until I got here, but I've done a lot of thinking. I called Karis and told her the same thing. I told her I didn't love her . . . that I went back to her out of habit. I panicked."

"Listen, I'm sorry for all of your personal trouble, but I can't help you." I hung up the phone and slid to the floor holding the receiver tightly to my chest. The phone rang moments later, and I let the machine pick it up. I grabbed my keys and fled to Brady, my closest friend other than Jessica.

Over the following days, I received several messages begging me to answer when he called. Finally, I did.

"Hello," I said hesitantly.

"Thank God." He sounded winded, frantic.

"What is it, Brit?" I asked, not really wanting to hear the answer.

"You need to hear me out."

"I don't need to do anything," I challenged, acutely aware of how glad I was that he was halfway around the world.

"Please, I'm begging you."

"Brit, I'm not sure why you keep calling me, but there's nothing left to say."

"I love you." My heart stopped for a moment. A thin sheen of sweat broke out all over my body. "I was afraid of how strong my feelings for you were. I couldn't resist the urge to run away. I started to see Karis to test my feelings. I figured if I still had feelings for her, then I wouldn't have to fear my feelings for you. I couldn't even stand the sight of her. It lasted about two weeks before I told her it was over, for good. No going back, ever." I mustered all of my courage and spit out a sentence.

"I'll never trust you again, Brit."

"I know you're hurt and angry."

"I'm not hurt," I spat defensively, not wanting to reveal how deeply I was wounded by his mendacity and abandonment.

"I'll spend the rest of my life working to earn your trust."

"I don't believe you," I said quietly and hung up the phone. I took to bed as I had in the days immediately following our breakup.

43

The flowers arrived each morning, always a dozen white roses with pink ribbon and a card reading Answer the phone.

Unlocking my front door one day, I heard Brit's voice. "I don't know what else to do but come home," he spoke to the recorder.

I ran for the phone and picked it up.

"Brit, don't come home. I don't want to see you," I lied and hung up. I longed to see him, but knew it would result in more heartache for me. The flowers continued arriving with no card. I had no intention of answering the phone or listening to messages, which I deleted as soon as I heard his voice.

I accepted an invitation to go dancing with a girl I'd met in one of my summer writing classes. I hadn't been to my favorite underground club since meeting Brit. During our relationship, it didn't occur to me to do anything without him, and after, I couldn't bear to hear all of the music to which I had introduced him.

As each song played, I danced away the emotions threatening to over take me. Ann Marie grabbed my arm.

"That hot guy has been staring at you forever."

Through the thick, dry-ice fog, I saw that hot guy was Brit. He was leaning against a pillar, Miller Lite in hand. He hadn't shaved in a couple of days, leaving his scruff exactly how I liked. A mischievous smirk danced on his full, gorgeous mouth. He raised his eyebrows to me, challenging me.

"You should go talk to him," she yelled. I turned to her and shook my head.

"Talk to him? I dated him," I yelled back. She seemed aptly impressed. I looked again and he was gone, and I wondered why he hadn't approached me. In the dim light, it could have been Ash, which would have made more sense with Brit in Brazil.

I lingered at the end of the evening, talking to friends. I regretted drinking so much. My defenses were down, and I couldn't risk running into either Brit or Ash. I was relieved we'd taken Ann Marie's car and asked if I could crash at her place to avoid being alone.

Arriving home the next morning, I found a letter on my front mat.

I will pick you up at eight, it read, in Brit's familiar hand. Against my better judgment, I was ready, waiting downstairs for him, not wanting to relive the last night we were in my apartment. He screeched to a stop, got out of his truck and ran to me. Sweeping me up in a hug, he held me tight.

"My God, I was afraid you wouldn't see me. I've been going crazy without you," he said in a thin, tight voice.

"Why didn't you talk to me last night at the Underground?" I asked when he set me down.

"What? I wasn't at the Underground last night." He looked bewildered, then concerned. "Was it Ash? Was he there? He was with me in Brazil. When I told him I was coming home, he wanted to come, too. We've been trying to work on our relationship. It isn't working." He grabbed my hand and led me to the truck, opening my door for me. He helped me in and gazed at me for a long moment. He brushed a curl from my face and held it for a moment.

"You are so fucking beautiful," he breathed and inhaled deeply. I contemplated bolting from the truck and remembered I had resigned myself to hearing him out. My face flushed hot, and I tried to breathe normally.

"I thought we'd go to my place. I want you all to myself so we can talk." I would have preferred to remain in public in case it got ugly, but didn't say anything.

As we arrived, I felt great apprehension returning to the scene of the lascivious moments with Ash. My skin crawled just thinking about him kissing me, exploring my body with his hands and mouth, and ultimately violating *me. Surely Brit didn't know or he wouldn't be attempting to mend either relationship.*

He opened a bottle of wine and I sat stiffly on the couch. The Couch. I tried to repel the thoughts flashing in my mind. He settled in close to me after putting on some music. Candles were lit and I could smell something fabulous cooking. I feigned indifference.

"I can't tell you how beautiful Brazil is. Everything reminded me of you." He reached down next to the couch and brought out several packages. "I shopped for you the whole time, hoping you'd give me the chance to win you back." He unleashed a boyish smile causing my heart to ache.

"Brit, I can't accept these."

"Open them first, then decide.'

I slowly unwrapped the first package. Inside was a large, gorgeous silk scarf. I pulled it out, stunned by the colors. Without thinking, I rubbed it against the side of my face.

"It was soft, like your hair. I couldn't resist." I set it down quickly.

"Really, I need to go," I stood, reaching for my purse.

"No!" he yelled, and I nearly jumped out of my skin. He put his hands on my shoulders, eyes wild. "I know you're upset with me, and I deserve every bit of it. I need you. Please stay. Let me feed you. We'll talk." He begged. I caved.

He had prepared a marvelous chicken cordon bleu. I tried not to get lost in the familiarity of the evening, reminding myself we were not a couple; he had left me for another woman. I tried to tap into the despair and depression I had felt in the weeks following his abandonment.

"I've never felt so strongly about anyone in my life. It made me afraid. I don't remember my mother—I've always felt an emptiness inside. When I was with you, I didn't feel empty anymore. I didn't understand it. That's why I scheduled the trip to Brazil. I wanted to test my love for you. I didn't get back with Karis until after you refused to speak to me. I was afraid."

He reached for my hand and I let him take it. Tears ran the length of his beautiful face. I felt overstimulated. All at once I wanted to laugh, cry, hold him, hit him, go to bed, take his pain, cause him pain, and run.

Stories abounded of Brazil, Tracy's family, and his attempts to reconcile with Ash. I had a strange feeling he took Ash to keep an eye on him. I listened more intently than I had planned, wishing we'd never been interrupted. I considered all the ground we'd lost, all the time and the trust. The simple fact remained: I was in love with him, but didn't trust him.

He took me home and didn't attempt to kiss me or force a commitment of any kind. In all, it had been a lovely evening. I was wide awake, so I started to pack. I would soon be moving into a new apartment.

Over the next week, I limited Brit to lunches and casual coffee dates. Understanding and eagerness had taken the place of his former aggression and impatience.

Once I was all moved in and my dad had departed after helping me unpack, I ran to the store for a few cleaning products. I returned to find an ice-cold six-pack of Miller Lite on the door step to my new condo with a cork dated one week from that day. The note read: I am going to Amsterdam to spend a few days with my sister. Patrick is driving my truck to NY with his girlfriend, Kaylee. Patrick is entering culinary school and he can't afford a flight. Go with them. I will meet you at the Waldorf-Astoria one week from today. Patrick will call you with the details.

Had this actually worked in my favor? Had I been given the time to come to my own conclusions about Brit? I felt ready—more ready than I ever had to give this relationship an honest, fresh start.

44

Lynden was surprised to find the other side of her bed empty.

"Brady?" she called. Certain he had fallen asleep on the couch, having told her he was going to read for a while, she snuggled into the spot where he had held her close, and breathed deeply his scent. It had been so long since she had been involved with a man on any intimate level.

Other than her parents, Brady had been the only constant for most of her adult life. He had been her sanity, and for his kindness, he had nearly died. If she hadn't been so wrecked and confused, she may have realized Brady had loved her since the day he'd met her. He'd told her so last night.

She had failed to see as anything sexual the rangy, toned and tanned body, the soft, dark curls he had let grow in recent years, the compelling brown eyes with which he'd lured her into his arms last night.

Even now, her body longed for him. Brady had been so gentle, touching her in ways only he could understand she needed. She had never revealed all of the details of her self-destructive relationship with Brit, and Brady never pried, just listened when she had something to say. She was grateful for him then and even more so now.

Remembering she had a lunch date with Gia, she grabbed her phone to check her messages. She'd assumed Brady would be with Dorrie today, but, blissfully, Dorrie was not here. Two messages. Gia cancelling. Excellent. Now she could spend the entire day with Brady. She debated a few minutes before returning the next message.

"Joel Goldstein, please," she said politely and almost gave her name when asked. "It's personal," she stated instead.

"This is Joel."

"Mr. Goldstein, I'm returning your call from last night. This is regarding Ms. Marks?"

"Yes . . . Yes, thank you for calling. Wow." Joel pondered methods by which to force this woman to part with her name. "It would be so much easier for all involved if you would tell me your name."

"Yes, it would be easier for everyone but me," she responded.

"Do I need to remind you that *you* contacted *me*? Why would you do so if you're so worried about your identity being revealed?"

"Mr. Goldstein—"

"Joel."

"Joel. I have spent the past twelve years of my life under an assumed name. My family doesn't even use my given name. I don't trust anyone. For all I know, you are actually Brit Holden. How do I know? You could be using a fake name, stalking your favorite client to drum up some press." Joel took offense but remained calm. As for Lynden, her words were for effect only. She'd know Brit's voice anywhere.

"You didn't answer my question."

"The man stalking Ms. Marks, or, I should say, the man I believe is stalking Ms. Marks, devastated my life. He nearly killed one of my closest friends. The thought of this escalating to murder motivated me to write. I know Ms. Marks is better insulated than I was, but I know the person you're dealing with is either Brit or Ash."

"We appreciate the information, but thus far the police have been unable to find these men."

"I told you the Michigan police were also unable."

"Do you have any other names we could run down?"

"I know they were adopted, but I can't guarantee it was official. Further, I don't know if the last names they used were their birth or adopted names. Shouldn't there be adoption records? I think it needed to be official for their uncle to handle their estate."

"Estate?"

"Yes. They're very wealthy. Look, Mr. Goldstein. Joel. I'm not comfortable with your questions."

"Why don't we arrange travel for you, and we can all sit down and share information. Between all of us, we can put a stop to this. For both of you."

"No."

"Videoconference?"

"No."

"Perhaps you'd be more comfortable speaking with the police."

"Is that a threat?"

"No. You don't seem to understand we aren't dealing with an ordinary citizen."

"Yes, you are. Me." Lynden was furious.

"I didn't mean that."

"Yes, you did. My life should be sacrificed in order to save her?"

"No. I meant we're concerned and would like the opportunity to sit down with you and determine whether this is the same guy or guys and, if so, how we find them."

"It is and I don't know." Lynden hung up the phone abruptly, her stomach in a white-hot knot. Who the fuck did he think he was? *I never should have written. Let her deal with this on her own*, she fumed.

~

"Mr. Goldstein? I have a fax from Detective Ford," Barb announced as she entered Joel's office. He skimmed the evidence list until he reached the corks. There were three. One Roederer Cristal cork with the date 3/24 written in black marker. Damn. It was a match to the date he, Meridan and Roz had consumed a bottle of this particular brand of champagne. The second cork was from a bottle of Grgich cabernet dated 3/31. He made a note to ask Meridan about that one. The third cork was found at the Texas ranch with a date of 4/23. Joel had no doubt this was the same guy or guys. They had to get through to this woman.

45

When Roz's phone rang, she was surprised to see Meritime's main number popup on the caller ID. It was Saturday morning. Who the hell was in the office?

"This is Roz." She was surprised to hear the breathy, panicked voice of the receptionist, Agnes. "What is it?"

"Well, I stopped into Meritime this morning because I forgot something, and I checked the e-mail—" Agnes stopped short. She hadn't read all the e-mails yet because she wanted to run from the office screaming for help.

"And?"

"B e-mailed."

"What? He's never e-mailed before. Forward them to me."

"Roz. I didn't mean to read them, but I was confused by the sender name. I started reading and now I'm afraid to stay here. I'm also afraid to leave. He says he's coming here."

Roz told her to call security immediately.

The forwarded e-mails from "Marksman" started coming over almost instantaneously. She opened the first one and trembled at the name's ominous double meaning as a shiver stole its way up her back. Once she had finished reading the first e-mail, she understood Agnes's discomfort. The thought of him lurking outside Meritime was unnerving.

April 7th, 9:10 a.m.
Subject: Where are you?
From: Marksman

Meridan,

I'm growing tired of your little hide-and-seek game. I got e-mail so we could communicate better. I'm e-mailing Meritime because I forgot your personal e-mail address. Hey, if someone gets this before Meridan, please forward her personal e-mail to me. I would appreciate a call to let me know where you are. Or you can e-mail. Isn't this fun? Maybe I'll just go to Meritime and wait for you. Lunch?

B~

As the messages came to Roz in a sudden avalanche, the phone rang, startling her.

"Agnes?"

"That's all of them for now. I set the computer to forward to your home."

"Excellent. Is the guard with you?"

"Yes."

"Let me speak to him."

"Jackson here."

"This is Rosalind Lescher. Please escort Agnes to her car, and, while you're at it, could you please search the street and garage? If you detect anything suspicious, contact Detective Ford or Detective Adler. Their contact info is on my desk."

"Yes ma'am, I can do that. Is this man armed?" The word "Marksman" glared at her, and she told him it would be a good idea to assume so.

Roz hoped Joel would be close to his computer.

"Where are you?"

"What's wrong?" Joel answered.

"He's e-mailing."

"What? Who's he e-mailing?"

"Meridan, at Meritime. Agnes went in this morning and there were tons of them. Can we catch him?"

"What provider is he using?"

"FreeMail Express."

"Fuck, another free account. We've had no luck tracking down that woman using her e-mail."

"Has anything materialized? Have Detective Ford or Cameron turned up anything on those men?"

"Not a thing. It's like they don't exist."

"Maybe they don't."

"She said there was an adoption. Cameron's combing adoption records for a five-year range."

"Maybe we're on the wrong track with her."

Joel sighed heavily and brought Roz up to speed on his conversation with the mystery woman. "She speculates this will spiral out of control, and that ultimately he might try to kill Meridan."

Roz felt a little tremor in her stomach as it rejected the thought of Meridan dying. "All the e-mails I have here from him are within one hour. As we talk, the office is forwarding them. It's creepy. I've only read one. I need to read the rest."

"What's his user name?"

Roz hesitated. She couldn't get the image of a shadowy figure with a sniper rifle out of her head. "Marksman."

"Marksman? You're shitting me."

"He means Marks's man, right?"

"I fucking hope so. Now I know why you're nervous. Forward everything to me and also to Detective Ford."

"What about Meridan?"

"Noah is babysitting her. God knows what she has on the agenda. Shopping probably. I did ask her to stay off Rodeo, out of Neiman Marcus and away from Melrose. She'd have to go downtown. It's better if we keep this quiet for now. Let Cameron and Detective Ford get some more work done.

I might try to call the woman back. I got the evidence list and the corks are dated. The Cristal was from March twenty-fourth."

"Wow. She could have signed an autograph for him."

"Do you know where she was on March thirty-first?" Roz rifled through her desktop copy of Meridan's schedule and informed Joel she had gone to a premier with Christian. Having the third cork date confirmed, they terminated their conversation on a confused note.

April 7th, 9:15 a.m.
Subject: Where are you?
From: Marksman

I had to run out for a bit, I think someone is trying to poison my water. Anyway, I think I missed your call so call me. Or you can e-mail me. This e-mail thing is cool.
B~

A little demented but non-threatening, Roz thought as she continued reading.

April 7th, 9:16 a.m.
Subject: Where are you?
From: Marksman

I think my phone is broken—you haven't been able to get through. That would explain no e-mail, too. I've been by your house, there's no sign of you. I drove by Roz's place but she isn't home either. I should check with Joel. He usually knows where you are. I am assuming you're in a hotel somewhere after what happened at your place. I can't believe someone broke into your house. I'll have to start checking hotels if I don't hear from you.
B~

Roz bolted from her chair, setting it to spin. She snapped closed the blinds in her office and headed for the front door. Her alarm was set and her door locked. Looking around, she noticed there were no lights on. She'd gotten up and made coffee, headed to her office and started working. If he had driven by, it would look as if no one was home. My God! What if he had crept around, looked in her office window?

April 7ᵗʰ, 9:50 a.m.
Subject: Call me!
From: Marksman

I was out and about today. I went by Joel's office, but I guess he doesn't work on Saturdays? Must be nice. I wouldn't mind a day off every once in awhile, and moving doesn't count. I have to get out of this place . . . my water is bad. I think it's making my hair fall out. Do you think I would look good bald? Just give me a ring when you get in—I'm starting to worry about you.
B~

April 7ᵗʰ, 10:00 a.m.
Subject: E-mail
From: Marksman

I'm confused by your silence. It's not like you to be so out of touch. Are you mad? You don't still think I'm your stalker, do you? How can you stalk someone you have a relationship with? Are you upset because I have not been able to spend enough time with you? I just need to get this water thing under control. It isn't safe for you here. Besides, you will end up having to leave to shower—it isn't safe.
B~

April 7th, 10:05 a.m.
Subject: Christian York
From: Marksman

I've got to tell you, I am feeling a little harassed by you. I hope you're not with Christian York. I have driven by his place. It's difficult to see in with the gates and all the foliage, but there was no sign of you. Did you ever think he might be your stalker? Maybe he's upset about your breakup? I don't want to hear you're with him.

B~

"Nice," Joel said when he picked up the ringing phone.

"Did you go into work today?" Roz asked.

"No, no one's there."

"I don't understand a fucking word he's saying. He's on this Christian York thing again. Should we warn him?"

"Hold on. I have Detective Ford beeping in. I'm going to try to do a three-way call here. Hold on. If I lose you, I'll call you back."

"Joel?"

"Yes, Detective. I have Roz on the line as well. Roz, you still there?"

"I'm here, Joel. Hello, Detective. Have you been able to read any of these e-mails?"

"Actually, I'm out of the office. I got Joel's message, so I had Detective Adler read them. She thinks there's enough cause to send someone by all mentioned locations. We'll try to identify suspicious vehicles. I don't know how far she's read, but she mentioned Christian York and Roz's houses and Joel's office. Oh, and Meritime. Sounds like he's been busy today."

"I don't know if he's actually doing anything. Listen to this." Joel read, stressing the time of the mail.

April 7ᵗʰ, 10:07 a.m.
Subject: Where are you?
From: Marksman

I drove by Christian's place again, and I have to tell you, I'm starting to think you're lying to me. You told me it was over with you two, and now—now I don't know where you are. You're not going to get away with this, Meridan. I have worked too hard building a life for us. As soon as I can get this water thing squared away, we'll be fine. I'm looking into a nice two-bedroom house, water purifiers on all faucets, a water cooler. You can have all the fancy bottled water you want.
B~

"These e-mails are only minutes apart, yet he's saying he's driven by Christian's again." Joel pointed out.

"Right. How many e-mails are there total?"

"Detective, they're rolling in about one every three to five minutes."

"That doesn't sound good. Well, on the other hand, maybe it is. Maybe he's just having fun and fantasizing. Keep reading, Joel."

April 7ᵗʰ, 10:10 a.m.
Subject: Fuck you
From: Marksman

What the fuck is your problem? Do you think you can treat me like this without any type of repercussions? I'm going back over to Christian York's, and he and I are going to have it out. I'm tired of the lies and the harassment. You of all people should know that. Now I have a headache. See what you are doing to me? That may have bought Christian York some time. I need to see someone about my head right now. Who's open on Saturday? Maybe you could just come over? Take care of me? After all I've done for you, you'd think you could be less selfish for five seconds and think of someone other than you. You are quite a piece of work.

B~

"What is with this water thing?" Joel asked. "Has he ever mentioned water or being poisoned or anything like that?"

"I don't recall anything?" Roz answered.

"It kind of sounds like he's going nuts right in front of us, live on e-mail." Detective Ford sighed.

April 7th, 10:15 a.m.
Subject: Bad water
From: Marksman

I just got back from the doctor. He said I may have a brain tumor from the water problem. He thinks maybe I should move in with you. I could protect you from that stalker. You realize it's that boy toy of Roz's, don't you? I see him around, lurking outside your place. If Christian York is such a badass, why doesn't he take care of it? Never mind, I'll do it myself if I see him again. What's going on with that big bald guy, by the way? I think he's following you. The way he looks at you makes me insane. I should probably just get with the FBI. I've worked with them before, and it's time we stop screwing around with this. You're not safe. Let's just cut the LAPD out of the loop, they are so fucking incompetent.

B~

"Okay, that settles it. He's at home, jerking off the machine," Detective Ford insisted. "There are only five minutes between those e-mails, and he says he went to the doctor."

"God willing, he really does have a brain tumor. One that's metastasizing rapidly." Joel snorted a little, and they all shared a chuckle that was more a tension reliever than anything.

"Can you have an officer drive by anyway? Let's inform security at the

Four Seasons. Someone needs to find out where Jim is. I think Meridan said he was in South Florida. At least he's safe halfway across the country. Christian, too."

"Yeah, no problem. I'm going to talk to Noah and security at the Four Seasons, but I'll tell you, I feel great about how frustrated he is. It means he has no earthly idea where she is. That's a first. I've got to run. Keep me informed if you notice anything unusual."

"I've noticed about twenty unusual e-mails." Roz joked, then promised to let him know if she saw anyone around her house.

46

The living room was dark but Lynden could see Brady sleeping in the dim light. Her mind involuntarily drifted back to a similar incident so many years ago.

"Brady?" she called as if to convince herself that it was, in fact, Brady, and not Brit or Ash.

She could see he had fallen asleep reading and, as she crept closer, was horrified to find he had been reading her journal. Closing the gap between them, she snatched the book from his chest, startling him into an upright position.

"Christ, Reese!" His hand was over his heart, his eyes wild as he tried to orient himself. "What is wrong with you? You scared the life out of me." He reached for the lamp next to the couch.

"How dare you read this! It's none of your business!" Her voice was loud enough to shatter the windows and he held up his hands in futile defense.

"Hold on, Reese. I was looking for something to read. I stumbled onto this. I debated, I did, but as soon as I started—"

Her hands flew to her face as if it would in some way shield her embarrassment. "What? What, Brady?"

"I needed to know."

"You know everything! You were there!"

"No, I don't. Not really."

"So? What? You need to know all the bloody details?" She asked tightly and began to pace. Her eyes darted to the windows and doors. From where she stood, they all appeared to be locked. Pacing triggered the need to create order.

She had to distract herself.

"I *deserve* to know."

"Oh, my God, you resent me. I knew it! After all this time, the truth."

"Hold on, Reese. Come here."

"No."

"That isn't what I meant. Believe me, after you moved, and I was still in the hospital, I couldn't help wondering how it had gotten so bad. What had driven him to come after you? What drove him to . . . Reese, sit down."

"Stop calling me that." Her movements were frantic, manic.

"Baby, sit down. I'm sorry. You don't want to talk about it. I get it." His apology caused her to snap out of her patterned behavior. She looked him straight in the eyes. It was Brady. Brady loved her. He wouldn't leave her. She could be honest.

"I'm sorry." She lowered her gaze.

"It's okay. I just, if we're going to move forward, as more than friends . . . How did he hurt you? You know how he hurt me." Lynden bowed her head in shame. What she had brought to Brady's door was inexcusable. "You're so different now. I want to know how that happened."

"I'm embarrassed. I don't know what you read. I don't know what will make you not want to be with me!" Her hands flew to her face, which was hot to the touch. Her mind was running wild; she couldn't imagine what he thought of her. She was relieved when he folded her into an embrace.

"Reese, don't be embarrassed. Look at me." He forced Lynden's hands from her face and was struck by how purely beautiful she was at that moment. Her face was flushed, as it was after they made love, her eyelashes were thick with tears as they had been so many times, her full lips were naturally pink and bee-stung. He longed to kiss her, but feared her response.

"Can't we talk? As friends, if nothing else?" She nodded and her hand flew to smooth her hair and check the knot in back. She brushed the wrinkles from her robe, trying to create order. He watched, knowing now where all of this had started, marveling at the lingering manifestations of her past.

"I don't want to be friends with you anymore," she said, and Brady jolted back, a pained expression emblazoning his face. "That's not what I mean." She reached for his hand. "I want more."

"Jesus! You had me worried for a second. Reese, let's talk about this."

"What do you want to know?" She steeled herself against his questions and hoped he would ease her into it.

"Why were you so attracted to him? I mean, despite the obvious physical attraction. Hell, it sounds like I'd be attracted to him." She joined him in a smile.

"I think about it all the time. It wasn't just an attraction. It seemed I'd willed him into existence. He was not only my outward ideal, he was interested in everything I was enthralled with—cars, motorcycles, fashion, food, wine. Granted, I didn't know anything about food or wine back then. My idea of a great wine was white zinfandel." She laughed hollowly at the memory. Somehow, here with Brady, she wasn't nearly as afraid as she was every minute of every other day of her life.

"He was really abusive, emotionally. Actually, I should say *they* were, and not just emotionally." He had read of Ash's violation. She forced herself to continue, nonplussed.

"I never saw it. It came on so slowly, so covertly. I didn't realize he was belittling me, trying to break me down, make me weak, all so he could control me. I was impotent from the beginning."

"The whole dynamic is really scary. He was so aggressive."

"I was terrified most of the time, not just of his temper or his physical aggression, but of him ending the relationship. I was overwhelmed by my attraction to him, but I wasn't ready." She saw him flinch as though her words were little slaps. "I'm sorry. Is this hard for you?"

He shrugged and leafed through the pages of the journal. "No harder than reading this. No harder than what we went through in the end." He reached for her hand.

"I had just come out of a wholesome, wonderful relationship built on love and respect and, well, boredom. I didn't really have the skills necessary to deal with Brit."

"Looks like you got a little more excitement than you bargained for."

"Like asking for a light rain and willing a typhoon."

"Was the money a factor?"

"Definitely, in that we could go out and do things, which I loved. With money, though, comes a different . . . perspective."

"Like, you can have anything you want?"

"Yes. Exactly. I think maybe I was a challenge."

"That and a competition? With Ash?"

"Ash." Her eyes glazed over as her emotions swelled. She held up a hand to stop him from asking any more questions.

"Reese. I'll never leave you. I love you. I've always loved you. I loved you the first day I saw you. I won't deny I was crushed when you started seeing Brit. That's why we didn't talk. When you came to me, hurt and afraid, I didn't turn you away then. I won't turn you away now." He reached out and touched her knee. She drank in the warmth.

"You don't understand how stupid and naïve I was. All the signs were there. Everyone, including my own father, saw straight through him. I was blind and rewarded appropriately."

"You were young. You fell for the wrong guy."

Desperate to stop the conversation, she stood and slowly untied the belt to her robe. She heard Brady's breath catch as she slowly opened her robe.

"Are you sure you want to do this?"

"Yes." She smirked seductively.

"We're not done talking." She dropped the robe to the floor. "My God, Reese." He rose to look at her. She stood unabashedly, allowing his eyes to roam over her. She unbuttoned his shirt slowly; her turn to stare. He was not wearing an undershirt, and a perfect landscape of tanned skin and muscled chest emerged. She watched him watch her and grew more excited by the second. His dark eyes were riveting, and she could almost read his lascivious thoughts. His defined oblique muscles disappeared into faded jeans. Brit popped into her mind for a moment and she deftly pushed the memory away.

47

"These are all from today?" Meridan held the stack of printouts in the air in protest. The floor was covered with pages Meridan had discarded after reading.

Cameron nodded.

"This is insane." She shook her head and collapsed, appropriately, onto her fainting couch, hand at her forehead in the classic gesture of only the most desperate of damsels.

"Precisely." The e-mails had been coming fast and furious all day. Al Roenick had an inside track with the host company Marksman was using, and they were all on a hair trigger waiting for word. In the meantime, they worked to familiarize themselves with B/Marksman's intentions and overall state of mind.

"He has a brain tumor?" Meridan asked.

"The question is how he found this out in, what, three minutes?"

"He's crazy. What's this about the water? It's poisoned?"

"He sounds like a paranoid schizophrenic to me, in addition to being delusional."

"Yeah, I'd say. He's just babbling . . . most of this doesn't really make sense. Did he really go to Roz's house? And Christian's?"

"Detective Ford said no one's reported anything unseemly, but that doesn't mean nothing happened. Christian's security has been alerted."

"There's nowhere more secure than his estate. Hell, maybe I should be there."

"He has this real fixation on your relationship with Christian."

"Sometimes. Other times he says Christian is my stalker. Or Jim. Or you. I can't believe Joel hasn't been fingered."

"Jim's safe, right? In Miami?" Meridan nodded. "I'm just glad this whacko has no idea where you are." Meridan sighed and read on.

April 7th, 11:20 a.m.
Subject: What is going on?
From: Marksman

Hey, I was thinking maybe something different tonight. I'll pick you up. It is so much more gentlemanly, don't you think? I know you've been insecure in the past about other women hitting on me, so this is the best way to do it. Wear that silver Versace number, the one with the plunging neckline. I'm feeling better—I took a nap. That always helps. Did your mother ever tell you that? Oh, that's right, you don't talk to your mother. I haven't in a long time, mine is dead. I can't wait until you meet her.
B~

"I'm afraid it's looking more like a crazed fan than a setup, Mer."

"It's almost like he believes all this stuff—us talking, meeting, dining. It's spooky." She nibbled a thumbnail while she read. "His mother is dead? He looks forward to me meeting her!"

"Yeah, not cool." Cameron opened his phone to call Joel but was interrupted by a knock on the door.

"Cam, it's Joel and Roz."

"Come in. Have you read all of these?" Roz nodded and Joel rolled his eyes.

"I'm not a lawyer anymore. I'm stalking a stalker who isn't really stalking."

Meridan hopped up to greet them and make sure they knew how troubled she was. They all settled into their chairs set up around a large, oval table. Roz pulled out her copies, which were covered in highlighter markings.

April 7th, 12:20 p.m.
Subject: Where are you?
From: Marksman

I'm worried you're not getting my e-mails. I've had quite a day today with the tumor, the doctor, the x-rays. I'm tired and probably very sick. I'm willing to go out, but you are starting to piss me off. I think you're at Christian's house. I'm headed over there now. I'm going to put a stop to this.
B~

April 7th, 12:25 p.m.
Subject: Christian the coward
From: Marksman

Lucky for the bastard, he wasn't home. I've had all I can take from him. He actually had the nerve to accuse me of stalking you. Would you please let him know that isn't true? I bet it's that big, bald guy. He stalks you and then you hire him to protect you. I have a headache so I'm going to lie down for a while.
B~

"Do you think he knows these are time-stamped?" Joel shook his head, baffled by the senseless babble.

A knock at the door gave them all a start. "That'll be Detective Ford," Cameron announced, putting them at ease.

"I had Detective Adler read these to me on the way." He waved and joined the group. "Let's e-mail him back and set up a location for them to meet. Let's bust him."

"I have my laptop," Joel said. "She can say she was with me all day and just now stopped at Meritime."

"I'm in. I want it over," Meridan said decisively. Detective Ford told Roz to call the guard to check for observers in front of Meritime while they spent a few minutes drafting an e-mail.

B,

I'm so sorry I've been out of touch. I've been with Joel all day going over your scripts, which I think are brilliant. Let's talk more over dinner. I am staying at the Grafton in West Hollywood. Please meet me in the Balboa bar at seven. I will wear the silver Versace.

M~

"What if this wigs him out? He isn't used to having any interference from the real world," Joel asked, mouse poised above the send button.

"We don't have any options. We're never going to catch this guy if we don't start taking more radical steps," Detective Ford insisted as he took out a legal pad. "I'm sure Cameron told you he uncovered nothing regarding the information the woman sent. This new e-mail about a dead mom interests me. The initial matches, the corks are dated, and now he mentions a dead parent. He could be adopted. These could be our guys. "

"Al Roenick is working on her identity through the cell records," said Joel. "Her phone apparently is registered to a company. It's a Dallas exchange, which could mean nothing or everything. It's a whole spider web of red tape. He's got a guy inside FreeMail Express working on getting B's information."

"I can use any help I can get. We've scarcely been able to authorize the amount of work we've done thus far. If he would just make a move . . ." The detective was interrupted by the chime of incoming mail. All eyes turned to the laptop.

April 7th, 5:08 p.m.
Subject:
From: Marksman

Thank God! I was losing hope I would see you tonight. Brilliant. Balboa. Seven sharp.
B~

"Don't you think that's odd?" Roz asked no one in particular.

"What specifically?" Joel asked.

"That he responded?" said Detective Ford. "Doesn't that seem inconsistent with his methods so far?"

"He seems to be evolving or changing somehow. Maybe this is a new phase of his illness." Joel asserted.

"Should we write back?" Meridan asked.

"Would it kill us to ask for a name? We could end it right here."

B,
I'm so tired of calling you that. What is your name?
M~

They waited patiently, hoping for a response that also included his social security number, driver's license number, last and current addresses and, if it wasn't too much to ask, a photo.

April 7th, 5:10 p.m.
Subject:
From: Marksman

Marksman

"I really hate that. It's creepy." Meridan shivered.

"Let's move," Detective Ford barked.

48

"Wow, Reese, you're a fabulous cook." Brady pulled her by the waist down onto the sofa with him. They'd spent a glorious day in bed, shopping for dinner, and cooking together. Brady had been kind enough not to bring up the journal and she had waited until he had a few drinks in him to reveal the details of her conversation with Joel Goldstein. She decided to ease into it.

"I want you to know last night was, well, I mean this . . . this is great."

"I'm a little on edge about everything."

"About us?" Her heart started to thump and she felt adrenalin slosh into her stomach.

"I have a lot to sort out with Dorrie. You and I have so much to look forward to." He raised his eyebrows, seeking confirmation.

"We do?"

"Yes."

She handed him his wine glass and proceeded. "I spoke with Joel Goldstein today. Meridan Marks's attorney?" As casually and unaffected as possible, she delineated her conversation, all the while bracing herself for his anger.

"I agree with the way you handled it." Brady swirled his wine and looked into the glass thoughtfully.

"What are you thinking?"

"I'd like to read some more of your journal."

"Brady—"

"Please? It's important to me."

"If you really want to read this, I'm going to read in my room."

"Are you sure?" She nodded and kissed him on the cheek. Before retiring with the book that sat largely unread on the table next to her bed, she refilled his wine glass. He settled in for what looked like the long haul, and her heart was heavy as she plodded to her room.

49

I kept to myself in the back seat of Brit's truck, busying myself with a novel until falling asleep. Patrick never asked Kaylee or I to drive and he guided us safely to New York City while we dozed. I awoke to the familiar honking, banging and crashing I knew to be Manhattan. It was twilight and I was dizzy with excitement; I'd never been there as an "adult." I couldn't wait to experience this city in love and with Brit.

The hotel was aglow as we pulled up. A troop of professionals rushed the truck, opening doors and removing luggage. I was offered a hand and led from the back seat. I'd only gotten out once since we'd left and felt nearly crippled. I wished I'd have been able to freshen up prior to seeing Brit, but my enthusiasm overshadowed my fear of inadequate hygiene.

The splendor of the Waldorf always stunned me. Its majestic old-world setting drew you in, captivated you, and made you feel like visiting royalty. The bellman whisked me straight to the elevator without checking me in. I immediately sensed Brit's hand in the situation.

"Ms. Hatcher, we are delighted to have you with us for the weekend," the porter offered kindly, and, in turn, I expressed my absolute delight at being there. I was completely unprepared for what I confronted when the door to our suite was opened for me. The room was lit only by candles, and vases filled with white, long-stem roses were perched on every available surface. I entered slowly, wanting to prolong the experience. Brit was nowhere to be found.

Single roses and petals covered the large king-sized bed, the sight of which reminded me the long standing sex issue would be resolved this trip. I walked toward the warm glow of the bathroom. The enormous marble tub in the corner was filled to the rim with bubbles, and a bottle of Roederer was chilling on its ledge. An envelope with Brit's writing on the front was propped against a collection of bath and body products.

I slid a finger under the seal and read the note.

I know you've had a long journey, not just today, but throughout the past few months. Please enjoy a bath, think of me, and join me in the Terrace bar when you are ready. No hurry. There's a surprise for you in the armoire.

I could think of nothing but Brit while trying my hardest to relax in the tub. I pondered the one-bed setup, wondering how many nights I would be able to withhold sex. I could more easily give myself to him without reservation if he didn't pressure me, if I felt as though I was deciding. Like I had on his couch that day with his brother. I shuddered as the careless memory slipped in.

Brit's intense focus on the role of sex in a relationship was foreign to me. My ex, David, had been patient, loving, and kind, making it clear he wanted me, but not under any demands or ultimatums. With Brit, I couldn't shake my fear of abandonment. If I withheld sex, I had a modicum of power. He consumed me completely.

Eagerly anticipating seeing Brit, I cut short my bath and champagne enjoyment. Additionally, I was curious to see what the armoire held. I toweled off and liberally applied my new lotion and mist, which smelled sinful and indulgent. I wrapped my head in a towel and headed to the bedroom, pausing a moment to internalize my surroundings. I truly felt like a princess.

The armoire held a virtual wardrobe. I ran my hand through the stable of new garments, my mouth gaping. I had never seen clothing so glamorous or sophisticated; Neiman Marcus sale racks were the extent of my couture experience. I pulled out one of the evening dresses, a slinky backless black jersey halter dress with a plunging neckline. I dried my hair, making certain it was extra curly and wild, just the way he liked. The phone rang as I applied the final touches of makeup.

"I need you."

A grove of butterflies took flight in my stomach at the sound of his voice.

I had slipped on the dress, which fit me like it was tailor-made; it took sexy up about three hundred notches. I tried to ignore the overt sensuality oozing from my appearance, but ultimately embraced it. Why shouldn't I enjoy it?

I entered the bar slowly, keenly aware of the eyes on me. I was betting everyone thought I was a high-dollar whore. I looked around but did not see Brit, and I racked my brain trying to remember if he'd said Terrace bar. I felt his breath on my neck and his hand graze the small of my back. Goose bumps spread like fire and my nipples stood at attention. I crossed my arms self-consciously and he brought them back down to my sides.

"I want everyone in the bar to see you, to want you, and to know you are mine." He inhaled deeply. His hands locked into mine firmly. "See that man to your left? He almost came in his pants when you walked in." A slow burn smoldered between my legs and traveled through my body. What I felt seemed like fear, but of what? Of feeling turned on, of feeling like a sexual being, of being objectified? Of enjoying that men found me attractive? Or, of Brit saying I was "his"? He turned me to face him, and I tipped my head up to look in his eyes. He lowered his mouth to mine, touching it ever so slightly.

His tongue flicked out and wet my lips. After an excruciating moment, he placed his open mouth on mine and seduced me. His hand was firmly placed at the small of my back, holding me tight to him. I couldn't help but wonder what type of scene this was creating, and I almost didn't care. I felt him growing firm and tried to diffuse the passion by pulling away.

"You know better," he said into my mouth, and I relented, melting into him. He had spoken, and I obeyed.

As he led me to the bar, I saw him throw a braggart's wink at the guy he had mentioned. "That should've finished him off," Brit smirked. My thighs had gone up in flames, and I knew I'd be sporting wet panties for hours.

Brit ordered a glass of Roederer and a double Tanqueray on the rocks before asking me to stand up and turn around so he could admire my outfit. I complied self-consciously and sat back down.

"Fucking phenomenal. You have the body of a whore, the face of a goddess, and the composure of a princess. What a combination. You make me

weak." He smiled, bringing a hand to his heart. So much to absorb, I decided to take it as a compliment. He took a handful of my hair and leaned in to bury his face in it. "I've missed your smell, your taste." He brought my hand to his crotch, which I instinctively jerked away. He grasped my wrist tightly and returned it to his hardness.

"Feel how much I want you," he breathed.

"Brit, people are watching!"

"That's because every man and woman in here wants to fuck you as bad as I do."

I choked on my champagne, his comment searing through me. I didn't quite know how to process his crudeness. It was exciting, but terrifying.

"Are you alright, sweetheart?" He patted me lightly on the back. My bare back. God, the signals I was sending in this dress.

"Yes, I just, I don't . . ." I trailed off, not knowing what to say. "Where are we going?"

"Back upstairs so I can rip this dress off of you," he said and took a long drink of his gin. Panic. Stark, unadulterated panic. My eyes raced, searching for exits. "I'm kidding. I thought we would go to Kinetic. It's the hottest restaurant in Manhattan." It was as if he had never propositioned me. I was more than happy to let it slide.

"Can we get in?" I asked and he cast a "don't be silly" glance my way.

50

A town car awaited us, and I realized we were to dine alone.

"Are Patrick and Kaylee joining us?" I asked. He shook his head no and we rode in silence. We hadn't yet discussed his trip to Europe. I wondered if he truly went to visit his sister or another woman.

"How was Amsterdam?"

"Filthy and perverted." He must have been right at home, I thought to myself.

"Your sister lives there?" I knew nothing about his family.

"No."

"Visiting?" I prodded.

"Sure."

"How many sisters do you have?"

"One."

The car stopped outside of a nondescript door, outside of which a line snaked down the sidewalk for nearly a city block. People were jostling one another, clamoring for position. The women postured and made eyes at two men in black suits and earpieces aggressively guarding the door. I finally glimpsed blue neon letters that spelled "Kinetic." I turned to Brit with a skeptical glance, nervous about being potentially turned away at the door in front of the throngs of hip New Yorkers. My trepidation caused a seductive smirk to spread across his remarkable face.

He helped me out of the car and strode straight to the front of the line. The bouncers opened the metal door without pause.

A blue glow cast over the interior, and I inhaled the heady aroma of clove cigarettes. My body reverberated with the heavy bass of the industrial music. We walked a dim corridor, which opened into the spacious, warehouse-style club with a bi-level restaurant.

An enormous bar spanned most of the first floor and part of the second. Dinner was available on the second floor and beyond the stanchions and red rope marking the entrance to the third floor. The noise was deafening, a combination of the music and one thousand conversations. Pure dissonance.

"Mr. Holden!" The backslapping, hand shaking and half-hugs commenced with, it seemed, everyone. I felt insignificant, as I was not introduced or acknowledged. The maitre d' led us to the third floor, and we were ushered through the cordon. Our table was on a jetty of sorts, positioning us in a veritable fish bowl. I tried to fight the feeling of vertigo.

"Babe, are you okay?" Brit reached for my elbow to steady me.

"Yes, I'm fine, just a bit dizzy. It'll pass. This is some place!" I looked around, absorbing the details. Fabulous glass pendant lights in a variety of colors hung throughout, casting a warm glow in some places and hot spots in others. I felt twelve years old.

"You are the most beautiful woman in this room." He reached for my hand, and I laughed.

"Brit, look around." I scanned three floors smattered with supermodels, goddesses, and basic beauties. "I feel so ordinary."

"You don't honestly think I would bother with someone who was ordinary, do you? I mean, let's be honest, Reese, look at me." My eyes must have bulged out of my head, because he burst out laughing. I did, too, when I realized he was kidding.

"You make that dress spectacular."

"Brit, the room, the flowers, the clothing, it's too much. I don't need anything but you. I'm very thankful to be here."

"Who, I mean, what did you do while I was in Amsterdam?" he stumbled purposely.

"What's wrong with you? " I demanded.

"I didn't mean to say that. It must be my suspicions talking."

"Suspicions?"

"You fucked that guy, the guy with the motorcycle. I saw him leaving your apartment. You went straight to him the minute we broke up." His cold gaze chilled me through.

"'We' did not break up. You broke up with me!" I said indignantly, not believing his gall.

"I said maybe we should take a break. I was asking for communication," he challenged. I instinctively looked around for an exit.

"You were leaving for Brazil. You didn't know what my 'problem' was, as if that wasn't enough to piss me off. I thought we were in a relationship, yet you were out making plans that didn't include me, without even running it by me. I had every right."

"Who are you—my mom? I have to run everything by you? Oh, that's right, my mom's dead." He squinted his eyes at me, poised to attack. Bastard.

"I'm sorry your parents are dead. That is, however, irrelevant."

"No, it isn't. I told you I went to Brazil because I was afraid of my feelings for you."

"You told me that after you came back."

"It doesn't matter. I wanted you to ask me not to leave. I wanted you to tell me we didn't need a break. You say you don't trust me or believe in my intentions, but look at you! You just hung up the phone and went on a fucking spree!" I gasped sharply.

"That's right! I don't trust you. I don't believe in you. I don't even know you! You frighten me, you intimidate me, and, for the record, Brady is a friend. He has a girlfriend." I had gone too far; I had tipped my hand. I never wanted him to know I was afraid of him. I needed to reel that back in. *"I'm afraid you'll leave me again, that you'll decide you're tired of me."* He leaned back in his chair and drained his glass of Tanqueray. I reached for my purse and he grabbed my wrist.

"Where do you think you're going?" My wrist throbbed but my face remained impassive.

CONSUMED

"To the restroom."

"Watch yourself," he warned, and I had no idea what he meant. My heart pounded as I wove my way through the crowd that had collected on the stairs leading to the third floor. Attempting to be subtle, I cast a casual glance up to our table. Brit stood at the railing, his eyes trained on me. He looked huge and imposing, a king holding court.

I scanned the room and was surprised how many people were also looking at him. I took a deep breath and braved the crushing throngs of people. I searched for a restroom sign and was thankful when a tall, attractive man read my mind.

"Go all of the way around the bar and take a sharp left. It isn't well marked, but you'll see the line." He smiled and I thanked him graciously. I didn't have to go to the bathroom at all, so I didn't mind standing in the line. The women around me chatted loudly about their options for the night ahead.

"Did you see that guy that went up to three?" I heard someone ask from just inside the door, out of my sight line.

"The guy in all black that walked in like he owned the place? Yeah. He was with someone, wasn't he?

"What does that matter?" They all went up in gales of laughter.

I emerged from the bathroom and saw the handsome gentleman who had provided directions leaning against the bar. He had a glass of champagne in one hand and what looked like scotch in the other. I averted my eyes and headed toward the third floor staircase.

"Hey, where's the fire?" he said, moving toward me.

"Oh, I need to be getting back." I smiled. He held out the champagne to me, and my heart stopped for a moment. Glancing upward, I saw Brit chatting with the waiter. "I really need to get back to my date. He'll be wondering where I am." I shrugged, but he stood in front of me.

"Just one sip," he urged. "You aren't from around here."

"No. I'm not. My boyfriend and I are here for the weekend. I haven't been here in years." I smiled politely.

He raised his glass and I met it with mine. "To New York being even

233

more alluring, at least for the weekend." I took one sip and attempted to hand back the glass, but he wouldn't accept. "Take it with you." I looked up at the jetty and Brit was nowhere to be seen. My pulse quickened as I said goodbye. I turned and ran smack into Brit's chest. He grasped both of my arms, champagne splashing my chest and dribbling into my cleavage.

"What the fuck is going on?" His eyes shifted back and forth between the man and I.

"I—this gentleman helped me find the bathroom." I wiggled loose of Brit's grasp and tried to smile. I was acutely aware of the champagne glass in my hand, as was Brit. He eyed it as if it were poison.

"Relax, buddy, I only bought the lady a drink to help her endure the trip back to her table." He extended his hand, which Brit ignored.

"Go back to the table," Brit demanded.

"Brit, please. He didn't know I was here on a date."

"Because you didn't tell him? Looking to trade me in?" His gaze met mine and my breathing became jagged. People were starting to notice the mounting storm.

"I wouldn't want to be with anyone on earth, let alone this bar, but you," I forced myself to say.

"I apologize," the man said, attempting to diffuse the situation. "I had to give it a shot, right?" Brit lunged and nearly knocked me over, the delicate flute shattering on the floor. The guy turned tail as quickly as he could and made for the door. I leaned against a column, thankful he had had the sense to bolt, wondering where the evening would take me.

I wanted to go back to the hotel and pack my things, but knew that wasn't an option, unless I was certain I wanted to end things for good. I was going to have to figure a way to make things right with Brit.

Guiding me around the mess of broken glass and champagne, he led me firmly by the arm back to the table. I steeled myself for the fight that was looming. He ran a hand through his head of thick, dark hair, which resettled seductively onto a furrowed brow.

"What kind of asshole buys someone else's date a drink?" He sighed

heavily, and my mind settled on the word "date." "Babe, are you okay? You looked terrified down there. I didn't mean to make a scene. He was just acting so nonchalant!" I was relieved Brit wasn't mad at me, and I couldn't stop a smile from spreading across my face. Everything was fine. Here we were in the most fabulous city in the country, and I just wanted to enjoy it.

"I'm fine. Thank you for coming to get me." I batted long, dark lashes at him and twirled a chunky curl around my finger. Distract him. He brought a hand to his heart.

"You will be the death of me."

Or vice versa, I thought.

51

"I don't think it's a good idea for us to go back there," Joel said to
Meridan. The sting operation had accomplished nothing. As they feared, no one
showed. Detective Adler managed the situation with help from several other
officers and Al Roenick. She and two detectives in plain clothes covered the
Balboa bar, while the others canvassed the lobby of the Grafton.

"I'm bored, Joel. At least send Roz." Joel pulled the phone away from his
ear. He detested whining.

"For the first time, he has no idea where you are. You've never been safer,
and I'm not going to jeopardize it."

"Well, if he thinks I'm at the Grafton, there's no reason Roz shouldn't be
able to come here."

"We don't know if any of us are being followed. It's too risky. Detective
Adler checked into the Grafton under your name. She'll be especially aware of
anyone who asks for you or is snooping around. Maybe he sensed a setup."

"When is something going to pop?"

"Pop?"

"You know, when is this going to be over? I can't handle it anymore."

"I don't know, Meridan, but you can be certain we're all doing our best to
keep you safe. Try to be nice to Noah."

"I hate Noah." Joel refused to indulge her petulance. She'd been
complaining about Noah's lack of attention for days.

"Call Jim. Relax. Why don't you take a bath and get into bed early?"

"I don't want to go to bed. I want to get out of this fucking room, Joel. I feel like a prisoner."

"How about better there than dead?" Joel snapped and regretted it instantly.

Meridan slammed the phone down without saying goodbye and flounced onto the bed.

"Problem?" Noah asked, not really caring. He'd had about all he could take of her indulgent superstar attitude and feared it was only going to get worse.

"As if you care! All you've done is ignore me and read that stupid gun magazine. You don't have any idea how hard this is for me. I'm tired, I'm scared, and I'm bored."

"What would you like to do?"

"Go out."

"No can do. Next?"

"Can we at least order out? You can go get it."

"Negatory. I'm not leaving you."

"Then you need to have someone from here go get me some cheese ravioli from Ago."

"Meridan, it's seven o'clock. Ago is a madhouse right now."

"And I want ravioli. Just do it, Noah. Isn't this what you get paid to do?"

"No."

"No?"

"No. It isn't what I get paid to do. I get paid to make sure you're alive."

"Well, I don't want you here anymore. Go away. Get Joel on the phone. Now!" Noah left the room to retrieve his cell phone and make the call in private. He could barely resist killing Meridan himself. "Mr. Goldstein? Noah here. We have a bit of a problem." He didn't want to appear he couldn't handle his job, so he downplayed the drama.

"What?"

"Well, Ms. Marks would like to be left alone for the evening, and she also would like cheese ravioli from Ago. What should I do?"

"You know what? I don't perceive any threat whatsoever. We offered her up on a silver platter, and the guy didn't show. She has a battalion of security at the hotel, so you're on call."

"Are you sure? I have no problem staying."

"As long as you sneak out of there, we should be fine. She's at the Four Seasons, for God's sake. What could go wrong?"

"What about the ravioli?"

"The what?"

"She wants cheese ravioli."

"Right. Let me call a courier and have them deal with this."

"Understood. I'll leave on foot and catch a cab on Olympic."

"Great idea. Hey, Noah. Don't take it so hard. She tends to eat people alive. She'll be fine tomorrow. This whole situation has actually strained her. I know it's hard to be sympathetic when she acts up, but I appreciate your effort."

"Thank you, sir. I'll speak with you in the morning." Noah hung up the phone and walked into the living area. Meridan was still on the bed, half pouting and half watching TV.

"Well?" she asked, a disgusted and defiant look on her face. Noah wondered how anyone actually found this woman attractive.

"You win. I'm leaving, and Joel is having your ravioli delivered."

"When?"

"I'm sorry?"

"When are you leaving, and when will my ravioli be here?" she demanded.

"Now, and I have no idea." Noah grabbed his sport coat and computer case and left without another word.

"Well! Of all the nerve!" Meridan gasped and began prowling around the room.

52

April 7th, 8:15 p.m.
Subject: Where are you?
From: Marksman

I don't know what to say to you right now. I am going to have to think about this.

April 7th, 8:18 p.m.
Subject:
From: Marksman

You are a self-centered bitch. How dare you invite me to dinner and then blow me off. It's one thing for me to invite you and be stood up, as usual. But quite another to be invited by you and stood up. I don't know what to say. I feel harassed.
B~

April 7th, 8:30 p.m.
Subject:
From: Marksman

I've decided you need to be punished for what you've done. I'm not sure yet what that punishment should be. Preliminary thought has generated some

ideas. No spa treatments and maybe no shopping. I haven't decided whether
this is severe enough for your infractions, but we can start there. I'm depending
on you to monitor yourself until we sit down and agree on this formally.
B~

Roz sat, riveted, scrolling through the post-setup e-mails. It was mind-bending. He vacillated from anger to forgiveness in minutes. She lost herself in thoughts of his apartment or house. Was it lined with tin foil? Was there simply a table, a mattress and an exposed light bulb dangling from the ceiling? Did he function in society? Was he wealthy? Did the woman who e-mailed know anything? Was this the same guy or guys?

Startled by the ringing of her phone, her martini glass tumbled into her lap and onto the floor. "Fuck!" She looked around for something to mop up the mess but decided to answer the phone and let it soak into her robe before getting up.

"Hello?" Her annoyance was obvious to Joel, who was in a mood of his own.

"What's your problem?"

"I just spilled my fucking martini. I need a vacation. Why can't someone get a line on this guy?"

"Tell me. Did you read all of them?"

"No, I was just getting started. Have you talked to Meridan?"

"Are you shitting me? I tried to explain this is for her own good. I left my laptop there. I told her to surf the net. She said she doesn't know how," Joel said, and Roz could almost hear him rolling his eyes.

"Yes, she does. She's being obstinate," Roz sighed.

"The guy's a harmless whacko. I'm just about done with all of this drama. She wants to call the e-mail woman. She thinks it's the only way to solve this problem."

"What do you think about that?"

"We have nothing solid that ties her to this case. How can someone supposedly emotionally disturbed outwit a team of really smart people?"

"Oh, but don't forget Meridan—the idiot from a village we call Hollywood."

Roz snorted. "Joel, you're so funny. You ever think about a career in stand-up, let me know. "

"Sure, I might throw away my education, job security, and lucrative practice to be a starving artist."

"Can I have your car?"

"Sure, and my house, as long as you take my wife."

"See? So funny."

"What do you think? About having Meridan make the call?"

"What does Detective Ford think?"

"Does it really matter? He had to pull her guards to aid with the bust and now she's run off Noah. I alerted the hotel security and offered an incentive to keep a close watch on her room. Detective Ford wants to try to set him up again tomorrow. There's been no activity at the Grafton at all. How can they be so inept? I don't imagine you and I will emerge as new caped crusaders, but fuck! This is what they do for a living. I'll make sure the bastard rots in jail or a mental institution, but they need to find him first."

"Let her make the call," Roz said.

53

Meridan shivered as she read the latest e-mail from B. At first she felt bad about invading Joel's privacy by looking at his mail, but since it all was for her, too bad. Further, he told her to use the laptop if she wanted. It was time to take matters into her own hands, literally.

B,

I apologize for missing our dinner last night. I fell very ill, bad water I think. You can relate. I was thinking maybe we need to get to know each other better. Either that or you leave me the fuck alone!!!!!!!!!!!!!!!

B,

I've been giving it some thought and, well, I think you're an excellent writer/ crazy fucking bastard, and we do need to get together. I've enjoyed your letters and e-mails about as much as jabbing a shrimp fork into my eye. It's wonderful to have such a devoted and stark raving mad fan. I appreciate all of your gifts. They were very thoughtful and imaginative, psychotic and demented! How nice of you to remember important nights in my life and attempt to ruin them. Especially the cork from Ago, that will always be the night I broke it off with Christian York as far as you fucking know you creepy, crazy asshole. You were so right about him. Thanks so much for listening and being there like cancer, I couldn't get through without your support. How about lunch on Monday? I'll swing by the asylum.

She laughed as she created a few more and sent them to the draft folder with the others. Later, she would pick one to mail. She wasn't sure what tack she wanted to take. She was furious he had changed her life so drastically. What did he want? A friend, a girlfriend? A relationship? Sex? All of the above? To be published? To make a movie?

The phone jangled and she nearly knocked her wine onto the keyboard. Joel.

"Can I go home?

"Meridan? Knock it off. Just give me until Tuesday morning. It's been tough to run down information over the weekend. Roz and I talked, and if you want to try and reach that woman, go ahead."

"Really? Should I call her or e-mail her?"

"I don't care." The call ended abruptly. Meridan had gotten at least one thing she wanted.

Copying the number from the e-mail, she pushed send. Two, three, four rings, then an answering machine.

"Hi, um, right. Hi, I wish I knew your name, it would make things easier. This is Meridan Marks, and I was calling regarding your e-mails. If you could call me back? My cell number is 305-555-9871. Thank you."

Damn! She had really expected her to answer and talk and be a font of information about this guy or guys or whatever. She threw the phone onto the bed, releasing a loud sigh. What was she going to do with herself?

She wanted company so badly. She called Christian, but he didn't answer. She left Jim a message asking him to call her as soon as he could. She flipped through the channels and stumbled onto one of her own movies on cable. Her mood lifted a bit, and she raided the mini-bar and called the woman again before settling in to watch one of her first romantic comedies.

By the time the ravioli arrived, she had left the woman a couple more messages. She devoured it, the only thing that would keep her from waking with a crashing hangover.

Just before passing out, three quarters of the way through a bottle of Cristal, she drunkenly drafted an e-mail to the woman.

Ive called you fouur timees tionight. I guess youre not going to call me back. If you are so scared wy did you get into it at all.. forget I tried you are just a hpnoney anyway.

Eridan

54

"Reese?" His voice broke through her slumber. She rolled onto her side and propped herself up.

"You look like you're coming down with the flu," she said, leaning into him and putting her hand on his forehead.

"No, I've just been making myself ill." He held up the journal to indicate the source.

"I'm sorry you had to read that."

"I didn't have to. I wanted to. I had no idea how much he fucked with your mind."

She was quiet for a long moment, formulating her thoughts. "When my dad would get mad when I was little, I would do anything I could to diffuse his anger. While reading all this, it seems at times the same response. It was as if I was blindly doing whatever he wanted."

"Don't beat yourself up. He used love, or the promise of love and affection, to manipulate you."

Brady stretched his long body out on the bed and laced his hands behind his head. Lynden explored his face, wondering where the conversation would go next. She had no idea how much he'd read.

"Why did you keep going back to him, Reese?"

"I couldn't help it. Do you hate me?"

"Hate you? Why?"

"For being weak?"

"Weak? You're the strongest woman I've ever known. You carried all of this alone, with no help, no one to talk to. You've built an amazing life for yourself, with no help from anyone. As far as hating you? I love you, Reese." Lynden couldn't help but succumb to emotion when the sincerity of his words settled on her.

"I love you, too. What will happen now?"

"With what?" He wiped at her tears and kissed her cheeks.

"Dorrie?"

"Hmm." He kissed her lightly on the mouth and looked at his watch. "Well, Dorrie is about six hours away. What do you say I lose myself in you for the next two, then get on a plane and deal with her then."

She gazed into his soft, loving eyes and dreaded the moment he'd have to leave. She feared Dorrie's power over him.

"What if she wants to work things out?"

"I'm on the cusp of having everything I've wanted since I was nineteen years old. Do you really think she has any power over me?" Lynden shook her head before getting out of bed.

"Are you hungry?" she called from her closet.

"Surprisingly, yes. Earlier, I thought I'd never eat again."

"I'll whip up something for us?"

"Sounds perfect. Do you have those *Glitterati* articles? I'd like to read them."

"They're in my library next to my laptop."

He went to the library, while she headed to the kitchen.

When breakfast was almost ready, she called to Brady, who had been conspicuously absent.

"No wonder you e-mailed the attorney!" he said, bursting into the kitchen, both *Glitterati* magazines in his hand. "The fucking balls on these guys!"

"You think it's them?"

"There's no doubt in my mind. I'm sorry I was angry with you the other day. I can see now, after everything I've read today, she's in for a world of hurt if you don't get involved."

"So, what do you think I should do now?" She flipped an enormous omelet and savored the delicious aroma. Cutting it, she placed the larger half in front of Brady.

"Reese, I understand your need to help her. I had no idea how bad it was for you."

Lynden nodded her agreement as she chewed a bite of rye toast. "If he, or they, end up harming her, I would feel horrible and partly responsible."

"She has protection. You didn't. You were a defenseless young woman in love with a man who preyed on you."

"I'm not going to L.A. I don't want to testify. I don't want to get involved any further. Quite frankly, I don't know anything else that will help them."

"How about if we agree to monitor the situation? If something heavy goes down, we'll deal with it then?" She nodded and tried not to think of Brady's departure.

55

Meridan's curiosity overrode her crashing hangover, and she dragged
herself from bed and to the computer. She was dying to know if the woman had
written back. She closed the heavy drapes before fully opening her eyes.

Two new messages, one from Al Roenick and the other from B. B?! She
looked at the draft folder and realized instantly what she had done. All the
e-mails she had written out of frustration, anger and hatred were gone, released
when she sent the message to that woman.

Her heart thundered in her chest as she tried to mentally recreate the
e-mails. The subject line of his reply read "Watch yourself." As if her spine had
dissolved, she slumped, aware she'd done the stupidest thing in the entire realm
of stupidity.

She opened Al Roenick's mail first.

*Joel, the information you requested. R. Lynden Hatcher, 5948 Edmondson,
Dallas, TX 75205. The phone was ultimately traced to this address. Don't ask
me how. Don't reveal me as your source unless absolutely necessary. AR*

Wow, a name. Lynden? Was that a man? What did "R" stand for? Wasn't
there a president named Lynden? Or Landon? Something. She'd never heard
the name for a woman. Maybe this was her husband?

She decided she'd need a drink before proceeding to B's e-mail. Almost a
half a bottle of champagne remained in the chiller, enough to make a couple of
mimosas. She wheeled in her room service cart from the hall and grabbed the

pitcher of orange juice. Brilliant. Carbonation danced on her tongue and for a moment she forgot her dilemma.

Bracing herself, she opened the e-mail. It was empty. Perplexed, she leaned back and noticed, for the first time, a long floral box on the bottom shelf of the service cart. It was gorgeous and pristine, with a large pink ribbon. B? No, he'd never put flowers in a box. Jim. He missed her as much as she missed him. She slowly undid the ribbon, imagining him slowly undoing the belt of her robe. *Soon*, she reminded herself.

The smell hit her before her eyes focused on the rotting flowers, hideously slimy and black. She retched, vomiting onto the floor. She threw down the box and vomited again. The stench was consuming. An envelope sealed in plastic bearing her name rested atop the flowers. She inched her way over to the box with her nose plugged and her mouth shut. With a fork she snagged the baggie and raced to another room so she could read without being assaulted by the acrid odor of decomposition.

Meridan,

You have awakened in me something that, until this moment, I was unsure still existed. I have to say the murderous rage humming through my body right now is almost orgasmic. I'm savoring your e-mails. They are so raw, just the way you are going to be after the sixth, seventh, eighth time I fuck you. This, of course, will not be as pleasurable for you as it will be for me, since you won't be conscious. Hell, I can't say with absolute certainty you'll even be alive. I actually had misgivings about my plans for you. I even felt you weren't ready when last I touched you. Now I know you are ready to experience the ultimate pleasure and price for your behavior. I have really had it with you.
Looking forward to your demise,
Britten Holden

"JesusfuckingChrist!" she yelled, the letter slipping from her grasp. She raced to the computer. Britten Holden. That was one of the names! That woman, that R. Lynden or whatever the fuck her name is, she knew this guy!

Her e-mail still was in Joel's inbox.

Britten. Blood screamed through her veins as she called security and requested transportation to the LAX charter area. She demanded two guards escort her from her room to a private car. She would not be calling Roz, Joel, Cameron or Noah; she needed to do this on her own.

She raced around the room, throwing things into a suitcase. She'd already brushed her teeth, thank God, because a ponytail and jeans and T-shirt would have to do—she was out of here!

The knock on the door caused bile to rise in her throat again.

"Ms. Marks? Security." She approached the door tentatively, trying not to breathe or look at the flowers.

"Prove it."

"You just called, ma'am. We have your car waiting."

"Oh, thank God!" she said as she opened the door to two imposing gentlemen in dark suits. "Come in! Turns out it was a very bad idea sending my security home." She pointed to the box on the floor. "Get rid of that. I'm ready." She threw her gigantic Louis Vuitton bag over her shoulder. "Get the suitcase. I need to get the fuck out of here. Make sure no one is out there. Send him first."

"Do we need to call Mr. Goldstein?"

"I'm a grown fucking woman. As a matter of fact, a grown fucking woman who pays all of the bills, so you listen to me. There's a crazy fucking maniac out there, and, I mean, he could be right out there, ready to kill me."

"Ma'am." The bigger guy held up his palms in an effort to stop her from exploding.

"Don't call me ma'am. I will fucking handle Joel Goldstein. Now go!" She yelled, pointing at the door. The bigger guy took the lead and called clear when he reached the elevator. Meridan broke into a dead run and took off toward his voice. They loaded into the freight elevator and utilized the service area in the underbelly of the hotel to get to the limousine in the cargo area.

"LAX, no stops," one of the guys informed the driver. Meridan's heart was roaring and she was nauseated. Customarily, she consulted with at least one of her people on every move she made. This time, though, they'd be furious with her for inciting B by sending those e-mails, even if by accident.

R. Lynden has been so right, she thought. He *was* potentially murderous. He had brazenly signed his name, and he was ready to come for her, unafraid of being caught. She shuddered despite the car's perfectly controlled climate.

56

The void created by Brady's absence jettisoned Lynden back to a time when depression was unavoidable and inescapable. Over the past few days together, so many emotions had been unearthed. She had transitioned easily from best friend to lover, but sex was not the only factor. There was love, and it had changed from brotherly friendship to the poignant intimacy shared by lovers. Lynden couldn't help feeling uneasy about Brady's return to Atlanta.

Lynden glanced at the bedside clock. She knew Brady was still in the air, and her stomach roiled with dread. Dorrie would be picking him up from the airport, and he planned to start negotiating tonight. Lynden was certain Dorrie would never give up Brady, just as she would never forgive Lynden for nearly getting him killed. Dorrie may not want him, but she wanted Lynden to have him even less.

She lay in her bed, surrounded by pillows soaked with mascara and tears, wondering what it was going to take to make her whole again. She knew the answer. Brit and Ash had to be located and put in jail or an institution. She could relax knowing they were captive. Certainly, Meridan Marks's people would be able to find them. She stared at the ceiling and racked her brain for a way to help without exposing herself. She dozed off, sleep having long ago become her primary coping mechanism for depression.

The doorbell rang and Lynden bolted upright, confused and disoriented. Her clock read five-thirty p.m. She swore heartily and got up when the doorbell chimed again, fishing a small-caliber handgun from under her pillow and heading to the door.

The house was flooded with light and warmth, which lifted her gloom somewhat. After she determined whatever this urgent matter at the door was, she promised to get out, call Dane, have a late lunch or an early dinner, and tell him everything that had transpired.

She stopped dead in her tracks when a storm of thunderous pounding issued from her front door. Afraid to call out, she inched closer to see the kitchen monitor that showed the view on the front porch. A woman. She wasn't in a FedEx uniform. A neighbor? She was frantically pounding on the solid wood door. There was something familiar about her—dark curly hair, big sunglasses, and then, straight at the camera, Lynden's own face.

"Can I help you?" Lynden asked through the intercom.

"Oh, thank God. It's Meridan Marks. I'm looking for a woman who lives here."

"Jesus Christ!" Lynden jumped back from the panel as if shocked, wondering how in God's name Meridan Marks had found her way to her front door.

"What do you want?" Lynden asked.

"Please, are you the woman who sent the e-mails to me? I need to see you. I'm terrified." Meridan's voice was tight, not at all the mellifluous voice to which fans were accustomed.

"Hold on," Lynden said, slipping the gun into the back of her pants and pulling down her shirt. "Are you alone?"

"Of course I'm alone. Who would I bring?" she snapped, as if it were nothing out of the ordinary for a famous actress to show up on a stranger's doorstep, with or without an entourage.

Lynden unlocked the door slowly and was nearly knocked over as Meridan burst through.

"Good Lord, it's three hundred degrees out there," she announced, walking directly to the kitchen to set her enormous handbag on the counter. She fished around inside for her sunglass case and put away her favorite Gucci shades. Finally, as if remembering what she was doing, she turned her attention to Lynden. "I'm . . ." she began, stopping when her eyes met Lynden's. "Stunned.

How—how did you do this?" she asked, eyes narrowed and inspecting every inch of Lynden, approaching slowly as if she were a dog who might spring suddenly.

"Do what?" Lynden asked, confused and surprised herself. Meridan looked more like her in real life than she did in the movies or in print.

"Make yourself look like me." She bent at the waist to observe each side of Lynden's face. While they weren't identical, the resemblance was eerie.

"You'd have to ask my parents. They did it."

"When?"

"The spring of 1977." Lynden quipped, annoyed.

Meridan rolled her eyes. "I mean, the cosmetic surgery," she condescended, as if speaking to a toddler.

"I haven't had any. This is what I look like. I'd be willing to whip out my high school yearbooks and family albums if you don't believe me." Lynden raised her left eyebrow in a challenge.

Meridan reached out toward Lynden, who raised her hand defensively.

"What's wrong with you?" Meridan demanded, furrowing her brow.

"What are you doing?" Lynden scooped her hair back with the rubber band on her wrist.

"Is that natural curl?"

"Yes."

"How do you walk around looking like me and not get mobbed?"

"I usually wear my hair up or back, and I almost always wear glasses."

"Why?"

"Why what?"

"Why not get contacts and wear your hair down?" Lynden ignored the personal question and countered.

"Can I help you?"

"Oh, right. It's just spooky. I mean, I'm looking at someone who could be my sister. Are you adopted?"

"No, and a lot of people look alike."

"This is really alike, though. Look." She grabbed Lynden's hand before she could snatch it away and led her to the mirror behind her dining table. Meridan was right. Spooky.

Meridan's hair was longer, but the basic color was the same, despite highlights. Unlike Meridan, Lynden had a widow's peak, which kept her from wearing her hair parted in the middle as Meridan often did.

"These teeth are caps." Meridan tapped her front two teeth. "I'm telling you because I think it's pretty obvious. I mean, I have nice teeth anyway, but this is more alluring. It draws more attention to the mouth." Lynden cocked her head a bit and had to agree.

Meridan turned from the mirror and folded her arms in front of her, one hip cocked out, her eyes riveted to Lynden's.

"Why are you here?" Lynden asked, trying to ignore the surreal sensation settling over her.

"Do people say you look like me?" Meridan asked, clearly not ready to move forward.

"Every day."

"Do you consider it a compliment?"

"No."

"What?" Meridan gaped with obvious offence.

"I think I look like me. Lynden Hatcher." She shrugged her shoulders for affect. She was one of the little people.

"You *are* the woman. What does the R. stand for?"

"What R.?" Lynden asked weakly, wondering how Meridan knew about her first initial.

"Your name came up R. Lynden Hatcher. I didn't know if you were a guy or maybe your husband."

"I don't have a husband. How did you find me?"

"My private detective found you, something about your cell phone. He didn't get specific. Do you have anything to drink?"

"I'm sorry. Please, come in." Lynden was horrified by her manners and gestured toward the great room and its inviting couches. She was relieved she had taken Brady to the airport that morning; she was dressed and wearing a touch of makeup, not looking nearly as bad as she should for laying in bed all day crying.

"Can I get my suitcase?"

"Suitcase?"

"I need to stay with you. I need to talk to you."

"Why don't you pull your car into my garage?"

57

Once both women were settled on opposing ends of the massive couch in front of the fireplace, the tension began to abate. Lynden had reluctantly opened her guest room upstairs for Meridan and left her alone to unpack while she busied herself in the kitchen. She arranged several cheeses on a marble cheese tray with some grapes, apples and blackberries, cheese knives, thick slices of toasted garlic bread, and water crackers. She emptied a container of mixed Greek olives into a bowl, popping a large Alfonso into her mouth.

She pulled a perfectly chilled bottle of Roederer Brut from the wine captain and popped the cork. The smell wafted up to her nostrils and she inhaled deeply, her mouth watering a bit.

What had propelled Meridan Marks to Texas? She seemed genuinely afraid, but the jury was still out. Lynden tried not to be judgmental, but she seemed completely self-absorbed, arrogant, and not very bright. She admonished herself for being so quick to form an opinion. She was, after all, worshipped and adored by millions.

"Did I hear champagne?" Meridan called as she walked down the back steps into the kitchen. Lynden made a mental note to comb the stairs once Meridan was tucked into bed.

"It's not every day I have visiting royalty." Lynden smiled and removed two hand-painted flutes from a glass-front cabinet.

"Roederer! I love Roederer. Cristal is wonderful, too. Have you ever had it?"

Lynden responded with a quizzical look and then reminded herself

Meridan had no way of knowing what she did for a living. She poured them both a glass and led Meridan to the couch after sliding the bottle into an ice bucket. Meridan looked around, seeing the house for the first time.

"You live here all alone?" she asked after a long pull from her glass.

"Yes."

"Why aren't you married?"

"Why aren't you?"

"Well, my life is a little intimidating."

"Why would it intimidate someone as famous as Christian York?" Meridan tilted her head and seemed to contemplate.

"Well, not for Christian, but definitely anyone else."

"You and Christian have been dating forever. Why don't you get married?"

"Hollywood marriages never last."

"What about Ronald Reagan and Nancy Davis?"

"Who is Nancy Davis?"

"Nancy Reagan."

"She wasn't an actress. And he was the president," Meridan said as if Lynden were the imbecile. Lynden resisted correcting her.

The women sipped their champagne silently, both waiting for the other to begin.

"Meridan? Why are you here? Has something happened?" Lynden asked sincerely and Meridan nodded, her eyes tearing up a bit. "Tell me what's going on. I'll try to help you if I can," she assured, and Meridan wiped a tear from her cheek.

"It's so much worse." Meridan paused either for effect or to collect herself, Lynden wasn't sure which.

"Worse than what? Since when?" Lynden asked. Meridan shook her head and wiped another tear. Lynden handed her a tissue from the box on the coffee table. Meridan had looked at it, but made no attempt to get one.

"Thanks." Meridan was silent for a long moment and then rose to replenish her glass.

"Here, let me," Lynden offered, also refilling her own.

"Everything is so much worse than we, my people, have let on."

"I'm sorry," Lynden said honestly, knowing she deserved pity if she were being stalked by Brit or Ash Holden.

"It's horrible. I'm terrified. I don't know what he looks like, but he's everywhere I go. He knows everything I do, what I eat, what I drink. He sends me cards, letters, scripts, faxes and now e-mail." Her voice rose gradually until she was almost yelling at Lynden. "I can't believe you never called me back."

"What? You called me?" Meridan nodded and Lynden looked around for her cell phone. She got up and searched her purse. She had turned it off after talking to Meridan's attorney Saturday. She thought for a moment and remembered seeing it next to her bed. It had been there the whole time, off.

Oh God, Brady might have tried to call her! She raced to her room and a moment later sat back on the couch with the phone pressed to her ear. Five messages. Meridan.

"Sorry," Lynden erased the first message. "You again." She listened, her left eyebrow arching at Meridan's bitchy tone in her voice mail. She erased the message.

"You again, you're mad. I'm sorry I didn't call you back. Maybe this whole trip could've been avoided." Meridan shook her head. "My, you are persistent. You e-mailed?" Meridan told her to forget the e-mail.

"I was upset. I thought you were ignoring me. You can't imagine how many people came forward to help, but they were just fans taking advantage of my pain!" She stressed the word pain, and Lynden sat motionless, watching the actress pontificate.

"I need to know about him."

"Them."

"Is it really *them*?" Lynden nodded. "Why do you think it's both of them?"

"When I read that *Glitterati* article about your ranch here being broken into, it made me wonder if one lived or was based in L.A. and the other one here." Lynden shivering at the thought of either one of the men being anywhere near her.

"His e-mails sound like he's crazy!" Meridan sighed.

"Ash is mentally imbalanced. Hell, I say Ash, but they both are. I only know what Brit told me." She shook her head.

"He threatened to kill me this morning," Meridan said softly.

"What?" Lynden was on her feet. "How did things escalate? I read he was sending gifts and there was a break-in or two, but you weren't harmed at all."

"The police tried to set him up, but it didn't work. I accidentally e-mailed him yesterday." Meridan, still ashamed, told Lynden about the e-mails she had sent.

"Oh, my God! It's almost funny. No wonder he was pissed off! If it's Brit, he's not crazy about being confronted, and if it's Ash, he's not too excited about people accusing him of being off kilter." Lynden's eyes widened, and she tried to comprehend Brit or Ash's reaction. Rage. Pure and simple. "What happened this morning?"

Meridan launched into a lengthy soliloquy detailing the past days' events, holding Lynden rapt with her dramatic prowess.

After what seemed like an hour, Meridan paused to shovel a Roquefort-slathered cracker into her mouth. "I'm starving," she managed, struggling to swallow.

"Let me make us some dinner," Lynden offered, relieved at the break in the conversation.

"Dinner? It's only, like, five o'clock in L.A.," she snorted. She picked up a small chunk of hard Parmesan cheese and held it up, raising her eyebrows in question.

"Parmigiano Reggiano—hard Parmesan cheese."

"Like on a Caesar salad?" Lynden nodded and sipped her champagne. She was more than content with fruit and cheese and alcohol, the last of which was welcomingly relaxing. Lynden watched as Meridan inhaled the grapes and blackberries while issuing compliments.

"This is like a restaurant. I mean, the snacks. Are you a caterer?"

"No." She paused and wondered briefly what she should be calling herself. "I'm a consultant of sorts."

"What sorts?"

"I'm a food critic. I have my own column. I also consult with people who have restaurants or want to open restaurants. I give advice." Meridan nodded seeming content.

"How does someone become a food critic?" A valid question, Lynden thought, ruminating over her answer for a moment, nibbling on a huge black olive.

"I have a degree in writing. Actually, a couple of them. And I love food. It seemed a logical choice."

"But how did you get a column?" Meridan seemed impressed, as if becoming a box-office smash was commonplace.

"I was writing freelance for a magazine, fresh out of college and trying to earn a living, and our critic passed away. He'd been a part of the magazine for, like, a thousand years." She chuckled. "Everyone got to submit reviews of local restaurants. They wanted to hire either from within or one of their contributing writers." Meridan nodded and chewed.

"What did you leave out of the articles?" Lynden asked, trying to conceal her intense interest.

"My God, you won't believe it!" Her eyes were wide again, and Lynden knew nothing she said would surprise her in any way. She nodded for her to continue, and after Meridan was done chewing the last of her mouthful, she launched into the harrowing tale of the break-in.

"He left something under my pillow. He'd been that close to me." She held up her thumb and forefinger to indicate about an inch.

"You didn't wake up?" Lynden couldn't imagine sleeping through anything like that.

"I'd had a few drinks. Anyway, he left something for me on my dining room table."

"What?" Lynden prodded.

"One of my PR photos and a note. A pair of my panties had been, um, used." Meridan expected a questioning glance, but the statement sent Lynden's hands to her hair to evaluate her ponytail. Meridan furrowed her brow and expounded unnecessarily. "He used them to get off."

"I got it!" Lynden paled a bit and Meridan placed a hand on her knee.

"Are you okay? You should eat something." She spread some cheese onto a water cracker and handed it to her. Lynden smiled graciously, not yet prepared to share much of her side of the story.

"What was under your pillow?" she asked, dreading the answer.

"Oh, yeah. A scarf. One that he could have used to choke the life out of me."

"What did it look like?"

"It was gorgeous. I wish the police hadn't taken it." Lynden's stomach rolled, knowing before Meridan spoke it was shades of fuchsia, purple, blue, and red.

"It was mine," Lynden said, regretting saying the words the second they left her mouth.

"I don't think so," Meridan replied, indignant. Suddenly, it occurred to Lynden that Meridan knew nothing about her relationship with Brit or Ash. "When did you meet these people?"

"1997."

"Mmmm." Meridan paused, tilting her head, and searched the ceiling for answers. "I think I have the answer." Lynden's almond eyes widened, anxious for the "answer". "My first film came out in 1996."

"And . . ."

"And, they fell in love with me then. You looked like me. They stalked you until they could get to me." Lynden choked on her champagne. She coughed and hacked and cleared her throat for what seemed like twenty minutes, all the while digesting Meridan's absurd statement.

"Meridan," she began and coughed again. "That's not the case."

"Lynden, it doesn't take a brain scientist to figure this out. They're obsessed with me. And, now that you've given me a time line, I understand how it's all come down to this."

"What are you talking about?"

"Can you imagine worshipping someone for over, what? Ten years! No wonder he—they are fucked up." She gulped her champagne and held out the glass for more. Lynden wanted to snatch it from her and smash it against the side of her head. Brit had never compared her or mentioned any resemblance to another woman. It was incomprehensible to Lynden, having been destroyed by Brit, that she didn't own that destruction.

It shouldn't come as a surprise that Meridan was arrogant and self-absorbed, she told herself. She tried to reel in her own emotions and make sense of them. She poured more champagne for Meridan and got up to make another selection.

Meridan continued prattling on about her various other less-than-stable fans, stopping abruptly when she heard another champagne cork pop.

"Cristal! You're so good to me!"

"Maybe I should cook. Do you like red meat?"

"Are you kidding? Doesn't everyone?"

"Actually, a whole bunch of people don't, and most of them live in Los Angeles. I thought I should check. Potatoes? Spinach?" Meridan nodded to all.

"How do you know how to make all of this stuff? Do you have a cookbook?" Meridan said, as she observed the steam rising, the bacon crackling, the vegetables portioned, washed and waiting.

Lynden shook her head from her position seated on the island.

"When you eat out as much as I do for work, you pick up on tastes, smells, you learn what goes together. I guess I have a knack for it." She shrugged and nibbled on a leftover piece of baguette, the rest of which was broiling to make croutons for the salad.

"What are we having?"

"To start, we have Caesar salad, a bed of romaine lettuce, topped with crisp, uncured bacon, green onions, hardboiled egg and homemade garlic butter croutons with fresh Caesar dressing."

"What else?" Meridan leaned on the counter, and Lynden was struck again by how similar they looked. Meridan was at least two inches taller and wearing very high heels. Lynden felt like the ugly duckling version of this elegant swan. She reminded herself to make an effort the next morning.

"Mashed potatoes with spinach and a bit of cream." Meridan clapped, reminding Lynden of Gia and the fact she hadn't spoken with her since Brady arrived, since the *Glitterati* article. "Filet mignon with a wild mushroom reduction."

"I'm impressed. You're so normal." Lynden let out a deep laugh. It may have been the least accurate assessment ever made.

"I was, at one time."

"What happened?" Meridan asked, but Lynden wasn't ready.

"Life, I suppose," she said simply, and pulled the croutons out of the oven, turned them with a spatula and put them back under the broiler on the lowest rack so they would crisp without burning.

"I know what you mean! I swear."

"Tell me about Meridan Marks. Is that your real name?"

"What? You really don't know?"

"I write for a magazine; I don't tend to read them."

"Hmm . . . You aren't interested since you look like me?"

"I've never been interested in celebrity."

"Come on, everyone is star-struck."

"Not me. I wouldn't want to be famous for anything."

"Why?"

Lynden let her question sink in and searched for the right answer. She was lying. She had wanted to be a novelist, and being a successful novelist brought fame and notoriety.

"It seems like a hassle is all," she said.

"I love it."

"I believe you." Lynden laughed.

"I do. Every bit of it. Well, except for Brit."

"Brit." Meridan's conversational tone nauseated her. As though she were speaking of a friend.

"Yeah. Britten Holden. He signed his name to that letter this morning," Meridan said nonchalantly, and Lynden excused herself, barely making it to the bathroom before the torrent of champagne with a few chunks of bread and cracker cascaded into the toilet and splashed on the floor. She sank to her knees, her feelings swirling like darkness threatening to consume her. The shrill scream of the smoke detectors cut through her fog and she wiped her mouth, bolting from the bathroom.

"The croutons!" she yelled, rushing to the kitchen. Meridan seemed confused by the smoke and the noise; she had managed, however, to put on an oven mitt. Lynden pushed her aside and extricated the burning cookie sheet, dropped it into the sink, and flooded it with water. Effortlessly, she hoisted herself onto the island and fanned the smoke detector with a towel. After a couple of minutes, the shrieking stopped and she jumped down.

"Sorry about that," she said. Meridan's eyes were red and watery from the smoke, providing the perfect cover for her own tears.

"No problem. I can live without croutons. They hurt my mouth sometimes, you know, like Captain Crunch?" Lynden erupted into laughter, and Meridan joined her.

Lynden laughed until she didn't feel like crying anymore. She removed the potatoes from the stove and dumped them into a waiting colander. Once rinsed, she put them back in the pan, adding cream, pepper and a pat of butter.

"Could you get in that drawer," she pointed, "and hand me the masher?" Meridan jumped to task.

"What does it look like?" Lynden suppressed a giggle.

"Like a flat coil." Meridan held up a black whisk and then the masher. Lynden reached for it as she continued to sauté the mushrooms and onions in red wine, swirling them gently, coating them thoroughly.

"Thanks." Lynden mashed strenuously and folded the spinach into the warm, soft blend.

Meridan watched in awe as Lynden set two places at the large square nook table and finalized all of the preparations. Feeling a tinge of insecurity, Lynden had purposely pulled out all of the stops. After all, the kitchen was the stage on which she performed.

"Dinner is served," Lynden announced.

"A girl could get used to this." Meridan smiled warmly. "This is one of the corks."

"What?" Lynden stopped, fork poised in front of her mouth.

"This wine was one of the corks he left for me. I thought Christian had done it because it's his favorite. Brit must have been there. He must have seen us. He hates the fact Christian and I are together. As a matter of fact, that seems to bother him the most. He's so jealous."

"Wow, my eyes are still burning from all of that smoke." Lynden smiled weakly, hoping Meridan wouldn't notice her tears. She doesn't even know she is driving a knife through my heart, Lynden conceded. It was bad enough Brit had destroyed the person she was, but for Meridan to insinuate he did so for reasons having nothing to do with her was unbearable. She pushed the thought away and poured them each a glass of Grgich Hills cabernet.

"So, anyway, Brit insisted I break it off with Christian. You can imagine what Christian thought of that. As a matter of fact, Christian has extra security because Brit keeps threatening him." Lynden swallowed hard, wondering if it were really possible she had been nothing more than an accessible version of Meridan Marks for them.

Meridan demolished every single bite on her plate with unbridled enthusiasm. "Meridan . . . what are you doing here?"

"I need to know everything about Brit and Ash." She wasn't yet comfortable with Meridan, not enough to confide the most significant and tumultuous experience of her life; to tell her about the man who had altered her infinitely, left her a shell of herself, some watered down, tepid version. "I want them captured. I need to feel safe. I haven't felt safe in months. He's changed my life. He's forced me from my home. I live in a hotel, for God's sake. You can't imagine."

Yes, she could. Meridan wanted to talk, but Lynden was spent, acutely aware she had not heard from Brady. She left Meridan in front of the television and, after cleaning the kitchen, alone, promised her cooperation the next day and dragged herself to bed.

58

"What's that smell?" Meridan asked as she made her way down the back steps Lynden had just finished combing. Lynden cringed. She would have to figure a way to get Meridan to use the front steps.

"Shouldn't a movie star make more of a grand entrance?" she hinted and nodded her head toward the front staircase.

Meridan smiled. "Good point. I'll try that later." She headed straight for the coffee pot as Lynden put the finishing touches on breakfast and brought it to the table.

"I thought you might enjoy eggs Benedict, Lynden style." The skim milk she offered Meridan for her coffee was refused.

"I love eggs Benedict. What makes it Lynden style?"

"Spinach."

"Sounds wonderful. You must have dates lined up around the block, wanting you to cook for them." A pang of sadness seeped through Lynden's cheerful façade. She'd settle for a phone call from Brady. Lynden smiled as she led Meridan to the table.

"Do you . . . have a busy schedule today?" Meridan asked in between enormous bites.

"I have one meeting later I can move if I need to."

"I kind of crashed your life, didn't I?"

"Not really. I have a flexible schedule and tend to work at home most of the time."

"Writing?"

"Writing, planning, prospecting, I do many different things to keep from getting bored."

Lynden sat back in her chair and admired the enthusiasm with which Meridan approached eating.

"So, tell me all about Brit," Meridan said, not even capable of fathoming how hard his name hit Lynden. What appetite she'd had dissolved immediately.

Lynden preoccupied herself with her coffee, her mind racing. To her dismay, she felt an overwhelming sadness approach like the grim reaper. Slow, subversive, and set on stealing her soul. "Don't you need to call anyone? Let them know you're okay?"

"I will. I probably already should have. They're going to be furious with me." Meridan seemed so innocent, so honestly afraid, Lynden considered letting her in.

Perhaps it would be therapeutic to open up, to talk about it again so soon after she and Brady had opened the wound. She spent so much time trying not to think about that time in her life, it was difficult knowing what to say.

"Meridan, I don't mean to seem coy, but I'm not very comfortable talking about Brit or Ash. I should never have gotten involved. I recognized them, I was afraid. I could empathize with you. I know what it's like to be that afraid, even more afraid."

"Oh, no," Meridan interrupted and Lynden bristled. "You can't imagine what it's like to wake up with him in your house, to have had his hands close to your neck, to find that he, he, you know, all over your underwear, threatening your life." Images flashed through Lynden's mind at lightning speed, that year of her life she spent every waking and sleeping hour trying to suppress rushing forward. Meridan didn't know what it was like to love the man who had done all of those things and many more. "I mean, this has been going on for months!" *Try twelve years*, Lynden thought. *How about twelve years of shadowboxing, obsessive-compulsive disorder, therapy, senseless heartache, and nightmare-ridden nights?*

"What does he look like? You said handsome. Why wouldn't he approach me if he were attractive? Do you think something has happened to him? Like, maybe he is misfigured?"

"God willing," Lynden muttered, finding it difficult not to correct Meridan's solecism. "I don't know, I haven't seen him in twelve years. I suppose anything is possible. Maybe he's intimidated." Lynden knew it was unlikely.

"Probably. Most men are. Thank God for Christian or I'd be alone." Meridan smirked as if she had a secret, but Lynden didn't press.

"I doubt that," she managed.

"So, what does he look like?" Meridan prodded and popped the last bite of eggs Benedict into her mouth. "Mmm," she chewed.

"Well, he's tall, six foot four, brown eyes, brown hair. And yes, he was handsome at twenty, but I have no earthly idea what he would look like now. He ate well and drank a lot, so for all I know, he could weigh three hundred pounds and be very unsightly." She tried to laugh, wishing that were the case, knowing full well Brit was far too vain to let himself go. Ash, on the other hand, perhaps.

"That makes sense. If he's fat, he'd be embarrassed. I mean, look at me." She heard the last few words in Brit's voice, as it was something he said often.

Meridan drank the rest of her juice and nibbled on grapes and blackberries while she finished her coffee. "Aren't you going to eat your breakfast?" Lynden shook her head and was surprised when Meridan reached over and appropriated her plate.

"Can I warm that up for you?" she offered.

"Sure." Lynden headed to the microwave, wondering how she was going to get rid of Meridan Marks.

59

"Joel, I know you're upset, but don't be. Lynden's really nice and cool. She's not involved in any type of conspiracy with this guy."

"I cannot believe you did this." Joel sighed loudly and threw his hands up to Roz, who was equally stunned.

"Tell her I'm furious with her. I should've gone with her!"

"I heard that," Meridan said before Joel bothered to repeat it.

"What possessed you to run out like that?"

"I didn't want to tell you this last night but, I, well, I really pissed him off."

"Tell me you didn't e-mail him on your own. Have you lost what little sanity you have?" Joel roared, and Meridan held the phone away from her ear and cringed.

"No, Joel. I'm not stupid. I was reading the e-mails that came in from him after the bust. I don't know, I guess I was angry—at him, at you, at everyone. I wrote some e-mails and saved them in the draft box. I was going to read them later and decide which one to send."

"What kind of e-mails? Hey, Roz, grab my laptop for me." He pointed to the case on the table at the far end of his office.

"Well, some were nice-ish and some weren't. I wasn't going to send them. I was just entertaining myself, you know, venting?"

"And?"

"Well, I'd been calling Lynden all day and she hadn't called me back. I'd had some drinks and, well, I was in a really foul mood."

"I am truly on the edge of my seat."

"Well, I read her e-mail and replied. I was kind of a bitch. I told her to go to hell, I didn't need her help."

"And then you pressed send and all, let's see, eight of your e-mails were sent to B because my computer is set to mail all drafts when you push send."

"I didn't know that, though, Joel!" she yelled into the receiver. "He has a name."

"Marksman."

"Britten Holden."

"Like she said."

"Yes."

"And?"

Meridan set about reconstructing the morning. She used a little baby talk, hoping to garner some sympathy, but Joel was impervious.

"Wait, I have to put this on speaker. I don't want to have to tell Roz." Meridan heard a little click, and she and Roz exchanged tense greetings.

"There was a letter, in a baggie."

"Where's the letter?"

"I have it with me. I was terrified, Joel. Really fucking scared. I couldn't think straight. I packed a bag, called security, ordered a car, chartered a jet and came straight here." Despite his unadulterated fury, Joel was proud of her. She actually had accomplished something without the aid of a legion of professionals.

"I didn't even know she knew how to do any of that," Meridan heard Roz snicker.

"Very funny, Roz. I happen to be quite able to handle my own affairs." Roz's apology was empty, but Meridan accepted.

"So, I came here. I'm in search of the truth. Lynden knows these guys. She can help us figure out a way to find them, catch them, something."

"Can you fax me that letter?"

"Hmm . . ."

"She can charter a jet but can't fax a letter," Roz grumbled in the background.

"I don't know if she has a fax machine, Roz!" Meridan screamed. "Stop being so mean to me. I didn't do anything on purpose!"

"I know, I'm sorry. We've been worried sick since the Four Seasons called. I mean seriously, Meridan. I don't see how this, what's her name, Lynden, can help us."

"She knew them. She likes me. She'll help us. When you read the letter, you'll understand why I bolted. I've never been so scared in my life. He wants me dead. He intends to kill me."

"What?" Joel and Roz shrieked in unison.

"He threatened me. I almost want to puke thinking about it."

"Let me talk to her." Joel demanded.

"She's in the shower, and . . . I don't think she likes you."

"Tell me about it. She all but told me to fuck off."

"Do you want me to come?"

"No thanks, Roz. I really like her, and she cooks like you can't believe. I've done nothing but eat since I walked in the door."

"Maybe she dated one of these guys. Appeal to her on that level." Joel suggested.

"How?"

"I don't know, just figure out a way to open her up. Oh, and fax that letter to me right now. How about if I e-mail you some of his e-mails for her to read? See if it triggers anything."

"Good idea. Do you think I should show her the letter?"

"You haven't? What have you been doing there? You've been there, what, like, three days?" Meridan knew Roz was furious. She had never made a major decision without Roz before.

"I just got here and, well, I was side tracked."

"By food?"

"She looks like me."

"What?" Joel asked.

"She looks like me. And not just a little bit."

"Be more specific."

"Imagine me, a few inches shorter, with slightly bigger boobs and my old teeth, and before that little lip thing."

"Come on, Meridan."

"I shit you not. I'll fax you a photo of her if I can find one."

"Don't bother, I'll have her driver's license photo within ten minutes."

"Don't come here."

"We won't, but you have two days, depending on what that letter says, to get her on board, and then I'm pulling the plug on this whole stupid idea."

They all hung up, and Meridan mocked Joel for a while to make herself feel better. She looked into Lynden's office. The light was on, and there was a fax machine on top of a small filing cabinet. Lynden's desk was immaculate. Her laptop was closed, and there were no papers, pens or paper clips on the desktop.

There was a picture of what could have passed as Meridan herself with two people she assumed were Lynden's parents. How odd, Meridan thought, that two people who don't look anything like her own parents could produce a child who looked so much like her. Maybe she was adopted and didn't want to admit it, although, there was a striking resemblance to the woman. Maybe I'm adopted, Meridan thought, not for the first time.

~

Lynden had left Meridan to her breakfast and was now standing lifeless in the shower. Tears blended with the rivulets of water cascading down her numb body.

"Hey, Lyn?" Lynden yelped at the knock at the door. "Are you okay?"

"Yeah, yes. I was just relaxing a bit in here. I'll be right out."

"I talked to my attorney, and he asked me to fax the letter from Brit. Can I use your fax machine?

"Help yourself. It's in my office. I'll be right there." Lynden raced to rid her hair of the heavy conditioner. She dried off and slipped into a comfy workout outfit. Her hair was pulled back tightly, wet, and she had no makeup on, a stark comparison to Meridan, who had come to the breakfast table ready for a night on the town. Her tresses were wild and curly, hanging loosely, Lynden envied her for a moment, feeling so carefree. If she wore more makeup, the similarities would be mind bending.

"You should wear more makeup."

Lynden, annoyed, replied, "Why, so I can look like you?"

"No, you have really nice features. You could enhance them more."

"I don't want to enhance them."

"You should wear your hair down. There's a picture of you in your office. Are those your parents?"

"Yes."

"You look really good in that photo—hair, makeup. It works for you."

"It's a really old photo. I would hope I looked good at twenty." She smiled and tried to change the subject.

"You look good now, too. I think you should put more effort into your appearance is all."

"You know, you caught me on a bad day yesterday. I'd been in bed feeling depressed. I tend not to hit the salon for hair and makeup right before I take to the bed." Feeling defensive, Lynden crossed her arms and gave Meridan an eyebrow.

"I didn't mean that. Why were you so depressed?"

"Never mind." She dismissed the actress with a wave and headed toward the office. "Did you get your fax off okay?" She called just as she saw the piece of paper resting in the tray. She picked it up absently and began reading.

60

The letter floated to the ground as Lynden slumped down onto the chair, catching the edge and almost slipping onto the floor.

"Lyn? Are you okay?" Lynden's mind went numb faced with the reality that Brit was an equal opportunity sexual predator. *Had he ever even loved me? Was Karis even his girlfriend, or just another woman they had terrorized? This isn't even about me. It never was. How many other women have been destroyed by them?*

"I'm sorry, what?" Lynden tried to pull herself from her chaotic thoughts and make sense of what Meridan was saying. Tears had formed fully, and Lynden was struggling to hold the vestiges of her dignity inside her lower lids.

"I don't think I should've let you read that. Not until I know what they did to you. Let's not read those e-mails Joel sent, okay?" Meridan crept closer. "Lyn, let's go sit down. How about some coffee?" Lynden nodded and let Meridan lead her to the couch in the great room. She longed for the comfort of a fire, despite the seasonal heat.

"Here." After a few moments, Meridan handed her a large coffee mug emitting a fabulous aroma.

"What is this?"

"Let's just say I know my way around a bar."

"This smells familiar," she said, scrolling through her massive memory bank, comparing smells with notes and articles and flavors. Losing herself in the task, she snapped her finger, "Morton's coffee!"

Meridan clapped. "You're amazing, Lyn. I almost said you should do this for a living, but, duh, you already do. How'd you know?"

"It's what I do for a living." Both women laughed. "I've been trying for years to get this recipe. I was there last week, but left without having this."

"Why didn't you have the coffee?"

"Why are you so curious?"

"I figure if I ask you enough questions you might answer one or two."

"How did you get the recipe? Oh, I forgot, you're a movie star."

"Exactly. I promised the bartender a kiss. With tongue. I was pretty hammered. Luckily, it didn't end up in the tabloids."

Lynden was stunned by Meridan's temerity. They were so alike on the surface—but the similarities ended there. One lived her life boldly and unapologetically; the other hid. One was broken; the other was not. Lynden wanted to be fixed, to not be afraid anymore.

"You're so sad, Lyn, what happened? Can I help?"

"I don't think so. Several therapists, a wonderful best friend, and the most understanding, compassionate, and supportive parents on earth have not helped me."

"What do you need? What do you want? Is it your career?"

"What?"

"Is my being here hard for you? I'm so successful . . . we look so similar. Do you feel like a failure? Like you could have done more with your life?" Lynden's mouth dropped open, and her eyes nearly burst from their sockets.

"What?" Meridan demurred.

"Tell me you didn't just say those things to me. Look around, Meridan," she said, gesturing widely with her arms to display her home. "Not that I need to justify my life to you, but I live in a million-dollar home, I have a successful writing career, I own my own business, I'm about to own a restaurant—"

"What kind of restaurant?"

"What in the hell is wrong with you? You just insulted me, attempted to diminish me, my life, and my career, and then you just move on?"

"I'm just curious."

"About what? What are you so fucking curious about? Maybe you should be curious as to how you ended up being famous. It isn't something I'd ever want. I love what I do. I'm very happy."

"No, you aren't."

"You're so annoying."

"No, I'm not."

"You are, Meridan. Why don't we just get this over with so you can go back to wherever people like you come from."

"Hollywood."

"Right." Lynden took several long gulps from her coffee cup, the liquid heating her further. The woman wasn't living in reality. "You don't think I could've taken a different route?" She couldn't believe she was allowing herself to be dragged down into the muck with this vacuous, insipid woman. "I could have. Things changed for me after I met Brit and Ash."

"Why?"

"Why? How? There's too much to explain."

"But, I really want to know. I've thought about you constantly since you sent that e-mail. I want to know what happened. I didn't mean to make you mad. Sometimes I just can't believe everyone wouldn't want to be famous. It's so fun."

"What about now? Is it fun having someone threaten your life? Has it been fun being forced to relocate? Your boyfriend is being guarded and you're on the run. You're holed up with someone you don't even know, asking very personal questions."

"I'm having fun. I like you." Lynden sat back puzzled, perplexed by this woman, so multi-faceted and yet one-dimensional. She alternately insulted and praised you, repelled and sucked you in with innocence and honesty. Lynden knew her Oscar was well deserved. "I like you, too, but you're really arrogant."

"No, I'm not!" Meridan pondered a moment. "You think I'm arrogant?"

"A little."

"Why?"

"I don't know, little things?"

"Hmm. I think you're overly sensitive. You think I'm arrogant because you don't care how you look and I do?"

"I do care. You know what? Never mind. I apologize. That was a rude thing for me to say." Lynden picked up her phone and stared at it. There were no voice mails.

"Expecting a call?"

"Actually, I was waiting for my appointment to confirm," she lied, knowing she was confirmed and wondering whether she should cancel. She and Gia needed to walk the space and approve the walls before any further progress could be made.

"Can I come?"

"Are you shitting me? You're not leaving this house. You're in hiding, remember?"

"What am I supposed to do?" Just then a thought occurred to Lynden.

"Do you read?"

"Like, do I know how?" She threw Lynden a disgusted look.

"No, as in, do you like to. Some people don't."

"It depends on what it is."

Lynden stood slowly, fighting rapidly descending vertigo. Her eyes darted to the journal and she resigned herself to the knowledge that there was no other way. Meridan needed to know everything, maybe to save her life, but Lynden didn't have the strength to walk her through it. The thought of another person delving into her past, her heart, and her mind was terrifying. Brady had to know in order for them to move forward, to build a life together. Meridan was different. Her knowledge was a matter of survival. Traversing the room slowly, Lynden made her way to the bookcase, stopping in front of the journal. Her hand found the cool leather, which she held fast to her chest after easing it out of its resting place.

"What's that?"

"Well, it's my relationship with Brit, well, and Ash, I guess."

"What do you mean?"

"I had a relationship with Brit."

"What do you mean, like, you knew him?"

"No. We dated." Meridan tilted her head, not unlike a dog hearing a scarcely discernible sound.

"I thought they stalked you or terrorized you? I don't understand."

"Me either, but this might help."

"Is it a diary?"

"Kind of."

"So it's real?" Her eyes were wide, as though viewing the Hope Diamond. She reached out her hands to accept the precious gem, but Lynden was not quite ready to relinquish.

"I need assurances. I don't want this stolen, published, or made into a movie."

"That's awfully arrogant, isn't it? I thought you said you didn't write fiction."

"This is my life. I don't want to share it with the world. I don't even want to share it with you, but I have a difficult time talking about this."

"I'm not interested in making a movie of your life, Lynden. I hate to be a bitch, but look around. You're single, your phone hasn't rung since I got here, you don't go out to eat . . ."

"You know what? Forget it! Get out! Go back to Hell."

"Why are you so mad? First you accuse me of wanting to steal your life, and then you get mad when I assure you I won't."

"That was the most insulting assurance I've ever received."

"Can I have it? I'm actually a really fast reader. I have to be because about all I ever do is read at work."

"Whatever. Knock yourself out." Lynden handed Meridan the journal, transferred her Morton's coffee into a portable cup and nearly ran for the door.

61

I stayed in the bathroom long enough for Brit to pass out, waiting until I heard him snoring before I snuck out. I stared at him for a long time; he looked so innocent in a deep slumber. I had never been so attracted to, afraid of, intimidated by, in love with and in a state of complete loathing for anyone in my life. I'd never felt that strongly in any one area, let alone all of them, for anyone. My whole heart told me to run as far as I could before he destroyed it along with my mind.

Despite his constant acknowledgment of my physical attributes and his obvious interest in the physicality of our relationship, I continued doubting his intentions. At times he talked of the future, and at others reduced me to a "date."

I slipped into bed next to Brit, terrified of waking him. Tomorrow was another day and I would be on my best behavior. I lay awake replaying the details of the evening at Kinetic until I fell fast asleep.

I was awakened by Brit's growing erection in the middle of my back, and I had prepared myself for this eventuality. I turned slowly, gauging his breathing. He was not yet awake. In an act of self-preservation, I slipped beneath the sheets and took him into my mouth. He moaned, stretched and reached for me. I had to act fast and not give him the opportunity to interrupt. I needed to work him into a state of euphoria impenetrable by thought.

"You're so good at this," he sighed, his hands filled with my hair. I pulled out every trick outlined by Cosmo *and felt his body begin to tense. His hands dug deeper into my hair.*

"I want you," he said, and my pulse quickened. Please don't let him stop me. "I want you to take me deeper," he asked, and I complied. I could tell from his breathing he was getting close. When he was about to release, I pulled my mouth away and continued with my hand. He didn't seem to mind. I was surprised by the amount he ejaculated and fascinated it had reached up his toned and flat stomach to his firm and defined chest. The primal essence of his climax thrilled me. I loved being in charge.

I got up quickly before he could recover and ran a hand towel under warm water. I returned and gently but thoroughly cleansed his body. He watched me and I pretended not to notice. His hand came up and snagged a long curl in his fingers.

"You're so beautiful in the morning. I'm sorry about last night. I hope you weren't disappointed. I didn't mean to pass out. I guess I had more than my fair share." His hands massaged his temples. I held out two Advil and handed him some water.

"I had a bit more than I should have, as well," I smiled, secretly hoping some of his memory of the past evening had been lost in an intoxicated sleep. "Shall I order up breakfast or do you want to go out?" At that very moment, a knock on the door sounded. That "silly girl" smirk played on his lips. I hopped off the bed to open the door.

"Wait! Put on a robe. No one sees you like that but me. At least not anymore." The T-shirt I was wearing barely covered the essentials. Once robe-clad, I let the waiter in. He set up breakfast by the window and Brit signed the check from bed.

I munched on bacon and a bagel while he devoured eggs Benedict and fruit. He read the paper and I watched. My heart thumped just at the sight of him. He was, without question, the most beautiful man I had ever seen. His hair was a sexy mess, his beard a full day old, his chest hairless and smooth under the partially open robe. I hated being such a girl, but I needed to define terms.

"Last night you called me your date," I broached, gently.

"That's what you were, no?" He raised thick, heavy brows at me.

"Is that all I am to you?" I couldn't disguise the hurt in my voice.

"It is until you tell me different. You're in the driver's seat, don't forget. I've been waiting for a commitment from you all along. I'm trying to be patient." His eyes locked with mine, and I could barely fight my urge to smile. I then realized much of his behavior was driven by a lack of commitment on my part.

"I want more. I want it all. Does that scare you?" I asked.

"What do you mean? Why would it?"

"Last time you felt yourself getting too close, you ran off to Brazil. You got back with Karis. Should I brace myself for another flight?"

"I don't think so. I need you to understand something, however. If we are in a committed relationship, you are mine."

"Of course. We wouldn't see anyone else." As if.

"I mean that you belong to me." I liked the way it sounded, in theory. "It also means we are going to have sex." My eyes narrowed.

"We will have sex when I'm ready, Brit. I don't feel I have to consummate this commitment for it to be valid. If you care about me, you'll give me time." He raised an eyebrow at me.

"Then, we're friends," he said casually.

"What?" I gaped.

"Do you fuck your friends?"

"No!"

"Well, you don't fuck me either, so we're friends." He diverted his attention to the paper and ignored me. I was dumbstruck.

"This is about sex, not love. You don't care about me!" I was outraged. "If you did, you'd give me space and time."

"Well, if it isn't the Queen of Mixed Signals. Who just sucked my dick? Who comes on overnight trips? Who wants to play house? Who wants a relationship, but won't give it up?"

"Just because I'm not ready to have sex now doesn't mean I won't ever be. In the meantime, we can do other things. It's a progression with me. I don't just jump into bed with someone!" He cast a skeptical glance at me, and I wondered if he was still pairing me with Brady. I wanted to commit fully, *without reservation, and when I was ready.*

Darkness settled over the table. He had shut down completely. He rose and walked to the bathroom, and I heard the shower start.

Brit exited the bathroom a virtual GQ advertisement; I could almost hear the cameras snapping away. His faded jeans were slightly frayed at the pockets and the cuffs settled softly on a stylish pair of loafers. He wore a crisp, white T-shirt bearing the message "NO!" under a black cashmere blazer. I had to wonder if the shirt was a dig at me.

"You look amazing," I said, sliding from my chair. I wanted to hug him. I needed to smooth this over.

"You'd better get ready. I told Patrick and Kaylee we'd meet them for some sightseeing and then lunch with friends." He turned away from me. I didn't look forward to a day of people I didn't know with my "boyfriend" angry at me. He called to me as I started to shut the door.

"I've laid out clothes for you. I'll meet you down in the lobby. I need to make some calls."

My heart plummeted. I showered quickly, scrunched my hair a bit and slipped into the outfit he had purchased for me. Low-cut jeans with a slim boot-cut leg; a tight-fitting black bodysuit with a thong back; and a gorgeous, black kid leather motorcycle jacket with gold zippers. I added a belt and cowboy boots and was very happy with the end result. I felt very New York and stylish.

Brit was nowhere to be found in the lobby. I picked up the sports section of the newspaper and read while I waited.

"What are you doing?" Brit demanded, startling me from my article.

"You told me to meet you in the lobby."

"I told you I was going to the lobby to make some calls and that I would meet you in the car." He hadn't, but I didn't want to further exacerbate the situation. I grabbed my jacket and purse and followed him to the door.

"These jeans are awesome. Thank you for buying them for me," I said, hoping to thaw him a bit.

"They're men's jeans. I figured since you don't have any hips, they'd look fine." He didn't look at me to evaluate or to acknowledge, and my stomach took

a nervous dive.

We joined Patrick and Kaylee in the town car and they all chatted excitedly about Patrick's orientation at the Institute of Culinary Education. I was happy for the diversion. I wasn't expected to interact or even interject other than a "Cool" here and there. We spent most of the morning in Times Square. Brit didn't speak to me at all other than to inform me of the next portion of our agenda.

We ended up in a tiny restaurant in Little Italy for lunch. We were to meet a few of Patrick's new classmates, who had recommended the place. I loved Italian food, but my heart was not into the day. I needed to defrost Brit, but didn't know how.

I was fairly knowledgeable about Italian, and when Brit ordered for me, as he usually did, my stomach clenched. He said carbonara. I hated carbonara. He knew I didn't like creamy sauces or fatty dishes, and that was the worst of the lot. I leaned into him and placed my hand on his arm.

"Brit, I really don't like carbonara," I said with all the sweetness I could muster. He ignored me completely. He was chatting with the two new couples that had joined us, who sat riveted.

"So, Reese, are you from Michigan also?" A guy named Jared asked me, likely out of pity. It must've appeared I was without a friend in the world, as that was how I felt. It turned out we had a lot in common, so I busied myself with Jared and wine.

My stomach lurched when the food was delivered. The carbonara looked revolting. Globs of slimy bacon bobbed in a sea of cream and fat. The pasta was drowning. The smell made me want to vomit. Brit turned to me for the first time since we'd been seated and locked eyes with me.

"I don't—"

"Don't you dare embarrass me, Reese. You're going to eat that." I felt like crying. I hoped no one had overheard him. "You need to try different things," he said, handing me a fork. I choked down a few bites of what truly was the most disgusting thing I had ever had the displeasure of experiencing.

"Don't you like it?" Jared asked.

CONSUMED

"No, I do. I guess I pulled an amateur move and ate too much bread." I smiled, relieved by my recovery.

"May I?" he asked, raising a fork. I silently blessed him as he scooped up a large portion, thankful also Brit was too engrossed in yet another story about Brazil to notice.

The ride back to the hotel was quiet until Brit broke the silence.

"Why didn't you invite your boyfriend back with us? What was his name? Brady?" he smirked. I wanted to slap him in the face.

"I thought you were my boyfriend."

"Well, I am a boy, and I am a friend, and we don't have sex so, technically, you are correct."

I rolled my eyes at the window and folded my arms defensively across my chest. Once in the room, I eased down onto the bed on top of the covers, wearing my jacket, and fell asleep instantly.

62

A low whimper drew me from my sleep. I was experiencing the hallmark disorientation caused by afternoon naps. What time was it? Where was I? How long had I been sleeping? Further, what is that sound? It sounded like a child at the tail end of a massive crying jag, resigned to exhaustion and frustration. I rolled over and in the dim light saw Brit lying next to me. His face was contorted with sadness, wet with fresh tears, and I realized the whimpering was coming from him. I was stultified by apprehension. I didn't know whether to wake him, but ultimately decided against it. Even when Brit appeared to be vulnerable, I distinctly sensed it was a façade.

His strength, to me, was his defining characteristic. Watching him, I understood why I kept coming back—simply, I responded to authority. I was submissive. I felt a perverse satisfaction creep over me as I watched him squirm and whine. As I eased myself toward my side of the bed, his steel-like grip enclosed around my wrist, causing me to yelp more out of surprise than pain.

"Where're you going, cupcake?" he questioned sharply, and I willed my heart to slow itself.

"I—I didn't want to disturb you. You were sleeping so soundly, and I have to pee." I smiled weakly and, most likely, disingenuously. His eyes narrowed and he forced me to hold his gaze. His tears had mostly dried, and gone was the vulnerability I had reveled in just moments before.

"Hurry back," he said, tossing a casual glance at his watch. I nodded and rushed from the room. I sat on the closed toilet seat with my knees drawn up close to me and tried to identify my feelings. My heart was racing, and my

stomach weak. I was feeling either excitement or fear. Was I afraid of Brit?
Was I afraid of loving Brit? Was I afraid of losing Brit? Was I afraid of being
consumed by Brit? The unfortunate answer to all questions was yes. I quickly
brushed my teeth and checked my makeup. Not too bad for post-nap, I decided,
and returned to the bedroom.

The room was candle-lit, and on the table was an elaborate spread of
cheeses, none of which I recognized; fruit, most of which I did; and breads.
There was a bottle of Roederer chilling in a bucket of ice and a bottle of
Cakebread cabernet next to the tray. I marveled at Brit's speed in pulling
together such a beautiful feast and my stomach growled in anticipation.

Brit slipped his arms around my waist from behind and I felt his breath on
my neck. Goose bumps spread like buckshot over my entire body.

"Is this to your liking?" he whispered, and I nodded, not trusting my
voice. His large hands found my hipbones and he squeezed, pulling me back
into his enormous erection. My hands instinctively went to his. "Just let me
smell you." I wondered if he could hear my heart crashing into my ribs, and I
struggled to keep my breathing even.

He explored every crevice on my neck and somehow worked my collar to
reach my shoulders. I visualized him, so rakish and dark, smoldering and sexy.
I could feel my knees weakening and felt a mixture of relief and frustration
when he kissed my cheek and by the hand lead me to a chair. He sat me down
and laid my napkin gently in my lap.

"What will it be, madam? I'm at your service." He bowed to me, and I
couldn't help but giggle.

"I don't even know what most of these cheeses are," I admitted, knowing
full well he did and would delight in my education.

"Roquefort." He named the greenish, soft cheese he was spreading on a
slice of French bread. It looked repugnant and smelled worse. I steeled myself
against a rancid assault on my tongue as he fed it to me. The pungent taste
caused me to reach for my glass of champagne, but by the time I did, the flavors
had mellowed.

"You like?" he asked, one eyebrow peaked, skeptical.

"Actually, I do. I was unsure at first, it smells so strong."

"The stronger the smell, the more intense the flavors. I should've started you on Havarti," he smirked, probably at my pedestrian palate, and I felt childish.

"No, I like it," I fired, defensively.

"Good, that's the harshest one. The rest of them are flavorful, but not so forceful."

He introduced me to the assortment of the cheeses slowly and with explanation, pairing them with different fruits.

"You were tossing and turning. Did you have a bad dream?" I asked, the curiosity finally too much for me to bear.

"Umm? Dream?" he mused, a slight tilt of his head. His dark eyes searched the ceiling for clues. I watched the storm clouds roll in and hoped it was a small one, not a typhoon. He dropped his napkin on the table, grabbed his wine glass and settled back in his chair. I regretted having asked.

"I dreamed about Ash. We were in an orphanage. We were, like, eighteen, and no one had adopted us. All of the other kids had come and gone, hundreds, thousands, ten thousand." His gaze was far off, overlooking Manhattan, his voice deep and distant. I was riveted.

"My aunt would visit but kept explaining she had two children of her own and couldn't handle the extra burden. My parents would visit and explain they were sorry, but they just didn't want children, they hadn't realized. Ash was afraid, he cried all the time; he wanted a family."

"But, none of that happened right? Your aunt and uncle took you in."

"Fuck." Brit pulled himself from his chair and dragged a hand through his hair. He loomed above me, hands on his hips looking ravaged, exhausted.

"I'm sorry. I shouldn't have asked."

He dropped to his knees and placed his head in my lap. The shuddering of his body was almost undetectable, but I knew he was crying. I ran my fingers though his hair and massaged his neck and shoulders. "Don't leave me. Please don't leave me." He began to sob, and my heart seized at his words. "I need you. I need you to make it all go away." I was paralyzed by his display of emotion. My mind whirled.

He sat up suddenly and settled his back against the bed. His beautiful face was deluged with tears, his eyes full of angst and desperation.

"They didn't take us right away. I remember it was dark a lot. There was so much crying. I don't know, it could've been me crying. It smelled. Ash took care of me. He was so strong and so, I don't know, he made me feel safe." I held my breath and waited for him to continue.

"My parents didn't have a will. My dad's parents were deceased. He had been an unplanned child, and we didn't know my mom's parents at all. I was so young, but Ash says he doesn't remember ever meeting them. To this day I never have. My aunt is my mom's sister. Money was really tight, and my uncle didn't think it was fair to his kids." He buried his head in his hands and, though I wanted to go to him, I remained firmly affixed to my chair. "Ash has always taken care of me. Fights, bullies, my uncle. We always had each other."

"But, your aunt and uncle loved you, right?" Knowing he still spoke with them regularly, I tried to make sense of what he was telling me.

"Oh, sure. They loved us, for our money. Once the estate was settled and my parents' attorney informed them of our finances, they rushed right over to take us. I guess my dad inherited a bunch of money when his parents died, but he had put it in trust for us. We were not to receive it until we were eighteen, but the court ruled my uncle could use a percentage of it to take care of us and to take the burden off of them. He was just getting his own business started as a stockbroker, which was why money had been tight for them. He used our money as his first 'client' and was entitled to commission on the dividends. I guess we're lucky he was a good stockbroker. It gave his family a whole new life. They had money and nice things, all because my parents died." I felt tears stinging my eyes. I didn't want to cry. I wanted to be strong, and, most of all, I wanted him to share. I had never felt so close to him.

"They told their friends we were their cousins. I remember always feeling embarrassed when I would call my aunt 'mom' and the other kids would roll their eyes. She told us to call her that. Part of me wanted to and the other part hated it. We never called my uncle 'Dad.' He was always Uncle Rodger. I hated *the questions from other kids. I always felt like an interloper. So did Ash. I felt like we were outsiders, when, actually, if it weren't for our money, they wouldn't have had that nice house, or the cars when they graduated and, hell, maybe not even college." The tears continued to roll and I was baffled by his strength. "I tried so hard to fit in. I just wanted them to love me. Ash hated them. All of them. He was always in trouble. Drinking, girls, stealing cars, drugs. He was never busted, you know, by the cops, but my uncle was a real asshole. They fought like crazy, fistfights and everything. We really grew apart toward the end of high school. He said I betrayed him. I had sided with 'them.' I wasn't siding with anyone. I didn't agree with his actions. He was so full of hate. He always has been. I understand it. Really. He tells me all of the time how alike we are, but we aren't. At all." It was at that moment I feared they were almost identical.*

The doorbell to our room rang, confusing us both. Brit looked at his watch and I waited for direction.

"Shit, it's Patrick and Kaylee. They were going to come for drinks before dinner." He pulled himself up, checked himself in the mirror, and went to the door. I cursed them vehemently for interrupting what could be the most significant moment of our relationship. I was finally gaining some insight into not only Brit, but Ash. I was beginning to understand why emotion simmered so close to the surface for Brit and perhaps why it was impossible for Ash to conceal any. I heard Brit jovially inviting them in, backslapping and a kiss on the cheek. Pleasantries. I wondered how he managed to shift emotional gears so quickly.

63

"*I made a reservation for eleven-fifteen at this gallery-slash-restaurant in Soho. That should give us plenty of time to visit,*" *Brit announced.*

Kaylee and Patrick helped themselves to wine and champagne, while Brit ordered up more drinks. I sat quietly with my wine. It was hard to keep my eyes off of Brit. Self-assuredness personified, each movement had purpose and intent. I was still reeling from the disclosure. My heart wept for him, for all he had endured, for all of the pain he internalized.

"*Babe!*" *Brit called impatiently from the sitting room. I noticed Kaylee and Patrick had settled onto our bed to canoodle. Brit had spread a down comforter onto the floor in front of the couch, and the television was on.*

"*Slumber party,*" *he said and patted the floor next to him. His smile lit the room.*

I settled in next to him and asked what movie we'd be watching. He turned off the TV and put in a CD. Nine Inch Nails filled the room. Brit was well aware their music always ignited an erotic flame in me.

"*So much for visiting before dinner,*" *I laughed, and he took my wine glass from me. He reached up and dimmed the light. The door was open, and I could hear Kaylee and Patrick talking. I felt comforted by their presence, knowing things could not get out of hand.*

"*There's a song on this disc that makes me think of you. Actually, I think it was written for you. Did you ever date Trent Reznor?*" *A malicious smirk curled one side of his mouth in question. I rolled my eyes in response.* "*No, for real. I swear you were the inspiration.*" *As my mind fast-forwarded through the beginning of each of the first three songs, the sounds of "Sanctified" began. Apprehension slowly descended upon me. Brit settled himself on his elbow and stared down at me. He sang the words in a low voice while twirling one of my curls through his fingers. I understood the lyrics were Brit's message to me. His anger, his disdain, his actions were justified by my emotional and physical distance. As the song concluded, he took both of my wrists above my head and held them firmly as he straddled me. I knew struggling was futile and would serve as nothing but lighter fluid on an already-smoldering situation.*

"It's time to punish you for everything you've put me through. You're trying to destroy my life, and I won't let you." Punish? *I thought. I was terrified.*

Hot tears formed in my eyes as his bored into me. He leaned down to kiss me and, without thinking, I turned my head. Deftly, he held both of my wrists in one hand and grabbed my chin with the other. "Don't do it again. Why do I have to keep telling you? You never listen!" His voice was condescending and fierce.

When his mouth met mine, the tears spilled over.

"Kiss me back. Stop pretending you don't want me!" I acquiesced, meeting his tongue, and wondered if he tasted fear. He bit my lower lip gently and then more forcefully until I whimpered in protest. "You love it." Kisses turned hot and brutal, and I clung to the reassurance that Patrick and Kaylee were just outside the door.

Powerless under Brit's absolute control, his hand slowly worked the buttons of my blouse, while I envisioned Patrick walking in.

"They're going to come in," I pleaded. His mouth worked its way down my neck, alternately kissing, licking and biting my shoulders and neck, while his free hand expertly freed my breasts from the constraints of my bra. He sighed briefly, as if taking in a majestic landscape.

Despite staunch emotional resistance, my body ached for his touch. I strenuously pushed thoughts of submission away. It would not happen like this.

"They're fucking in there. If you listen close, you can hear them. That's what we should be doing. Listen." For the first time, I actually did hear sounds from the other room, despite Trent Reznor, who had not tired of launching

accusations at me from the CD player.

"I want you, Patrick. Please . . . please . . . please. Don't make me beg. Oh, God. I love it when you do that," Kaylee mewed quietly. A wild mélange of feelings and emotions provoked my mind and body. I had never heard people have sex, except in movies. It was disturbing and captivating. I tried not to listen or to feel Brit biting my swollen nipples.

"Stick it in. Please, Patrick," Kaylee begged.

"I want to hear you beg," Brit whispered into my mouth. I shook my head as tears continued erupting from my eyes. A low groan in the next room confirmed the begging was over and that Patrick had given Kaylee what she wanted.

"Do not move your hands from above your head," he demanded, letting go of me to use both hands to remove my jeans. "I'm going to fuck you now."

"Please, don't," I choked, and he put a finger to my lips.

"Shhh. At first you'll consider it rape, but when I go into your panties and they're soaking wet, remind yourself of that. Your body doesn't lie, even though you do." I tried to make it difficult for him to pull down my pants, and he slapped me hard on the side of my hip. My hands instinctively came down in defense.

"Brit, stop!" I yelled before he clasped his hand over my mouth. With his other hand, he removed his belt. Taking his hand from my mouth, he fastened the belt around the leg of the couch and my hands, swiftly, as if he had done it before. I resisted the urge to scream, but tested the strength of the binding, disappointed to find it secure.

"Listen to me," he whispered into my ear. "I know this is what you want, but you're afraid to admit it. I'm going to help you." He smoothed my hair off my forehead, which was moist from fear. "Once you've been punished, we can move on." His hand worked its way into my panties and they were, as he'd guessed, soaked through. "See," he reasoned.

"I'm not ready. I don't want this." My voice was strangled into a whisper by my mounting hysteria. I didn't want to hear them having sex, and I didn't want to have sex. As if to torture me, Patrick came with unrestrained force not

even the music could drown out. Fresh torrents of tears spilled down my face, becoming lost in my hair.

"Yes, you do, baby. I may not be Ash, but I know you want me." Fear crashed through me, setting off all of the alarms in my body. He knew.

"What?" I whispered.

"Ash seems to think you knew it was him on the couch that day. He said you were coming on to him?" My head shook violently, and the lies tumbled forth.

"I swear to God, nothing happened. I thought he was you. I swear, Brit. Please, can we talk about this?" He shook his head to let me know this was no time for talk. I had to talk. I had to make him understand. He was about to punish me for something I didn't do. Well, not intentionally.

He inserted three fingers into me, and, despite my readiness, had to put force behind it. I caught my breath sharply. "Do not call out. Do you understand?" I nodded at his deadly seriousness.

I refused to allow even the tiniest noise to escape from me. If he was going to rape me, he would get no fight, no response; I would lay inert. "I want to hear you. I know you love it. You are so hot and wet. Show me. I want to hear you." I held my breath to keep from screaming as his fingers plunged into me hard and fast.

"Stop holding your breath." He slapped me again. Suddenly his mouth was on me, twirling around that most sensitive spot, which was erect and responsive. His tongue, firm and hot, was inside me when Patrick knocked on the door.

"Brit, time got away. It's eleven o' clock," he announced from outside the door. I pulled myself into a ball to shield my nakedness, but Patrick didn't enter.

"Be right there," Brit called out. "This isn't over." He pointed a finger at me. But I knew it was. Forever. I had to figure a way to bide my time until we left, get home and break it off. He was stark-raving mad.

64

"What about this one for sheer panels?" For the past two hours, Gia had flitted about, babbling excitedly about the walls, the floors and the fabric swatches. Lynden couldn't help but wonder what was going on at her house. Her innermost thoughts and personal details were on display for someone she had met yesterday.

"What? Oh, I'm sorry. What were you saying?"

"Panels, in the front? Or do you want to go with a treatment of some type on the windows?"

"Give me a little more time with material and fabric before we decide. I just wanted to bring these swatches to you and plan for us to meet with Novel Designs."

"Who are they?"

"They'll most likely handle all the furniture."

"Okay, so we're done? Are you feeling alright today?"

"I had a rough weekend. I wasn't feeling well at all. I almost cancelled on you."

"Why don't we talk over lunch? How about Green Papaya? It isn't too far from here, and we can relax. You probably need a glass of wine." *Or seven,* Lynden thought, knowing if they shared lunch, she wouldn't get back to the house until five o'clock.

"Can I make a call first?" Gia nodded and headed toward the kitchen to make some notes.

"Lyn?" She had to tell Meridan how much she hated that.

"Hi. Everything okay?"

"When are you coming back? I'm kind of scared." An unfamiliar tone resonated over the line. "I want to talk about this."

"My meeting's running late, I can be there by five or so. Have you eaten? I'll pick up dinner on the way home."

Lynden walked to the kitchen, and Gia eyed her wickedly. "Are you hiding someone at your house? A man, perhaps?"

"I had a friend come in town unexpectedly last night. Not a man. We haven't seen each other in a while."

"Do you need to go home?"

"No, no, she's fine. Just looking for some relaxation. I gave her a good book and left her to fend for herself."

"How about you both join me for dinner tonight? Let's show her the Big D."

"She's kind of a mess, a bad break-up. I appreciate the offer, though. I still feel bad for bailing on you and your parents. Maybe we all can get together after she leaves."

"Daddy asks about you all of the time. I told him you were fine. You are fine, right?"

"Of course. I get to working and forget to eat, and then it hits me like a brick. Next thing you know, I'm nearly fainting."

"Nina thought it was something she said."

"No! No, not at all." Lynden was desperate to end the conversation before it led to Meridan Marks or the *Glitterati* article. *I may look like Meridan*, she conceded, *but I'm certain I can't pull off any Academy Award performance lying.* "I'll meet you there."

65

There was nothing I wanted to do less than get ready for a late dinner with "friends." As a matter of fact, I was distinctly aware I hadn't a friend among the group. Somehow, I pulled myself together in five minutes, touching up my makeup and changing into evening-appropriate attire. Kaylee gave me a curious once-over when I emerged from the rest room, sullen and laconic.

"You look spectacular," Brit said, leaning in for a kiss. I gave him a perfunctory peck and moved to the door. I had selected one of the few outfits I had brought with me and sternly refused his admonition to wear the coat he had purchased for me in Amsterdam. "It's cold out there, babe." He threw the coat over my shoulders, cloaking me in possessiveness. "Hey, Patrick, grab the car, it should be out front. I forgot something," Brit yelled out to Patrick and Kaylee, at the same time grabbing my arm and pulling me back into the room. A fresh sheen of sweat broke out all over my body as the door slammed shut.

"Look at me. I was only giving you a hard time. I would never force you to do anything you didn't want to do. I love you." He tipped my head up to his so our eyes would meet. His penitent gaze made me cringe; he wasn't sorry. I felt lucky to have escaped his nefarious plot. I knew he honestly believed if he forced me to have sex, it wouldn't be rape because I "wanted" it. "Okay?" He raised his eyebrows, and his face fell smoothly into an angelic expression. Without a measure of sanity, I reached for the doorknob. He caught my wrist, brought my hand up to his mouth and kissed it gently. My heart fluttered, expecting violence.

"You were pretty excited." He smiled. I wanted to tell him my body was

preparing itself so it wouldn't be torn to ribbons when he violated me, but
didn't.

I just wanted some air. "Hey, look at me." I did. "I love you." He pleaded,
but I didn't know what to say. I scrambled for something to pacify him.

"We'd better go."

Patrick and Kaylee were settled comfortably in the limo. We were slated to
leave around noon the following day, which seemed a lifetime away. I wondered
how I would make it through this night, let alone the ride back to school. I was
grateful Kaylee was returning with us.

"Driver, could you play the disc that's in the console? Number eight?"
He lounged next to me, leaning his long body back into the couch-like seat. I
looked away until I heard the music.

"'Pretty Hate Machine,' for you, because that's what you are," he
breathed in my ear. More Nine Inch Nails. The music would never fall upon my
ears the same way again.

"I don't hate you," I snapped quietly.

"You don't love me," he baited.

"I don't trust you." I couldn't shut my mouth and was thankful he started
singing, until I started listening to and internalizing the words coming from his
mouth. I could feel him staring at me, but refused to engage. I closed my eyes
and tried not to hear the words I used to enjoy but had grown to dread and
abhor.

The restaurant was very small, noisy, and crowded. There were about
fifteen tiny tables, and the standing-room-only bar spilled into the dining area.
Cigarette smoke hovered in thick, noxious clouds.

"The wine prices are so high," I said, finding forty dollars for a glass of
wine to be outrageous. Kaylee burst out laughing, following Brit's lead. My
faced flashed hot. Patrick took pity on me and explained.

"The wine is sectioned into what they call flights. For example," he
said, pointing to the cabernet sauvignon heading on my menu. "Here is the
cab flight. You pay forty dollars for a two-ounce sample of each of these six
different cabs. Or . . ." he continued, and I lost myself in his lengthy lecture in

order to avoid my feelings of embarrassment.

When my lesson concluded, I mustered some confidence and ordered my own flight without consulting or even looking at Brit. His hand on my leg reminded me to be nice.

"What are you getting?" My voice was obsequious, but I didn't care; I needed some levity. He ignored me and addressed the waitress.

"Double Tanqueray on the rocks, several olives." I made a mental note to take it easy on the alcohol so I could remain alert. The three chatted about matters out of my realm. I tried to look interested but felt uneducated and immature. Brit ordered for me and I restlessly awaited some horrific form of punishment on a plate. I was pleasantly surprised when what he had ordered in Italian turned out to be mushroom-stuffed ravioli with a light Gorgonzola cream sauce. An olive branch, perhaps.

"This sauce should be pretty mild. We tried the sweet Gorgonzola this afternoon and you really liked it," he reminded me and kissed me on the cheek. "How is it, sweetie?" I nodded as I chewed. From Hate Machine to Sweetie. Amazing. What depth of character.

"It's really good. Would you like to try it?" I took my fork away so he could help himself.

"Feed me," he directed, and I did.

"You guys are so cute," Kaylee said saccharinely.

"Cute? They're hot," Patrick said, and both Kaylee and Brit snapped their heads around to face him. "What? They're a great-looking couple," he justified. Having thawed no one, he continued. "Come on, Brit, you know I've always had a thing for you," he laughed, and everyone joined him.

I could only imagine the images flashing through Brit's head behind the laughter. I was sure they included me being ravaged by Patrick and loving it. A long drink of gin confirmed his discomfort.

"So, are you guys getting married?" Brit asked Kaylee. She seemed startled and broke into a huge grin.

"Actually, Patrick asked me this afternoon in Central Park. It was so romantic," she gushed. Patrick was beaming. "We already talked to my

parents. Naturally, they're thrilled. I'm going to transfer to NYU!"

"You're still coming back with us, right?" I said without thinking. I could feel Brit's eyes on me. "I mean, don't you need to come home and pack?" I floundered.

"Well, I'm going to get a job on campus and register this week, and then I'll fly home, pack, and drive my car back. I'm soooooooo excited!" I wasn't. I wasn't going to be able to sit in the truck with Brit alone.

"Congratulations, I'm really happy for you guys," I lied.

Patrick and Kaylee finished their meals and went to the bar to smoke. I was conversely grateful for the airspace and dreading the Brit-space. He slouched into the booth and took large swallows of his fresh cocktail. I was still sipping my way through my third small glass of cabernet.

"Do you want to try any of these?"

"No."

"The first one was really good. What was it?" I reached for my menu, and he got up from the table. He didn't announce his intentions, but I assumed he was headed for the restroom.

"You have two choices." Before I could process what was happening, Brit had reached over my shoulder and snatched my unused steak knife, his other hand deeply enmeshed in my hair. "Reese," he whispered. "Take me back or I will end up in an institution for killing you. No more games." Immobilized by fear, I could do nothing but watch as he slowly brought the knife to the side of my throat. Blood thundered through my veins and I could feel the knife's edge flush against my jugular. No one was paying us any attention, and I prayed he was not drunk enough to kill me in the middle of a crowded restaurant.

"I've given it some thought," I choked through tears and the strain on my neck. "And I'm looking forward to getting home and back to where we left off." He threw the knife on the table in disgust and hefted himself into the booth.

"Stop crying. I wasn't going to hurt you."

Unable to speak, I nodded my understanding and cringed when Trent Reznor issued forth from the DJ booth. I braced myself for another dose of Brit's hatred.

CONSUMED

"I'm so glad you introduced me to Nine Inch Nails," he smirked. Yeah. Me, too. As glad as I am there's no cure for cancer, *I thought. "He's a brilliant lyricist, so honest. I really identify with him. I wonder who she was."*

"Who?"

"The woman who ruined his life."

Thankfully, Kaylee filled the limo with wedding dreams on the ride back, saving me from potential intimacy with Brit. As the door to the suite loomed ahead, I considered my options. Run. Hide. Wait until he passed out. Stay in the bathroom. Feign illness. No, he wasn't nearly drunk enough; he wouldn't pass out for a while, if at all. Excuses didn't seem to be an option.

He opened the door for me, and I entered our dimly lit room. The door closed behind me, and his hand stole into my hair, grasping it firmly at the base of my skull. Reversing our positions, he pinned me against the door and buried his tongue in my mouth. My crashing heart left me short of breath, but I did not pull away. Suddenly, he stopped kissing me, his hands against the door, blocking potential escape routes.

"Tell me you love me," he baited with a devious smile.

I weighed my options. "I'm afraid," was all I could manage to spit out.

"Afraid of what?"

"Of you." I hated my honesty, but was running low on resources.

"Why?"

"You put a knife to my throat. You said you'd kill me."

"I said I would kill you if you didn't take me back."

"I, we—I will. I did."

"Make up my mind."

"I did. I'm confused."

"I'm not." His gaze was firm. "Feel this." He lifted his shirt to expose his stomach. I kept my eyes riveted on his. He took my fingers and rubbed them *against the head of his penis, which had cleared the waistband of his jeans. It was wet and slick.*

"Brit—" I turned on the water works, hoping to invoke some sympathy.

"I just want you to feel how much I want you. I can't even keep it in my pants anymore." He closed my hand over his erection.

"Brit—"

"It's over, Reese. You knew the stakes. I told you that if we were back together, we were going to have sex. You took me back, so . . ."

"You threatened me!"

"I gave you an ultimatum, Reese, don't be so dramatic."

"With a knife!"

"Stop it!" he yelled in my face. "You're driving me insane." He brought his hands to his temples and squeezed. With the door behind me, there was nowhere for me to go. "It's time."

"No. NO! My God, no, Brit, please." I shook my head violently, tears spattering his shirt. "I'm not ready."

"Now you're just fucking insulting me. You fucked that guy Brady!"

"I didn't, I swear."

"I'm not good enough for you! Admit it!"

"That's not it. You are everything I ever wanted, but you—"

"You're so fucking selective, Miss Purity," he interrupted, seemingly not hearing my previous statement. "What was with Patrick tonight? Calling you hot? Is there something going on? Don't answer." He held up a hand when I shook my head. "You're a liar. You're a lying whore!" He was screaming at me now, and I wanted to scream as loud and long as I could, but feared the repercussions.

Pulling me away from the door, he worked me toward the bed. I decided to fight. At this point, rape was the least of my worries. His murderous eyes and tone caused me to wonder if I was going to make it out alive. I struggled wildly, but he held my wrists fast; the futility of my struggles only heightened my terror. "Don't fucking bother!" he screamed at me, and I tried to ignore the pain. "You've pushed me to the absolute limit!" One last effort freed me, and

I stumbled blindly backward and crashed into the open closet. My head struck something cold and metallic, stunning me briefly. Instinctively, I curled into a ball.

He put one hand on each side of the closet and stared in at me. His eyes were crazed, making him unrecognizable to me. We were silent and immobile until he began to undo his pants. I closed my eyes tightly, trying to shut out what was happening.

"Look at me!"

I refused. I plugged my ears. I couldn't take anymore.

67

I woke with a start at the sound of a door slamming. It was dark. My head was thundering and I couldn't open my right eye. I brought my hands to my face. It was crusty and my hair was matted. Inhaling deeply, I was assaulted by thick, sweet and fetid odors. My mind raced, trying to sift through remnants to figure out what had happened, finally honing in on the closet in our suite at the Waldorf-Astoria. I was in the closet. I had fallen into it. Or had been pushed.

I listened intently, wondering who had left or entered the room. My shirt and pants were intact as far as I could tell in the pitch-black closet. My eyes watered with relief. I hadn't been raped as far as I knew. Hearing silence, I reached for the door but was stopped just as my fingers touched the knob; my hair was stuck in something.

I wrestled with the hair for a moment, finally able to pull free after leaving a fair amount tangled in something. My legs screamed as I unfurled my body and blood roared through my head, causing it to pulsate forcefully. I slowly opened the closet door and brought up a hand to shield my eyes from the searing sunlight. Once they adjusted, I was able to see my hand was covered with something white and crusty, along with something dark that resembled dried blood.

Brit was nowhere in sight, so I crawled across the floor, certain I would fall if I stood. The tile in the bathroom was cold, and I fought the urge to lie on it until my head ceased to throb. The counter provided a stronghold to help me to my feet.

Once stable, I lifted my head to see myself in the mirror and nearly passed out at what I saw. I looked like Alice Cooper. Or Ozzy Osbourne immediately after one of his alleged bat mutilations. My hair was stringy and clotted with blood and . . . something else . . . oh, my God, it was ejaculate. My right eye was sealed shut with it, and it had dripped down my face and covered my shirt. The back of my head was a tangled mass, and I flinched at the tenderness when I touched it. I must have cut my head open.

I fought the fresh tears filling my eyes. Last night's makeup was smeared all over my face. I was a horror show. Turning on the water, I willed it to warm up quickly. I had to get out. Now. I cleaned myself up as much as possible without investing in a shower. There was no way I was getting naked and vulnerable with Brit lurking somewhere in this city. Attempts to cleanse my hair were useless.

I changed into a pair of jeans and a T-shirt, slipped on my boots and grabbed a baseball cap I had yet to wear. I balled the length of my hair up in a hair tie and put on the hat, hoping to completely conceal the blood and semen. My face was unmarred, thank God, as I didn't want to raise any suspicions on my way out of the hotel.

After cramming the bare essentials into my purse, I let myself out of the hotel room, leaving all of my other belongings and the key behind. I scanned the long hallway for signs of Brit, and, not finding any, bolted for the far elevators, knowing he never took them.

The elevators opened on the first floor and I burst forth, fast walking toward my freedom. I jumped into the first cab in line. "La Guardia, please," I announced and settled back to inventory my wallet. I had two credit cards, one my parents paid for, and another I'd applied for and never used. One way or the other, I was flying home that day. No one would know about this. I would charge the ticket to my own card and take a cab home from the airport.

I was terrified someone would notice the blood in my hair or worse, smell me. I maintained great personal space in line and my eyes darted wildly. Each moment I expected to see Brit race into the airport.

"One way to Ann Arbor, Michigan, please." The clerk eyed me suspiciously, and I realized that with no luggage, a baseball cap and no makeup, I looked like a twelve-year-old runaway. "Going back to school. We shipped my clothes. I have a real weakness for clothes," I smiled. She seemed satisfied. Or uninterested.

"It's cheaper to purchase a round-trip."

"Okay."

"It's also much cheaper to fly into Detroit." My mind whirled. I wouldn't have enough money to take a cab all the way back to school.

"What's the difference?"

"Five hundred and thirty dollars to Ann Arbor, and four hundred to Detroit."

"Try this card." I said, handing her my new personal Visa. "If it'll take the Ann Arbor amount, let's do that. My roommate is not back to school yet. I won't have a ride home." I willed myself to stop talking; she was not requesting my entire dossier. She gave me the eye again, and I wondered if I smelled like rotting protein.

"It went through." She smiled and went about organizing my tickets and boarding passes. "Here you go, sweetie, have a good flight." I took the ticket and tried to stop myself from running helter-skelter to the gates. Security seemed to take forever. I wanted more than anything at that moment to clear the terminal so I would be out of Brit's sight line should he burst through the doors.

I sat patiently at my gate with a book I didn't read. My heart was aching and my stomach sick. I had several hours before my flight, so I wandered about, surveying the area for food. Pizza sounded pretty good, so I bought a slice of New York-style pizza and vowed it would be the last New York-style anything I experienced again.

I nibbled slowly, sipping a diet soda. My stomach gurgled happily, as I hadn't eaten very much the night before. What a fucking mess I was, inside and out. My crusty, stinking hair was nagging at me. I wanted nothing more than to shower.

I laid down in an empty row of seats at the rear of the plane, flinching when I heard my hair crunch under me, and dozed off for most of the flight between New York and Chicago. Much of the second leg was spent in the *bathroom, trying to clean my hair. I surrendered my efforts the third time someone pounded on the door. I wanted so badly to be clean.*

I knew my machine would be loaded with messages from my parents. It wasn't completely unusual for me to go a weekend without calling, but I felt guilty for all of the lying. They would be so disappointed if they knew what I had done. I loved my parents, and out of respect had never rebelled or caused them problems.

I should have listened to my father. He had been so right, so long ago. Brit was absolutely mad. It felt good to be free of him and I forced myself to relax. It was over. It was finally over. I was free.

I gave the cabbie my address and in less than twenty minutes I was home. My body ached with relief, fear and sadness. Despite my exhaustion, I raced for the shower. It took me almost an hour to carefully clean my hair and head wound. A hand mirror showed a small gash in the back of my head. I assumed it wouldn't require stitches, as the bleeding had stopped. Hot water loosened the crust, and the sight of red spiraling down the drain caused me to vomit what was left of my New York-style pizza and soda. Once I felt a modicum of cleanliness, I dragged ass to bed and crashed instantly.

68

Meridan, curled up in the corner of the couch, was so engrossed in her reading she scarcely acknowledged Lynden as she entered the back door.

"Hey, I brought pizza," Lynden said, and Meridan looked up. There was an open bottle of Corona Light on the coffee table and discarded tissues covered the floor and couch.

"I'm really sorry," Meridan said, for the first time having no interest in food.

"For what?" *For the whole list of infractions*, Lynden wondered, *or just the top ten?*

"I made this all about me. I didn't realize you were involved with Brit and, I guess, Ash." Lynden nodded somberly, not knowing what to say. "I feel really bad."

"Why?"

"I haven't finished it, but this all must be very hard for you."

Lynden nodded. "In more ways than I ever would've thought."

"It must be hard for you to know he has moved on and is, well, fixated— Brit used that term—on someone else. Maybe he likes me because I look like you."

"Honestly, I really don't know what drives him, or them. All these years later, I'm no closer to understanding."

"Have you read this lately?" She tapped the journal gently.

"Yes, I've been reading it again, going through slowly. It's pretty painful. Embarrassing, really."

"Embarrassing? I think it's fantastic." Meridan sat up. "I'm totally into it. I mean, don't get me wrong, I feel really bad for you, but this is like a movie. Oh, here, I printed these out. I thought you should read them and tell me what you think."

"What's this?" Lynden looked at the first page of a stack of papers. It was a printout of an e-mail, to Meridan from someone named "Marksman."

"Marksman? That's a rather disturbing play on names."

"Tell me. Everyone is so over it."

Lynden settled into her corner of the couch and began reading.

"These don't sound like Brit."

"I knew it! Ash?"

"I can't say, but not Brit. The letter I read this morning, that was Brit— angry, lucid, decisive, and intelligent."

"So, this makes the two-man theory seem more likely?"

"Again, I have not seen these men in years, more than a decade. I don't know, even now, which was crazy and which wasn't, which is assuming they aren't both insane."

"Yeah, because you said at one point you felt Ash was a lot more sane than anyone was giving him credit for, and, um, he didn't ever seem drunk, though everyone talked about his drinking problem."

"True."

"So, we don't know what's happened in the last twelve years? What if they've both escaped from an asylum or—"

"Meridan, you're in too many movies."

"No, for real. Anything could've happened."

"This isn't Michael Myers in *Halloween* or any other crazy horror flick."

"You're from Michigan. I have a lake house up near Traverse City. Maybe when this all blows over, we could go?"

Lynden sat back and evaluated the actress for a moment before responding. She tried to imagine hanging out with Meridan Marks—having some drinks, sitting on a dock, watching the sunset. It was too surreal. "That would be nice," she said simply.

"Do you love him?"

"Do I or did I?"

"It's obvious you did."

"You know what? I'm very uncomfortable."

"You should have another drink then, because I've started this and I'm not stopping until I know everything about him and about what the future holds for me. You're still alive. That's good news."

"By the grace of God."

"What's that supposed to mean?"

"You need to read more."

"God, it's so intense. I guess this doesn't have a happy ending?"

"Not unless you call this—" Lynden gestured with her arms, looking around "—a happy ending. I'm alone, I have few friends, I haven't had a productive relationship since I met him, them. I'm afraid of everyone and everything, I have obsessive-compulsive disorder . . ." Lynden buried her face in her hands.

"You have a wonderful life, Lynden. I've been sitting here, with this, feeling so happy, sad, upset, nervous, anxious, furious, horrified, the whole spectrum. I'm serious. I feel so close to you. Don't be embarrassed. Let's talk about it." Lynden struggled not to correct Meridan's misspeak and resisted her cajoling.

"I don't want to talk about it. I lived it. I just want you to take what you can from what I lived and move on. Save yourself."

"How bad does it get? It's so sad, Lyn . . ."

"Den." Lynden finished her name, correcting her for what she hoped would be the last time. "I prefer Lynden."

"Oh, sorry. People always call me Mer, it's just habit to shorten." She smiled warmly, and Lynden hoped she hadn't come across as rude or harsh. "I came here hoping to help myself, but I met you, I read this, and now I want to help you, too. I think we can get through this together."

"I'm not involved in what is going on presently."

"You have the answers. I've made a list of things we can check out or have checked out." Lynden shook her head vehemently.

"No way. You can use whatever information you have and try to find them, but I will not make calls or do research. I already feel too close."

"What do you mean?"

"I feel like you're a portent."

"I am important."

Lynden tried not to roll her eyes. "I said 'portent.' It means omen. I'm worried you represent something."

"I don't follow."

"I can't explain. I feel the fact he is so close to you will bring him close to me, and I can't have that."

"The incident with Ash. Is all of this real?"

"Yes, it is. I wish it weren't, believe me." Lynden felt Ash's hands on her hips, moments before he violated her. She swallowed hard and forced herself to breathe.

"Is this too much?"

"No, just give me a minute." She counted in her head and focused on her breathing. "I know it's silly."

"No, it isn't. I'm sorry, is it weird I'm so interested?"

"No."

"Every time you were ready to, um, go to the next level, something horrible happened. The couch."

"Oh, God. It was the most horrific moment of my life."

"Ash raped you. Did he ever tell Brit? The suspense is killing me."

"I would have no way of knowing." Lynden stood and prepared two plates with cheese pizza and brought them back to the table. Meridan was busy in the bar opening a bottle of Cakebread chardonnay. It was early, but Lynden was exhausted.

She answered a litany of questions for the next couple of hours, leaving her nauseated and depressed. She could tell Meridan was intensely interested in finishing what was left of the journal, so she cleaned up the dishes and said good night.

CONSUMED

After a long shower, Lynden left yet another message for Brady. Was he waiting until he had finalized everything before bringing her into it?

Far too early, the doorbell snatched me from sleep. I ran to the landing and peered down to the front doorstep. My heart seized at the sight of the flowers sitting majestically in a large vase—white roses in a pink, blown-glass vase. After ten minutes, I felt reasonably sure he was not lingering outside. I brought the vase inside and threw the card away without opening it. I couldn't bear a hollow apology. The flowers were glorious, but nothing more than a sickening reminder of the suite in Manhattan for me. I deposited them on the balcony and closed the drapes.

Each morning that week, the same bouquet arrived. I followed the same regimen each time, setting them out on the patio. I didn't want them in the house. I had to ignore him.

Returning from the grocery store, I found the light on my machine blinking. I pressed the button to play the messages and my mind reeled when I heard his voice. Brit sounded breathy and exhausted, his voice rough. I wanted to lunge at the machine, but I was paralyzed.

"You didn't answer my questions. I know what you're doing—more playing hard to get. It won't work. We belong together. Forever. You may think this is over, but it's just a rough patch. I apologized. I'm sorry. I lost my head. I'm losing my mind. I need you. Reese! If you are there, pick up the phone. Reese!" He was screaming now, and the speaker in my machine was vibrating as if it would blow. "Why are you doing this to me? All I did was try to take care of—" The machine mercifully cut him off, and I was angry with myself when I began to cry. I slid onto the floor and let my emotions overtake me.

CONSUMED

"Please," I begged no one in particular, "give me the strength to walk away from him. I can't take it anymore."

The phone screamed again and my hands flew to my ears.

"Honey, it's Mom. Listen, Daddy and I want to make sure you're okay. We haven't heard from you in a week. Give us a call." Just the sound of my mother's voice prompted a fresh tide of tears. I was anything but okay. I stretched out on the floor and eventually fell asleep, my mind craftily trying to rewrite history.

When I awoke, the light was fading. I wasn't sure how long I'd been asleep, but felt I needed to get out, to drive my car and see people, avoid my misplaced nostalgia.

I switched into auto-pilot knowing exactly where I needed to be: Brady. He had always provided me with a shoulder to cry on. My heart leapt when I saw his car and no others in the drive. His tall, rangy body filled the doorframe as I trudged up the front steps.

"Reesey, where the hell have you been?"

"You guessed it," I sighed, and he furrowed his brow in question. "Hell." He opened the screen door for me to pass through and engulfed my entire body in a long hug. My attempts to withhold tears were futile. His embraced lingered as I sniveled and struggled to regain my composure.

"Let it out, baby girl," he cooed, his hands kneading my back in a tender but effective massage. I started to relax a bit and eventually felt I could pull away. He led me by the hand to the couch, and I was distinctly aware of how hideous I must look. I glanced about for tissue, a futile search in this home of three men, and dried my eyes with my sleeve, discreetly wiping my nose.

"What did he do to you?" Brady asked. I didn't want to tell him the truth. He vaguely knew about Brit, and, in telling him bits and pieces, I realized I had deliberately kept the details of my relationship secret from everyone. I was embarrassed by how defenseless I was against him. Despite all my efforts to make it seem as non-threatening as possible, Brady had still detected malice in Brit. It frightened me that he was disturbed by broad strokes that omitted the seriously dangerous moments.

315

"He's dangerous and he's hiding something," Brady contended, promising to be at my beck and call should trouble arise.

"I have no idea. I swear, after four months, I don't feel like I know anything about him at all."

"I can't believe you would take off with him to another state."

"I know. It was stupid."

"Your parents would kill you if they knew what you'd done."

"Don't I know it? I had to use almost every dime of credit I have to get back home."

"You could've called me. I would've done anything to help you." He reached out to brush a stray curl from my face and I swatted his hand away.

"Whoa, Killer," he chastised.

"I'm so sorry!" I gushed, and reached out for his hand. It had been an involuntary response. *"I hit my head and it's really been tender,"* I lied, and he looked skeptical. It occurred to me just then that since I'd returned from New York, I'd worn my hair in either a loose ponytail at the nape of my neck or a high ponytail. It also occurred to me I hadn't wanted Brady to touch my hair.

He soothed me with a big bear hug and I wished, not for the first time, I hadn't met him when I was in a relationship. We had a strong bond, but he had started dating Dorrie over a year ago, and they now were on the marriage track. He told me Dorrie was out of town, as were his roommates, and I was welcome to stay over. I jumped at the chance to avoid returning to my apartment in the dark.

70

Brady and I spent the day together buying books for next term. We enjoyed lunch at Middle Kingdom, my appetite strong for the first time in months. I wondered if it was partly a result of Brady's protective and reassuring presence. I had one eye out for Brit at all times. I wondered where he was and what he was doing. I dreaded going home to my empty apartment, but Dorrie was on her way back to school and Brady could have no evidence of my visit. She was not comfortable with our friendship and couldn't believe we were simply good friends with no romantic involvement. I found it absurd, and wondered what the hell he saw in her anyway.

It was nearly dark when I returned to my apartment. I cursed myself for not leaving on a light and looked to the blinking VCR as a point of reference. Instead of flashing twelve o'clock as it had since I had moved in, it read seven forty-seven p.m. Sweat leaked from my pores and I resisted the urge to run for the door. There was an explanation. I flipped on the light closest to me and did a visual search of the first floor. Nothing was out of place. I approached the entertainment center, wondering if we had lost power and the clock had reset itself. My stereo was on and the pause symbol was up on the LCD screen.

I reached for the remote, which didn't appear to have been disturbed. Clearly, there had been a power outage.

I depressed the pause button and Nine Inch Nails roared from my stereo. The remote flew from my hands as I juggled it, trying to turn down the volume. As it skittered under the couch, I whirled about, certain Brit was in my apartment. I did not own the disc. He was here or had been. The ominous and haunting music paralyzed me. I tried to be optimistic. This song was sad. It was about resignation, about something the singer could never have. I manually lowered the volume and backed against the wall, a torrent of tears washing over me.

"Brit. I'm sorry." I lied. "I never should've left New York the way I did." I choked the words out and wished for the first time in my life I owned a gun.

"Brit!" I screamed, feeling desperate to confront him once and for all. Trent Reznor was the only one answering.

From where I stood, I could see no signs of forced entry. How did he get in? At once, I knew. I had left the patio door unlocked. I must have. I turned to it slowly and saw the dowel I used as an added safety measure standing up at the end of the track. The blinds were pulled open enough for me to edge out to the patio to deposit his latest gift. My God, he had seen the flowers.

"Brit!" I called, growing more confident each time he didn't appear. I wanted to search my apartment. I wanted to end it forever. I was willing to do whatever it took. I would lie to him. I would tell him I loved him. I would have sex with him, and the moment I could flee, I would. I would run and hide. If I could just make it through the night.

What should I do? The police? What would they say? Brit didn't emerge, so I crawled to the phone and dialed Brady's number. After a frantic explanation he assured me he would be over immediately.

After turning off the music, I huddled in the corner of my first-floor landing. If Brit came down the stairs at me, I could run out to my car. If he tried to come through the front door, I could bolt to the balcony and jump off.

Brady searched the house and confirmed I'd left the patio door unlocked. I put on the bravest face I could, knowing Dorrie was already mad he'd come.

"Do you want me to stay? I will. I'm worried, Reese." I wanted him to stay, but didn't want to be the reason he and Dorrie broke up.

"I'm okay, thanks for coming. I'm sorry if I ruined your night." He held me tight, and I didn't ever want to let go.

71

The phone rang early, too early. Without thinking, I grabbed the receiver and held it to my ear.

"Get him out of your fucking house, Reese, or I swear to God, I'll kill you both!" Brit screamed, causing a white-hot bolt of terror to crash through my body. He thought Brady was still here! I slammed down the phone.

Police? No. Brady. I frantically dialed and resisted the impulse to peek outside for Brit's truck. My body was electric as I braced myself for Brit's thunderous knock on my door.

"Brady! Brady, I need help. Brit is somewhere near my apartment. He called. He knew you were here. He thinks you still are! He threatened to kill us both!"

"Whoa! Reesey, slow down, I was sleeping. What happened?" I crawled to the landing with the cordless clutched to my ear. I peeked out the window and saw nothing.

"He just called and said to get you out of my fucking house or he'd kill us both!"

"What? Jesus! I'll be there in less than five. Do not open the door for anyone but me."

I crouched in the corner of the landing and prayed Brady would arrive before Brit took off my front door or crashed through my window. I crawled down the stairs and over to the sliding glass window. Mustering all of my courage, I peeked through the curtain, fully expecting to see Brit, foaming at the mouth and wielding a weapon.

I put my back against the wall and waited. I heard the police sirens long before they arrived. I ran to the window as a cavalcade of motorcycles screeched to a stop in front of my condo. First, Brady, then our friends Nick and Alex, and finally, a cop car, lights blazing and sirens wailing. I raced to the door, threw it open and rushed to Brady, hurling myself into his open arms. He held me close while Nick approached the cop car.

"You won't believe this. We were breaking the speed limit by about fifty miles per hour and got busted. Once I took off my helmet, the cop and I recognized each other from high school. I told him to follow us. Let me talk to him." I stepped back and let him dismount. He shook hands with the cop and gave him a "guy" hug. They talked for a moment and Brady pointed to me. They both approached, overwhelming me with apprehension.

"Hey, I'm Matt." The handsome young cop extended a hand to me and I shook it firmly. "Brady tells me you've been having some problems?"

"I, well, I don't think the police need to be involved. I called Brady because, well, I was afraid." I shrugged my shoulders and beseeched my friends nervously.

"Reese isn't the type to cry wolf, Matt," Alex interjected. "If she called us, there's a problem," he said, committing me to dealing with law enforcement.

"Why don't we go inside," Matt suggested, and all of the guys dismounted and placed their helmets on their seats. Once inside, I served juice and we settled in. I wondered if Brady had imparted any details to Nick or Alex from when we spoke, but doubted it; there had been no time. I now had to decide what was to be shared and how I wanted the situation portrayed.

"Tell me what happened," Matt prompted, opening a small pad he had taken from his pocket.

I looked at the anxious eyes of my rescuers and tried to find a starting point. "I've been having some problems breaking up with someone. I thought he was in my apartment last night—"

"He was. I came over and checked the grounds and the apartment. Reese was really rattled. I wanted to stay, but Dorrie . . ." Everyone nodded, knowing.

"This morning, the phone rang, it was my ex—uh, my, the guy I'd been

seeing, and he told me to get Brady out of the house." My explanation was intentionally vague. I was hesitant to involve the police in what was a personal matter and most likely just another one of Brit's games.

"Reese!" Brady reprimanded.

"He said he would kill us."

"Are you sure it was your, I'm sorry, what is his name?"

"Brit."

"Are you sure it was Brit on the phone?"

"His voice, it's unmistakable."

"When was the last time you saw him?"

"Over a week ago, in Manhattan."

"Does he live there?"

"No, he lives here. We were there together. I flew home." I tried to appear calm. I was reluctant to have the police call or visit Brit.

"What other trouble have you been experiencing?" Matt asked.

"None. Well, he's really persistent." I walked to the balcony and opened the drapes to reveal the bouquets.

A cacophony of responses rose from the ranks.

"Are these all from him?" Matt stood and came closer to inspect. "They're all the exact same arrangement . . . they must be."

"Yes. I threw away the cards."

"You're kidding. So you don't know what they said? They could've been evidence!" Brady yelped, coming out of his chair.

"I didn't want to read them! I just want it over." Reflexively, Alex rose from his seat and put an arm around me.

"Okay, relax, Brady. He hasn't physically harmed her, so there isn't much we can do. He actually has to make a physical move toward her for us to step in." I burst into laughter; I couldn't help finding the humor. Matt had hit the issue square. I was a fucking mental case, wracked with guilt, my self esteem was in the toilet, I had given up friends and viable relationships, I was looking over my shoulder everywhere I went, I couldn't bear to be alone, but Brit hadn't physically harmed me in any traceable manner.

"I'm sorry for laughing," I said. "Relief, I guess." I wiped the tears from my eyes. "Thanks for not throwing these guys in jail, Matt, and thank you for coming. You can make whatever report you need to, but, honestly, I think he was driving by, maybe saw Brady arrive and assumed."

"What?" Pencil poised, Matt tried to catch my eye.

"Oh, sorry, he has a thing about Brady and me. He thinks there's something going on. I'm sure he was just angry. You know how people get." I couldn't stop thinking of Brit outside, fuming at my involving the police.

"Listen, Reese. I'm not saying there's nothing we can do. We can talk to him."

"No! I mean, really. Obviously, I don't perceive a threat that would involve the police. I called Brady in a moment of weakness."

"I don't think I'm entirely comfortable with leaving this alone. What does he drive?" I gave him the make and model of Brit's truck and motorcycle, but couldn't remember the license plate numbers. I reported his full name and apartment number, but didn't know the street address of the complex.

"Reese, if anything frightens you or you find anything out of the ordinary, call me at this number." Matt handed me a business card listing his direct line. "If I'm not reachable there," he said, scribbling on the back of the card, "this is my mobile number. Additionally, I will notify dispatch to send a car over immediately if your phone number ever connects with nine-one-one."

"Thank you so much, Matt." I smiled genuinely for the first time that morning.

Brady wanted to stay, but I suggested he go back to Dorrie. I packed a bag and headed to my parents' house. I even contemplated coming clean with them. I no longer felt safe living alone.

I lasted one day at home with my parents nagging at me before I fled back to school—afraid I would tell them everything. Turning into the driveway, I noticed a black BMW sedan in my parking spot, odd, as parking was assigned. I slammed on the brakes and retreated, slowly reversing around to the opposite end of the tiny complex to park. I scanned the area for Brit's bike or truck. I walked between two buildings and navigated through the bushes, trees and shrubs lining the small pond in the center of the complex, my eyes fixed on the back of my building.

I nearly wet my pants when Brit rounded the side of my condo and hoisted himself up onto the patio. I ducked quickly behind a large bush and fought the urge to vomit. He was completely disheveled. He had at least a week's worth of growth on his face, his hair was matted, his jeans had a rip in the knee and his T-shirt was old and faded. He looked more like Ash, but even in the quickly fading light I was certain I was watching Brit. He used his hands to shield the glare on the sliding glass door and peered into my apartment. He tried the door, which was locked.

"Fuck!" I heard him hiss.

He turned and slid his back down the glass, ending in a crouch, his head cradled in his hands. I held my breath and waited. He let out a bone-chilling scream and clasped his hands against his temples as if he were keeping his head from exploding. I wanted to run but couldn't; I was completely mesmerized by the horror unfolding before me. He grabbed a vase and hurled it over the balcony into the drive. It shattered, scattering white roses all over the pavement. One after another followed, and he cursed me with each vase he threw down. Dissatisfied with his progress, he braced himself against the balcony and heaved a vase at my patio door, which exploded into a rain of shards ricocheting back at him. I covered my ears.

He launched another vase at the door, unfazed by the blood dripping from his head and hands. It penetrated the glass and disappeared into my apartment. Brit stopped a moment before kicking at the glass. Blood was pouring from his head, transforming his face into a ghastly mask. Once he'd cleared an opening, he slipped inside. I shuddered imagining what he was doing in there.

I ran back to my car as if my life depended on it, reasoning it might, and drove straight to Brady's. Alex opened the door and I burst into frantic, unintelligible babble through my tears. I collapsed into Nick's arms and sobbed uncontrollably. They both tried to calm me down so I could communicate, and Alex inspected me for injury. Nick guided me to the couch and Alex handed me a beer, which seared my throat as I chugged.

"He's there."

"What? Where? Your apartment?" I nodded wildly.

"Do you know Matt's number?" Alex barked at Nick.

"Nine-one-one!" Alex raced to the phone and dialed. I leapt from the couch and ran to the bathroom, dropping to my knees and vomiting the beer into the toilet. My stomach empty, I dry heaved at the visual of Brit's crazed face and vicious attack on my home.

"Sweetie?" A gentle knock on the door interrupted the convulsive heaving.

"Yeah," I answered weakly.

"They're on the way over there. They told us to stay put." I nodded, wondering what would happen, assuming Brit would be held for vandalism and bailed out immediately by his attorney.

An hour later, Matt arrived with Brady on his heels. They had been out together for beers when Matt received the call about activity at my address.

"He was gone . . . your apartment is fucked," said Brady.

"There was a fresh bouquet of flowers on your dining room table, blood all over the vase. We were terrified it was yours," said Matt. "There were prints, but it's unlikely he's ever been printed before. The arrangement was different than the rest. It had one pink rose in the middle of white ones."

"Honey, there was a card." Brady looked down at me and kissed my head when I didn't meet his gaze. "It said, 'I told you I'd never say goodbye.'" He ran a hand through his thick chestnut curls. "Jesus! What're we dealing with here?" I didn't answer.

Matt later told me he'd found semen and blood splattered all over my bed. My parents arrived later that day to discard what was left of my belongings and move me home. I arranged to complete my last three writing courses through independent study.

~

Weeks later, my quiet was shattered by a phone call from Brady's parents. I raced down the hospital corridor, my parents trailing behind me. The group of police officers gathered in the hallway made Brady's room easy to find. I dreaded seeing Dorrie and was relieved to learn she and her parents were resting at a hotel. Brady's parents were in the room with him. Matt was the first to notice me and approached.

"My God, Matt! What happened?"

"Reese." He nodded somberly and introduced himself to my parents.

"Is he okay? Is he going to be okay?"

"He's stable, but not well. He has a serious head injury. If the fire department hadn't arrived when they did, he'd be—"

"Oh, my God! This is all my fault!" My dad collected me in his arms, and I pulled away, not feeling deserving of comfort. "I need to see him." I swiped angrily at my tears, trying to be strong.

"You can't. He hasn't regained consciousness. At this point, it's immediate family only."

"Is there someone here named Reese?" an elderly doctor called out from Brady's room.

"Me! I'm Reese!" I charged the door, but the doctor blocked my path.

"I'm Dr. Marshall. I'm only letting you in because he's calling for you. His parents agreed to it, but you mustn't excite him. He's been unconscious for more than twenty four hours." I nodded my understanding and ducked under his arm.

Mr. and Mrs. Harold rose to greet me. I feared they would be angry with me, but realized they probably didn't know the full story yet. After a quick embrace, I turned my gaze to Brady.

His head was completely bandaged and faint red stains seeped through the dressings. My heart was clasped tightly by guilt, knowing I had brought this to him.

"Reese." His eyes were closed, so I sat next to him and held a thoroughly scraped hand. It looked as if he had been in mortal combat, which I knew he had.

"Brady." I could barely speak through my tears. "I'm here, Brady." I waited. Finally, one eye opened slowly, and I flinched at the red hemorrhage *that had overtaken the white of his eye.*

"Reesey, you're okay." I sobbed. He was nearly killed and only concerned about me. I held his hand gently to my lips. "You have to leave."

"I don't want to. I'm sorry. I know this is my fault." I whispered.

"No, I mean forever. He's coming for you. He wanted your parents' address." He spoke slowly and with great effort.

"Oh, my God," I whispered, my thoughts swirling. Brady had refused to give me up. He'd risked his own life for me.

"Go and never come back."

"I can't leave you. Not like this."

"I love you." He closed his eye and I felt his dad's hands on my shoulders.

"Reese. Matt told us everything. Brady doesn't blame you. He's right though." I kissed Brady's hand and trudged to the door.

"It was so old, it went up like straw. Thank God no one was home. He caught Brady outside when he arrived. It's a miracle he's alive." I could hear Matt talking to my parents.

"Get her the fuck out of here!" Dorrie shouted, closing the distance between us faster than I was prepared for. Matt stood between us, trying to soothe her.

"Dorrie, calm down."

"The fuck I will. She nearly got Brady killed! I want her gone. Daddy! Make her leave!" I was more than willing to go, not only from the hospital, but the state. I was heading to Texas, where I'd been accepted to the University of Texas M.A./Ph.D. program.

72

"Meridan?" Lynden spoke softly and gently tried to rouse the sleeping actress, who had fallen asleep on the couch, the journal closed and held tightly in her arms. "Meridan?" she said a bit louder, and Meridan snapped awake with a yelp.

"Jesus, Lynden! You scared the shit out of me. No, *this* did." She set the journal on the table and stared at it. "Oh, my God. I was having the worst dream. I was you."

"I know what you mean."

"I'm serious. I finished it. I was so upset. I wanted to wake you up, but you were out. I have to pee. Are the doors locked?" Lynden assured her the doors were always locked. She watched Meridan climb the front stairs, grateful she wouldn't have to comb the back steps.

Meridan reappeared moments later. She had removed her makeup, changed into a different pair of jeans and a T-shirt, and pulled her hair into a high ponytail. Lynden stopped in her tracks.

"Wow. You really look like me."

"I think I like it, too. I feel so, I don't know."

Lynden handed her a mug of coffee, and they both sat down at the island.

"I read it all. I feel ashamed." Meridan looked at Lynden sheepishly.

"Why?"

"I was so selfish. This is about you. Not me."

"It *is* about you now."

They shared a long silence. "Does he want to kill me?" Meridan asked softly.

"That's what he said."

"Why?"

"I don't want to make this about me, because clearly it isn't, but what if it's as simple as you looking like me? Like he never finished the job?" Lynden hesitated to make the statement, but it was the only thing she could imagine being true.

Meridan nodded. "At one time he seemed to really like me. I guess I changed all that with those e-mails. I have no doubt this is because of you. I look like you."

"My doctor says his fear of abandonment, you know, his mother and father dying, and even Ash's psychological problems, play a huge part in his rage. He's angry with Ash for not holding it together for him, despite their problems. They both felt all they had was each other."

"How do you leave the house?"

"It's not easy. I think I see them everywhere. It nearly shuts me down." They sat in heavy silence, the winds of fear whispering through the house.

"I don't know how you came out of all this, not just alive, but sane."

"I'm not completely sane. I harbor a lot."

"I guess I know why you surround yourself with food and wine." Lynden nodded. "The hair. You poor thing. I understand now. And the hand washing. I feel like I need to shower, and it didn't even happen to me. It's pretty scary though, him in my apartment . . ."

"It is. I'm surprised he didn't make a move of some type. I'm sure he's still enjoying torturing you."

"What do you mean?"

"He was always fucking with my emotions. I think he enjoyed it, and now he's enjoying pushing your buttons, watching you squirm."

"He never raped you. Right? You didn't leave anything out?"

"No."

"Is Brady okay?"

Lynden winced because at this moment, she didn't know; he hadn't called.

She chose her words carefully. "He survived, barely. There were a couple close calls after I had moved. He moved, too, to Atlanta, and married Dorrie. We talk every once in a while."

"It isn't your fault."

"Yes, it is."

"I'm worried about Christian. He's focused on my relationship with Christian." And Jim, she wanted to say. She wanted to tell Lynden the truth about Christian, but she knew he'd kill her.

"You said he was protected."

"He is. Always. We have to find him, Reese. I mean Lynden. Sorry."

"It's okay. I can't help you any more than I have. You know what he's capable of. You know why I've been in hiding. I know he isn't after me, but it doesn't stop me from being hyperaware. I think you should be, too."

"Do you care if I give these names and leads to Al? He's my P.I. He found you, after all."

"I really don't care, so long as my name never comes into it. Without question, I want him in custody. After that, I'll take a nice dip in the Lethe and move on with my life."

"What's a lethe?"

"The river of forgetfulness. I need amnesia." Lynden tried unsuccessfully to laugh.

"I feel sick."

"You're hungry."

"No, I'm sick to death. I don't want to go back. I want to stay here." Lynden was surprised by Meridan's reticence. Normally full of questions, she appeared exhausted.

"That won't do you any good. You need to stay safe and let your people find him. You're lucky he's so angry. Maybe that will make him careless, like he was with me in the end."

"You know what's sick? I fell in love with him a hundred times while I was reading. I can't imagine going through it for real."

"I'm sorry I can't help you more."

"Thank you for helping me understand. For helping prepare me. For taking me in. For feeding me. For being so nice to me even though I was a horrid bitch when I got here."

"I feel better someone can understand me. You've had a taste of the fear he generates. Now I have someone I can talk to."

"My God, I need to call my people. Joel is probably going insane. I checked your e-mail. He said he had not heard from Brit at all. No one has."

Lynden shivered. "Silence follows rage. It's his way. He's plotting. You're well-insulated, right? You're protected?"

"I have two bodyguards, well, one, but hopefully the other will forgive me for being such a wretched bitch to him. Joel, Roz, Al and now the cops are really involved. When I get back, they'll want me to go into a safe house."

"I think it's for the best. Should you call your bodyguard to come get you?"

"Joel said he's been staying at the Mansion and going by the ranch frequently. He wanted to see if Brit would show up there."

"Just the thought of him being this close to me, several times, perhaps."

"Yeah. How far are we from my ranch?"

"Where is it exactly?"

"Off Lebanon and the toll way."

"Fifteen minutes. Good Lord."

"Can Cameron come and get me?"

"What about your car?"

"Oh, yeah."

"Further, we can't risk that he's followed. Maybe you should meet him at the Mansion?"

Meridan cocked her head to the side and tears began to fall in fat drops from her eyes.

"What is it?" Lynden grabbed Meridan's hand in hers and waited a moment.

"I don't want to leave here. Leave you." Meridan squeaked and embraced Lynden tightly.

Lynden returned the hug, keenly aware she felt no need or desire to break the embrace prematurely.

"We're going to be okay," she reassured Meridan quietly and patted her back.

As Meridan got into her rental car, she hoped to herself she and Lynden would remain friends.

73

Phone in hand as she backed out of her garage, Lynden could not resist trying Brady again.

"I'm concerned about what's going on. Please call me as soon as you can." She wanted to add that she loved him, but thought of Dorrie and decided against it.

Lynden felt restless and charged. She had nothing scheduled for the day, and her next review wasn't due for weeks. She considered calling Gia or Dane, but hesitated. She still was trying to wrap her mind around the strange events of the past few days.

With Meridan gone, Lynden was left to digest the long-dormant memories and emotions that had risen to the surface. The sight of a Starbucks jerked her from distraction. She pulled into the lot and parked, unaware of the car pulling in behind her and parking two spots away, the driver not emerging.

She stood patiently in line, ordered and waited next to the barista for her name to be called. The hair stood up on the back of her neck as she suddenly sensed someone watching her.

"Hey, beautiful," a man said from behind her. She shrieked loudly and turned to bolt, running smack into Dane's chest. "Whoa, Lynden, calm down!"

"Jesus, Dane, you scared me to death!"

"I called to you outside. What's wrong with you?"

"Nothing! I was just lost in my thoughts, I suppose." He led her by the hand to a table and left her while he ordered an iced latte.

Bearing their beverages, he returned and sat. "Why haven't I heard from

CONSUMED

you? It's been, like, weeks."

"So much is going on. Let's see . . . Oh, I've been offered a partnership in a restaurant. Can you imagine?"

"By . . ."

"Gia Androvaldi."

"As in Androvaldi Excavation?" He was duly impressed when she confirmed with a nod.

"He's like Midas, that Luca."

"Tell me. She's an attorney. He wants her to work for him, but she wanted her own business. He's funding the whole thing, and they both want me on board."

"Do it. Like I said, everything he touches turns to gold. What's she like?"

"She's gorgeous and whip smart."

"Like someone else we know?" Lynden, ever self-depreciating, rolled her eyes at him.

"I'm seriously considering it."

"Would this be the end of Hatcher Consulting or your column?"

"Wouldn't necessarily have to be, but I've been thinking also of getting back to writing fiction." She let the comment dangle in the air.

"Are you serious? I think it's a brilliant idea. Will you write about me? I'm a perfect subject—tall, dark, handsome, heartbreakingly gay." He batted long, dark lashes at her and she laughed, relieved to be in the company of a familiar friend.

"Absolutely."

"You know Luca Androvaldi's a gangster, right?" Dane lowered his voice and shifted his eyes dramatically.

"Don't be ridiculous. There are no gangsters anymore." They both laughed heartily.

"I know people," he said. "I'm serious, Lynden, there are rumors."

"Yeah, there also are rumors you're straight."

"How does that happen? I work so hard!" He poured on the diva attitude to deliver his last line.

"How's it going at the restaurant?"

"Spectacular. Come tonight. Call Gia and bring her with." Lynden promised to call. Somehow, she felt slightly unburdened knowing Brit was busy terrorizing someone else.

74

Gia was thrilled with the invitation to Mexi-Waiian Island and offered to pick Lynden up later that evening.

Lynden spent a few hours putting her house back in order, stripping the beds and washing the sheets, combing the steps. Once finished, she wanted to relax awhile before getting ready. Her mind kept returning to the fact she hadn't yet heard from Brady. She instinctively assumed the worst—that he'd rethought the entire situation upon his return to Atlanta, and that Dorrie had convinced him to reconcile. She dialed and got his voice mail.

"Hey, I'm getting worried. I'd expected to hear from you by now. I'm dying to fill you in on what has been a very bizarre few days. At least let me know you're okay." She hung up disappointed, resigned she'd done all she could.

Lynden lingered in the shower and let the events of the past few days wash over her. She hadn't digested how surreal it was to have Meridan Marks in her house, let alone how unnervingly alike they looked. She doubted Meridan's detective or the Los Angeles Police would have better luck in finding Brit or Ash than the Michigan police had years ago. He was out there, and he was going to hurt Meridan Marks.

~

"Oh, my God. Stand still, I need a photo!" Gia gushed when Lynden opened her front door.

"What?"

"You look gorgeous! Where are your glasses? Why is your hair down? Are you seeing someone?"

Lynden laughed. She'd selected a black, corset-style Dolce & Gabbana dress that was far too revealing and high, sexy Gucci signature sandals. Her hair hung loose around her shoulders, but she had a black ponytail holder around her wrist for the inevitable anxiety and ensuing ponytail.

"I felt like dressing up."

"Daddy was right, you really look like—"

"Meridan Marks."

"Not so much with the glasses and when your hair is back, but with makeup and hair, it's spooky."

"Tell me about it," Lynden laughed and poured her guest a glass of champagne.

"Thanks for inviting me out. I've been dying to go there. You consulted, yes?" Lynden nodded. "Perfect, I can see one of your concepts in action."

"You can meet my friend Dane. He—"

"Dane Paige? You know him? Oh, my God! We've been trying to get Dane involved in a party for us, but his people said no. And I don't mean cater. Daddy's planning a huge vendor appreciation party at the house and wanted a celebrity chef."

"Well, maybe his people never explained it to him. You'll meet him tonight and you can ask him in person. You'll love him. He's one of my closest friends." Gia was more than impressed and launched into a verbal fantasy about stealing Dane from Clifton Fox.

"Perhaps he's not the best choice for us. He doesn't love doing Italian, and, anyway, there are tons of chefs who would kill for what you're paying."

"What *we* are paying, right?"

"I've yet to speak to my attorney, but I'm definitely interested."

"Daddy will be devastated if you don't come on board."

"I'm on board, I just don't know if this is the right time for me to get involved in such a deep project. I plan to help you until the doors open, but I've been thinking about exploring some different career paths."

"What?" Gia stood back, stunned.

"Relax, I meant on the writing front."

"Good lord, you scared me. Surely, working with me would leave you plenty of time to do that."

They finished their champagne and walked out to Gia's new Bentley Continental Supersports convertible.

"This car is sublime."

"Should I sweeten the deal?"

"What?"

"You can have my car if you partner with me."

"Gia, this is a three hundred thousand dollar car."

"So?"

"So, it's *your* three hundred thousand dollar car."

"I know, but I'm not really a Bentley girl. If I were, it would be the sedan—not *this*. Daddy bought it for me for graduation. What do you think?"

"I don't know. You boggle my mind at times."

"How so?"

"I just can't fathom such wealth."

"Partner with me, and it'll be just the beginning."

"You sound like Satan. Do you want my soul, too?" They both laughed as they roared down the tollway.

~

As Gia and Lynden entered the front doors Clifton clapped his hands and announced dramatically, "Ah, people! We have visiting royalty!" Lynden smiled and hugged Clifton warmly. She hadn't seen him since the opening and her subsequent review. "You, my dear, look radiant. And this hair! Who'd have thought it was this glorious." He reached out to touch, but she dodged him and shifted the focus to Gia. "And who is this?" he asked, eyeing Gia, calling his questionable sexuality, once again, into further question.

"Clifton, this is Gia Androvaldi. She's opening a new concept." He extended his hand to enfold hers and smiled like a schoolboy.

"Androvaldi? As in Excavation?" Gia nodded. Clifton explained Androvaldi Excavation had helped him transform his own concept.

"Great, I hope they do as well for me. Your place is beautiful, so eclectic." Gia poured on the charm and had Clifton tripping along hanging on every word as the hostess led them to a wonderful table on the deck. As they walked by the kitchen, she saw Dane bustling about, happy and productive. He settled several dishes into the window for the expeditor to check prior to handing them off to the waiters. Noticing her, he did a double take, pretended to faint and popped up waving. Lynden rolled her eyes and laughed.

Gia gushed about the restaurant, insisting she know every facet with which Lynden had helped. Clifton stationed himself at Gia's right elbow as they toured the restaurant, and regaled her with each of Lynden's contributions.

"Ms. Marks! Oh, Ms. Marks!" she heard Dane call as he strode up the deck stairs. "Oh, you're not Meridan Marks, but the fabulous, the one, the only Lynden Hatcher. Ladies and gentlemen, Ms. Hatcher will not be signing autographs this evening," Dane announced to the other guests on the deck, none of whom were interested in anything but a moment of his time. Gia appeared star-struck. She stood and introduced herself.

"Welcome, welcome, please sit! So wonderful to meet you, Gia. Lynden has told me all about you!" Gia smiled widely and Clifton sighed. Dane turned to Lynden. "Now, what possessed you to wear your hair down? Are you ill? Dying? Is this your last night on the town? You can tell me. I'll make it. I have people." He clasped Clifton's hand, which Clifton shook off immediately to everyone's amusement.

"I was just feeling adventuresome. Why does everyone have to make such a big deal?"

"We aren't. You look great," Gia reassured. The waiter arrived with drinks and they chatted effortlessly until longing stares forced Dane to mingle with guests.

"Should I ask him? You know, for Daddy?" Gia whispered and Lynden nodded. Clifton seemed confused until Dane returned to the table.

"Mr. Paige."

"Dane."

"Dane, my father's people have contacted your people about the possibility of you acting as celebrity chef for a party we're having. It's a vendor appreciation party, and he wants nothing but the best of everything."

"How can I say no? What did my people say?"

"They said no."

"Hmmm. Why don't you and I come to terms on it personally?"

"Are you serious?"

"As a rattlesnake, sweetie."

"Oooh, Daddy's going to be so thrilled," Gia squealed and wasted no time dialing her father on her cell phone to deliver the news.

No one called attention to Lynden's hair, which, at some point during the evening, ended up in a ponytail. Once tucked in bed, she felt she had experienced close to a perfect evening, despite the fact Brady had yet to call.

75

When the coffee cup slipped from her hand and shattered to pieces, a searing pain in her foot penetrated Lynden's stupor. Impossible.

". . . met with the actress over the weekend in Dallas." Mouth gaping, Lynden stared at her never-used PR photo taken nearly seven years ago when she launched her column. At the time, the similarities between the women were not as strong, but, as the talking head on *Your Hollywood Morning* had pointed out, the resemblance was uncanny.

She raced to her laptop and brought up Google. Once "Lynden Hatcher" and "Dallas" were entered, the address for Hatcher Consulting appeared along with a direct link to her consulting website. She scrambled for her cell phone and left a frantic message for her assistant not to go into the office for any reason until further notice.

After scrolling through her address book for the number Meridan had programmed, she dialed.

"Meridan, you need to call me immediately. You promised me." Meridan's face appeared on the big screen, and Lynden lunged for the remote and turned up the volume.

"She's a very courageous woman. For her to come forward, to help me, is very brave. I will be forever grateful as soon as we find the men responsible for terrorizing not just us, but probably countless women. We are asking for the help of the public. We know they're from the Detroit area . . ."

"Noooooo!" Lynden screamed and threw the remote. She needed to ground herself before she had a full-on panic attack. Brady.

She reached for her phone again and dialed. The thundering of her heart made it difficult to hear his recorded voice mail greeting, but the sound of his voice calmed her a measure. After a few deep, bolstering breaths, she called Brady's home number. It was apparent from Dorrie's curt greeting that caller ID was in effect and it would do no good to hang up.

"Reese. You need to stop pursuing Brady."

"What? I am not—"

"Don't lie to me. I know he was with you over the weekend. I need you to understand whatever happened between you is over. I'm pregnant. We are working on our marriage. We're both overjoyed with the news. I need you to butt out. For good. Find someone else to help you through whatever crisis you are having. It's always something with you. It's not enough he almost died for you? You'll notice he isn't returning your calls. He doesn't want to speak to you."

"I need to hear this from Brady."

"Let the fact he's not returned your calls speak for him." Dorrie hung up.

Her mind was screaming at her to pack a bag and get out of the house, but she was immobilized by betrayal, terror, and pain. I'll just lie down for a minute, she thought as she collapsed to the floor. Darkness seduced her.

The next thing she knew, her cell phone screamed next to her ear, jerking her from slumber. Her shoulder felt paralyzed and she could barely move it to reach for her phone.

Meridan.

"How could you fucking do this to me?"

"I didn't. You have to listen to me."

"I listened to you on TV!" Lynden yelled into the receiver. She pulled herself up to her knees and slowly got to her feet.

"I was trying to do damage control. While I was in Texas, Joel researched you. He got all of the information. We don't know how it got leaked. I swear."

"You're an opportunistic bitch. Is this some fucking publicity stunt for you?"

"No. I swear. I don't know if some documents were sold from my movie studio or one of my security team. Probably that Noah. I fucking hate him."

"I don't really give a shit. I hope he finds you and kills you."

"I don't think—"

"That's the problem, Meridan. You don't think. But, if you ever wade in those unchartered waters, try thinking for yourself and not ME!!!" She pressed the end button so hard she shattered her thumbnail and burst into tears. Pull it together, Lynden, and get the fuck out of here. She snapped the hair tie on her wrist, hoping pain could bring some clarity to the situation.

Speeding down the driveway, she nearly cut short the life of the lawn guy. It was impossible to concentrate with the constantly ringing phone and her humiliation suffocating her. Meridan. Brady. Fuck him. Fuck her. This was her reward for opening up to them. She turned off the phone. Nothing anyone had to say was of any interest to her.

~

"Welcome to the Four Seasons. Under what name is the reservation?" asked the guest registrar.

"Actually, I have a layover here, unplanned, of course, and I need a room for the week."

"We have a large suite on the sixth floor, overlooking the golf course."

"That'll be fine." She pulled out her credit card and it flew across the marble counter and slipped off of the other side, falling to the floor. She apologized and pleaded with herself to calm down. After signing the necessary paperwork, she was pointed towards the elevators.

"I need to make certain no calls are allowed through to my room, please. If you need to reach me for any reason, please have a message left at the desk or under my door."

"Absolutely," the clerk said.

Once inside her spacious and luxurious suite, she sprawled on the bed and went to sleep.

76

Lynden was surprisingly lucid when she woke up. She knew she was at the Four Seasons, but couldn't remember the details of how she had gotten there. She gazed down at her disheveled appearance. Blood was caked on her foot and sandal; close inspection revealed a huge gash on the front of her ankle.

The coffee cup had shattered. She had dropped it when she saw her own image on television. It was all flooding back. Dorrie. Dorrie was pregnant and Brady was "overjoyed." Lynden inspected her throbbing thumbnail; it had broken to the quick. She must have appeared wildly out of sorts when she checked in with her bloody foot, jeans and a T-shirt. She vaguely recalled rifling her credit card at the hostess. She ran the events through her mind, trying to piece it together. She grabbed her phone to check her voice mail.

"Lyn, it's Meridan, please call me."

"Bitch." Delete.

"Sweetie? Dane here. Hey, funny thing. Saw *YHM* and there was a photo of you, and it seems your life has been in danger, and, oh, yes, Meridan Marks was staying with you all weekend? Call me back, we need to talk."
Delete. Tears leaked from her closed eyes. She was horrified and embarrassed and had no intention of involving anyone else in her mess. That included Brady. He'd already come close to losing his life.

"Lynden, it's Gia. I just got a call from Daddy. Nina was watching some show that said that you had met with Meridan Marks over the weekend to help her figure out a way to stop this person from terrorizing you *both*? Daddy wants you to come out to the house. It's completely secure. Call me." The tears turned

343

to sobs she couldn't hold back. Delete. As kind as Gia and her family had been, Lynden simply could not endure another betrayal. She couldn't open up to anybody else.

Her phone rang and Brady's name appeared on the face. Her heart hammered as she debated through three rings.

"What do you want?"

"Reesey—"

"Do not call me that."

"Come on. I can't believe you're mad at me. I thought you'd want me to do the right thing."

"The right thing would have been for you to tell me you were still sleeping with your wife regularly, despite the fact she was sleeping with another man, before you put what could be a diseased penis inside me."

"Reese."

"It's Lynden!" she screamed.

"Listen, I didn't mean literally we haven't in years. I meant we haven't been regular or happy or in love."

"No, just fucking . . . making babies."

"I know that kid isn't mine."

"Dorrie will be so disappointed. She told me how overjoyed you were at the prospect of being a father."

"Where are you?"

"Don't worry, I can take care of myself."

"I don't want you to."

"I don't want you anywhere near me, now or ever. I trusted you, I believed in you. I shared my life with you!"

"I love you, Reese. Don't shut me out. Not now. We're too close to having it all."

"You have shut me out for almost a week!"

Silence.

"I don't want your kid," Lynden offered, filling the void.

"It's not mine. I swear we haven't slept together in months and the doctor said she's eight weeks."

"It's possible."

"She has agreed to a divorce if the paternity test is negative."

"You should have insisted on a divorce, period. We made plans." She hung up while choking back sobs.

She felt nothing for Brady—not anger, not hatred, not love—nothing. Meridan was another story. She had trusted her to do the right thing. There would be no more opening up to people, no more confiding, no more sharing her feelings, her thoughts, or her past.

Brady, who had been such an enormous part of her life, her happiness, and her well-being, had committed a most traitorous act. He'd made her believe he loved her and was intent upon building a life with her. Now he possibly had a baby on the way, content to live a lie until he knew for sure.

Just as she turned on the bath, Meridan's name appeared on the face of Lynden's ringing phone.

"How could you do this to me? I trusted you," Lynden asked.

"My bodyguard Cameron is convinced his partner, Noah, was the leak. He hasn't been to work in days. The minute I got back, we were bombarded with calls from the press. They knew all about you; there are several old Michigan Police reports with Brit's name on them. I was just trying to downplay your role, especially now. I tried to take the hit. Please don't hate me."

"I don't know what to say."

"Say you're relieved. I think the media's plan backfired in our favor. They hoped to create a shit storm, and, instead, he's not communicating, which is totally weird."

"A lull in the storm."

"I don't think so. I feel really good about it. Christian and I are being watched twenty-four seven. There hasn't been so much as a peep. Are you mad at me?"

"I'm mad at myself. I've never trusted anyone except my parents and Brady with this, and now . . ."

"I don't want you to be alone. Come out here."

"No fucking way. I know him. He's planning. He's laying low so he can attack when you don't expect it, and I don't want to be anywhere near you when it happens. No offense."

"No problem. Everyone out here wants to meet you."

"After they sold me out?"

"None of my close people did that. Joel was just scared to death when I took off. It's in his nature to, what does he call it, information-gather?"

"Yes, that's about right for a lawyer."

"Not just a lawyer, a friend. They all are, and so are you if you'll stop being mad at me."

"I'm not mad. I said I'd help, but you don't understand. My whole life has been exposed."

"Nothing personal, just your career, your accomplishments, and the fact you were once stalked. This is almost over. We played our cards right and we exposed *him* to the world. How long can he hide? Joel says if we can get an address on him, even a former address, we can hit him with a restraining thing."

"A restraining order?"

"Right."

"Really? I don't imagine he would adhere to it, but what are the chances of adding me to it?"

"I'll ask. They're still running down the notes I made from the journal. We're not coming up with anything, though. I say *we,* like I'm in the dredges with them." Lynden smiled at her unintentional slip of the tongue. Pure Meridan.

"Sorry I overreacted, but I don't like people in my business. I'm not like you. I'm not a public person."

"Maybe it's time."

"Time for what?"

"Time for you to stop hiding."

Lynden was just about to get in the tub when her phone rang. Not recognizing the number, she decided not to answer, but putting it down, she fumbled, and accidentally answered it. She was just about to hang up when she heard something that piqued her interest.

"Did you say detective?" she squeaked.

"Yes ma'am. Your alarm company forwarded your contact information to us." Her heart thundered in her chest and she dreaded the answer to her next question.

"What is it, detective?"

"Am I speaking with Lynden Hatcher?"

"Yes, please, tell me what's happened." Her mind was ablaze with possibilities. "Ms. Hatcher, your home is on fire."

"My house? Are you sure?"

"We need you to come to the scene." Scene?

Adrenaline rushed through her system as she sped toward her home. She racked her brain, trying to remember if she had ensured all appliances were off before leaving her house in a fury. Wasn't that one of the ironic benefits of obsessive-compulsive behavior? Wasn't she always assured the appliances were off?

She saw the smoke billowing all the way from Interstate 635 and the tollway, nearly six miles north of her home.

Her bastion, her safe haven. Ruined. After a whiplash-inducing stop, she bolted from her car. Ignoring the crowd of neighbors who had collected in the street, she accosted the first firefighter she encountered. "This is . . . was my house. What happened?" she pleaded. He pointed toward two men in sport coats approaching.

"I'm Lynden Hatcher. Can you please tell me what's going on?"

"I'm Detective Harris and this is Agent Deason," he gestured toward his partner with his thumb.

"Agent?"

"Arson."

Darkness swirled and Lynden reached for her hair tie. It was gone. She'd left it at the hotel. Reaching out blindly, her arms desperate for purchase, she began to fall. Agent Deason caught her and lowered her to the ground.

"Ms. Hatcher!" Disoriented, she looked at the men with glazed eyes for a moment before her muddled thoughts began to gather.

"Good Lord, what happened?" she asked, her eyes wide as she got to her feet.

"You almost fainted."

"I know that! Why do you suspect arson?" She flicked herself in the wrist sharply, hoping the pain would keep her focused.

"We found a can of accelerant in the great room area. With all of those books, this place went up fast." The books! First editions, signed copies. The journal! All gone. The detective's words resonated like the thick, dark smoke threatening to engulf her. She stood vacantly, staring at the rotten carcass of her sanctuary. Only when the arson agent touched her arm gently did she realize her phone was ringing.

"Yes?" She answered and listened carefully. "I know who did this," she muttered numbly after hanging up.

"Really?" The arson agent inched closer, pad at the ready.

"I need to go to my office. No. I need to get out of here."

"Ma'am?" Detective Harris' eyes evaluated her for signs of shock.

"We have to leave here. I have to leave here." She stepped back, tripping on fire-fighting equipment, and fell down, bursting into tears upon impact. These were not the tears of an adult, however. These were the tears of a child; wild, gulping, desperate, and inadequate. After many long moments, she reluctantly accepted Agent Deason's hand and stood. "My office has been, uh, I guess, vandalized? That was my assistant on the phone. Someone broke in."

"And you know who that someone is?" Lynden nodded somberly. The specter of her home threatened to spawn a new crop of tears, so she turned away.

"Is there somewhere we can speak privately?" she whispered, gesturing with her eyes to the throng of onlookers.

Detective Harris extended an arm and led Lynden through the crowd. "Do you know how to get to the police department?" She nodded and drove the short distance to the Highland Park headquarters. Lynden slid her small convertible into one of the several open spaces in front of the beautiful building and followed the officers inside. They settled in a small, Spartan meeting room.

"His name is Britten Holden. I think. Or it could be Ashland Holden." She offered the spelling for the bewildered detectives. "I'm sorry. They're brothers. To the best of my knowledge, they both are from Bloomfield Hills, Michigan."

"What business do they have here, with you?" His tone was saturated with skepticism.

"That is a very long and involved story."

"We've got nothing but time and interest," the arson agent smirked.

A gentle knock on the door came as the interview concluded. A young female cop stuck her face into the already crowded room. "Detective Harris, a word please?" He nodded and she entered.

"Ms. Hatcher?" Lynden turned her tired, red eyes to the young officer. "We've just finished processing the scene at your office." Scene. That word again. Lynden nodded, steeling herself against what the officer had to impart. "It was a God-awful mess. Your assistant was on hand to help us determine what was stolen."

"Nothing."

"I'm sorry?"

"Nothing was stolen."

"Right."

"He was looking for something."

"What?" Lynden held them rapt in her momentary silence.

"My address." Her face collapsed, but she refused to cry anymore.

"If you had to guess, what's his agenda?" Detective Harris asked.

"I have no idea." The plot had thickened, the cast of characters had grown, and Detective "You've Got to be Shitting Me" and Agent "This is a Load of Shit" were now on board, jazzed to be involved in a big-shot, movie star-related case.

"Do you want to stay here for a while?" Lynden declined, wanting instead to go back to the Four Seasons. She required sleep.

"Officer Hoffman? Could you drive Ms. Hatcher back to the Four Seasons? Have your partner follow in a squad car. I need to okay some type of protection." Officer Hoffman agreed and Lynden was too tired to argue. Was this her punishment for interfering with his plan for Meridan? *Hey, as long as I'm in Texas harassing the shit out of Meridan, I can burn down the house of the bitch who's helping her.*

77

"Ms. Hatcher. I've spoken with hotel security and they're aware you're not to receive visitors until either I or another officer returns. If I need to reach you, I'll call you on your cell phone." Lynden nodded and crumbled onto the bed. By the time the door clicked shut, she was asleep.

The noise shot her straight up in bed. Disoriented and confused she sat completely still and waited. What was it? A knock? The lock? Was someone in the room? Was someone trying to gain access? Each beat of her heart was like rising flood water, obscuring her usually keen hearing.

Not another sound. Had she dreamt something? Her phone. Muffled but somewhere here in the bed. Meridan.

"Lynden! How are you?" Meridan chirped happily. "Lynden? Are you there?"

"He burned down my house."

"He who? Did you just say your house burned down?" Meridan asked.

"No. I said *he* burned down my house," Lynden said, slowly articulating every syllable.

"What?" Meridan shrieked loudly.

"Meridan, he destroyed my office and burned down my house." Lynden struggled with the word *destroyed* and images of her townhouse flashed through her mind. She was grateful her assistant had offered to remain at the office and attempt to put it in order. Lynden had asked her to throw away anything unsalvageable.

"There has to be a mistake. It's been so quiet. Could it be a coincidence?"

"No. They found a can of accelerant in my great room. The arson investigators are pretty confident ruling it intentional." Lynden fought back tears, desperate to maintain some composure.

"You've got to come here. Please, I'm worried about you. I have so much security here." Lynden heard Meridan mutter something to someone else and inquired. "Oh, Joel. He wanted to know what was going on."

"Lynden? Joel here. You're on speaker. Call security on the land line, get them to your room immediately. Make them show you identification and look at their faces through the peep hole. You're getting out of there." Joel said firmly with deadly calm. Lynden could hear Meridan rambling in the background. "Meridan, shut up." Lynden wondered momentarily what was going on in Los Angeles; Meridan sounded as frantic as Lynden felt.

She brought the receiver to her other ear and rang the operator. After three rings, the phone was answered, politely, by someone far too composed.

"This is Lynden Hatcher. I need help. Please send security to my room. At least two people." She hung up the phone and sat on the bed. She could hear Joel and Meridan arguing on the other end of the phone, but couldn't piece anything together. Someone's hand was over the mouthpiece or they were off speaker.

"We were already setting up a safe house for Meridan. We are going to put you in it. You're going to go straight to Love Field Airport to Jet East. By the time you get there, I will have arranged a charter for you . . ."

78

The wheels of the Escalade SUV sunk into the soft earth of the driveway as Lynden slowly approached the lake house. The directions had been perfect; she'd made excellent time. It felt good to have emotional and physical distance between herself and Texas. Thoughts of relocation pervaded throughout the flight to Traverse City. As long as she was house-hunting, perhaps it was time to lose herself, again.

The full moon cast a brilliant glow onto a modest two-story dwelling, enhancing its charm. The moment she opened the truck door, she was consumed by the sensations of home. Pine; fresh, clean air; sand and earth. Her heart ached for her parents, and she wondered briefly how she was going to tell them about all this. Mr. Richey, the elderly caretaker, waved to her from the small porch.

"Lynden?" She smiled and nodded.

"Thanks for waiting. I'm sorry to keep you." He held up a beer to let her know he had brought entertainment with him.

"All you need is this and the sunset up here." She agreed wholeheartedly.

They shook hands and she reluctantly allowed him to help her with her bags. Conducting a thorough tour, he opened every closet and room to allay any fears she might have. Joel had obviously imparted her concerns to him. Once every window was locked and the house secure, he said good night.

She thanked him profusely and relaxed a measure at a time while she milled about the kitchen, putting away the groceries she had purchased on the way.

Famished but exhausted, she opted for wine over food. Meridan had a decent selection of glassware and she found a cabernet glass. She settled onto the couch and looked around. It was lovely.

At the front door, a staircase separated the kitchen from the great room. The golden hue of the wooden staircase and banister and tongue-in-groove pine floors cast a warm, amber glow throughout the entire space. The furniture was simple and well-worn. There was no television, but a small bookshelf stereo was nestled into the shelving under the staircase. There was no evidence of Meridan Marks.

Alone with her thoughts, she let them wander. It had been the hell of all days. It seemed that perhaps she'd had more than her fair share. The Grgich Hills cabernet brought Brit to the forefront of her mind. She didn't want to think about him anymore, but it was unavoidable. Where were the brothers, and what did they have in mind? Had they raised the bar on their games? Did they remember her? Or, was she simply being punished for getting in the way?

It wasn't long before she was overcome by exhaustion and slipped into a deep but fitful sleep.

~

The sound of a car door nearly caused a cardiac episode. In the streaming daylight, Lynden familiarized herself with her whereabouts and stood to greet the caretaker.

"Hey!" She recognized the voice immediately and rushed to unbolt the door.

"What are you doing here?" Lynden asked Meridan, who stood on the porch with a huge Christian Dior everything bag over her shoulder.

"Don't you ever check your messages?"

"In my defense, I was having a problem with reception."

"Oh, yeah. It's pretty in and out." Lynden stepped aside so Meridan could enter her own house. "Pretty decent setup, huh? I inherited it from my mother's sister."

"It's great." Lynden smoothed her hair back and redid her pony tail. "I fell asleep on the couch. It was surprisingly comfortable. I was so dead."

"I convinced everyone it was safer for me to be here. Cameron wanted to come, but they got some kind of hot lead he wanted to check out."

"What lead?" She shrugged and set down her bag.

"Can you help me with the rest of my stuff?" Lynden followed her out to a Hummer H2.

"Is this yours?"

"Yeah. I keep it at the hangar."

"How often do you come here?"

"Pretty often. I love it here. It's a perfect little love nest," she giggled.

"Speaking of which, how is Christian with you being here?"

"Oh, he, he wanted to come, but he's shooting." Lynden nodded her understanding and unloaded a shockingly heavy suitcase from the cargo area of the truck.

"I love this truck. The Escalade is sweet, too." They hefted the luggage into the house and, while Meridan was settling in, Lynden took a shower. She was glad for the company and surprised by how happy she was to see Meridan. If she pushed Brit, her homelessness, and her fear of being killed from her mind, it was like a vacation.

Rummaging through her clothing for something casual, she settled on a button-down halter and jeans. It was comfortable but cute in case Meridan wanted to head out for anything.

"Lynden! Breakfast!" Meridan's voice rang out from downstairs.

"Breakfast?" Lynden repeated, not sure what to expect from Meridan and the kitchen.

The scent of roasted coffee wafted up the staircase and Lynden followed the rich aroma. Meridan handed her a mug of coffee, pointing to the small table in the great room. It was set, complete with a daisy in a bud vase.

"What's this?"

"Breakfast tacos. You inspired me. I took a private cooking lesson with Wolfgang Puck." Lynden made a great show of being impressed and sat down to what looked like a delicious meal. "I made the salsa fresh. Just now."

"What, are you playing a chef in a movie soon?"

"No. I just want to be more, um, normal. Like you."

"Ah. Thanks." Lynden had learned not to take Meridan's lack of touch with reality personally. She just didn't know how to express herself.

"I mean, I want to have a family, a life. Outside acting."

"Have you and Christian talked about it?" Meridan cocked her head and seemed to contemplate deeply for a moment.

"Yes. We are definitely thinking about moving our relationship forward." She smiled.

"Good for you."

"I love him so much. I never thought I was capable of loving anyone so much."

"Wow. I'm so happy for you."

"It's just gotten so intense lately. Crazy, passionate. He worships me, and I can't get enough of him."

"I'm jealous."

"Don't be. The right guy is out there for you. I know it. When this is all over, we're going to get you fixed right up."

"The journal was in the house."

"No!"

"I know. I feel so weird about it."

"What're we going to do? Can you recreate it?"

"Maybe it's supposed to be this way. Maybe it was a sign I need to let go. With it on the shelf, I couldn't move on."

"But it was so good!"

"I know, but it wasn't fiction. It was reality. My reality, and I don't think it was healthy."

"But, I thought it was part of your therapy to talk it through."

"Yes, well. Maybe this is the next step of the therapy. Burning it."

"How weird Brit is the one who did it." Meridan shivered as if a cool breeze had blown in. "Whew! Check it out. That gave me goose bumps." She offered her arm for inspection. Lynden didn't want to admit the chilling irony was not lost on her either.

"So, what should we do?"

"I don't know. Lay low?"

"We are as low as it gets, believe me. Other than the caretaker, I never see a soul out here, other than on the lake."

"Sweet. Hey, this is really good, by the way. You're quite the budding Julia Childs."

"Who's that?"

"Baby steps, Mer." They both laughed and enjoyed mimosas made with freshly squeezed orange juice and Roederer. Once the kitchen was clean, they changed into swimsuits and headed outside to relax on the dock. The sun beat down warm healing rays and Lynden felt herself actually beginning to uncoil. She let herself sink into a relaxed state and dozed off.

79

"Joel." Even over the phone, the excitement in the detective's voice was immediately detectable. A lead? "We just got a call on the hotline from a Kevin Williams. We'd had a call in to him, but turns out we called an old number. He saw it on the local news in Detroit."

"Tell me."

"He confirmed he was roommates with Brit Holden and knew Ash Holden, but that was about it. He'd spoken with police in Michigan after a Brady Harold was nearly beaten to death, but Brit had already moved out of his apartment. He'd never visited either of them in Bloomfield, but twice the brothers had taken all their friends to a lake house in Northern Michigan—"

"Northern Michigan? Where?"

"Traverse City, he thinks."

"Shit. Anything else?" Joel's stomach took a nervous dive at the proximity to Meridan's place.

"No, but I'm going to start researching the name in reference to properties. He didn't know they were adopted."

Joel hung up and immediately lunged for his cell phone.

"Cameron."

"What's up, Joel? You sound upset."

"Something isn't right." Joel recounted the conversation with Detective Ford. "I'd feel better if you'd head up there."

"No problem. Can Al hold things down here? I think we're getting closer. Someone has to know these guys personally."

"I'll stay on top of it," Joel promised and immediately left a message for Meridan to be very aware of her surroundings. He didn't want to alarm her, but let her know that Cameron was on the way, in case.

~

"Thirsty?" Meridan asked. Lynden opened one eye. A halo created by the sun surrounded Meridan, and it took a moment for Lynden's eyes to adjust. She reached out to accept what she was overjoyed to find to be an ice-cold Corona Light.

"Thanks, this is awesome. I actually haven't thought about the fact my house was reduced to a pile of ash in, like, four minutes."

"I feel horrible about everything." Meridan said softly and picked at the lime pulp that remained at the opening of her bottle. "I led him right to you. I'll buy you a new house."

"I have insurance, and you didn't lead him anywhere. It's not your fault. I should never have gotten involved."

"I might not be alive if you hadn't. I have a feeling something in the journal will crack the case." Lynden diverted the conversation from the journal, not wanting to discuss the past.

"You've gotten too much sun. Should we go in?"

Lynden made turkey Reubens, which Meridan gushed over with every bite.

~

"I knew it was about to break!" Detective Ford sang into the phone.

"Tell me!" Joel rose from his desk and began pacing behind it.

"We just got a call from a woman named Marsha Graves. She claims to be the sister of Brit and Ash. She's been out of the country, works a great deal in Amsterdam. The family name is James. I've been waiting on faxes from the Michigan State Department of Transportation. Turns out their licenses haven't been renewed in ten years, so they aren't in the system. The faxes will have their photos."

"At least we'll be able to put a face to the name. Meridan will never be surprised again. This is as good as over." Joel smiled, relieved and confident for the first time since the whole thing began that they were on the right track.

"Oh, by the way, about there being two of them at work . . ."

Joel paced and did as much research on Google as he could on the family name while he awaited the faxes. Turns out Rodger James was, indeed, a successful stock broker with his own prestigious firm in Bloomfield Hills, Michigan. He had properties listed in Traverse City, West Bloomfield Hills, Lake Tahoe, and Florida.

A bio on a recent book jacket listed a wife and two children. Interesting. As the first page began to emerge from the fax machine, Joel chewed on his lower lip. Cover page. He growled and threw it to the floor. Come on, come on.

Dark hair, dark eyes, strong nose, full mouth. Even upside down, he could tell the man was attractive. Turning it upright, he saw not a hint of insanity in the eyes or on a handsome and vaguely familiar face. Ashland H.C. James. The fax machine sputtered a bit and lost connection.

"Fuck!" He bent over and peered at the screen. Paper out. "For the love of Pete!" Joel raced around, trying to locate extra paper, and realized he hadn't for the life of him any idea where it would be. Barb was not at her desk, but there was a fax machine in the exterior office.

After raiding the supply, he hoped the memory on the fax machine would retain as much information as a photo. He loaded the machine then reset it, and was rewarded with whirring and whining as the fax began to draw from memory. He tapped his foot, hands on hips, and each second seemed to last four life times.

Dark hair, dark eyes, strong nose, full mouth. Even upside down there was no mistaking the face of Britten H.C. James. Joel knew exactly who he was.

"Holy Christ!"

80

Speed dialing Roz, Joel wrestled with his knowledge, knowing it would undo Roz completely, but he needed her help.

"Roz, I've already left Meridan, Mr. Richey, and Lynden messages. I need your help. I'm flying to Michigan right now. Please, while I'm in the air, call Meridan every few minutes. We have to reach her. We have to warn her. I've sent the devil after her."

~

"What's that noise?" Lynden asked, setting down her wine glass. "It sounds like a car."

"Oh, yeah! I have a surprise for you. It's my boyfriend." Meridan stood, clapping.

"Christian York is here? Now?" Lynden couldn't mask her interest at the prospect of meeting such an attractive and famous actor. Meridan was different; the circumstances which had brought them together made her much more real, less famous.

"No. I guess I should have told you. Christian's gay. We date for his cover. Sean, I told you about him? He was Christian's boyfriend for years. Jim and I have been dating for several months. He's amazing. I wanted you to meet him. I knew if I told you, you'd say no." Lynden was shocked by the information flowing freely from Meridan's mouth.

"Are you sure it's him?" Lynden's face took on a worried expression.

"Yeah, it's his car." Meridan had her face pressed to the window. Lynden heard the car door slam and was mildly disappointed she was not about to meet Christian York.

"You should turn on the outside lights for him. It's pitch black out there." Meridan nodded and did so.

"He works out of Chicago part of the time, so he has an apartment there. I was allowed to come up here if I agreed he could babysit us. We come up here all the time. It's like a three-hour drive. You'll love him." Lynden shrugged and went to retrieve her wine.

"Nice car," Lynden said, as he rummaged in the forward trunk of the 911.

"Oh, yeah. He has great taste. He's in advertising. He does *really* well. I think he's close to proposing."

"Really? Why didn't you tell me all this?" Intrigued, she struggled for an angle which would reveal his face.

"No one knows. Christian insists the whole thing stay under wraps. When we're in public, Jim poses as Roz's boyfriend. The whole thing is soooo sophomoronic."

Lynden burst out laughing at Meridan's unintentional yet quite brilliant sniglet, but the laughter died in her throat when the trunk slammed shut and she saw his face.

"Brit," she gasped.

Her wine glass slipped through her fingers as his name slipped from her lips. Meridan whipped her head back and forth confusedly when the glass shattered on the floor.

"Don't be paranoid, Lynden. That's Jim. He's my boyfriend." As if Lynden had but a minimal grasp on the English language, she spoke slowly and clearly. "We're getting married. You're just confused!" Just the sound of her voice was enough to free Lynden from disabling fear. Meridan reached for her arm, but she was already racing toward the door.

"I'm not confused, Meridan!" Lynden insisted at the top of her voice. "Is there a deadbolt? Anything?" She was shouting frantically, but Meridan was dumbstruck. Jim was clearing the distance from the Porsche to the house in record speed.

"Lynden! Calm down! It's dark." She was hot on Lynden's heels, trying to instill reason, but Lynden would not be deterred. "Are you drunk? Please! He's here to help."

"No! No!" Lynden pulled the blinds on the door shut just as the doorknob started to rattle.

Meridan approached the door as Lynden scoured the kitchen for a weapon. In the time she had been there, she'd spent little time in the kitchen and was holding out great hope that Meridan had a state-of-the-art cutlery collection featuring a fifteen-inch butcher knife. "Lynden," she said quietly. "I'm going to open the door. You're confused. Jim is tall and dark. That doesn't make him Brit. You've got to calm down."

"No! Meridan. I'm not fucking blind." Or was she? It was dark and she'd had a couple of drinks. God, was she insane? She put her back against the kitchen counter with a hand to her head and looked Meridan straight in the eye. "Are you sure? I swear to God, I thought . . ."

"You said so yourself; you always think you see them." Meridan nodded reassurance. There was a knock at the door.

"You're sure?" Tears of embarrassment spilled over Lynden's lashes. "I'm sorry." She held her head in her hands, averting her gaze to the floor. She needed to pull it together before she met someone new. *Breathe. Ten, nine . . .*

Meridan unlocked the door and was knocked to the floor when it crashed open. Jim stepped into the light.

"Hi, Reese." He leered lustily at Lynden, who remained motionless, immobile as she realized her worst fears.

"Jesus Christ, Jim, what's wrong with you? Don't call her that." He reached out his hand to Meridan to help her up. "What's gotten into you?" Meridan struggled to her feet and stood, pausing to brush herself off as if she had landed in dirt. "Stop fucking around. You're going to upset her. Lynden! Come out of the kitchen. I want you to meet my boyfriend. I told you that in confidence," she whispered the last part to Jim.

He shoved Meridan hard and she stumbled blindly before collapsing onto the couch. He pointed a finger at her. "You. Don't call me Jim. It's Brit. And thank you, by the way, for your confidence." He smiled brilliantly and Meridan cracked. She screamed his name and demanded that he stop.

"Do not move from that spot and do not say another word to me unless I address you," he demanded, and she sat back obediently, her hands flying to her face, covering it as if that would in some way stop the horror from unfolding in front of her.

Brit leaned his tall, lithe body against the handrail leading up the stairs. He put his strong hands on slim hips and cocked one. He eyed Meridan with disgust. "Reese. Come out of the kitchen. Now. I need to see you. Oh, and take your hair down before you do." Meridan could hear what sounded like panting from the kitchen and knew Lynden was having a panic attack. "I really missed you, babe. Come to Daddy." His gorgeous face grimaced when he heard vomit hit the floor. "She vomits when she gets stressed out," he told Meridan conversationally, but she was shaking her head, whimpering like a baby.

While she continued to dry heave, Lynden's hands probed the drawers, finding only a small, serrated knife to brandish. She stood stock still and waited, weapon in hand. She had a clear shot through the door, but she would have to pass him. Would she have time to stab him? Was he armed? She couldn't see. She listened to Meridan snivel and tried to form a plan.

"Reese, whatever it is that you're going to try and defend yourself with is pointless. Meridan doesn't have a knife worth a damn in the house; I would know." The door was her only chance, but that would leave Meridan alone with him. Lynden knew there was nowhere to go for help within at least a mile.

She clutched the knife, and, to bolster herself, she took a few deep breaths. Without consulting her nerve, she bolted for the door and made it through without interference.

"You be careful out there, Reese. We're going to fuck you up." Brit's voice grabbed her and held her fast as the ominous statement settled over her like wet cement. For the first time, Ash flashed into her mind, and she knew what Brit meant. Ash was maintaining the perimeter. There was nowhere to run. She forced herself to turn around and face him. He was still leaning against the railing, arms crossed, looking not a day older than the last time she saw him hurling flowers from her patio.

"Give it a shot, but you won't get far. Meridan and I are going to have so much fun here." Lynden comprehended his tacit meaning. Meridan sat motionless on the couch, her eyes pleaded for her not to leave. Now that Meridan knew who he was, it was end of game. A bone-rattling shudder crashed through her body and Lynden sank to her knees as they gave out.

"Why?" she said softly, her head hanging in defeat.

"What, honey?" he asked in a tender voice. She closed her eyes and shrank away from the approaching foot falls.

"Why are you doing this to us?" It would be of no benefit to try and kill him. Ash would be prepared to take over; there was a plan in place.

He removed the knife from her lifeless hand and bent down to her. She squeezed her eyes shut and waited for him to stab her three hundred times or so. Instead, he carefully removed the clip from her hair and let it cascade to her shoulders. She could hear him breathe deeply several times. She heard a soft groan in her ear and choked back terrified sobs.

Instead of slitting her throat with her own weapon, he folded her hand in his and helped her to her feet. Brit guided her back into the house and led her to the large armchair adjacent to the couch where Meridan sat, rigid and befuddled. He leaned against the large wall so he could see them both. His long-sleeved black T-shirt clung to an impossibly fit body. Lynden knew that underneath he was a likely candidate for the Presidential Fitness Award.

"So we are clear, ladies? I'm not doing anything to 'us,' I'm doing something to Reese." The words slapped Meridan and her eyes bulged. Lynden wondered if she was breathing at all.

"What's going on?" Meridan asked through tears.

"I told you not to talk unless I addressed you, but I'm going to let it go this time, because it's a really good question. Where should I start?" Brit asked cheerfully and clapped his hands together loudly, causing both women to start. "Wine, anyone?" He took the bottle from the coffee table and poured the remainder of its contents for Meridan and headed to the kitchen. "If I know you two, there's more where this came from, eh?"

"Run?" Meridan whispered, her eyes clearly evidencing her terror.

"Nah." Brit advised from the kitchen, but Lynden had already shaken her head. There had to be a better way.

Who knew what Ash's mental state was or where he was lurking? Brit emerged from the kitchen with three champagne flutes and a bottle of the Roederer Meridan had picked up in Traverse City. "Look what I found. You girls are so well-trained. I love it." He smiled broadly. Lynden searched his eyes for insanity and saw none. That, in and of itself, exemplified his instability. A true sociopath, he had no capacity for sympathy or remorse.

When the cork popped, she jumped involuntarily. "Remember the first time we had this?" Lynden shook her head violently as if trying to avoid the memory. "Yes. You do. She's being difficult, Meridan." He handed her a glass, but she merely stared at it. "Meridan? Unless you would like to be sent away, you will cooperate." She reached for the glass, unable to meet his eyes. "*Salute*," he said after setting a flute on the table in front of Lynden. Her stomach roiled at the word.

"A food critic, Reese? I'm so proud. It's like you took a bit of me with you when you abandoned me. Do you think about me all the time?" he asked, raising his thick eyebrows expectantly. Silence. "Come on, you couldn't make it through a frigging menu without my help, and now the restaurant community of Dallas is hinged on your word?" He chuckled. "She's giving me the silent treatment. She'll warm up, she's pretty shy," he informed a truly devastated Meridan.

"Are you mad at Lynden for helping me?" Meridan squeaked.

"What?"

"Why did you burn down her house?"

"Meridan, do you have any idea what's going on?" She shook her head honestly. Lynden wasn't exactly certain what had led them all here, but pernicious thoughts were taking shape.

"Did you stalk me because I look like Lynden?"

"Okay, okay, enough of this Lynden shit. It's Reese." He turned to

Meridan with deadly seriousness. "No more screw-ups?" She shook her head as tears made their way down her cheeks. "God, Reese, you look hot." Meridan choked on the compliment until Brit trained an eye on her. "Alright, Meridan. Q-and-A time. Did I stalk you because you look like Reese? Mmm. Yes and no." Meridan's face collapsed from anticipation to confusion.

"Did you date me because I look like Reese?" Meridan's all-powerful ego was at center stage. Lynden was stunned these were her questions. Did it matter?

"Yes. But, let me make myself clear. We weren't dating. I was, how shall I say, on a mission."

"What?" Meridan pleaded, and it seemed to Lynden she still held out hope this was a mistake.

"I've been looking for Reese for—what has it been, honey, like, twelve years?" Lynden sat, immobile, dreading every word that came out of his mouth. Her mind struggled for any avenue that would get her out alive.

"Anyway." He took a long drink of his champagne, and she watched as a huge amount of amber liquid slipped beyond undeniably beautiful lips and disappeared into his mouth. An idea formed. Was it possible to get him drunk? Was it possible to change her tack? Was it too late to respond to him? She shifted in her seat and took a less terrified posture. She reached for her glass and he smiled at her. As she lifted it to her mouth, he wagged a finger at her. "Do it right, Reese." She went through the familiar motions of tasting. "Why did you leave me?"

"I was afraid. Things got a little crazy. Someone attacked a friend of mine and nearly killed him. I was worried."

"Now, Reese. I appreciate your consideration of my feelings, but Brady wasn't a friend. You fucked him. You fucked him, and I fucked him up," he stated matter-of-factly and took a drink. While he closed his eyes for a moment to savor the champagne, Lynden gestured for Meridan to drink.

"Anyway. I took Michigan apart looking for you. Not a trace. No one at U of M knew where you were. I couldn't locate your parents. I want you to know I tried, though." Lynden was certain of that fact, now more than ever.

"What about me?" Meridan's ego couldn't help but ask.

"You. Wow, talk about the right place at the right time. Don't think I hadn't noticed the resemblance in movies. Hell, I have the whole Meridan Marks collection at home. Some are a better masturbatory aid than others." He let the weight of the words settle on Meridan and watched her ego shrink a bit. "Get this, it's priceless." He laughed and drank. "So, there I am with this friend of mine from school, you remember Tracy Ellis, don't you, honey?" Lynden nodded and wondered if Meridan's people had ever made contact with him for questioning. "Well, he goes by his full name now, Trace Jameson Ellis." Meridan's eyes widened as Brit used his hand to exhibit an imaginary marquee.

"The director? The one from Brazil? My God! It was right there in the journal. Why didn't I think of it?" Meridan queried. Brit nodded. Lynden cursed her lack of interest in pop culture and wondered if she would have recognized him if she'd seen a photo.

"Anyway. He invites me to this big party and there you are," he said, turning his attention to Meridan. Lynden was shocked when she batted her eyelashes at him. Was she going to try to seduce him? What was she thinking?

"I hatched my plan that night. I was going to date you, make you fall for me, build a confidence with you, delude you into thinking that I loved you . . ." He took a sip of champagne and let the nasty words hit home. Meridan struggled to maintain what was left of her composure.

"Mission accomplished," she said sharply.

"Hey, Mer. Don't sell yourself short. You led me right to her. I couldn't have done it without you." As he raised his glass to her, Lynden watched as the realization she'd been nothing but a pawn settled over Meridan.

"And Reese. You're as predictable as AIDS in a bath house." Again he raised his glass and she knew he was right. She had walked into his trap. "Don't get me wrong. I had a ton of fun terrorizing you, Meridan. It was masterful, really. I found a bunch of old letters Ash had never mailed to Reese and borrowed some of his material." He took a long drink, then refilled his glass and topped off theirs.

"I didn't expect Reese to be so guarded, though," he continued, uninterrupted. "Remember the night you called me to tell me you were going to the press? Remember me coaching you? Telling you what details the public would find interesting? You know, from an advertising and marketing perspective? Hilarious. By the way, I don't have a job at all, Meridan; I'm just really fucking rich. I have a fabulous house on Beverly Boulevard in addition to that townhouse you visited. I was never too far away from you. Every day you told me where you were going and what you were doing. It was like playing chess with someone in a coma!" He let out a thunderous laugh and slapped a firm thigh.

"It was beautiful. I thought Reese would fly out immediately. When she heard the description of those flowers, I bet she came unhinged. I always bought her white roses, but I left the same fabulous arrangement for her at her townhouse." He paused to allow either woman to interject, but neither seemed capable. "I actually expected this to all come down long before I had to tell you I loved you." Meridan's mouth flew open and she narrowed her eyes at him. "I regret that it went that far, because I don't want to diminish what I feel for Reese in any way. So, now you know, Reese. I did tell her, but I didn't mean it." Meridan burst into tears, and, through her own stark terror, Lynden felt bad for her.

"Don't you say that!" Meridan launched herself off the couch at Brit, who adroitly guided her to the ground using her own momentum and put a knee on her chest. Meridan sobbed and railed against him. A gash bled on her forehead where it had clipped the coffee table.

"Reese? Hand me my bag. Now." Lynden stood and retrieved the bag that lay between them. She held it out for him, squelching the desire to run, knowing that she couldn't make it past him. "Nothing stupid from you. Go sit down." He ordered and she did. She considered smashing her glass and stabbing him in the neck, but how far would she get with Ash outside?

"Don't hurt her."

"What happens to Meridan is up to Meridan," he said, looking Meridan straight in the eye. She nodded her understanding.

"I love you," she cried, and Lynden felt something disturbingly similar to jealously punch her in the stomach. "Please, Brit. Don't do this. We can be happy. We were happy, weren't we?" Brit furrowed his brow at her. "Meridan Marks. Are you trying to play me?" Brit asked, and Lynden wondered and hoped the same thing. Was she going to sell her out? If Meridan had been the one who bolted out the front door, would she have come back?

"No. No! Brit, I love you. I need you. I want to marry you. We can just pretend nothing has happened."

"No, we can't, because I have no interest in you whatsoever." He smiled coldly.

"Why are you trying to tell me that this had nothing to do with me? It was me you made love to! It was me!" she screamed.

"Reese. I didn't want it to come out this way, and, quite frankly, 'made love' is not the exact term I would use. Fucked. It's true. We fucked. Again, this in no way diminishes my desire for you," he told Lynden.

"Why are you punishing me?" Meridan begged through her tears. *I'd like to thank the Academy?*

"With the lights off, I could barely tell. Reese has a much better body than you do and I imagine she is sublime in bed. But then as all good fantasies must come to an end, there you were." Lynden buried her face in her hands and plugged her ears with her thumbs. She couldn't bear it. Meridan was turning on her. Meridan's ego was bigger than she ever imagined.

"Stop it!" Meridan screamed at Brit, who rendered her silent with a fist to the face. Her head slammed into the floor and she went completely limp. Lynden pulled herself into a fetal position and rocked herself gently back and forth.

81

The voice mail icon was blinking as Joel emerged from the underground parking lot of his office.

"Fuck, I've been out of range for like four seconds!" He cursed himself for making calls from his office instead of on the way to the airport. He'd lost at least a half hour not reaching anyone.

He grappled with his phone and it hit the floor of the car, sliding under the seat. "Damn it!" Pulling over to the side of Wilshire Boulevard, he narrowly missed a valet stand. Unable to reach the phone, he threw the car into park and opened the door for a better look, his Mercedes nearly sideswiped by a speeding limo anxious for his spot at the valet stand at Mr. Chow. The light was failing, so he ran a hand under the seat. He exhaled sharply when his fingers touched the cool, metal surface.

He depressed the voice mail icon, not trusting himself to drive while he listened to the voice mail message that could be from anyone. When he'd called Detective Ford after receiving the fax, even the detective was frantic.

"Joel, the Grayling PD isn't answering. They have deferred all emergencies to the Kalkaska department. I've paged them and am waiting for them to get back with me. I'll put a call into the state police as well. Don't worry. She'll be fine." Joel detected a lack of conviction in the officer's voice.

~

Lynden pressed her eyes closed tightly, not daring to open them. After what felt like an eternity, she felt a hand beginning to unwrap her arms from around her shins. She considered resisting, but knew better. She pressed her eyes shut even more tightly and kept her forehead on her knees, hoping to garner some sympathy. Brit's breath was slow and controlled. Patient. Hers, short and choppy, a heartbeat away from a full blown panic attack. It might as well have been 1997. He was in control . . . again. "I apologize for that, but she is so fucking annoying," Brit said softly and Lynden's eyes searched the room for Meridan.

"Where is she?"

"She's fine. For now." Lynden blinked back tears, trying to reconcile her situation.

"What now?"

"What now?" He dropped to his knees, still holding her face in his hands. He was every bit as stunning as she remembered. He probably hadn't shaved in a day or so, his shadow thick and sultry. "We have a lot of catching up to do." He smirked wickedly.

"Where is Ash?"

"Ash?" he repeated, surprise in his voice.

"Is he outside?" Brit sat back and squinted his eyes at her.

"Oh, you mean because I said *we're* going to fuck you up? Smart, huh? I knew you'd be afraid. No, he's not outside. He was as good as dead the day he fucked you." A sharp intake of breath caused Lynden to cough uncontrollably.

She put as much distance as possible between them, sitting back, drawing her legs up to her chest. "It's sad, really. It's his own fault for telling me. He should have known better than to let me find out. You, however, are not blameless. You let my brother fuck you." She was shaking her head wildly, back and forth. "Now, Reese. Don't lie to me. He said you loved it."

"What did you do to him?"

"What did I do to him? Oh, no. He did it to himself. They ruled it an accident."

"Because of that? Because of me?"

"You act as if it isn't reason enough to kill."

"Did you kill your brother?" Brit smirked, and Lynden's heart threatened to tear through her chest.

"Don't feel bad. He was so fucked in the end, I think he would have done it himself. He was manic-depressive, bipolar, and a functioning alcoholic."

Lynden went slack with the realization Brit had killed the only remaining member of his immediate family. Because of her. After a few moments of silence, Lynden spoke.

"How did this happen?"

"You were hiding, but I knew you'd help if you thought for one second I was threatening someone." He handed a champagne flute to her and refilled it from the bottle on the coffee table. "Man, it was so fun. It was the best game ever, especially knowing the prize. Meridan was taking forever, though. She's so fucking stupid, she barely has the capacity for fear. That's why I took it to the next level by breaking in. I needed more information from you. The cell number helped, but it was a dead end. Thank God for Al Roenick. He cracked it. Meridan called me when she got back from meeting you. She leaked the story, you know." Lynden shook her head. "She did. To Noah. She set him up to be sold. It was rich. Meridan can't resist publicity. She's like an addict." Lynden's mind reeled. "Once I had your name, it was a piece of cake. Google gave me the office address. From there, I found your home address."

"Why did you burn down my house?"

"I guess I was really pissed off you weren't there, and I had to flush you out. Besides, you have no home without me. Then Meridan told me you were at the Four Seasons. I was in the room with Joel and Meridan when you called after getting my message. I was the one who suggested to Joel he set you up here. I promised to head straight up and keep watch while they tried to apprehend me." Brit burst into laughter and Lynden tried to keep up. It was brilliant and she had fallen right into it.

"Where's Meridan?"

"Tied up. Don't worry. I didn't hurt her. I want her to watch later." Lynden's mind resisted his implication.

"What then?"

"Well, for starters, we're going to relocate. I have this gorgeous house in Carmel. It will be a bit of a drive, but the Porsche is great fun. You'll love it." She held her head high to give the illusion of strength.

"What about Meridan? She knows it's you."

"Oh, she's going to have to go. I just want her ego to go first. I have to destroy it. She's so fucking full of herself. I loved watching her fall head over heels for me. She was so easy. When you're this attractive and rich, not much gets in your way." Lynden knew that for certain. She herself had been powerless against him.

"I guess if someone really wanted to do the research they could've figured it out. My given name is Britten Holden Cooper and Ash was Ashland Holden Cooper. Holden was our dad's first name. Our uncle forced us to take his last name, James, as if we'd walk around with his name a moment longer than we had to. So, we decided to go by our first and middle names."

"So, Jim now?"

He nodded. "Okay, enough talking. I need to start enjoying you." He turned his back on her and dug into his overnight bag. There was no way out. Lynden decided to try and perpetuate the present state of affairs, hoping someone would come to their rescue.

"Are you upset with me?" she asked, and gasped when he pulled a Beretta nine-millimeter from his bag.

"You cost us twelve years, Reese. We'd have three kids by now." Lynden searched his eyes, which revealed nothing. He waved the gun around and she wondered if there was a bullet in the chamber.

"Did I do anything to make this . . ." she stalled.

"Just being you, beautiful. I'll tell you, that fucking Brady guy? He should've been dead. When I found out he wasn't, I was so pissed off." Lynden shuddered at his nonchalance. He'd meant to kill her and Brady, and he did kill Ash. He planned to kill Meridan. Letting him have sex with her was not going to help. She needed to figure a way to fight him.

He gestured with the gun for her to get up, and once she was on her feet, the room began to spin. "Are you okay? Reese?" Just the sound of his voice, the smell of him, threatened to push her closer to blackness. It was the voice she had been running from, and it was here. She wanted to give in to the feeling, to pass out, but she was afraid of what he would do to her.

"I guess I've had too much to drink." With a hand to her head, she tried to steady herself. He had a firm grip on her arm.

"Nah, the party's just getting started." He set the gun down and began to unbutton her shirt. "I knew you weren't wearing a bra. What's gotten into you? That's kind of whorish." His hands slipped into each side of her halter and held her firm. His eyes were riveted on her; his thumbs caressed her breasts slowly. "Why are you crying? Because I called you a whore? You fucked my brother, Reese. That was totally out of line." His voice became stern. "You left me in New York. I had to explain that. You made me look like a fool. You were fucking that Brady and God knows who else." The mere thought of Brady brought a new level of pain to the moment. She would never have the chance to say goodbye to him or to her parents. There was no good way for this to end. Even if she did make it to Carmel, how could he keep her prisoner for the rest of her life?

She looked at the gun, so powerful but so far away. He leaned in to kiss her, but instead wiped away her tears. "God, I love you. Not a day has gone by I haven't dreamt of this moment." When he lowered his mouth to hers, she turned her head. Before she knew what had happened, her head snapped back from a brutal slap. Her hand flew to her face protectively and she was able to cover herself simultaneously.

"Still feisty as ever, but, see, now you're really pissing me off. When I think about all the men who have given it to you, and you're still pushing me off." He backed away, running a hand over his stubble. "Take off your shirt, Reese. Slowly." She shook her head and his eyes darkened instantly.

As she opened her shirt, he sat down in the chair opposite her. With his legs stretched out, she could see that he was fully erect through his faded jeans. The shirt fell to the floor. She unzipped her jeans and pushed them down over her hips. He groaned softly and gripped his impossibly large erection. She refused to allow him to debase her. She was giving of herself freely. She stepped carefully out of the jeans.

"Nice panties, Reese. Keep them on and come over here."

She walked to him slowly and dropped to her knees. Earlier she had entertained the thought of removing his penis with her teeth, but the gun changed her chances of making it out alive. "Are you excited?" he asked, the gun pointed directly between her eyes. She nodded. *Excited-slash-scared beyond all reason,* she thought.

"Do it." She undid the first button on his jeans, not surprised to find his erection had cleared the top of his jeans and he wasn't wearing underwear. She bit back tears and forced herself to do whatever necessary to save not just her own life, but Meridan's. She closed her eyes as she worked each button; he raised his hips slightly so that she could lower his jeans. "Open those eyes, Reese. I want you here with me. No checking out mentally." He tapped the side of her head with the gun. She opened her eyes and pleaded with them. His gaze was steely. How could someone so beautiful be so purely evil?

"Reese. You owe this to me. Do you have any idea what you put me through? I've been a fucking mess without you. I need you." As she worked him aggressively, he buried his non-gun toting hand in her hair and pulled it. "Wait!" he demanded, but she wouldn't. There was no way she was going to let him have sex with her if she could stop it. She took him deep into her mouth the way she knew he loved it, and he tried to pull her away by the hair. "Reese, stop! Oh, God. Reese. I knew you wanted me. I knew you still loved me. Reese. Reese. Wait!" She held him fast with her hand and refused to stop. "Reese!" he thundered, at the last moment pulling himself away from her mouth, spewing molten liquid into her face and hair.

In her periphery, she could see it clinging in her curls and suppressed a violent urge to vomit. He threw her shirt at her and she used it to cleanse herself as much as she could. She cringed at the thought of her hair drying into a crunchy, sticky mess. Her shirt became saturated long before she was free of the gooey discharge.

"Shower?" He raised his thick brows suggestively. Her eyes ran, either from the burning or the disgust and shame enveloping her.

She sat back, drawing her legs up to cover her bare chest and watched him. He ran his hands through his hair and sighed loudly. "Who taught you how to do that?" he asked and she would die before she gave him any more ammo.

"*Cosmo*," she insisted, as she had so many years before.

"Sticking with that story, eh? You're so charming. Stand up. Let me look at you." Relatively confident she had bought herself at least a half an hour, she stood up. "You haven't changed a bit. You're a little stronger, though. I'll give you that. Are you wet?" She shook her head and hoped to God she wasn't. She had read that if your body senses you will be penetrated, it would ready itself. He wouldn't understand that. "Come here, let me feel." Fear cemented her to the floor. "Reese."

She took a few steps forward and he dropped to his knees in front of her. He buried his face between her legs and inhaled deeply before pulling the front of her panties down and caressing her with his tongue. She instinctively pushed his forehead away, and he brought the gun up and aimed it at her face. She weighed her options.

"Let's leave, Brit."

"Reese. I'm not stupid. I know every scenario playing out in your mind. I'm not going to spare Meridan's life. I had to endure all these months with her. You'd want to kill her, too. Further, nothing is going to interrupt our lives; I can't risk letting her go." Lynden silently prayed for help. Brit sat back and looked up at her. "What're you thinking? Are you going to placate me, let me fuck you? Are you going to fight me, try to kill me? Are you going to beg for her life, sacrifice yours?" Lynden fought tears. Taking advantage of his pause, she backed away slowly and he came to his feet.

"Why don't we relax? Hell, it's going to be at least fifteen minutes before I can take you after that. Sit down." He gestured toward the couch and she reached down for her shirt. "No. No. Here." He slowly peeled his long-sleeved T-shirt from his hard, muscular body. His lateral muscles bulged for the brief moment he had both arms captive in the body of the shirt. She tried to avert her eyes from the seductive rippling of his abdominal muscles, but couldn't. Her heart replayed each time she had fallen in love with him. When he handed her the shirt, she felt grateful for the cover, but it enveloped her in his smell. The heady aroma launched a barrage of memories, none of which were productive.

Brit set the pistol on the coffee table as she pushed herself to the furthest corner of the couch. He held out her champagne. She thanked him as she took it. *God,* she chastised herself, *this isn't a date.*

"So, tell me about you and Ash. I think I can get over it if we talk about it," he said, watching a tear slip from her eye. He reached out to wipe it away, but she slapped his hand. She absorbed her tears with his shirtsleeve and silently apologized to Ash; despite his deceit, he didn't deserve to die. "Come on, Reese." He leaned back on the couch and extended his long legs. The top button on his jeans was still undone, and she tried not to look at the thin trail of hair disappearing into them.

He was slightly more built than he was in college, and age had made him even more rugged and captivating. Poor Meridan. She never had a chance. Lynden tried not to blame her for loving Brit; she tried not to be jealous of the time Meridan had had with him; she tried not to think about them making love; she tried to avoid thoughts of him telling her he loved her in tender moments after sex; she tried not to entertain thoughts of them as a happy couple; she tried not to remember any good times she herself had shared with him; she tried not to wonder how her life would be different if he was sane; she tried not to feel, at all, but it was impossible.

"Well."

"What?" she cried, yanked from her emotional Odyssey.

"Tell me."

"He raped me. I thought he was you."

"What were you wearing?"

"My bra and panties." He settled his hand on his crotch and groaned a bit. He eyed her to continue. "He woke up immediately. I called your name," she choked back a sob, hating the feel of Ash's hands and mouth on her body. "He did it anyway."

"Now, of all the lackluster, lame-ass recollections. A little more detail."

"No."

"I'm sorry?"

"I won't do this. Just kill me if you want," she said, prompting a laugh from Brit. He stretched his long body over to her and kissed her full on the mouth. Before she could even consider pulling away, he told her not to. Deeply suppressed tendencies took over, and she relented. His tongue explored her mouth thoroughly. Hot tears burned down her face. He brought his hands up and cradled her face affectionately.

"Tell me," he whispered into her mouth. She wiped her mouth and nose of mucus and forced herself to speak. "Were you wet?" She shook her head.

"He . . . he . . ."

"Went down on you? Oh, my God!" He covered his face with his hands and tilted his head to the ceiling. It was but a moment, but she lunged for the gun. The wind was knocked out of her as she hit the floor, but the gun was firmly in her hands.

Frantically, she rolled onto her back and faced him. He stood. His body towered over her. She clicked off the safety and aimed directly at his heart. Acidic tears obscured her vision and she was sobbing loudly. He exposed his chest to her.

"I think we should talk about this, Reese."

"I'm done talking to you," she screamed and pushed herself backward with her feet. She needed some distance in case he rushed her. The pistol shook violently in her hands and she felt security in the tension on the trigger.

"I love you, Reese. We belong together." His eyes grew moist and soft.

"Stop it. You don't love me. You want to own me. You want to control me. You were going to kill me twelve years ago."

"I was upset. I'm sorry." She shook her head vehemently.

"It's too late for that." Through her hysteria she considered an extremity shot. He was strong, though, and she doubted she could live the rest of her life fearing his release from an institution. She squeezed her eyes shut and pulled the trigger.

When the hammer drove home and clicked hollowly, Lynden's eyes widened in horror. She stared at the traitorous weapon before throwing it at a howling Brit. She struggled to crawl away, but he was on her instantly, his weight driving her to the ground. Her hip bones ground painfully into the wood floors, and she fought for breath under his two hundred pounds.

"Do you not know me at all? Why would I need to load a weapon to keep you in line? It was fun though, eh?" He panted into her ear from behind, but she could barely hear him over her sobbing. She had stupidly squandered her only hope of leaving the cabin alive.

"I can't decide whether I want you to fight me or beg me."

"I refuse to do either one." She let her body go limp, resigning herself.

"Now, that isn't an option." He rolled off her onto his side and propped his head up on his elbow. "Reese." She didn't move. "Reese." He slapped her on the behind hard and she fought the urge to yelp. "Reese. Stop fucking around. I swear to God you're trying my patience. Don't force me to do bad things to you." He slapped her again. "Okay, if you want it this way. You can pull the dead fuck routine this time, but eventually you'll fight me, maybe from pain or exhaustion. Or, you'll beg me to stop, maybe from pain or exhaustion." Her fight-or-flight kicked in, and she brought an elbow back hard and felt it connect with ribs. She kicked and fought her way into his vice-like grip.

"That was so lame, Reese. What if I were a stranger attacking you? You need to take some self-defense courses. Well, you don't need to worry about that anymore, though, because you will never be far enough away from me for anyone to hurt you." He held her from behind by the upper arms, his fingers digging into her flesh with searing strength.

"You *are* a stranger," she screamed.

"Don't be absurd, Reese. You just had my dick in your mouth."

"I hate you!"

"No you don't. You're upset."

"I hate you," she crumbled into hysterical sobs, and, with a shove, he put her face first on the floor.

"God, this is so annoying. Why don't you just act right?" he demanded.

"What do you want from me?" she screamed at him.

"I want you to be quiet. You're giving me a headache." His fly was open, revealing his hardness. His hair, a tousled mess, conspired to remind her of happier times.

"I want this over."

"Well, again, over isn't an option."

"Meridan!" Lynden screamed, trying to convince herself Meridan was still alive.

"Meridan? What, you want her to help you? She can't even help herself. Hell, she's probably dead from that head wound. Either way, she's firmly bound to the bed. When I was tying her up, she thought I was going to fuck her. Can you believe that? She tried to get me to kill you and pretend this had never happened. Can you imagine? I bet you thought you were friends." He pouted, mocking her.

His words had horrific potential. She'd seen the look in Meridan's eyes when she told Brit she loved him. She had begged convincingly. Regardless, Lynden couldn't have another death on her hands. She scrambled into the corner of the room and watched him. He pulled a fresh clip from the bag and expertly dropped the empty one, which bounced noisily on the wood. He shoved the clip into the stock and pulled the slide back. Lynden closed her eyes and prayed. She prayed for Meridan, for herself, for Ash and even for Brit. She was relieved to hear him disengage the hammer. At least he wasn't going to kill her now.

"While I don't need bullets to control you, my love, I do need them to kill Meridan. I am, however, going to keep this way over here so you can't get to it." He placed the hand gun on the table just inside the door at the base of the steps. He held his hands up to indicate he was unarmed. His lats sprang out, his upper body taking the shape of a cobra. As if he needed a gun.

Lynden buried her face in her arms, which were folded across her knees. Counting backward from ten, she took deep, focused breaths.

He gripped her ankles and pulled her from the corner. She did not resist in any way. "Come here, baby doll. It's time. I've waited for so long. Come to think of it, I'm glad you gave me head. Now I can last longer." She cursed herself roundly. He straddled her knees and took her face in his hands. "You're so beautiful, Reese." His mouth met hers with savage aggression. Her top lip busted open, flooding her mouth with blood. She winced, but didn't cry out. Kissing him back, she let him consume her.

He removed her shirt to plant fervent bloody kisses over her throat and chest. As he worked her breasts hungrily, she closed her eyes, let her head tip back and tried to drift away.

"Look at me, Reese." She squeezed her eyes shut tightly until he landed a kick to her shin. She yelped at the abuse. She winced at his readiness as he slowly stepped out of his jeans. "Spread your legs. Don't worry about the panties." She did as she was told, turning her head away as if it would somehow separate herself from the inevitable. Her panties tore free, relatively painlessly. "Okay, how did Ash do it? Missionary or from behind?" he asked in a conversational tone. She fought the memory, but answered with a cry when he slapped her hard on her thigh.

"Missionary," she whispered.

"Then you get it from behind. Let's get you over here to the picture window. I want to see your face while I fuck you." A light kick prompted her to move. "Crawl," he ordered.

"I fucking hate you," she said boldly.

"No, you don't, you love this. You love being controlled. You love my strength. You love being dominated. It's why you respond to me, Reese. I'm your perennial weakness."

"I hate you." Raw emotion bubbled up as unadulterated hatred as she crawled toward the window, feeling dirty and exposed. His reflection loomed like a specter behind her, but she felt eerily calm. She watched him take one knee and then two.

He moistened her with saliva and she was thankful she wasn't wet. She hoped he was offended. His huge hands settled on her hips. He gripped tightly and drove himself into her and the force propelled her forward, but he pulled her back, brutally violating her again.

"You're so fucking tight! Have you been waiting for me all these years?" His eyes were closed, his head back in the throes of ecstasy. She squeezed hers shut against fresh tears. He groaned thunderously each time he crashed into her. "God, I love you, Reese. Tell me you love me. Open your eyes, Reese! I want you to see this," he roared and when she did, she saw a barely recognizable Meridan in the reflection.

"Stop it!" Meridan screamed and leveled an enormous firearm on him. At that very moment, the sound of sirens was unmistakable in the distance. Lynden could no longer see the reflection of what was going on behind her as it was suddenly obscured by bright lights through the picture window. Meridan looked to the door, seemed to consider briefly and fired.

Lynden's eardrums exploded at the sound, and in the brief moment before the picture window was transformed into a rain of deadly shards, Lynden witnessed life's essence explode in a hailstorm of gore.

~

As he raced up the steps, heart lodged in his throat, Cameron could see a crumpled body on the stairs just inside the cabin. Meridan. Was she alive?

"Meridan!" He dropped to his knees and reached for his client, trying to ascertain whether she was breathing. Her face was hidden by masses of curls, but listening close he could hear a low whimper. "Meridan. Look at me. Are you hurt? Have you been shot?" His eyes quickly assessed the room. Jim, well, Brit Holden, was lying partially outside the pane where the picture window used to be. It was an unfathomable mess. In addition to a fatal gunshot wound, falling fragments of glass had sliced him to ribbons, and several were still protruding obscenely from his neck and back. Cameron gave an involuntary shudder at the still-widening pool of blood and returned his attention to his client.

"Meridan. Talk to me. Where is Lynden?" He'd only heard one gunshot, but that had been as he got out of the car. There could have been more. He shook her a little, hoping to snap her from the catatonic state. "Meridan. Is Lynden alive? Is she okay?" He softened his tone, but needed to raise the volume over the approaching sirens. "It's okay. I'm here. The police are almost here." He brushed the hair from her face and recoiled at the blood caked on her nose, mouth and in her hair. He swiftly evaluated the damage, and only then did he notice the bloody rope burns around her wrists. What in God's name had happened here? He needed to check the house. He had to find Lynden.

A second look at the carnage revealed a small, bloody foot in between Brit's splayed legs. He hadn't seen it before. My God! She's under him!

"Lynden!" He raced to Brit, careful not to slip on the shards of glass scattered everywhere, and dropped to his knees. "Lynden. It's Cameron. Are you okay? Can you speak?" He reached under Brit until he grasped an arm and pulled it out. There was a pulse and while it was faint, it was regular. Jesus.

"Lynden. The police are here. You're safe." With considerable effort, he was able to roll Brit's naked body off of Lynden. He grimaced at the sickening sound of the jagged pieces of glass crunching under the dead weight. Christ! What had Meridan shot him with? A surface-to-air missile? He looked around for a gun and spotted a Desert Eagle under an ottoman. Whose was it? How had she gotten her hands on it?

Lynden's gasp for air brought him back to task and he thanked God when she began to cough.

"Lynden? Lynden? It's Cameron. Don't move. I'm going to cover you." He removed his jacket and was just about to lay it over her naked, blood-smeared body when she emitted a deafening scream and pulled herself into a ball, placing her hands over her ears.

"No! No!" she begged, and it tore at his heart.

"Lynden!" Cameron heard Meridan shout next to him just as tires skidded in the drive.

Meridan, battered, bloody and bruised, enveloped Lynden in her arms. Lynden rocked slowly and Meridan rocked with her.

EPILOGUE

Dear Lynden-

I am sorry it's taken me a week to write this. I wish you'd have allowed me to visit you in the hospital. As you know, I'm not great with words, but it's important to me that you understand what happened at the lake.

As soon as you came back in, after running out the door, I knew you and I were in it together. I knew I had just as much responsibility to you as you felt for me. The only thing I could come up with was to try to seduce him—I thought he'd loved me—he was very convincing. I want you to know I was acting. I was trying to save our lives.

I grew close to you at your home when you opened up to me. You put your life on the line to help save mine, and that means the world to me. Unfortunately, I have been taught to use my looks to get what I want and need, and for some reason I thought he'd remember how much he cared. I figured if I could distract him, you could hit him over the head or something and we could escape. Together we could have dealt with Ash.

I hope you got my flowers. If you are reading this, I am begging you to let me visit. I just want to hug you and get through this together.

I fear you'll never forgive me, but please believe I was acting, and that I NEVER sold you out. I never spoke to Noah. I'm certain Jim, sorry, Brit was the one who pulled all the strings. I know he pulled mine.

Much love,
Meridan

Lynden folded the note in half and stood at the door to her hospital room, which was covered on every surface with flowers—every variety except roses. Having given it plenty of thought, she walked out of the room.

~

"Reese Hatcher for Meridan Marks," she spoke into the intercom, and the gates slowly parted. She traversed the driveway, which was, surprisingly, more than a mile long. Half way, she was required to stop and speak to a guard. He didn't give her a moment's trouble.

The house was mind boggling. It was difficult to fathom there was this much land in Bel Air, especially considering there was but one home within the gate's confines. Reese brought the car to a stop, rose from her seat, closed the door, and turned to confirm it was locked. She had barely reached the bottom step leading to a huge wooden door when Meridan came racing down the steps screaming her name. The actress enveloped her, and they hugged for a long time.

"Does this mean you're staying? For good? With me?" Meridan choked through her tears.

"It means I'm staying, for now—as long as you know a good therapist." The women laughed as they wiped tears and entwined arms as they headed into their home.

CONSUMED

Dedicated Charity

The Donor Project is a nationwide initiative to eliminate the wait list for organs. While many are willing to donate and have registered with their state or regional agencies, there is no single national database containing their names. The result is that few organs seem available, many in need are turned away, and only a small percentage of donated organs are actually transplanted. With their single database of potential donors available 24/7/365, The Donor Project expects the transplant waiting list will be eliminated by 2016.

This cause is so very meaningful to us, as Hilary's biological father is in renal failure and she likely will donate a kidney to him in the coming months. Additionally, Hilary's Uncle Paul, whom she adores, is in need of a heart transplant and has been disqualified due to his age and the condition of his other organs.

As a side note to all those concerned about our economy and the state of health care: if you are diagnosed at any age with renal failure, your treatment (dialysis) is covered by Medicare. The government is currently spending $6 billion annually on dialysis. Can you imagine the stimulation the government could offer the economy with that money diverted?

We plan to write about the vast benefits of The Donor Project in our second novel, as yet untitled. We applaud its founder, Steve Moi, for his conviction and tenacity. Bless you, Steve.

If you intend to become a donor or have already registered with your state or region, please faciltate and confirm your desire to donate by registering at **donorproject.org.**

LaVergne, TN USA
03 January 2011
210810LV00002B/3/P